Thank you for t...ns above.
Now you bring light ...

Morgan,
merci d'avoir introduit ta lumière dans ma vie au cours d'une décennie.
Maintenant, tu fais briller ta lumière pour le monde entier depuis les cieux.

To my Darling Fans
Jason & Derrick
Love Always

Introduction

In this Universe, there are places where reality is thin enough to meet fantasy. It is in these spellbinding spots; should you happen upon one by accident,
That the Faeries dance, weaving their enchantments in the air around the world tree.
Where Yokai and their kin enjoy the repast from chasing their many tails.
There's fun and frivolity as the Satyrs and Maenads recreate with their Bacchanalia with the drinks that flow from the bar.
It is a place for almost anyone, including the dark and brooding creatures of the night. The vampires, who come to contemplate their immortality.
Yes, even a place where djinn can come to make their deals. These little corners of intrigue can be uncovered by you in the most unlikely of places. However, in some cases, it makes perfect sense where they are to be found. For instance, Vancouver Canada. Sounds innocent enough. But when you look closer, you will see the melting pot of cultures, races, and lifestyles. It is no wonder that other beings also think to make this place their playground and their home.

Prologue
***

Family. Every being came from a starting point. In most worlds and dimensions, this was the Okāsan/お母さん (Mother). The Grand Design created these perfect receptacles of love and nurturing to further a species. The family began with Her. You came from Her.

My Skulk (Family) began with my Okāsan. Looking back, she was still the most magnificent creature imaginable, so graceful and powerful. When Zenko (Kitsune, Fox Spirits) pups were born, we were in our fox form for much of our youth. During this time, our Okāsan needed to remain to tend and nurture us and occasionally defend us. My Okāsan said we had an Otōsan/お父さん (Father) but had long gone to the place we could no longer reach.

I asked my Okāsan about how she met my Otōsan, and she always had a lost, wistful look about her. Their meeting had been simple; she and he were around the Age of Transformation. My Okāsan had been cultivating her abilities as was required for Kitsune. Cultivation was when we developed our abilities, the ones passed from parents to a pup and the ones that were the pups alone.
My Otōsan had interrupted my Okāsan's meditations which earned him a slap and a lecture on how rude it was to spy. And yet, he kept coming.

As my Okāsan suggested, "Usually one of you knows before the other one that it is a match." In my Okāsan's case, it had been my ever-persistent Otōsan. He had endured many slaps and lectures before they actually began to learn their cultivation together. And as these things did, Okāsan realized he was hers, and that was how it was to be. Kitsunes were promiscuous from the beginning, enjoying sex as much as any other being. But upon meeting their mate, all that energy would go into their significant other for the rest of their lives.

Growing up, my brothers and sister would play and rough house. I would occasionally find it more interesting to explore our home. We were born in the hills of an area that was now known as Kyoto. We called it something different at the time. It soon became evident that my exploration and curiosity had become a skill that I was developing. My family would quickly use it to help the family hunt. That would keep me plenty busy. That skill carried on through as one of the talents that were each pup's alone. Not passed on from parents – Ayaka

***

Part One
Chapter 1 - Doctor's Office (Sunday)

It smelled like a combination of incense and cooking spices, which made no sense at all because I was sitting in the semi-full waiting room of a doctor's office. Were they doctors? There were apparently a few working here. The waiting room looked standard. It had clean yet functional furniture set against the walls on the nondescript linoleum. There was the customary pile of magazines on an old table in front of me. They were a collection of gossip rags that pleaded desperately for attention, inviting readers into the most intimate and secret (and likely fictional) lives of various celebs.

I ignored my instincts to peruse the misfortunes of the rich and famous. There was a newspaper next to them. I tried to ignore that too. Unfortunately, it sported a half-page photo of one of the harbour side restaurants: the Romero cordoned off with police tape and looked like police and techs combing the scene for clues. The title said: "Another Body Found in Coal Harbour."

There'd been a series of weird wildlife attacks recently with no apparent pattern of animal behaviour. It kept the experts and authorities stumped and the public on edge. In Vancouver, there had been the odd gang shooting and some fights and assaults here and there. But such dramatic deaths were relatively unheard of. I was too nervous to read the article, but it did make me frown and offered a moment's reprieve from my anxiety. And why did it smell like a new age store in here? I flipped the New Year's red envelope in my hand nervously. A few other patients were waiting to see their various doctors. I wondered if they had similar troubles. I looked over at a middle-aged business type wearing his after-office look, complete with greasy salt and pepper hair and stubble. You could tell; he looked nervous. He was fidgeting, and a bead of sweat betrayed him, running down his neck. Definitely. Which brought my mind to my particular issue. And I was sure I visibly blushed while thinking of it. The said businessman raised an eyebrow at me. I must have been a cherry red for him to notice—the Asian blush without the benefits of alcohol. I looked again at the red envelope in my hand. It gave me a sense of comfort to look at it. This would be weird to most Chinese as these envelopes were generally only seen at Chinese New Year.

I was sure this was the right place. Neelas seemed reliable when it came to such things (given our brief meetings) as far as I could tell. And the sensitive nature of my issue lent me to follow her instructions with desperation. I shifted uncomfortably in my seat, remembering the past few days. They had seemed so simple. Dream-like, almost. Well, that dream had landed me here. *Arghhh*. My cheeks burned from cherry to beetroot, possibly purple. As a Chinese Canadian with pale skin, it was sure to make me look unpalatable.

I was not bad-looking. I just considered myself interesting to look at, unique maybe. And probably skinny. When I wished to attract it, I got enough attention. This was likely due to my Eurasian heritage. This gave me a nice mix of my French Maman's (Mother's) more prominent nose and the narrow dark Asian eyes and primarily straight hair of my Chinese Bàba/爸爸 (Father). The dark hair was at this time up in an out-of-style man bun, mainly for practical reasons than fashion. My hair would just stick to my nervous red face otherwise. I usually found my own company preferable to that of my close friends and parents. Like a good Chinese boy, I was close to my parents: my Maman, Marguerite, a French *tour-de-force*, and my Bàba, Jing/靖
 (or "James" to his Hong Kong friends), born in Guilin, mainland China. I actually enjoy speaking to my parents. They were good parents too. I was lucky. They got landed with an oddball of a child and took it in stride instead of trying to force me into some archaic mould to suit outdated values. Although that was mainly due to my Nǎinai/奶奶 (Gran) and an interesting woman named Ling/灵 (the "enlightened"). I flipped the envelope again.

Such a wonderful couple of days had now taken a downturn.

A nurse came out in her scrubs and called my name, "Mr. Li?" I used.

I didn't use my full name: *Li Yīng (Li/漓, our unusual family name after the Li River whence we originated, and my own name, Yīng/英, my Nǎinai gave me.*) That was me. My friends mostly called me Li. My last name. I didn't mind. I was reasonably sure that I was sweating more than the panicked businessman. As the nurse, an efficient Filipina lady, Jane, led me past closed doors to one particular entry, as I was in a daze. No real names for this clinic's staff. I bet they use "John" and "Jane Doe" for all the team here. It was to be expected. The past week had been magical, and then it wasn't. I almost crushed the red envelope in my hand but gathered myself. I had to take a deep breath to push down the swell of despair I was so used to feeling. Without remembering to check me, I had to be careful with my emotions and remember to breathe. I had tended to let myself wallow. I could do this.

"Dr. John will see you now." "John" and "Jane." The name thing was interesting. I followed Neelas 'instructions; she'd seemed to care about my situation. The nurse opened the door and smiled reassuringly. She looked Filipino, but one look in her eyes showed something else. Almost feline, cold, and calculating. Not chilling as one would expect, but I couldn't see an aura as usual with her type. I went In.

"Come in, sit if you wish. I'll just finish this," the doctor was writing in a notebook. I looked around the room. There was incense and shelves stacked with parchments and books whose covers could only be described as ancient. There were also charts on the walls, some modern depictions of human anatomy. Others looked like they belonged in an acupuncturist's office, showing the meridians and essential centers. There was even a poster showing the classic chakras on the body. I really hoped this was legit. I was terrified, and this had to be someone who could help.

He turned on his stool, still seated. I was pretty sure I yelped a little. But, if I did not, at least the surprise showed on my face.

He could not have been more than twenty-five years of age, maybe thirty, and handsome to boot. He looked like a beach bum who fell into a suit and lab coat on his way from a surf club. His hair tussled and sun-bleached, and his skin smooth and tanned. His eyes were almost an ocean hue. Was he a student? I thought. Was he a doctor?

"Are you the doctor?" Oh god, that sounded rude.
"Yes. Obviously not exactly what you were expecting. I know this looks more like a miniature 'Dumbledore's Office' than my exam room, apart from the exam table, of course." He smiled at that.

Clearly, he was used to this. I looked around the room again to avoid looking at his chiselled features. Good looks were now a recent problem for me. Well, not a problem. A disaster. Sitting at his desk with the notebook and a pinboard were various pictures and notes and reminders of this or that. A book lay in front of the notepad he had been scratching on. The diagram and language looked like a Lovecraftian nightmare that I couldn't even read. He grabbed a bookmark from the side facing away from me and placed it in the book. My heart jumped. The bookmark was a Chinese New Year red envelope, very much like mine. No one had these except me. He snapped the book shut. I jumped slightly.

"Sorry, just nervous, I guess," I mumbled.

"Relax, let's have a look at you," At that, he got up and came up to me while pulling on some latex gloves and took my face in his large hands. He stared, squinting into my eyes, which obliged by widening in surprise. A series of "*hmm*" and "*ahhs*." God, he was cute. And smelled of cinnamon and…something else. When he pulled away, I could see he was trying extremely hard to look stoic but almost failing. A smile kept breaking the façade. He was enjoying this a little, which always made for an uncomfortable 'medical' visit.

"You may as well show me so I can make a better judgment of what I am dealing with here." Oh, perhaps he was familiar with my issue?

I sighed. I had been mentally dreading this but resigned to my humiliation. I did what I had to. It didn't matter how I would feel; I needed answers. I was hoping he was the type who had seen it all and wouldn't be baffled or shocked by what he saw. But he looked younger than me, although in the circles I was now dealing with, looks didn't mean anything. Holding an indecipherable amusement on his handsome face, he stepped back. This was to give me room as I went to the exam table, unbuckled my jeans, pulled them down with my briefs in one anxious go, and bent over.

"Oh...oh dear." He said, stammering, before recovering his composure.

***

Chapter 2: MGV Publishing (Thursday)

I worked for a publishing firm, MGV, in downtown Vancouver, Canada. It was small but doing quite well considering the advent of eBooks. We mainly published graphic novels and some niche manga which kept us well above the red. My friend Patience landed me the job right out of college after I had gotten my degree in Visual Arts and a double major in Art History. I was an illustrator. It was a dream job, and I was grateful to Patience every day for it. Currently, I was working on some illustrations for a storyboard of a popular manga series. It was packed with fantasy and romance. I liked illustrating them the most, and Patience was good at sending them my way. Favouritism, probably, but I didn't care; I was happy in my work. I didn't like illustrating for the action-packed graphic novels of today. The 'graphic' part should be in bold everywhere they're sold. I found the violent scenes challenging to recreate on paper. When I sketched the piece, I would always immerse myself in what my Nǎinai called the 'soul of the painting.' My Nǎinai had been the one to first put a calligraphy brush and then a paintbrush into my hands when I was barely four. Painting violence made me nauseous.

Patience was my boss, and I was never questioned on her decisions to send manga romance work my way for two reasons. One, I had won the publishing house numerous awards with my artistry; and two, Patience never lived up to her name. She was, and I say this affectionately, a total bitch.

I did call Patience, my friend. In fact, I considered her one of my closest friends. She had been the one to tell me I was gay in college but always maintained that she would be the perfect woman for me otherwise. We had met in the Visual Arts program. She was a tough cookie and never took flak from anyone. Short, blond, pretty, but fearless, perhaps like a Pomeranian. I'd never tell her that, at least not without a few drinks in her. She ruled the art department of MGV with a diminutive but iron fist. My cubicle sat outside her office, so we would trade jibes and innuendos throughout the day. She once told me she wondered how I got so much work done while being such a clown at work with her.

Today, she was late. Which was not all that unusual. She sometimes had many meetings throughout the day, and some even began before the office opened. I could return the same question to her on how she got so much done while being a total bitch clown in the office. Or she could be at the rifle range to fire off a new pistol or some such. Guns gave me the creeps, but she owned at least three. She said it gave her a sense of 'always gonna be ok, no matter who's around the corner.' To be fair, that statement was true.

Todd from the mailroom was making his morning rounds. He was overweight, sometimes smelly, and always sweaty with a goatee on his red blotchy face. But that didn't stop him from being likable. Somehow, he managed to make anyone in the office smile, except for Patience. He was a riot when it came down to it, and I suspected a career in stand-up would have been in the cards for him had he tried. He rounded the corner at a brisk pace. The only person in the office that could rattle Todd was Patience, so he always tried to get his rounds done when she was absent from the office.

"Phew!" He puffed, wiping some stray sweat off his brow with a tissue. He kept a box with him at all times.

"I have this for Patience, probably from one of the reps." He gently shook the wrapped box he was holding. It made no sound. Which likely meant the sender anticipated a Todd on the other end and had packed accordingly. He put it on my desk for me to give to her. I smiled up at him from my seat in my cubicle.

"Hey, did you hear about the animal attack in Stanley park?" Todd was also an avid news watcher, and as I wasn't, he was basically my morning newspaper when I needed it.

"What? What kind of animal?"

"Apparently a bear, the place has been cordoned off all morning; I had to go all the way up Robson and down Bute to get here."

"Odd, I don't know much about bears, but they don't usually attack people from what I hear, must've been starved," I said. But I decided to put it out of my mind. "So, other than bear attacks and longer commutes, how's tricks Todd?" He still seemed slightly out of breath before answering, and I was only half listening.

"Oh good, good. Can't complain. Apparently, another body was found near Point Grey in the posh area, umm, Belmont, I think. Torn up by the same bear, they think." Ok, now I couldn't just put it out of my mind if there were more than one." They're not sure what to do, I think, but I'm going to Canadian Tire to get some bear spray."

Without looking up from my work, I opened my black leather messenger bag next to my desk drawer at my feet. I pulled out a small spray can with a picture of a bear and the label "Sabre Wilds" on it and waved it vaguely at him.

"We're having an after-work thing if you wanna come. Patience will be there, of course," he didn't shudder as he usually would. It was well known she liked to have fun, and it was the only time the staff could enjoy her company without being scared.

"Maybe next time. I gotta finish this storyboard," At this point, I did look up out of slight discomfort, "and, um, it's the anniversary." The mention of this sent a pang of hurt through my core. Deep breath, in and out, I said internally.

Todd had the good grace to look embarrassed.

"I'm sorry, Li, I almost forgot. Look, come by if you wanna just take your mind off things for a bit." My colleagues, like my friends, called me Li. It was easier for them, and I didn't mind. He really was a sweetheart, but it would always be a firm "no" at this time of the year.

"Thanks, Todd," With that, I went back to work and politely ignored everyone else. A small signal of overwhelming sadness that might sweep through my body tried to raise its ugly head, and I took another deep breath to banish it back to its hiding place. It had been five years to this day that Marcus had passed away. Another deep breath. I absently touched the puckered line along my wrist—a constant reminder of both my loss and my weakness.

A shimmer, more like a coloured heatwave, suddenly caught the corner of my eye. It took me a few seconds to register what it meant. Oh crap! I opened my desk drawer and found them neatly waiting at the front of the drawer, next to the organizer. The pill bottle was always handy these days. Among the others that I had been prescribed for the past five years now: some anxiolytics, some SSRIs, and the important ones for this occasion, a combination of NSAIDs and triptans for severe migraines. Migraines were not just "headaches." When someone was holding their head and saying they had a migraine and not swaying, clenching their eyes shut, seeing colours, or vomiting, they had only a headache. Migraines had been a long-standing curse for me, and my Nǎinai thought it was for reasons other than neurological. But hey, I just needed to follow the signals, usually starting to see auras around things. When that happened, I would take two of my pills pronto. Because the thing about a migraine was that if you left it too long, no matter what you took, the pain would continue pushing you into a debilitated state.

I gulped down two with some water from the cooler and went back to my seat. The package for Patience looked as if it had a haze around it, sporting different colours: pinks and purples with some black threaded in there. Closing my eyes, I hoped it was not too late for the medication to take effect.

I opened them. The haze was still there.

"Oh! Perfect!" A small, manicured hand snatched up the box, leaving a multi-coloured blurry streak in the air following it. I looked up to see my best friend, who was grinning down at me. A halo of colour surrounded her too: purples, greens, with weird smoky tendrils. Oh, this migraine was going to be bad if the meds didn't kick in.

"What's up, Li?" She looked concerned through the haze of psychedelic colour emanating from her and the box she held. She narrowed her eyes, "Migraine again?" I nodded.

"Yeah. I think I got it in time. My sight just hasn't quite gotten the message yet." I had told her about the colours that surrounded everything when my migraines came. She said it sounded pretty cool except for the excruciating pain." Where were you this morning," referring to her slight tardiness. Her smile faltered.

"I was with Hope in one of her sessions and then had to drop the girls off at daycare and school," she said.

"You're a good aunt," I reassured her.

"Apparently not as good as uncle Li," she scoffed, "the girls are always asking after you!"
"Hey, I can't help it that I am loveable and fun to everyone," I looked at her, guessing she was holding back something." How's Hope's treatment going?" Her face was impassive as she rolled the tiny package in her hand, almost thoughtfully.

"It's ok. It's taking its toll, but we are not giving up." She smiled and narrowed her eyes at me, almost annoyed at my diversion.

"Hey," she said softly, sitting on the edge of my desk, her skirt probably a little too high, as she clacked the heels of her stilettos together." I know what day it is. You know I'll come at the drop of a hat. You have always said that on this day, you'd rather be alone. But maybe that's not so healthy," she touched my shoulder with her tiny hand. We weren't really touchy besties, so this gesture was equal to a full-blown hug." A group of us is going out tonight. Perhaps you need a good distraction, or something else starting with D." She grinned, wiggling her brows at me suggestively. It was crass but well-intentioned, and I smiled up at her accordingly.

"I'll stay in. But thanks, you're the best. And the 'D' would always be nice, but I also have these boards to complete."

"You sure do, but if that migraine comes out or you need the day off," she looked pointedly at me. I was grateful. She'd had my back for so long now, I was not going to take it for granted by skirting my work responsibilities. My right thumb ran along the scar on my left wrist. I had hurt enough people with my selfishness.

"Nah, I'm good. Anyway, what is in that box? More perfume from reps, or a new vibrator because your other ran away and decided to join a convent? It was probably traumatized by the awful things you make it do."

She laughed, "You'll never know." She spun off my desk and practically skipped into her office before shutting the frosted glass door with her name on it.

"She seems really happy about that vibrator," I mumbled under my breath, smiling. Well, it looked like the pills had kicked in. There was no pain. Though I could still see the colours seeping through the frosted glass of Patience's office and around my fellow workers.

***

Chapter 3: Home Alone (Thursday)

Opening the door to my apartment was a relief. Usually, Patience would offer me a lift home in her Tesla, but I had wanted the time to myself. The walk and bus home had been weirder than usual. I saw colours around people and objects. Sometimes static, sometimes moving as if they were alive. This had happened a few times in my life when the migraines came. It just seemed more precise now and more vivid. I remember distantly being able to see them a lot without the pain when I was younger. But no more.

My apartment was a studio in the center of downtown Vancouver. It was spacious, and I had only been able to afford it with help from my parents. Bàba was a banker, so his financial acumen had gotten me an outstanding mortgage where I paid so little each month. My neighbours were the only other people on the floor. A lovely Persian family whose son Baraz would feed my fish and take care of my aquarium while I was visiting Maman and Bàba in Hong Kong. My parents had moved back there after my Nǎinai had passed away, and I missed their company. Baraz's Mother Afsaneh was always inviting me over for dinners, and I obliged them as often as possible. I was sure she was trying to adopt me. Afsaneh and her husband, Elham, ran a design and architect firm together and were responsible for the sleek and spacious contemporary look of my open plan studio.

The floors were light grey oakwood. White aesthetics. Clean. With black countertops and cabinets. Marble slabs in the bathroom with a free-standing tub and a large open shower with two rainfall showerheads. My furniture was contemporary but comfortable. It stayed pristine mainly due to the lack of visitors. I looked out the floor-to-ceiling windows. It was a beautiful city at night. I could see Coal Harbour through my window. An almost unobstructed panoramic view. I turned and went to the open kitchen. My refrigerator was black, like the counter. A smokey mirrored backsplash accentuated the lights from outside, reflecting them in a way that sometimes felt like the skyline was indoors with me. My aquarium gave the lights outside a complimentary sparkle with the bio lamps shining on its tiny inhabitants—little crustaceans in different colours, neon tetras, and a blue and magenta beta. The aquarium had its own stand and was edgeless, with the filter imitating a waterfall while trickling peacefully. My eyes saw the fish and the coloured halos around them that only I could perceive. At least, this was one of the blessings of my aura sight. They left rainbow trails throughout the water.

Though my apartment was largely monochromatic, this would change when my 'sight 'emerged. It turned the entire space into a kaleidoscope of colours. My Năinai had maintained the migraines were my fault, and the sight just happened. It was reminiscent of petrol splashed in a water puddle after the rain. The one thing that was entirely out of place was the garish, red, and gold calendar. I bought one every year. My Năinai would have loved it, no matter what and how much it clashed with. On the calendar on particular dates were red envelopes, the kind given out in Chinese New Year. Except these were handmade, and some of them by me. They, too, had a brilliant iridescent haze around each of them, which didn't surprise me. These days the auras were coming more frequently than the migraines. Opening the fridge, I looked at the desolate landscape inside. My Maman would be horrified. An empty fridge to her was an empty home. And whenever she and Bàba visited, she'd bring bags and bags of groceries in before I had a chance to even say hello.

***

Năinai: "You have a sore head because you're trying to not see Xiǎo yīng (小英, my Năinai would call me Xiǎo, little; yīng, hero/flower). Cut it out!" My Năinai was a mainland Chinese born. Her mandarin could sometimes slip into her Guilin dialect, and I'd get a little confused at what she had said. This time, though, she was making herself clear.

I spent much of my youth with Năinai. She was the one that gave me my name. My parents had moved the family to Hong Kong when I was a baby, so I grew up there with my Năinai refusing to learn Cantonese. She was a character. Stubborn, willful, and "always right." To be fair, she usually was. When I first started telling my parents about the colours I saw, they were worried and had looked to Nǎinai for guidance. She was pasting her annual red envelopes together at the time. She'd snap at them both, "Don't you dare tell him not to see them; you'll make him a madman," And that was the end of it for them.

My dear parents were great. They did their best. Bàba became a banker and did very well; Maman was a nurse. She was almost as stubborn as my Nǎinai. She had followed Bàba to China from France, where they had met and married. From what I heard, my Bàba had been terrified of Nǎinai's reaction to a French lady joining the family. Nǎinai seemed to ignore her most of the time. It seemed rude, but Maman did the same. Then one day when I spied them both in the tiny kitchen of our Hong Kong apartment. They laughed away with rice wine while Maman was making dumplings, and Nǎinai was correcting her technique. Perhaps they pretended to be aloof to keep Bàba on his toes. He was, after all, surrounded by the strongest women I knew. Which meant that French and Chinese women had those qualities in common. Clever and always keeping men guessing. I had kept that moment to myself. But seeing them both so happy, drinking rice wine together, and gossiping stuck in my mind.

I had only heard stories about Nǎinai's life in Guilin. Apparently, she used to go to the river a lot, but not to fish. Her husband had been, I suspected, like Bàba, knowing when to keep quiet about some things. The name she took when she'd gotten married to my Zǔfù/祖父 (grandfather) was not his. She had always maintained the surname Li/漓 (as I mentioned, the Li River in Guilin). We were never told why this unusual turn of events took place. My Nǎinai's decisions were rarely questioned.

It was said that she had learned the craft from a river faerie. My Nǎinai was what was known as a *Wunü*, or shaman. Many things she did weren't in the traditional sense. My maman told me that once Nǎinai had cursed a family for trying to ruin her husband's business of silk paintings. I wasn't sure how true it was. But it was undeniable that everyone treated her with a considerable measure of reverence.

She set up an unofficial business in Hong Kong when we moved there, helping people with her skills. Lifting curses. Charms for luck. Health. The usual. But what most people looked forward to was Nǎinai's New Year's red envelopes. She would make them herself. She refused to buy them from the shop. She dyed and painted them red and gold, with her own designs on them. She'd get me to help with the designing, painting, and gluing. To receive a red envelope from Nǎinai was a massive blessing on New Year's. And everyone we knew secretly hoped they'd get one.

"Xiǎo yīng, Cut it out!" She'd barked, seeing I had again been trying to ignore the 'sight.' Yup, definitely her own woman. She had been right. But everyday life and Nǎinai 's world didn't seem to go together all the time. I had learned over the years to calm the auras to a point where they weren't always there, and as she had predicted, the migraines would come. Nǎinai had once told me I was born under an incredibly '*xiōng xīng*,' or unlucky star. But then she had also said that it didn't matter because we could make our own luck, and fate could kindly go fuck itself. I hoped she was right. I did feel blessed at times having great friends though few they were, beautiful parents, and even neighbours who were fast becoming friends.

***

I touched the date for the next red envelope to open: a week and a half away. My cell rang.

"*Wei!*" I answered. Video chat was a marvel. My parents were in Hong Kong still and called almost every week to check up. I suspected they wanted to call me more, but they were trying to respect my boundaries. They knew what tonight meant. And they had called right on time.

We chatted about life, everyday polite things. Dancing around the subject of the night, which was typical for us Chinese. It was enough for me to see them and know they called to be here for me in the only capacity they could for now. They wanted to know, of course, if I was eating well (I had forgotten entirely about dinner, to be honest), but I lied to placate them. I didn't want them to worry for me again. Then, of course, Maman questioned my health, saying I looked pale (which I usually did). Perhaps I needed my iron checked because iron deficiency was expected in many people these days.

I waited for it to come, and it did: "Remember Dr. Pia? My old colleague from the hospital. We are always in touch, and she asks after you all the time. She said you can go see her whenever you need to, and she'll make room for you." And the next part, "you know she would, especially after what Nǎinai did for her family." Nǎinai had been alive while we lived in Vancouver for some time, and where she went, a need seemed to appear for her particular expertise.

"Are you being careful?" My Bàba yelled far too close to the screen. I could almost see up his nostrils. He hadn't quite got the hang of vid chat like Maman.

"There's been some kind of animal attacks; I think I read on the news," she jumped in, "apparently a bear is about. Poor things have nowhere else to go sometimes, but still." She was forever the caring type. I did as I had with Todd and grabbed my bear spray for them to see. That seemed to satisfy them. They didn't mention Marcus, which was good. I didn't want them to know it was still a heavy subject, especially after all they had done for me.

When we signed off, I was somewhat comforted by the conversation. I smiled internally. Another thing about Chinese and French, they both loved their food, and they constantly fretted. I loved my parents and missed them terribly. It was sometimes strange for Chinese parents to have such an openly close relationship with their children in a culture where many feelings were more implied than expressed. When they were still in Vancouver, and I was just out of college, I had called them. I wanted to set up a dinner to tell them that they shouldn't expect grandchildren anytime soon because I was dating a guy. When they answered, I was so scared that I almost didn't do it. Even though my parents had never displayed a lack of support for my entire life, I was still petrified. I forgot that there was a force stronger than my fear at play in my life and always ready to protect me… my Nǎinai. They had patiently listened while I told them. Then they said that they weren't surprised, and they loved me so much.

Nǎinai had been puttering around in the background and yelled, "Has Xiǎo yīng said it yet?"

Yup, a force of nature that almost everyone I knew feared. My Nǎinai. Who adored her little Yīng as she had always called me. Her beautiful flower, her little hero. She had "come out" for me. It had been comical at the time. When we finally had that dinner together that I had suggested, she said that her little Yīng had far more important things to do than pop out kids and marry some girl whom no one would be happy with.

I ordered a pizza and a drink. Knowing my stomach just needed something in it, anything really. The inevitable was coming, and I needed to be prepared for it. My annual ritual felt necessary, although I wasn't sure if it was anymore. The practice that made the year bearable at least and the medications less critical.

I went to my bedside drawer and opened it. I pulled out a photo. It showed a man with a square jaw, perfectly symmetrical features. To most people, his face would seem an unremarkable European face - roman nose, full lips. But those lips, I knew them by heart. Blue eyes that shone with mirth and joy. His hair was a mass of dark curls on top of his head. He had a tilt to his head in the photo as if waiting for the punchline of a joke.

I sat on the edge of the bed. There was no joke. No punchline would bring any relief to me whatsoever.

And then it came as it did every year, that blanket of dark emotion, like a black pit engulfing me. I would hold it in check all day, all year mostly, but I let it in today. The tears came. The memories. God, he was beautiful. Even to the last moment. I was able to push away the sight long enough to see my love. He was still lovely to me. Even hooked up to those horrible machines and tubes, barely conscious, I still saw him. His beautiful mouth was covered by the oxygen mask. I still saw him, tousled curls, ready smile.

Marcus had been the love of my life. He had come into my life just after college and swept me up with his charm and wit. Hailing from Montreal, Marcus had tried to speak to my Maman in French and my Bàba in somewhat broken mandarin. With this, he had managed to also charm my parents even though he hadn't yet settled on his idea of a career. His degree had been so diverse, it was almost as if he'd thrown darts at the curriculum to decide, which might have been the case. He had come to study at the University of British Columbia. I had been so busy; I hadn't noticed him at all at school. He said he had seen me and had been waiting for the right time. But when he had crashed into me at the dockside gelato shop, covering us both in my and Patience's gelato cups, I suspected it wasn't entirely true. Patience had adored and hung out with him even when I was in Hong Kong visiting my parents.

Marcus, young, beautiful. A light. And taken from me. Yet, there was absolutely nothing I could do about it. I had barely remembered the funeral. In fact, that week had been a numb blur of shock. What I did remember was the press of a razor against my wrist, feeling too empty, hollowed out. Like one of those crab shells, you'd find on the beach after seagulls had eaten the meat. Hollowed and about to shatter into a million pieces. The blade hadn't even felt like anything; I was so far gone inside my own grief.

I laid down on my bed and let wave after wave of despair do its work. Each year I was told, would be easier. It had been five. And it seemed that my soul was stubborn and didn't want it to be easier. I still held onto my grief. And I probably would always. But when Patience had found me in our apartment in the kitchen surrounded by my own growing pool of blood, I remembered only a little, fading in and out of consciousness at the time. Her face was twisted in horror and sadness. Then my parents came to the hospital. My Maman screamed and cried, yelled, and kicked the sparse furniture in the room. My Bàba, whom I had never seen overtly emotional except when it came to his wife, whom he doted on - but this time, his usually passive face was holding back tears and anger; he was trembling feverishly, like a volcano about to explode. At the time, I didn't care. Though looking back and seeing my Bàba: the stout

banker, with nerves of steel when dealing with billions of dollars and their manic investors, had rushed to the bedside, pushing Patience against the wall. He was only able to speak in his native Mandarin at the time:
"My Xiǎo Yīng, my beautiful boy. Never again. Never. You are family. We are family. Never again!" He repeated himself over and over until I passed into unconsciousness again.

A knock at the door startled me from my reverie. There seemed a muffled noise against the door like someone was pushing against it.

"FUCK!" a disgruntled but familiar voice yelled.

The despair crawled back to its pit as I got up and stumbled to the door, opened the smart lock, slightly annoyed at the intrusion. The door opened to what I had to assume was my best friend Patience, though the tightly manicured façade looked like it had been put through a blender. Her blond hair was at one time in the evening, in some sort of fun up-do. Now it looked like a pelican could nest there happily. Her makeup looked like she had tried to wash it off with her sleeve and her eyes were half-open. And she swayed.

"Fuck you!" She hollered.

"Shhhhh!" I dragged her in and dumped her on my couch, "the neighbours, dimwit."

"Don't you… shushushshhhh." She slurred, then she shook her head and put one hand to the side of it, "Every year you do this martyr thing, and I know I said I'd respect it, but it's shit. And you're not helping yourself."

"You're probably right," I mumbled, sighing as I went into the kitchen to boil some water for whatever hot beverage the next 30 minutes of tirade would require.

"Of course, I'm right! I came all the way," That was an exaggeration. Patience lived in a townhouse on the water, about a 15-minute walk to my apartment building. And likely, she hadn't actually walked that distance. Instead, she would have gotten dropped right outside my building from whatever bar the crew had gone to this evening." Because you need me," she carried on, no stopping her now, "Yet every year, you shut yourself away and do this morbid Twilight sorrow bullshit."

Ok. Patience was pulling out the big guns and comparing me to some sappy teen fiction character. She knew me so well. I hated the main protagonist in Twilight, that whiney moaning helpless moron.

She was right… to some degree. But to me, that was the only way to keep him. To feel what was left of him. I couldn't tell her that. And I most certainly didn't want to be a brooding Bella Swan. *Eww*.

She cared, but relationships weren't her forte. Like I said, our friendship, though close, was not touchy-feely. She went through men faster than I went through sketch paper. In fact, judging from her appearance, she had left one in her wake while coming here. So, her way of showing love was usually brusque and loud, involving some penis joke or other.

Her head hung back over the back of my couch. Although drunk, she narrowed her gaze, suddenly looking keen at my glass display cabinet. It held my Năinai's red silk box—a series of red journals that had belonged to her. There was also a framed postcard from France. I thought she was sending an angry gaze at the postcard. It was the last gift from Marcus. But she seemed to be looking at the journals. I had told her they had belonged to my Năinai. She knew my Năinai had been some kind of fortune-teller. And when she had met her, she had been slightly wary of her, like Năinai would either smack her with a shoe or turn her into dim sum and eat her. Năinai obviously hadn't obliged her paranoia. Eventually, Patience became more relaxed around her. Unfortunately, the same couldn't be said for Năinai. She liked Patience well enough but always showed a measure of guardedness around her. She had never explained why, but then that was Năinai.

Then she snapped her head up and groaned sickly. I guessed the room was spinning for her, and she was close to unconsciousness.

I smiled to myself. She was so good to me. I had told her early on in college about the migraines and about my eccentric Nǎinai. She had laughed and just said everyone had their stuff; some just hid it better. She never judged my flaws, and she never asked for anything in return, just my friendship. And, of course, at work, for my deadlines to be met. That made me chuckle. The crew would be in for it tomorrow. I heard the sounds of snores softly vibrating through a couch cushion and abandoned the jug of boiled water. I straightened her up on the couch. Her head rested against the arm and was supported by a pillow. She looked almost like a child sleeping. So tranquil looking. Almost like a tiny blond angel. That illusion was shattered with the rumble of a loud snore that croaked its way loose from her throat. Then she snuggled into the back of the couch, and the nasal roars subsided.

***

Chapter 4: Morning After (Friday)

Getting Patience up and out the door was the equivalent of trying to move the rock of Gibraltar. Her hangovers were epic and usually the reason people in our department would steer clear of her. She had crashed into my home on several occasions. So much so that I had just conceded to letting her have space in my walk-in to put spare work suits, shoes, and overnight things.
After taking my shower and completing my morning rituals, these consisted of brushing teeth, taking my meds, and cooking breakfast for us both. It continued with picking up the tiny but deceptively heavy Patience into my shower, with her mussed-up clothes, smeared makeup, and bird's nest hair into the shower. I turned it on and left her to wake up hating me for the next five minutes. It would only last until she dug into the bacon, eggs, and toast I had thrown together with a strong mug of black coffee for her.

My 'sight' hadn't changed since yesterday, and I was afraid a thumper of migraine would rear its ugly head. It didn't. Though some dregs of last night's depression still lingered at the forefront of my mind, especially when I walked past my display unit and saw the postcard from France. I pushed the feelings down and didn't bother to dampen the auric sight. Getting to the office was going to be enough of a mission.

She made it to the office with me only a few minutes late, wearing one of her black suit pants, a flowing white blouse, and severe-looking Louboutin six-inch pumps. At least her oversized, white-rimmed sunglasses matched her blouse this time as she click-clacked like the Devil wears a Hangover, walking through the department to her office. Already another steaming mug of black coffee awaited her next to its customary bottle of Tylenol. Her assistant Cherry (seriously, that's her name), a fiery red-headed lesbian who embodied what I found to be the weird straight male fantasy. She and her girlfriend were a gorgeous couple. Still, I never understood how straight guys could get into a lesbian couple. The two women would totally ignore them, or at best, demand the guy make them a sandwich. At the same time, they and they alone got down to strictly lesbian business. She always knew how to stay clear of Patience's firing line. Todd, on the other hand, tended to ride his mail trolley right into it. Usually, he'd slip up and knock her coffee over in his nervousness or bump her with the mail trolly. This would create the Chernobyl style flurry of expletives, curses, and threats, which he was always scared of receiving.

This morning, it wasn't the coffee or a bump from the trolly, but simply walking past her office the 'wrong 'way… I guess? His aura changed from red to mauve, then a kind of purple.
"Todd! Get in here, please!" He cringed and looked over to me for help. I smiled weakly and whispered, "Just get it over with. It's a five-minute moment of anguish that'll earn you a latte from me." I winked at him. No one was ever really in trouble at the MGV arts department. They just had to suffer the occasional bout of humiliation and shouting matches from our fearless leader.

Todd went in, resigned to his fate. At first, it was a "what took you! I've been looking for you all morning!" Lie." I have some documents that need to go upstairs now. They should've been delivered yesterday, but someone was in a rush to leave and didn't collect them." True. Todd and the rest of the crew were out earlier than usual, and it had obviously slipped Todd's mind. Though if they were actually necessary, she'd deliver them herself. But Todd had the bullseye painted on his butt today. It was the only thing that I did not like about Patience. Sometimes, she would act like a bully, even though she really cared about all her staff. Showing that caring nature publicly wasn't something she liked to do often. As I had said before, my friend was a total bitch. That was until her office door closed, and she was with one of our staff in a one-on-one. It was why everyone stayed. The money was good, but sometimes the shallow abuse was hard to take.

However, we had all seen it once or twice. Like when MGV was going through cutbacks a few years back when she had initially gained her position. Most people would have just toed the line and made firing decisions based on what the upstairs told them. Patience had refused to cut any of her staff. And it got around that she instead had taken a pay cut to cover the extra costs temporarily. The only way that worked was if she was able to bring MGV back into the black. And she did. And once she did, she demanded that her staff receive their due. They all got a pay bump and extra bonuses depending on the company performance for the quarters to follow.

And there were other times. Like when one of the Graphic designers was having trouble at home with her partner. Molly was her name. Molly and her husband had been together for 15 years. During that time, he must have spent the bulk of their marriage breaking down Molly's confidence and making her feel like nothing. Then the hitting began, and Molly would come to work with bruises and excuses. Patience had called Molly to her office and closed the door. A week later, Molly had filed for divorce and left him, and for some reason, she no longer feared him.

Another example was Gary. He was a dear old queen. He had lived through the AIDS crisis and lost many of his loved ones. All without any support from his family. He was single and happily so. He worked as part of the creative editing team, pulling the storyboards and graphics we had created together into a cohesive story that the authors would be happy with. And he was exceptionally good at it. Then he had been diagnosed with Parkinson's Disease. It had devastated him. It would mean that his once steady hands could no longer shape their masterpieces as they had before. We all thought he would be let go. Into Patience's office, the door closed. A few days later, an assistant was hired fresh out of design college. He was a sweet-natured Latino boy who was named Santiago. He was to help Gary with completing the work to the standard that satisfied Gary. After a few teething problems, they became an inseparable team with more cohesive work than before. And it was a surprise when Santiago got down on one knee and proposed to Gary, who was many years his senior. The pair seemed to have genuinely developed affection with their time together. So yeah, Patience was a bitch. But a bitch who garnered loyalty and passion for your work.

As I settled into my cubicle, I watched vaguely as the auras I saw settled into place around the objects on my desk. I looked at my sketchpad. I had to begin a new set of storyboards. Despite mental and emotional breakdowns, I had actually managed to complete my work yesterday before leaving.

This next manga I was to illustrate for needed a cover first. The author said that she wanted to see a good cover before trusting us with her whole line of books. The story was a "Donghua," Chinese animé. This time, it was another romance, a gay love story about a love that stretched into centuries between reincarnation and deities. I had read the manuscripts twice to get a good feel of the character and to find the "soul" of the art. The author had also stipulated that she wanted something different from the usual manga covers. Something that drew her readers into a fantasy. I looked at my sketchpad. Colours of auric patterns danced across its surface. I knew what I wanted the characters to look like, so naturally, I began cursory sketches of their faces, body shapes, and expressions. As my pencil scratched into the sketch pad, the auric colours left trails on the pages. Each character appeared to have its own halo of colours, just like people. They fluctuated with my intention and attention on the pages. Then an idea occurred to me. I could give her something no one else could in these pictures. I began sketching out the areas where the halos of energy began, melded into others or ended. I left notes along with the sketches of the colours I saw on the pages. She would definitely get something unique. I just hoped she would like it.

A hand on my shoulder jolted me out of my artistic musings.

"Li, hun, it's well past lunch, and you didn't eat much for breakfast. Get up; we're going to that vegan place you like, with the burgers." Patience squeezed my shoulder.

I let her lead me out of the office, watching the colours dance across the surfaces of everything. Some more vital than others, depending on if people touched or interacted with them more.
The café we went to was called "Below Ground," aptly named so because its food was all plant-based. It was also situated on the sub-level of a small shopping center near the office. I wasn't vegan, but for some reason, their burgers were amazing. Not the Impossible or Beyond Meat kind. I liked those, but these ones were old-school vegan, with chickpea and lentil paddies, flavoured with curry

powder and other spices. Everything from the bread to the vegan mayo was made on site.

This wasn't just a regular lunch place, though. Patience and I liked to come here and gossip about the office and what recent love match she had made on her dating apps.
The café had a very homestead, "Ma and Pa" vibe, completed with mismatched chairs and tables. House plants hung from the ceiling everywhere and in some places so low that they'd tickle your neck while eating your lunch. The pan flutes and other new-age-type music echoed between the plants where the overhead speakers were hidden. The place was aglow with life to my sight. Brilliant greens flew from one house plant to the next as if the leafy beings were communicating in a way too subtle for us to understand.

The staff was just as mismatching as the furniture in every good sense of the word. A charming blond boy served and delivered in his late teens, whose tight dreadlocks were pulled up into a pony. There were beads strung throughout his hair. He was cute in a boyish way. His tiny freckles still spotted his cheeks and hazel eyes that smiled when he did. Marcus would have liked him. The boy's hair and beads flowed with colour, blue, and gold that mixed in my 'sight'. I had seen those colours often enough on creative types. This just as they were to get a burst of inspiration before writing a masterpiece or playing something extraordinary and life-changing on an instrument. The boy would likely be someone special later on, given the right nudge, as my Nǎinai would have said. The Barista was another boy who had been transitioning from a female to a male. He was a mix of Latino and maybe someone Middle Eastern? Vancouver was a hub of diversity. So, it was sometimes hard to tell a person's heritage, which in my opinion, just added to someone's appeal. He had tattoos all up his bare arms, decorating his pale skin with scenes from various renaissance paintings. He had green eyes with hazel flecks, making his entire appearance exotic. His aura looked and felt like a tide washing in and out. It was a deep blue being engulfed by a sea green. I had also seen that in many things, including tadpoles and chrysalis, which were in the process of becoming something new. I knew a large-and-in-charge chef was out in the back, pounding away at the food orders, but we rarely saw her. She seemed in a rush or stressed, as most chefs did. I hadn't actually seen her aura as she visited the front so infrequently.

The blonde dreadlock boy, "Cody" on his name tag, delivered our food and my coffee and another black coffee for my still hungover boss.

We tucked in. Patience was having her usual nachos today. I had finished my burger in a matter of minutes. I must've been hungry as Patience had predicted. I sipped my coffee. Patience finished her nachos and was pushing the remains around with a fork. Her aura was a deep blue, like that of the trans boy, except with purple instead of sea green and dark threads of what looked like smoke shifting through the mass of energy she gave off.

She appeared to have reached a decision, her brow creasing. She grabbed my left hand in hers, and I felt a jolt, like before when I had been sketching but stronger. I gasped, but Patience didn't appear to have felt anything of the kind and continued holding my hand. I let her, curious as to where her hungover brain was leading. She ran her thumb on the scar there, the raised flesh on my wrist.

"You know I love you, right?" Strange question from her. She sounded worried. Almost sad.

"What's wrong?" I grabbed her hand and held it in both of mine, "Of course, and you know I love you too. We're ride-or-die buddies. Thick as panty thieves and all that. Why so mushy? What's going on? It's not the girls or Hope?" She shook her head.

She chewed her bottom lip, looking away. We still held hands, in fact. It had occurred to me that we had rarely touched ever. Maybe a hug here and there, I think? But our friendship consisted of mainly dirty jokes and hilarious stories from her love life. We'd go out shopping together occasionally, hang out and watch movies at her place on one of her many streaming services. My TV was barely in use, and she had called it an embarrassment of a flatscreen TV and should be downgraded to a large tablet instead. But this, the hands, hadn't really happened, not that I could remember.

"Yeah," she said nervously, "so…I have something to ask you." Oh, God. Please don't ask for me to be a sperm donor. This woman should not have children. I loved her dearly. But from her rampant nights out, her dedication to her work and team. Taking care of her sister and her family, and the addition of her prolific sexscapades…my brain was coming to a horrific conclusion…

"You can't have my sperm!" I blurted, looking terrified. Her seriousness broke, and she cracked up laughing, and I did too, probably more nervously than her laugh.
"No silly," still looking away, "I want you to come to Hopes birthday tomorrow." Oh shit, I'd forgotten. I forgot every year because it always rolled around the anniversary of my Marcus. But I hated forgetting because Hope was incredible. Her husband Dereck was a laugh, especially when it came to describing ice hockey to me. Then, of course, the girls. Little blond bundles of youthful energy that I always had time for.

"Of course! I love Hope! And the kids?"

"Not good. Hope can barely move, eat or play with the girls." Hope, unlike her sister Patience, lived up to her name. Patience and Hope's parents had both apparently died of some rare form of cancer. It was suspected that so did their grandparents and great-grandparents. Hope now had it. She had found out after her second child. But staying true to her name, she wanted to carry on enjoying her family regardless. They had done numerous genetic tests. The genes that were suspected to be linked to this form of cancer appeared to elude the doctors. While labs who searched for them were still hoping to understand the disease.

"I'm sorry, Patience. I love Hope. Her family is great. The kids. Dereck," Hope's whole family were keeping brave faces. Dereck, Hope's husband, worked hard in marketing. He worked in marketing for luxury hospitality. He kept up a tough façade and made sure his family had everything they needed. It was the only thing he could do right now. Hope couldn't work anymore. The girls, Faith, the youngest, three, and Charity, the oldest, six, had grown used to the lifestyle and tried their best to help mummy and daddy. This was endearing, especially when the tiny tots would try to do the laundry, cook dinner, or even get dad his evening beer for TV. This had resulted in Patience hiring a full-time housemaid to prevent any more floods, fires, or spills.

"It's ok," she said, her aura darkening, feeling almost like a storm that was about to break. She was still staring off to the side. I saw the well of tears gathering in the corner of the eye closest to me and knew the other one was doing the same. Both trying to hold back the crying. Patience was a strong woman. She wouldn't break while her sister needed her. I knew how close they were. Almost like twins. Not the look-alike kind because Hope was nearly half a foot taller than her sister, but in the way they communicated. Sitting next to them at dinner, you could almost feel their silent conversation going on between the looks they gave each other. It was uncanny. It put me in the mind of the plants above our heads. When Patience and her sister were like this, I sometimes saw sparks of blue shoot between them. Patience could not lose her sister. I suspected that she would move heaven and earth to change the outcome so Hope could live a long life with her family.

"Your migraines Li." A tear escaped from one eye and trickled down; she didn't bother wiping it away; she must really be feeling helpless about Hope's situation. Losing Marcus had destroyed me internally, and picking up the pieces and trying to put them back together again felt, on most days, impossible. Patience could definitely not lose her sister. But what did my migraines have to do with anything?

"Look, of course, I'm coming to the party, but let me know if there's anything else I can do. I know my mum has been looking for new doctors for Hope ever since she found out. "
"Li!" She almost raised her voice and stopped me mid-sentence, "Your migraines, there's someone I know who might be able to help. I know the doctors have done scans and all the rest and couldn't find anything, but this friend knows stuff like your Nǎinai did." She then turned and looked at me square in the eyes. It was then she pulled her hand away, leaving behind a slip of paper. Confused, I picked it

up—a post-it note with Patience's handwriting. In addition, there was a hastily scribbled address. It was downtown, not too far from my apartment.

"What's this?" I asked, and to lighten the mood, "It's not like that time you said you had a client for me to meet who had seen my work and loved it. And then I walk into the place, and it turned out to be a swingers club…for old straight people!" I shuddered with the horror of the memory.
She scoffed and chuckled quietly, "No, not like that," she said softly, "just go tonight and follow the instructions from the bouncer. That part is important. They're good people generally, and I am sure they can help."

"It's a club?" I said suspiciously. Ok, this might be an elaborate plot to get me into another weird-ass orgy, but at least we can laugh about it at the birthday tomorrow.

"Yes, sort of. But seriously, go. This chick can help. I promise. Please. I can't help Hope but let me at least help you."

I nodded and put the paper into my messenger bag—that settled things. Patience liked to be in control of things, and cancer she couldn't control. But this, me going to see this mystery friend of hers to help with my migraines, she could handle.

"Make sure you go tonight; she's expecting you." The storm in her aura appeared to open up and spill over her whole form. Briefly obscuring her from my view. It abated and went back to as it had been before.

"Ok, Patience. I'll do this. But you can't explain any further?"

"No. I'm sorry, you'll understand when you go." She said matter-of-factly. That left no doubt in my mind that I would not be walking into the horror of naked writhing couples and thrupples trying to rekindle the tired flame in their sex lives. Look, I know I shouldn't judge, and honestly, as long as no one is getting hurt, people should love as they please. But that doesn't mean I wanna see the loving happening in front of me with bodies whose ages were closer to my parents, who were 70 now.

The rest of the day crept on, and I tried to focus on my work. That was a bust. I thought about Marcus, and a pang of heartache rippled through me. He would've loved the café. Patience missed him too, I think, in her own way. I took my sketches to the scanner to load them into my Dropbox for later editing. I put the sheets of paper into the feed and pressed the button to scan. Sparks jumped from where my finger touched the scanner keypad, and my sight saw something like a dark thread that wove into the machine and vanish into its inner workings. Smoke rose. I looked around with an embarrassed look on my face. Patience was staring at me from her office doorway. Her expression was unreadable. The machine's lights had gone dark. A murmur rose from cubicles all around the office area. I looked. Screens on desktops had gone dark, and various laptops had small trails of smoke wafting from them. What the hell? A power outage. I guess I blew a fuse.

I looked back to the scanner, frowning. I went to pull my sketches out of the feed when Patience's small hand touched my sleeve.

"Don't," she ordered softly. Then she reached over to the feed and retrieved my sketches. They were burned all around the edges, veritably ruined.

"I'll call maintenance," she stated, looking at the sketches. Her eyes appeared to burrow into the pictures I had drawn.

"Take these home and try to recreate them by Monday," handing me the charred remains.
Then she was gone. Back to her office, closing the door behind her, alone.

By the end of the workday, I was confused by Patience's odd behaviour but more tired from my grief and just wanted a bed. I packed my messenger bag. Then I remembered something, opened the second drawer of my desk, pulled out an A4 sketch block, a packet of new Faber Castell paint pencils, and a handful of new paintbrushes. I stuffed them in with my ruined day's work and knocked on Patience's office door. I knew she was in there. No answer. Perhaps she was in one of her moods or sleeping off the remains of her hangover. I left. I'd text her later.

***

Chapter 5: Home (Friday)

The lift opened to my floor, tenth, and I exited, pulling out my phone to deactivate the smart lock. I was nearing the neighbour's door when it opened. Afsaneh poked her head out and looked around, then saw me and smiled. Afsaneh was a dark-complexioned Persian with those deep brown eyes. She wore her customary Hajib and a bright smile.

"Li! How are you, dear?" They had known Marcus for as long as I had lived with him in the building. We had shared the apartment before the renovation. My parents insisted on the renovation after Marcus' passing. It was to clear out the old energy of loss and sadness, the sad memories. Had they known the energy and sadness would just move into my heart and stay there reminding me of what I had lost, they might not have bothered. Then again, perhaps they would have. It was a lovely reno.

"I'm ok, Afsaneh. How's the family? How's Baraz?" She rolled her eyes slightly in irritation.

"You know boys; he's not focusing on his studies as much as we'd like, but he's still a good boy. He wanted to show you something."

"Oh, that's cool. I have something for him too." I pulled out the sketch block, brushes, and pencils.

She showed her beautiful smile again. Vancouver really had some good-looking people. And this woman in her prime, taking care of her family, was a good example. I had liked her the moment I met her. She had a warmth about her and a strength in her eyes that reminded me of maman.

"You shouldn't; he's happy to do things for you."

"No, I insist, and he loves his art. It's the only subject he's excelling at; still, I assume?"

"You assume correct," she sighed at that, still smiling and shaking her head in resignation.

"Li!!" That little brown face of Baraz, a small eleven-year-old poked its head around his mother, "Wanna see my new frog?" Baraz looked much like his mother. Even down to the long eyelashes, lashes Patience had commented that she was extremely jealous of.

"Totally!" I said honestly. I actually liked Baraz and saw a lot of myself in him. Especially with his penchant for art, "I found these and thought you could use them." He snatched the gift eagerly, his dark eyes alight with wonder and joy.

"Wow! I wanted these paint pencils! Thanks, Li!"

"I have to unpack my things. Just let yourself in with your code when you bring your frog over. Have you got a name for him yet?"

"Not yet."
"Perfect. Then when you've had your dinner, bring him over, and we'll come up with a kick-ass name for him, and you can feed the fish too." He positively leaped away like a bundle of youthful brilliance. If only his parents could see the plethora of possibilities that surrounded his aura, they'd cease worrying about his career path. He was going to do what he wanted and would do it exceptionally well.

"Li, we have plenty. You're more than welcome to join us."

"Raincheck? I have some late errands to run and some work that needs redoing. Don't ask. Work disaster." She didn't look disappointed. She just smiled. I knew the invitation was always there. And I loved her little family for it.

"I'll send Baraz over when he's done his chores. But definitely come for dinner when you can, Elham," her husband, "has insisted on asking you over. He's like a dog with a bone when he gets something into his head." Another resigned sigh. The men in her life were both a joy and a pain. I chuckled to myself and said my goodbyes, and went into my apartment.

***

"It's pink!" I remarked. Looking into the little plastic critter keeper, "It looks like a Pokémon."

"I know, right! He nips at everything too, even the cat." We were crouching on my living room rug, eyeing the tiny monster within the plastic habitat, which was eyeing us back. Probably deciding if we could make a nice meal.

Baraz opened the lid, reached in, and tenderly drew out the amphibian and put it on my coffee table's glass top. Baraz's family, Patience, and my parents were the only visitors I entertained these days. I found dealing with people would tire me out. So, I only dealt with people I liked. It kept things simple. And it made Marcus ' passing a tiny bit easier to deal with when it initially happened.

The pink and yellow lumpy blob on my table keenly looked at both Baraz and me. Its wide mouth, almost the width of its chubby body, and the beady eyes perched atop its head made it look cartoonish and cute. I saw the appeal.

"Can I touch him?" I asked. Curious to see what it would do. The aura around the animal was a light blue. It expanded and contracted slightly in time with the frog's breathing motions.

"Sure. Be careful." I touched his back gently. He was kind of rubbery, not slimy. I went to pull my finger away, and quick as lightning the beast spun around, mouth wide, and grabbed the tip of my finger. I squealed and flew back into the couch, the frog still holding tight to my finger. Baraz looked horrified and, as gently as possible, pried him off my digit.

I busted out laughing. A full-bellied laugh. So did Baraz. It was the best laugh I had had in a while.

"I think we have a name for him," Baraz exclaimed. A little worried about my finger, I waved him away.

"And what's that," still trying to calm my laughter.

"Azhi, it means demon." He said, putting little Azhi back into his plastic prison.

"Don't you mean 'asshole!'" We both laughed again out loud.

"Don't you dare tell your mother I said that word in front of you!" I insisted, "Now you take little asshole, I mean Azhi with you. Your mum will want you to get your homework done."

"Sure thing, sorry he bit you."

"Are you kidding? It means he's a tough little Azhi and will protect you. You want that in a pet." I winked at him and opened the door. He got his little plastic habitat, Azhi and all, and was ready to leave. I was standing at the door when he turned suddenly and hugged me.

"Mum says you're sad a lot, and love is the only thing that will make it better," he said into my shirt, his little brown face squished sideways on my stomach, "So you can have some of ours. We have lots. Even Azhi, I think."

I hugged him back tightly. Feeling his little warm body showing innocent and straightforward love towards me, the way only a child could. His parents were good people, and Baraz reflected their attention and love.

"Thanks, Baraz. You're awesome, and don't you ever forget it." I let him go, and he skipped to his family's door and opened it, turned and smiled, and was gone.

My Nǎinai had said that children were innocent and powerful in their own way. They could transform the worst situation into the best just with their laughter. She was right. As she often was. Such a simple gesture had lifted my soul a little bit. Nǎinai had loved children. She had extraordinary strong views on the raising of them, and I tended to agree with her. Once, she quoted to me: "Children should never suffer adult problems, no matter what." I made a silent promise to myself to keep an eye on Baraz in the future. Such innocence and kindness should be cultivated and protected.

I closed my door, went to the fridge, touched my calendar as I did, and opened the refrigerator. I opened the box of cold pizza sitting in there from last night and downed two pieces. God, my parents would be horrified.

As if on cue, my phone rung for a video chat.

"*Wei*," I answered. My parent's faces added to the brightness that Baraz had brought into the apartment, chasing away the melancholy for a little while.

"You guys are calling later. Have you had breakfast yet?"

"Yes," Maman answered. She loved food. Her French heritage, combined with my family's Chinese, had created a culinary beast of my Maman. She recounted that they had been to the restaurant downstairs and had had real New Zealand lamb for only ten Hong Kong dollars. And you could add sides for two dollars each. She had kept her love of food but lost some French snobberies and replaced them with bargain hunting. I listened, wondering how the hell an NZ lamp chop could be sold at such a price and settled on the fact that it was probably NZ-like lamb. But I wouldn't tell her that.

Bàba took over the call, aiming as he did, the camera at his nostrils. I laughed some more that evening. He was asking about work and Patience. So I told him about our lunch. Both my parents liked Patience a lot and had met Hope on several occasions. Maman sighed and shook her head.

"Those things shouldn't happen to good people," she'd seen her fair share of oncology cases in her work. It was rarely a pretty sight, especially in aggressive cases like Hope's, "Pia has a friend there who takes on special oncology cases. He lived in Cuba for many years after doing his residency in LA. Cuba is well known for its experienced oncologists. I can't remember his name. It was a while ago; Pia was much closer to him."

"I'll make a point of asking," I promised. And I would. Seeing Patience act so strange and out of character, today was almost disturbing. The call went on for a while longer, and then we signed off.

I felt so bad for Patience. I didn't have the right to laugh and enjoy myself when my best friend was in such a state. I pulled out the piece of paper she had given me with the address. The least I could do was to keep my promises. One less thing for her to think about.

I stood up and looked over at the display cabinet, commanding Google hub to start a playlist that used to be Marcus's favourite. He couldn't sing to save himself but watching him try had been such a joy. It was hilarious listening to him belting out off-key ballads from artists with considerably more talent and more of an ear for tone. Absently, almost by an automatic notion, I went over and opened the cabinet, pulling out the silver frame with the postcard in it. I put it on the sleek glass coffee table and opened the back, taking out the piece of cardboard carefully.

"Mon Amour, I am loving Paris. I wish you were here. I miss you so much. Mairée (cousin) is constantly wanting to see sights. I'll see you on vid chat soon, baby. I love you so much. Ps. I found the pillow you put in my luggage; it still smells like you. Love you. Marcus"

I dropped it on the coffee table. Marcus had been in Paris with his cousin Mairée who had always wanted to go but couldn't afford it. We were all supposed to go together, but Nǎinai had just passed away. I needed to stay with Maman and Bàba to help them make arrangements.

Regret. Hurt. Misery. These old friends climbed up again out of the pit. I snatched up the paper Patience had given me and pushed the feelings away.

Shower, I stroked my chin and shave. It's a club. I'd better at least try to look like I belonged. I looked briefly out the window and could barely see the city lights. Streams of rainwater pelted my windows. Rain. Not uncommon at any time of the year for Vancouver, but jeez, it made me want to snuggle up on the couch and watched some sappy K-dramas or some anime for inspiration. Pretty much the only time my "giant tablet" got any use.

I went to my closet and pulled out what I thought might be appropriate "club" wear. A long-sleeved (always long-sleeved) tight black top, crew neck. Tight (I'm gay, so they're gonna be tight, right?) jeans and black boots. The boots were ones that Marcus had insisted I needed. They were by a brand called Dior. He had sighed amusingly and asked how I made it through design without knowing who Christian Dior was. I also had a leather jacket that I wore often. It was a black biker jacket. I just liked it because it was comfortable.

***

To Kitsune, family is everything. Our Skulk was our lifeblood and our future. To understand what price would put me at Kentaro's disposal, it was my family. Our temples where we made our homes. They were on land that had been long claimed by a clan of vampires. For years it was a peaceful cohabitation between the two. Our skulk had even helped defend the territory on more than one occasion. As time went by and humans spread and their cities began to expand, it was easy for the vampires to integrate more thoroughly with the times. For Kitsune, it became more complex, and for my family, my skulk, it was especially so. We had lived lives near the Inari temples. Humans began to build their towers everywhere and pushed us further and further into areas that put us at risk of exposure. The temple disciples always worked tirelessly to help us, and we did our best to protect them.

When I was grown and I was able to transform into my human form, it was one of the most liberating things. I would sneak away from the safety of the temple's grounds just to see the humans going about their strange lives. My Okāsan caught me doing so one night, and instead of reprimanding me as I had expected, she encouraged me.

'Ayaka, my love, you should enjoy this new world that seems to be moving so fast for us. I think it is truly the only way for us to survive. Staying apart for too long has cost us an understanding that is vital to our Skulk. Our ignorance could be our death. Get the monks to teach you how to read more languages than ours. It will be useful to your future.'

I remember going out and trying to pretend to be one of the humans and not doing an outstanding job. Their rules of social engagement were so rigid and unnecessary. However, on many occasions, I found humans that I enjoyed so much that they became lovers for a short time. My brothers and sister had laughed at my choices, saying there was no point having relations with a human, let alone one of the same gender. My Okāsan, wonderful Okāsan. She was good at protecting our vulnerable bodies and also our hearts. She would tell them to hush and that my path was not theirs and they should find their own - Ayaka

***

Chapter 6: Crossroads (Friday)

Rain pelted down on my umbrella, pattering angrily and not being able to penetrate the stiff fabric. I hoped that I was dressed appropriately in all black, which matched my umbrella at least. I had just left the apartment and was almost there. The location was a little hidden, apparently. Maximal discreetness, with minimal fuss, I supposed. Only people such as I would be looking for it, according to Patience's last text. Apparently, she had only recently been made aware of its existence. The rain came down heavily, even this close to spring. Canadian winters could be beautiful, and in Vancouver, they were, but also very wet even when spring was just around the corner. I was wearing black on purpose. I supposed it would help hide me in the night. Lame. I wasn't a spy. I had almost lost the nerve, turned back, and gone home to settle into a night of Netflix K-dramas and chill, alone, with all that entailed. But I had done it; I was out, and I was determined to see this through now. I was walking in Davie Village, known for its gays, eclectic shops, and restaurants. There was plenty of streetlights for people to see by.

A brownstone building. A heritage building probably, with a stairwell leading to its basement level. It was mainly obscured, and the balustrade was being choked with ivy. Above the stair was a cast-iron sign that swung slightly in the rainy breeze with a single symbol on it, a tree design, like those Celtic World Tree designs. Lights of all rainbow-coloured colours shone from it, indicating clearly to those with the "sight," I presumed, where that stairwell led. Careful not to slip, I stepped down. A few stairs down, I noticed there was no rain at all on the stairs. Curious. At the foot of the stairs, the brownstone carved out a neat little two-metre by three-metre box with ivy hanging down. The entrance to the building was a huge black door with, in keeping with the theme, a cast iron door knocker with the same glittering rainbow 'tree' motif as the sign. Blocking the door was an incredibly muscular, bodybuilder-type male. He looked like a pairing of a smooth lumberjack and an Abercrombie model. Tight black tee and jeans to match. His skin was that lovely ebony colour, so smooth that it appeared to shine in the night's minimal light. His hair was dark as well and oiled, making its abundance of curls also stand out. It seemed to contradict whatever nationality he was, but the overall effect was distractingly attractive and sexy. His eyes kept changing hue depending on whether the light was reflecting off them or not. Strange!

"You won't be needing that in there," he said in a gravelly but warm voice. Likely a smoker. He pointed to my opened umbrella I was stupidly still holding above my head even though, for some reason, the rain declined to enter the area. I popped it closed and handed it to him, unsure of what to do next.

"Oh," I said. I always got a little tongue-tied around most hot guys. It was a perpetual problem that likely kept me quite single, that and my inability to move beyond my past.

"Now, who do we have here," he said, looking me up and down, almost hungrily. He had a tightly cropped beard, the kind that was practically stubble and well-groomed. His ebony skin complimented everything about him and reminded me silk or satin, and if I was bold, I would have reached out to touch his face. When he smiled, his teeth shone white in the night. A smile that would get me in trouble, and I might enjoy it.

"My name is L…." Almost like lightning, his giant hand came up to stop my introduction.
"Are you sure you are in the right place? No names, son." Son? Was he one of those daddy types? *Argh*. Mind out of the gutter and back on task. Patience was adamant that I listened to this guy's instructions.

"I think so…."

"You see the sign?" He pointed up.

"Yeah, it's hard to miss with the Studio 54 light show." At that, he grinned. I had guessed right. My 'sight' was some kind of ticket here. My nervousness and tension just washed away at his smile and headed further south.

"Well then, welcome…." He opened the large door, "to the Crossroads." He held his giant hand against the lower of my back, sending a desperate shiver through me, guiding me in. Had it really been so long that my body was reacting so irrationally to every hunk today?

"Head straight for the bar and don't stop to talk to anyone, you hear?" I nodded dumbly. He faced me directly, almost looking concerned. Then he was back out as the heavy door closed with a louder than necessary thud.

I looked around, and I did as he'd instructed and moved through a throng of bodies that appeared to dominate a dance floor. The figures moved and writhed; the colours in my 'sight' began to get confusing and mixed. I could almost feel the dancers, the same way you could feel power lines when you walked under them. There was a heady vibe of sensuality and sex filling the air. The air itself smelled like spices and perfumes that threw my mind into a spin and brought images of sweat, heavy breathing, and secret nights into my mind. In the center of the sizeable multi-level space was an enormous tree whose branches reached into the hidden depths of the ceiling. Looking at it gave me the strangest feeling of familiarity. Odd. Balconies encircled the place at every level, with two large visible staircases on either side upon entering. The floor looked like concrete polished to a high sheen, and it was hard to concentrate.

Music was playing. It was some kind of indie/dance mash-up, and bodies writhed around me, almost melting into one another before separating and joining another dance somewhere else. I saw the bar at the far end of the space and made for it. At the edge of my periphery, I saw semicircular couches which seated people of all kinds. I saw one, who was surrounded by well-dressed suited muscle, wearing a bespoke black Armani suit, if I was any judge. He had an identical man sitting next to him, wearing a white suit, just like his counterpart. The dark one was eyeing me as he held the hand of the white-suited guy tightly on the table. His eyes narrowed, and he leaned forward. His gaze seemed to glint blue and silver, which was strange considering the lights and colours I saw should have hidden such details. His face was passive. He looked almost

Romanian or some Central, possibly Eastern European mix. If perhaps Dracula and the guy outside the door decided to have a baby, this would be the result. A lovely result nonetheless. The suits around him were not bad looking either; they seemed to have Asian features, and one flashed a silver look at me. But their presence demanded less attention compared to this guy and his pale-dressed compatriot. His gaze was piercing. I kept moving, and he leaned back into his couch alcove, half carrying on a conversation with one of the suits next to him, still holding his eye on me. It unnerved me. I picked up my pace.

The heavy scent of musk, flowers, and spices suddenly assaulted my sense. It almost made me cough, but instead, it made my muscles feel leaden. I kept walking, trying to ignore whatever it was.

"*Mm*, nice to see a new face here? And who might you be?" I turned. What met my eyes made the bouncer, heck any guy I had ever met, seem a hideous old wretch compared to this. He was copper-skinned, with almond-shaped eyes. A smooth Asian face with long dark hair that swayed loosely about his shoulders. His smile held promises and his amber eyes had a feral hunger. What?! I tried to snap myself back to lucidity, but something about the scent and his fiery eyes held my attention. No, I yelled mentally at myself, to the bar and nothing else. Marcus' beautiful face floated into the forefront of my thoughts, sobering me. The guy flinched as if I had slapped him. I carried on toward the bar, ignoring the gorgeous interruption.

I made it around the giant tree. It was in the middle of the room (weird), and when I accidently brushed up against it, I felt like someone was giving me a hug. Not physically, just almost the notion of one (double weird!) to the back wall with the bar that stretched end to end. A woman of approximately middle years, wiping the sweat off her brow with a towel as she danced back and forward from one end of the bar to the other. This was an effective technique for serving the patrons and keeping up alone behind the bar. She had a tight bouncy ponytail and a no-nonsense face that saw me and came over immediately.

She handed me a glass of clear fluid and aided me in drinking it. I was suddenly awake. Like I had had a triple shot coffee with twenty sugars in the space of a heartbeat. I hadn't realized how foggy my thoughts had been just crossing the dance floor. I could hear the music and still smelled the sweat, perfume, and incense, but my mind was less distracted, "Thanks," I croaked out.

"That's better," she said, "you looked a little lost and out of it. This place can be quite a hit to the senses if you're not prepared for it." She gave me another shot of the liquid. It had no taste but went down quickly, and my fatigue of the day seemed to fade away." One second," She said, darting off to another set of patrons. These patrons looked like they were dressed for a Dungeons and Dragons convention, costumed as goat horns, but human bodies and bare chests, both men and women in the group. They were laughing jovially and lifting mugs of some liquid in a toast. The woman who had revived my senses with her beverage was literally just spraying an ale or beer hose over the bar at them. They were catching every drop in their mugs, barely spilling a drop. The show was mesmerizing. They showed such dexterity. They must have been a Cirque De Solei troupe. I had been to a show in Vegas called *Zumanity* with remarkably similar characters. All gorgeous and too sexually appealing to be authentic. She then rushed back to me, breathing hard, "Sorry… right."

"Now, the first thing I need to tell you. No names! It's dangerous. Keep it to yourself. Come up with an alias if you must," she looked up and down the bar, constantly aware of the patron's needs. "Second thing is, I know someone sent you to me, don't mention her name either. But you are gonna have to be really honest with me about what you are doing here. Think about that. I have to fill a few orders." She zipped off again to a different set of patrons while I mulled over her comments and question.

I got my bearings and looked out across the club. The same iridescent lights that were on the sign outside permeated everything in here. They were auras, like the ones I was used to seeing, only more intense. The reason I was here, I supposed. I had come to the right place, so hopefully, this was the right person if this was about getting rid of migraines. I'd have to thank Patience profusely if this worked out. It also meant she was right; I'd have to be honest.

She came back with an expectant look. "Well?"

"Yes. Well, the thing is," I continued to tell the particulars of my migraines and the auras but left out my Năinai and her theories about my "sight."
"There's something else, I'm sure, and maybe you're not aware of it yet." She eyed me keenly as she said it.

"Anyways, I'm Neelas," before I could question the use of her name, she said, "alias obviously, but I use it often here. This is a crossroads of sorts: A place where the veil between worlds is thin enough for beings to go back and forth depending on their nature. And by the looks on your face, this doesn't seem at all too strange for you," Well, it wasn't so much. I mean beings and all that was weird, but Năinai had lectured me about the possibilities of worlds within worlds. I had always thought it was her convoluted understanding of atomic structures, but she also told me, "Don't assume anything." Certainly not without all the information, my boy!

"My Năinai was old Chinese from the mainland. We're very superstitious there. I found that often applied to real life, no matter what people thought."

"I work here as a sort of 'overseer,' and as it turns out, a helper of the lost little talents who has fallen through the cracks. You, being one of them." She gestured to the club in general.

"I see," so succinct in my delivery tonight. I was either going mad, or the woman was telling me the truth. Which was more likely given my history and Năinai." So what is my talent exactly? Other than seeing psychedelic patterns without the fun of eating mushrooms?"

"I'm still trying to figure it out. My skills are limited compared to others. It's why I'm working behind a bar and not running a practice." She laughed at her own observation, "The next move is yours. What do you want to do with it?"

"What? I mean, I want it to stop, obviously. My life is complicated enough without 'latent 'abilities." I even made the inverted commas with my fingers.

"Ok, this I can do. In fact, it's kind of part of my duties here at the Crossroads. Depending on the nature of your latent abilities, they can be suppressed permanently or controlled."
"I see," I frowned. This was not what I had expected when I left the apartment this evening. For some reason, though, it felt right. My instincts told me to hear this woman out. Nǎinai had also told me to keep my instincts honed, especially when it came to people.

"Tell me, what do you see when you look around here? Other than the overtly sexual crowd and multitudes of weirdos?" She was again right; weirdos were in abundance, in the form of cosplay fans, armour, monster get-ups, and fairy wings were all in attendance… Only if she was telling the truth; these weren't all cosplayers and dress-up fans. Scanning the place, I saw again the heavy pall of colours seeping through everything and everyone. Waves of it cascaded from one individual to another. Some had more of the coloured light around them than others. Auras…

"I see auras, a lot of them, and a lot of energy, I guess, a giant aura within this place."
She nodded. She took the glass I had drunk from, held it close to her mouth, and gently blew upon its lip. Multi-coloured sparks bounced all around the rim, changing from one colour to the next.

"Tell me, are you much of a touchy-feely kinda guy? I'm betting no."

"Uh…Correct..." I was assessing her words and reactions as much as she was mine.

"I can see something else," she was peering into my eyes, "you probably experience bouts of unexplained bad luck, I'm guessing. Ha! Recently if I'm any judge."

"Correct again." She knew I was testing her. My Năinai had warned me in situations involving anyone from her side of the tracks not to give anything away. So, although the bar lady was helpful, I was cautious.

"And today, a big one," I thought of my scanner accident and the technical fallout through the office.

"What happened?"

"There was a power surge in the electrical that wiped out the office tech, including the scanner."

"And where did it start?"

"The scanner, I replied."

"Wrong," she said, pointing a finger towards my chest, "it came from you, my dear."

"I don't have some weird hexing powers; I would've noticed, and my Năinai would likely have told me."

"Would she now?" Neelas raised her brows at the mention of my Năinai. Oops. I didn't like talking about my Năinai and her… weird stuff. It elicited too many questions. Uncomfortable questions. "Give me your hand for a moment, please," I was hesitant and didn't move, "don't worry, it's nothing weird. I promise I'm here to help. Also, unlike most here, I'm 100% prime beef human." Ok, she said it. This place was filled with some "beings" that were not exactly human. I mentally sighed. Năinai! I was sure you missed a few things in my education.

I gave her my hand. She didn't stare at my palm as I had thought she would. She just touched it lightly, scrutinizing it.

"A Mimic. You're a mimic."

"I'm sorry a…?"

"A mimic. They, meaning you, are incredibly rare and mostly useless in a practical sense. But still great for party tricks if you can tame it," Neelas continued eyeing the hand in hers curiously. "I'm almost certain, though I can't tell you where the stray energy came from that blew out your office."

"How it works for mimics is that they touch anyone with a talent, and they can immediately for a temporary time copy it. Someone in your life has some talent, I'm guessing. They may not even know it."

"Can it go away?"

"Sure can with a tincture that's aptly called, 'Eraser,'" she laughed as if it was a private joke or something. "You seem quite sensitive, hence then aura seeing. You'll be fine as long as you don't touch anyone for a while. Stay away from these beautiful freaks here too. I have the tincture, but it's your decision. Plus, knowing you have this talent makes it easier to control. You might want to keep it. I would; I don't have any talents."

"What do you mean?" I laughed, "You practically divined 'me 'right here. That's a talent, Neelas." She snorted and waved an "aww shucks" look at me.

"No, Hun, that's just a lot of experience. I have been in this game a while," she went on to explain, "the 'eraser' basically shuts down your centres for a time. It gives them time to readjust to what is, I suppose, a normal…frequency? The mixology, not just cocktails (she winked at me), is my only talent, I guess, not inherent, just study."

I was about to say no, then suddenly realized what it meant. A piece of me would be shut down and gone. By choice, but still gone.

"Fuck, I need a drink." I huffed. I think I did too.

"Now that, darling, is something I can do. What will you have?" Ok. It had been a long time since I had been to a club, let alone drank alone. I felt kind of rebellious, naughty, or even dangerous. "I dunno," I gave her a sheepish grin.

"The gayest cocktail you can come up with, please. It's been a long week,"

"Coming right up." She spun on her heel and set about creating… something.

"Neelas, babe! What's a Yokai gotta do!" The voice came from my left. It also came from the man I had ignored on the dance floor. I continued to ignore him—nose in the air.

"Aya Hun! Give me a sec. I have a shiny new customer, and I wanna do this right," she had her back to me and was grabbing all sorts of bar-like paraphernalia. I saw her grab paper umbrellas, pineapple slices. Whatever she was building, there was sure to be a marvel.

"That you do," said the man. I could feel him looking at me. I kept my gaze on Neelas 'industrious back while she worked.

"Hey there," he had moved closer, and I could smell his cologne. It was intense but pleasant. Spicy and filling my air space. I was trying desperately to maintain my stone-like ignorance…. and failing.

"Um… hi," Wow, the epitome of eloquence was I.

"It's ok," he moved his face to the front of mine, "I'm friendly," he held his hands up like he was surrendering something. I barely noticed; his presence was as intoxicating as his smooth, mellow voice. It was like sorcery had given chocolate a voice and incredible beauty then sat it right next to me. He was wearing jeans similar to mine, tight, and I tried not to look. He had a tight long-sleeved shirt like mine, except his was red with a huge black mesh V from neck to navel. His dark hair, long and straight, sat about his shoulders like a halo of silk. I wanted to touch it. Snap out of it!

Neelas chose that moment to spin about to reveal a multicoloured monstrosity in an oversized giant glass goblet. It had layers of rainbow frozen liquor. At least six paper umbrellas were stabbed into it—every type of fruit imaginable balanced on top like a cornucopia of colour and frivolity. A miniature glitter-covered unicorn candy hung off the edge of the bulbous glass. There were little plastic pool boys, by the looks of them, swimming in the mixture around a tiny green bottle. The whole concoction had some kind of pink mist flowing off around and over the rim of the glass, making pink snowflake patterns appear along the side.

"Tada!" As if revealing the Mona Lisa for the first time. I laughed again, a second full belly laugh for the evening and entirely for the drink she'd so proudly presented. Out of nowhere, she flipped a plastic penis straw, the kind used for bachelorette parties, into the rainbow icy depths, penis head facing me. Ok, this woman was an artist.

"Wow!" I coughed out between laughter.

"Wow!" the man next to me echoed. He was giggling too.

"And what's this bit?" I pointed to the tiny green bottle. Something about it was familiar. It held an aura I had seen before but couldn't quite pin down.

"That," Neelas explained, pointing to the bottle, "is the 'Eraser.' In case you make the decision to say goodbye to all of this," she waved her hand vaguely around the vast room, "and him," pointing at the man who had now seated himself on the stool next to me.

"Rude," he said simply with a smile at the corners of his mouth.

"Yokai, be good and take care of my friend here; I have work to do."

"What about my drink Neelas?"

"What about it?" She yelled from the other end of the bar. He sighed. Obviously, something fun and friendly going on between those two. Who knows, I was more intrigued by the pink ice forming on the glass; how did she?

Still not looking at him and totally unsure how to deal with the guy, I decided to be polite and pleasant.

"You can share mine," I indicated to the carnival of alcohol in front of me, "this thing is huge, and I'm quite sure it's enough the get a whole frat crew drunk off their tits." He continued to look at me curiously, his pretty face alarmingly distracting. His cologne still clouding the air around us.

"Don't mind if I do," he leaned over the bar and grabbed a straw and proceeded the stab it into the rainbow lagoon in front of us, "but you first," he gestured to the drink.

I kept one eye on the beautiful interloper and on my drink. I put my mouth to the straw and took a massive gulp without thinking. My head felt like it was splitting open and giving birth to the drink sitting on the bench in front of me.

The man next to me snickered in amusement.

"Owe!" I wheezed. Brain freeze. God. How embarrassing, trying to look all cool and careful with my giant drink in front of this gorgeous stranger. Of course, I had to mess it up. Fuck it. The pain was where my attention was at the moment; embarrassment could wait a minute or two.

"Slow down. It's a big drink, and you're a small guy. Pace yourself. Neelas would murder me if anything happened to you now that I've been charged with your safety here."

I held my hand to the side of my head with one eye clenched shut, waiting for the pain to abate.
"Safety?" I looked around the bar again. Yeah, I don't think any of these people were human. They, like this guy, seemed too perfect. The idea of human sexuality and perfection had been condensed into one body. Their beauty put me in the mind of predators, like a tiger stalking its prey. My mind flicked to the guy on the couches with his harem of cute Asian suits around him. Yeah, I think I was right

there. Predators. Though Neelas was here, and she was ok. Perhaps she just knew the rules of this environment.

"It's nothing. Just enjoy your drink, and let me try some too." He leaned over, without moving the glass from in front of me, placing a hand on the seat edge of my stool and the other on the counter to balance himself. He kept both eyes on me, two glittering amber orbs. Then he wrapped his lips around the penis head straw and sucked up a hefty amount of the concoction. I'm sure I was close to creaming my briefs as my dick hardened and my heart pounded against my ribcage; this was getting absurd. No, I wasn't going to get horny with this obvious playboy and his…well, everything!

I pulled my eyes away from him and focused on the back wall. This felt weird. I had an erection for this stranger, and I was drinking a balloon of alcohol in a magical bar? I closed my eyes and thought of Marcus. My love. Again, my thoughts cleared, Marcus could do that for me, even when he was alive, be an anchor. I looked at the guy. Again, he flinched. The smile wavered slightly. I looked at his aura and focused on that. My face must have shown some surprise.

"What is it?" He said, his eyes with their amber depths showing amusement.

"Ah, um, nothing," I stammered. Not sure how to tell the guy that I couldn't see his aura for some weird reason. Everything had an aura of some kind. His just appeared to be not there. In fact, as I looked around, there were many patrons whose aura could not be seen.

"I see," he took another sip of the cocktail, still leaning in closer, "it's not uncommon for people such as I to keep it to themselves." While sipping, he looked down at my left hand holding the stem of the glass and saw the white line of the scar tissue disappear into my sleeve. I self-consciously pulled my sleeve up in a vain attempt to cover it.

"Keep what," had he known what I was doing?

"We call it a signature. Usually, humans call it an 'Aura' or energy field. And most, unlike you, can't perceive them without considerable effort." Humans?

"Humans?" Oh, I'd said that out loud. He was too close. It felt good, but it also felt like I was betraying Marcus in some way. There it was again, a slight flinch. I brought to mind Marcus again, remembering his tousled curls and his eyes, so blue and his laugh that somehow contained his French-Canadian accent. The guy backed away fully to his own seat. Interesting. I didn't know the rules here yet, but I bet I could learn some pretty quickly. Then Neelas's words came back: *Say goodbye to all this, and him!* Well, saying goodbye to the wet dream next to me was, in all likelihood, a good idea.

"Yes, humans. As in you are a human." He said it as if it were a fair statement. But he just confirmed my sight, my feelings of this place, and what Neelas had said. This was some kind of way station for "weird" folks.

"Well, yeah, we all…." I stopped and looked around. I saw the people that were missing auras, while others seemed to be flaunting them. Dancing with abundance on the dance floor. Năinai had told me about beings that existed alongside us that looked like us but weren't called Fae or Fairies. It was the only time I hadn't trusted what she said. But now…

"Huh," was all I could come up with to say. I looked at the stunning beauty next to me. He seemed suddenly withdrawn, the cheeky smile sad but still there. I sipped on the cocktail some more, careful not to let the icy beverage touch the roof of my mouth this time. It was good. And strong. I was already feeling a little tipsy. And then it occurred to me.

"Um, Neelas?" She was serving another group down the end. Somehow, she had heard me over the music and throng of sounds and bodies. She turned to me with a question on her face.

"I didn't pay for the drink." She laughed and carried on serving the group in front of her. They did pay, with some currency I couldn't see. They had auras, but their auras reminded me of the plants in the café earlier today. Vibrant and green, but primal, beautiful, and…not human. I could only see a few human auras now that I scanned the bar. Human auras fluctuated constantly but hugged tightly to their body, like a bubble. The others, their auras, seemed to permeate everything and mix together to create a cloud of dream-like energy floating overhead.

"Humans don't pay for drinks here," the man whispered, and somehow, I could hear him clearly. This situation was getting a little beyond Nǎinai's stories and quickly becoming something out of my manga comics.

"You're a human; you don't need to pay for drinks. It's one of the rules of this place."

Frowning at my drink, I came to a decision. I pulled the tiny bottle from my massive cocktail and pocketed it. The man on the stool watched me do so, still with a slightly saddened look. I pushed the cocktail over to him.

"Here, thanks for the weird time, but I think I'll be going." I stood up from my stool and turned to leave. His hand gently reached up to my shoulder, careful not to touch my skin.

"So soon?" I didn't really feel like explaining how odd this entire interaction was to me, nor how unbelievable this place was. Neither did I want to explain the thrill his touch sent through me and his apparent interest. Looking around: the giant tree in the middle thrumming with its own seemingly friendly aura of energy; the people here, all looking like they were from some ethereal dreamscape - alluring, graceful, and obviously dangerous. If even half of the stories Nǎinai had imparted onto me about the Fae when I was young were true, then I needed to get out of here.

"Yes, I can't be here." He looked disappointed and took his hand off my shoulder, "Thank you though, you have been very charming and hospitable. But I must go."

"Ok, sure," he stood up, "I'll walk you out, at least let me do that."

"Thank you, I don't even know what to call you. Thank you, that'd be good, I think." Did Neelas say Aya? I couldn't be sure.

I called out to Neelas to thank her. She just waved vaguely in my direction while serving another otherworldly group of patrons.

My escort stood next to me and placed his hand lightly on the small of my back, as had the bouncer not so long ago. I was so keenly aware of his hand. I couldn't ignore his touch there. He guided me to the door I had entered. We passed the group of suits I had seen earlier. The vampy wannabe was still staring. This time, though, he looked a little pissed, not so much at me, but at my escort. A detail to file away for later examination, like this whole messed up experience.
We got to the door, and my chaperone knocked twice. It was opened by the same bouncer I had met earlier. Now looking at him, I was convinced he was probably not human either. I turned to thank the guy again for being so hospitable.

"Can I see you again?" he asked before I could get a word out, a hopeful tone in his voice. Yet, everything he did seemed to reverberate in me, even this simple question—Yup, dangerous.

"I'm not so sure; I appreciate you helping me out of here," I didn't want to even begin to explain why seeing me would be a bad idea. Even if he was an average person, let alone something my Nǎinai had always warned me about.

"Well, perhaps we'll leave it to fate then." He said, almost tenderly; the bouncer smiled too as he saw me exit and handed me my umbrella. I thanked him and made my way up the steps and out of this mad dream. With every step, I could feel those amber eyes watching me. They both thrilled and scared me to the core. So, I did as I had earlier and brought Marcus' image to my mind. It comforted me, almost like a protective cover, because the feeling of those pretty eyes and their gorgeous owner disappeared. I popped my umbrella and headed home to the safety of my apartment.

***

Chapter 7: Home Safe Home (Friday)

Entering my home's safety, I put my umbrella on the stand next to the door and hung my coat on it. I went to the kitchen and got a glass of water. It vanished quickly down my throat, and then another. I was staring out the floor-length windows into the rain-soaked night—all in all, that had to be the strangest event I had encountered in my whole life. A few possibilities were edging into my conscious mind.

One was the air had been pumped full of some hallucinogenic compound akin to LSD and Ecstasy. Two, I was finally going lala over the edge of sanity into the sea of insanity. Possible. Option three, my Nǎinai, had been telling the truth the whole time. I'd have to flick through her journals. She had never been secretive with them around me. But upon discovering them as a kid, I'd only seen a bunch of Chinese characters, strange pictures, and diagrams that made no sense to me as a six-year-old. And I hadn't bothered to open them since. Maybe one held a notion of what I had just experienced.

The Crossroads.

It sounded like a fantasy fiction novel bar. The kind that leads the main character into a world of trouble. Was I that character in this story? If I were, I would be a total wimp and steer clear of places and people like that.

I opened the display cabinet and pulled out the eighteen small red volumes accrued over my Nǎinai's life. Her journals weren't a daily exercise. The type of woman she was, she wouldn't bother with, "Dear Diary" shit. She'd write down anything useful that she had encountered.
I gently placed my postcard back in its frame when I dumped the books on my coffee table. Then I put it back in its place in the cabinet, next to a few other treasures that my Nǎinai had left me. I went back to the coffee table and fanned out the books. They weren't thick, like a Harry Potter spellbook or anything. They reminded me more of the sketch block I had given Baraz, only about

one-quarter of the size. I just stared at them for a time. For some reason, I was apprehensive about opening any of them.

Leaving them there on the coffee table, I pulled out my cell and dialled Patience's number.

"Hey Li," She was panting like she'd been running a marathon.

"Are you on the treadmill? It's like three am?" I asked.

"Ah… yeah… the treadmill."

"Who's that?" A man's voice broke in. I blushed and laughed.

"Oh shit, sorry Hun," I had to apologize; she was busy.

"No, no. What's up?" She continued her heavy breathing. I heard the sounds of complimentary grunts and heavy breathing from the guy on the other end.
"I was gonna ask you for a drink, but not if you're-"

"How about breakfast at our café?"

"We're not having breakfast?" the man chimed in the background.

"Shut up; I'll give you something to eat in a minute!" I almost vomited. I loved patience, but TMI.

"Yup, breakfast, done. See you around 10?"

"Sure thing. Love you, bub." She hung up. I tried to shake the horrendous image of my best friend riding some guy's face while I was trying to talk to her on the phone. Calling Google hub to play some soft melodic instrumental music, I started to wind down.

I went to the bathroom and pulled off my shirt, and, without much thought, sniffed it. It smelled strongly of that spicy cologne the gorgeous stranger had been wearing. How?

I stripped off and went to stand under the hot water of a sobering shower. I was letting the water wash away thoughts of auras, monsters, Patience on some guy, otherworldly patrons frequenting a bar not far from my home, and even wash away some of the pervasive grief that haunted me. It even began to blur the strange lunch I had had with Patience. The water sprayed down hotly on my naked body, massaging as many of the cares of the world away—strange evening all in all.

***

Chapter 8: Korean Café (Saturday)

Downstairs from my apartment, I was lucky enough to have an abundance of restaurants, cafes, and bars. My favourite café was owned by a Korean family. The daughter usually worked the counter and took great delight when I would try and thank her in Korean that I had learned from my K-dramas. They sold typical café fare, but what I liked most was their coffee. I also liked the fact they played K-pop unapologetically in the background. A large double shot mocha in a mug. Even on a hot day, I'd order it. It was a great pick-me-up for any time of the day. I had ordered a strong long black espresso for the arrival of Patience. I also took the liberty of ordering her breakfast: bacon, eggs over easy, toast, and hash browns. We had known each other for so long that we knew our respective routines and preferences. I ordered my usual spinach omelet and an orange juice for when my coffee was finished.

The tiny bottle I had rescued from my jeans before last night's outfit was dumped into the hamper rolled around in my palm while I looked at it curiously. The bottle had an aura terribly similar to the package Patience had received the other day. And it didn't take a genius to figure they came from the same source - Neelas. I wondered what Patience had ordered. New birth control that was permanent with no side effects, or something to stop hangovers from ever affecting her again? I re-pocketed the small green bottle and began flicking through my phone's pictures, trying to avoid the "Marcus" folder. I was looking at some of the botanical garden pics I had taken earlier in spring. The flowers in bloom always inspired many of my paintings. I loved the tulips with two different colours, red and yellow or violet and white. It's hard to believe one bulb of these would fetch the cost of a house several centuries ago. There were pictures of cherry blossom trees in all four seasonal stages: bare and skeletal in winter, green and blooming in spring, with the blossoms floating their petals like pink snowflakes. I loved the brilliant deep green leaves that turned to orange and red flames during fall—my favourite. Perhaps I'd add some of that theme into the new manga cover I was working on.

The bell above the entrance doorway tinkled, and I looked up, squinting momentarily at the sea of colour around me and focusing on the new arrival. My "sight" was still in full force, though no migraine had presented yet.

Entered my friend Patience. She smiled sheepishly (strange....) and came to sit down. She was dressed in her athleisure wear. She usually went for an early morning run after a night of…whatever was happening on the phone last night. I knew that after we had attended her sister's birthday this afternoon, she'd probably head to the indoor range and fire off rounds. She'd do this until she felt the little paper men outlines on the targets had paid dearly enough for whatever crimes she imagined they had committed today.

"Hey," she squeezed my shoulder, her usual sign of physical affection for anyone close to her except her sister, who she treated as an extension of herself.

"Hey yourself, what the hell happened last night? Some mister was obviously disappointed to not be joining us?" I queried, raising one eyebrow in amusement. Seating herself opposite me in the little café, she sighed loudly and buried her face in her hands. At the same time, I giggled, knowing already the answers that'd follow.
"You know Heath, he's always trying to break the 'friends with benefits' zone." Heath was her regular when her prospects had dried up on the apps or in the bars. I had seen him once when I had barged in on one of their rendezvous on her couch when she had forgotten we had made dinner plans. He was a slam dunk hottie. Ebony skin African Canadian, muscled with a handsomely chiselled face, like a real-life sexy action figure. That is basically how she treated him. When I had first seen him, he looked at Patience hopefully, not caring that he was naked underneath her, wanting to finally be introduced to her GBFF, which everyone knows is a milestone in any relationship. He was sadly mistaken, as he must've been last night when she reminded him of the only "meal" he'd be having close to our breakfast, which would be her to the early hours of the morning. Gross!

"You could give him a chance, you know. He's cute and obviously smitten with you. You've been seeing each other for almost, what, two years?"

"Yeah," she sighed less obnoxiously, resigned to the mini-lecture that was to come.

"It's great having someone around to share life with," I thought of Marcus briefly. My grief somehow tapered off as another face floated into my thoughts…a Japanese beauty, long silken hair…I shook off the thoughts. Shut up, little Brain (little brain = penis)!

"That's what I have you for, silly. You don't ask for anything and are way more fun and less complicated than men. Every girl should have a Li." I smirked at her comments.

"Less complex? You forget what terror I put you guys through a couple years ago."

"Yeah, well, an anomaly that is highly unlikely to repeat itself as you had promised both your parents and me." Our order was being delivered by the pleasant young Korean daughter. She was sweet, slightly chubby but held such an appeal about her manner that I wouldn't be surprised if she had snagged herself a bf already, of gf, if I weren't too presumptuous. Patience dove into her meal, obviously needing to recover the calories she had been burning since last night's nocturnal workout. I waited till she was finished wolfing down her eggs to notice that I was staring at her expectantly.

"What?" She said with half mouthful of egg.

"Aren't you gonna ask about last night?" She swallowed her eggs and then slowly started picking up pieces of hash brown and dipping them in the small pottle of ketchup provided and started eating them one by one. She was avoiding my gaze.

"So what happ…." I cut her off mid-sentence, only half angry.

"What happened, my darling Patience," my voice came out almost a hiss through gritted teeth, ok, I was probably laying it on a bit thick, but I wanted to have a bit of drama at this moment, "what happened? I went to the address you provided and met your friend you mentioned."

She looked up and sunk into her chair, not just with embarrassment and shame, but something else…worry?

"Neelas did as you had suggested and gave me this." I pulled out the bottle and put it right in front of her plate. She looked at it. No surprise in her face, "A 'cure' for my migraines, and apparently for my latent abilities or something like that." She just looked at the bottle. Face impassive.

"Did you know?"

"Did I know what?" she snapped back.

"Did you know what was in that club? This isn't like the time you mislead me into going to an oldies swingers club."

"Yeah," She whispered, "yeah, I knew."

"Hmph," I leaned back in my seat, looking directly at her. She knew I was mad, but she was dying to know what happened.

"Have you been there? Inside that club?"

"No," she replied, "I met Neelas somewhere else. She's an old acquaintance; actually, someone I had consulted about Hope, but I swear I didn't know what was in that club; I just knew she'd be working there. I can't go in. Most people can't go in."

"I see," Still keeping my gaze steady, letting her stew in her thoughts a little more, "so Neelas, is she legit? Like my Năinai was legit?"

"Oh yeah," she also leaned back in her seat. Patience hadn't really been that curious about Năinai's work. Still, I had told her enough to understand some things, and she'd obviously taken some initiative to help her sister, I guess. Who wouldn't?

"So Neelas is human-like, she said?"

"Ha! She's just like you and me, buddy, well more me than you. She used to be a GP. Practiced medicine for a few years. She told me that she had received a patient late one night whose condition she couldn't quite diagnose, and the patient himself was some sort of doctor too, like an herbalist or something."

"And now she's tending bar in a magical club," my face showed doubt and disbelief with an unamused glare.

"It's more than that. After that, Neelas learned new kinds of medicine from this guy and is now quite well known in the circles your Nǎinai used to deal with."
"Will it work?" I asked quietly, wondering if one less burden in my life, no matter the beauty it brought with it, would help me move forward. Marcus had loved some of the things I'd paint just to show him how I saw the world when the auric sight took over. He was like a child ever curious and amazed by his Yīng. Those pictures were now stored away out of sight—just another reminder I shouldn't have around.

"It'll work, Li. I know your condition is more complicated than you ever let on, and I think you should take it," her voice was shaking when she spoke those last words.

"Perhaps I'll take it, but I have too many questions to rush things."

"Like what? It'd be goodbye to migraines and those weird colours you're always seeing. Look. Like I said the other day, I love you. You're family to me," she blushed slightly at that, "and I don't want you to get hurt. That world you glimpsed in last night is dangerous and seductive, I think. It's probably why your Nǎinai didn't tell you certain things about it. Otherwise, it wouldn't have been such a shock to you." I picked up the tiny bottle and rolled it in my palm, seeing its aura leave a purple trail on my palm before disappearing.

"As usual, you're probably right," finally, her usual grin broke the tension.

"Of course, I'm always right, you know that," she sipped her black coffee and looked away as she had in the vegan café the other day.

"Take it, Li, I think It'd be best to stay in the real world and away from all that stuff your Năinai was into," back to her serious tone from the other day, "No offence to her at all, but I always thought it was kinda scary what she did, and somehow it still does feel scary."

"Maybe I'll take it. Neelas said it was permanent, so I have to decide carefully." I put the bottle in my jeans pocket; yeah, I have more than one pair of skinny jeans; I'm gay, of course, I do.

"Do you wanna know what it was like...?" I teased.

"Hell yeah, I've only heard rumours, and Neelas never told me anything other than, 'Don't even think about it, you wouldn't get in.'"

"If what everyone is saying is true, then I practically walked into a den of monsters from fairy tales and emerged unscathed." I proceeded to tell her of the bouncer, which piqued her interest immediately; she loved the hunky muscled types. Then my entrance into the bar, the giant tree growing in the center.

"It looked like any other high-end club with some details added like the tree." I continued to tell her about my interactions with the infamous Neelas, a doctor/herbalist to the supernatural? Even in my head, it sounded ridiculous. We both laughed aloud, causing some patrons and staff to look at us oddly when I mentioned the cocktail.

"Yup, Neelas can be a little literal about her drinks, or so I've heard. But Li, there's something you're not saying. I've known you for almost a decade and know when you're hiding something." She had hit the nail on the head. I wasn't even sure I wanted to voice the other details to myself, let alone to my bestie.

"There was a guy."

"Hah! I knew it," she shouted, pointing accusingly at me. Again, garnering looks from the patrons. The chubby Korean girl just shrugged from behind the counter while she topped up the bakery cabinet. We were good tippers.

"What was he like?" I considered the question and tried to formulate an answer that made sense.

"He was…unearthly and beautiful. He looked like one of my manga covers," Patience leaned in like a child being told about Father Christmas for the first time and wondering what gifts he was going to bring. Her eyes were wide and bright, soaking in every word.

"I don't feel like it was real. He was kind and friendly, but I didn't understand why he was bothering with me." She slapped my shoulder, creasing the fabric of my long sleeve top slightly. I straightened it out, pulling the sleeve to cover my scar again.

"Don't be an idiot; you've never known how good-looking you are, Li. Marcus and I used to marvel at the ignorance of your own features when you could paint so many beautiful things accurately." She scoffed at that memory, then her eyes looked into her coffee a little melancholic.

"And then what, Li? Don't tell me you left without at least a number, a business card, or even without shagging him in the bathrooms?!"

"I'm not even sure that place had or needed bathrooms." It was Marcus, I said to myself. Marcus, I don't want to betray him, his memory.

"You are family, my darling Li Yīng, so I have to be harsh with some things to get them through that thick pretty skull of yours," She played at knocking inches away from my forehead.

"You've been living in a limbo, a half-life, for the past five years. We have all been pretty careful about it because of what happened after Marcus had passed. We didn't want to upset you," She again looked away from me. I saw again those tears swelling to the edges of her eyes, "Marcus loved you so much. And I know you loved him just as much. You both were perfect. And it's not fair," the tears were falling freely. Still, she held her voice and composure steady, "it was never fair that he got taken from you like that…from us," she took a shuddering breath trying to keep herself together, "but it is life. And life isn't fair. It just happens. To all of us." Her parents, grandparents were all gone because of some unidentifiable genetic illness that manifested as cancer.

"But you can't let life just stop anymore," she turned to me, her eyes red. Still, her voice holding its strength and conviction as to what she was saying, "Marcus loved you so much that he'd hate to see you like this, not loving, not moving forward, not being happy. He'd want you to be happy, Li Yīng. He'd want you to be loved. We all do." My mouth was agape with this barrage of truth and love being thrust upon me. Patience only used my full name when her point needed to be driven home like a jackhammer. What did I do to deserve this? This great friend and her constant, unwavering support. We finished breakfast and exited the café at that.

"I'll pick you up in an hour for Hope's birthday. I know you didn't get her a gift, don't worry, I signed both our names on the gift I got her." She winked at me.

"I do have one thing for her, it's a little bit of a surprise, though, but thanks, a double whammy always goes down well with gifts."

"Well, you'd know about double whammies going down on you," she challenged with her usual smutty sense of humour.

"Well tee hee, ha!" was my retort to her vulgarity. Not really being able to think of a viable response after what she had said over breakfast.

"See you soon then."

And we went to our respective homes to get ready for her sister's birthday. And I mentally prepared myself for the girls who tended to monopolize me the moment I arrived at Hope's house in any capacity.

The subject of Hope usually earthed both Patience and me, realizing that some things were more important than others.

***

Chapter 9: Gift (Saturday)

Ok, a confession: I don't really have a great sense of style. Marcus had usually been the one to pick my outfits. I had just never got the hang of it. So now I just have sets of specific outfits for particular occasions that he used to put together. Casual birthday outfit: I pulled the racks across in my walk-in closet. Polo shirt (pink, salmon?), a leather jacket (it was still cold out), and a pair of khakis? Meh, whatever. It's what I would wear.

I went to my glass display cabinet and opened it, pulled out my Năinai's silk box. I gingerly put it on the kitchen counter. I'd found it the other day and intuitively knew I'd have to bring it. I opened the box, which showed rows and rows of handmade red packets; one was lying on top of the rest. It had Hope's name, today's date, and a time on it. I didn't hang envelopes that were for others on my calendar. I only liked to bring them if necessary. I slid it into the jacket's inner pocket. Part of me silently prayed to my Năinai that it was something good. Yeah, you heard right; I prayed to my Năinai. I replaced the lid and put it back in its place. I turned to the fanned-out journals on the coffee table. I'd attend to those later.

Cell phone, wallet. Check and Check. I took a quick look in the full-length mirror in my walk-in. I tried to see what Patience had spoken of. My face? My slim body? I lacked a build for one thing. Well, I guess I'd leave other people's opinions up to them.

My phone vibrated with a text.

"Downstairs, Goober. Bring a bottle too." So, I went to the fridge and grabbed a random bottle of chardonnay and went downstairs to my ride-or-die to head to Hope's party.

***

Chapter 10: Glitter Bomb Party (Saturday)

Hope's family lived a fair bit away from both Patience and me. Their home was located in a suburb called Coquitlam. A residential area that had woodlands as well as strip malls dotting around. Their home was on a slight rise, with the garage leading downwards into a below-home carport. Above was their modest home. It had a well-tended garden all around the edge of the property that Patience made sure stayed maintained by hiring a gardener to tend it every few weeks. Patience had told me once her family came from old Dutch money, so she could afford it. The lawn had two instant canopies on their steel frames with fold-out tables laden with various party snacks on one table and gifts for the other. Soft rock from what I assumed was the eighties was playing, offering a frivolous, fun vibe to the event.

In between the two tables was a makeshift throne that sat Hope. She was just as pretty as her sister, just taller. Though a scarf hid her lack of hair, she had kept her looks well, and her smile beamed at all the party guests. A genuine smile, not a pasted-on kind that I sometimes felt I had to do for people. She was so happy to have this moment with her family and friends. We got out of Patience's Tesla when she parked it on the street, and I braced for the inevitable.

"Uncle Li!!!!" A pair of screeching blonde whirlwinds came barreling down the rise towards us. They both charged right into me, wrapping their arms around me. I patted their backs and smiled at Patience.

"Hello girls, what's new?" they both grabbed my hand in theirs and tugged me toward the presents. I flinched momentarily, remembering what Neelas had said about touching people. I couldn't see anything strange about their auras, nor did I feel anything different other than the warmth of human hands. Charity bounced up and down while her little sister copied her. Faith was dressed in an Elsa outfit, donning the blue ice queen's cape and all. Excellent, I silently said. Kids should be heroes in their own world. Charity was wearing a captain "Jack Sparrow" outfit. It wasn't news to anyone that Charity wanted to be a boozy womanizing pirate when she grew up, even though she had no idea what a womanizer was. When asked, I told her it was a type of sport that her aunt was good at and that she should only ask when she was thirteen and had fully decided a pirate was her future vocation.

"Come see what we got, mum." Charity rummaged through a pile to reveal a small stand holding a plaster cast with "Love you, Mum" scratched into the surface above two tiny handprints, one larger than the other but still unmistakably tiny.

"We did it yesterday; it took three goes because Faith kept moving in the plaster."

"No!" Faith said simply. Still, a wee tot was adopting a look of petulance I had seen on her aunt several times when she was immature and silly. It was utterly adorable.

"I love it, guys! You guys must be magical to know this is exactly what your mum told me she wanted for her birthday!" The two girls looked to each other, then me, eyes wide at the prospect.
"I just can't believe you made something so amazing; I only made your mum a special card." I pulled out the red packet.
"Where is all that smoke coming from Uncle Li?" both Charity and Faith fingered and poked the red packet.

"Smoke?"

"It's all colourful. And there's some glitter around it." *Hmm.* Children were prone to the 'sight' regardless of the latent gifts.

"Ooh! We have a new glitter set!" The "smoke" already forgotten, they again tugged me to the other side of the yard with a smaller children's table. There were three small plastic seats, each with a handwritten name in crayon on a label. The writing was that of a six-year-old. "Faith," spelled "Fath," and "Charity" with a backward capital "R" and the last chair, "Uncle Li."

"Mum helped me spell your name on your chair. Even though I'm the best speller in my class."

"Well, I bet you could have done it yourself, but it's very kind of you to let your mum try her spelling skills too; we don't want her falling behind in her homework." They both giggled.

We seated, and I saw Patience speaking to her sister, holding her hands. They were both engrossed in one of their "sister's" conversations. I turned back to my mini hosts, and we began playing with a glue and glitter pasting set that I was sure to see in my clothes for weeks to come. It didn't bother me in the slightest. Patience's nieces were the cutest. Sadly, my mind strayed to Baraz and his hug and then to Marcus. Marcus had wanted to be a father. He would have made a great dad. He probably would have spoiled them, and I would've had to have been the strict one with curfews and homework. And it would have been perfect. Instead, another dream was lost to time and circumstance.

"Uncle Li, you're doing it wrong!" Charity admonished, pouring more glitter from a multicoloured glitter shaker onto my pasted masterpiece, drowning it and my hands. I couldn't help but laugh. Laughter seemed to be happening more frequently to me these days. *Hmm.*

"Aww, man! I thought I was doing good, but at least I can do this," I tried to explain and threw the excess glitter into the air over my head. It settled all over me in a glitter bomb mess. Faith took that as permission to pick up the shaker and sprinkle some all over herself. Charity followed suit, but only with the pink glitter. We were a giggling sparkling mess.

"Li!" Patience's voice resounded from the thrown where Hope sat.

"Uh ohhhhh!" I said, giving the girls a conspiratorial look and a big uncle Li grin.

"Uh ohhhhh!" the girls echoed.

"I'll be back."

"Nope, I'm coming too." Charity stated as a matter of fact.

"Coming!" Faith said too.

"Ok, but don't get me into trouble."

We went to face our doom at the hands of Duchess Patience and Queen Hope. Hope couldn't contain herself when we arrived and almost fell off her little throne laughing, as did Patience.
"What on earth," Patience looking at me, the girls, then at me, shaking her head, trying not to laugh some more.

"It was a complete accident. The glitter exploded all over us. I think the glitter set is defective; you should call the company for a quick refund, or maybe even sue them."

"Who's Sue?" Asked Charity. Patience ignored the question and got down to wiping the girls with some wet wipes, then she gave up and took their hands to take them inside the house to remove the offending glitter as best she could.

"Li Yīng, I'm so glad you could make it; as you can see, the girls have missed you, and so have I. Where has the most handsome man in Vancouver been hiding?" Hope looked to me in mock admonishment (she would use my full name as mothers do when telling off their little ones, it was amazing).

Her skin was pale with a waxy quality to it, typical of chemo patients. What, in my experience, was also typical was what my 'sight' had shown me. Black pulsing veins crawling up her neck, presumably beginning at her middle spinal column. I knew that only I could see these—the clutch of the illness inside this poor but wonderful woman.

Five years ago, in a hospital bed, with tubes and machines, had lain Marcus. Almost a skeleton, the webwork of similar veins crisscrossing his face like some morbid and taunting tattoo. I had shut down my sight then for the longest time to make sure my last images of Marcus were untainted by the "sight." I had had migraine after migraine in the weeks that followed but didn't care. I refused to see those unsightly veins obscuring my love. And now, something similar was happening to Hope.

"Mainly at the grindstone your dear sister maintains." We were both holding smiles of genuine mirth and a kind of understanding about the truth of the situation. I sat in the seat next to her in a puff of glitter, which earned another chuckle from Hope.

"I brought you a wee something," I said shyly.

"You shouldn't, just seeing you with my girls makes me so happy. You're so good with them. "
Dereck chose that moment to emerge from the backyard with a plate full of barbecued meats.
"Li!" He put down the plate and reach over for a very manly hug, "How the hell are you?"
"Dereck, swear jar." Hope winked at me. Dereck pulled a dollar out of pocket and put it on the arm of the throne.

"For my queen," he did a mock bow, "and the guest queen," and bowed to me in a flourish—more laughter.

I pulled out the red packet from its place in my pocket. Both Dereck and Hope locked eyes on it immediately. They looked at each other, a mix of fear, anticipation, and wishful thinking. I didn't want this to be a nasty surprise for them or give them false hope, but my Năinai's instructions about her silk box were specific and could never be ignored. I handed the envelope to Hope.

"Patience has told me stories about these. And I remember your Năinai. A remarkable woman. Why would she-?" She was almost speechless. Suddenly I saw the weariness of her journey through the illness take her, and her shoulders sagged.

"Honey?" Dereck sat in the other chair next to her. All jokes gone now.

"Thank you, Li. Can you read the characters? I…"

"Of course, Hope. Of course. It has your name here in these two characters, and this is today's date exactly, and there is a time to open it here."

"What time does it say?"

"2:12 in the afternoon." Hope pulled Dereck's wrist over to look at the time. She couldn't wear a watch anymore.

"That's in less than a minute!" Her hand shook, making the hand-painted treasure flap slightly.

Her husband grabbed both her hands in his large hands, quickly covering hers and kissing them.
"It'll be all right, love. Just open it. Li's Nǎinai was a straight-up woman. And a good woman. I couldn't imagine her doing anything remotely cruel." He reassured her some more.

She looked again at his watch then carefully opened the seal. She pulled out the light rice paper inside and, with just as much care, unfolded it. There were words, not characters, on the paper.

"Oh, my."

"What, Li?"

"I didn't know Nǎinai could write English. I guess she's still full of surprises." Seriously. My Nǎinai had refused to speak English nor write in anything other than traditional Chinese characters....as far as we knew.

"That she is," Hopes voice was barely a whisper as she read the message that was for her eyes only. She gasped and put a hand to her mouth, eyes wide.

"What is it, Hun?" Dereck's concern was building, and he tried to move to look at the note. Hope abruptly snatched it away with a speed that belied her condition.

"It's precise." She said as she folded it and placed it back into its packet. Her countenance had changed and taken on a matronly tone. Interesting. Perhaps it was good news, but only she was allowed to know.

"Li Yīng? Can you please get that metal bowl there? And the lighter by the cake?"

"Sure thing." I got up.

"Hang on, love, what are you doing?"

"What is needed of me," She explained and offered no more.

I retrieved the implements she had commanded me to get. And sat them in her lap. She placed the envelope in the metal bowl and lit the edge.

"Hang on a minute, love." Dereck demanded, "what are you doing? Those things are more precious than gold! You know what Li's Năinai was."

"I know, and I do. I also know that it's not the packet or the letter; it's the knowledge they contain that makes them gold. And the knowledge was for me and for me alone."

He sighed at that. His wife was never to be denied anything. He would always abide by her. He loved her and his daughters more than anything. He nodded at her as the red packet burned away in the bowl. At the same time, he took the bowl from her lap just as Patience emerged from the house, wiping her hands on a hand towel, glitter falling here and there from it. Atop the steps, she saw the bowl and its contents, and her eyes flicked to me, a question, a wanting to know, a need to learn more. She kept it to herself. I stiffly shook my head in a way only she could see.

More guests were arriving. As it turned out, our glitter fun had made such a mess of the girl's hair Patience had resorted to putting the two little munchkins in the bath and hosing them down with the detachable showerhead. The girls loved it; apparently, it was all part of our game.

The evening wore on, and the girls had worn out both their aunt and me. Patience stayed, but I decided to Uber home. There were hugs and promises to return. Hope's determined and forceful gaze hardened after reading Nǎinai's red packet. I always wondered what the messages were, but my Nǎinai said it wasn't essential, and I wouldn't understand whatever it was if it wasn't for me.

The party had been a delight, and I loved Patience's family. They were good people. They had always made me feel so welcome, like part of their family. My parents and Nǎinai, and even Marcus, we had had barbecues like these during the summer months. I wished there were more that I could do. Well, for all I knew, Nǎinai just did something. But her packets were unpredictable and always private. But again, I prayed to my Nǎinai. Please, these people have shown me so much love. I need them to be ok. Like I said, I refused to pray to any gods at all since they never answered when Marcus was taken, so I say fuck the lot of them. If anyone would help me from the 'other side,' it would be my Nǎinai and my Marcus.

The Uber driver, Jeff, was one of those chatty ones and commanded my attention on the ride home. I welcomed the distraction from my own troubled thoughts and also from the too-full belly of cake and ice cream.

***

Chapter 11: The Boardwalk (Saturday)

The Uber drove steadily towards my apartment building while I looked out the window. We were past Stanley Park, and I could see the harbour on my left.

"Hey, Jeff, can I stop just up here on this side street?"

"You don't want me to take you all the way? It's just up ahead?"

"No, no," I assured him, "I think I need a walk; I overate goddamned cake," I said, rubbing my belly.

"I hear yah. Just be careful; that bear has been all over the city. You've heard, right?"

"Yeah, no worries. Thank you, Jeff." He pulled over to a side street nearest the harbourside. I got out and said my goodbyes and made promises for a five-star review. I kept immediately; otherwise, I'd absentmindedly forget and feel terrible about it the next time I opened the app. I also tipped him extra for stopping where I wanted.

I breathed in the cool evening air. The sun was set, and the lights of the harbour sparkled on the water around the boats, like the glitter that likely would stay stuck on my clothes and person for all eternity. My walk home was not far, but I wanted to process the events of the past couple of days. I was tired, and my bed called, but my head was so busy with thoughts. Too much had happened. My tiredness could wait for a little, then be heeded.

Marcus loved this walk; he'd often find me here walking off my thoughts. We had walked along with the harbour shops right on the water. There were cafés and restaurants. A memory of Todd's mention of one of the restaurants along here being subjected to one of the recent bear maulings. Gosh. What a terrible way to go. I had happened to see the article while browsing on my phone in the car. The victim's throat was torn out. I couldn't imagine how terrible that would be. I absently touched my throat. Not nice at all!

My ears and eyes were tuned enough to the area that I hoped that I would spot any trouble before it made itself known. There were others, some couples, some alone, doing their nightly stroll with me along the waterside. It was peaceful and calming. The sea always seemed that way when life had filled your head up too much. I leaned on the steel railing facing the yachts. They rocked quietly in the water. Not much noise at all, just the murmur of the water's edge on the rocks below and the people walking by on their way home.

The auras tonight were also peaceful in a way: blues and violets, some purples drifting around the boats docked in front of me. I was beginning to get used to just seeing the world like this. Would it be so bad? Well, apparently, this 'sight' and my 'gift' came with strings, like unwanted accidents should I bump into another supernatural person or thing. Or if I felt I 'saw' too much and tried to shut down the auric sight, a splitting migraine would occur on some occasions and lay me up for two days in constant agony. Perhaps the "Eraser" would be a good idea.
The 'sight' was part of my past with Marcus. It might aid in the moving-on process. Each morning, part of my ritual was swallowing a hefty antidepressant and an anxiolytic. Perhaps those drugs would no longer be part of my daily life. I let out a sigh and turned my back to the water, leaning on the rail. And yelped…! About three feet away from me was the Japanese boy/man/sex god from the club. His long hair waving slightly in the sea air. His tanned face sporting that cheeky grin and those pretty, pretty amber eyes piercing my soul.

"What the actual fuck!" A throaty laugh came from him at my reaction as he slowly sidled up next to me to look out over the harbour.

"It is beautiful, isn't it?"

"Wait a second, roll it back," he turned to face me, leaning an elbow against the railing, "where on earth did you come from? Are you stalking me?" I said, trying to sound angry but probably failing as my heart started pounding in time with other areas further south. But I had meant it; what the actual fuck!

"Stalking, no, never," he looked at me squarely in the eyes; I found it uncomfortable but was unable to turn away from his amber gaze, "tracking, yes."

"How is that any better?!"

"Tracking, I'm finding; stalking, I'm hunting," he moved his face closer. I swear I even heard myself gulp, "And you're not prey, are you?"

I tried to appear haughty and indignant towards his comment and likely again failing before his steady, confident look and the waves of strong spicy cologne rolling off him.

"Certainly not. I'm no one's prey to catch."

"I find that hard to believe somehow." He turned back towards the water, and I joined him.

"Can I ask you a question? It may sound rude, but I don't mean it to," I said nervously.

"You can ask me anything you wish." How on earth could he sound so sincere. Almost like promises were being made without being said.

"What are you?"

"Ah, interesting, that's your first question, but at least it's direct," a long tendril of hair fell in front of his face. I had the desperate urge to move it back over his ear to stop it from obscuring my view of him.

"You called yourself a Yokai at the bar," I reminded him, "then so did Neelas."

"That I did," he nodded, "though it's not entirely correct. It was an ironic statement, I guess."
"Ironic?" I repeated.

"Yes, but does it really matter what I am? Can't we just enjoy this evening?"

"We can," although the questions hounded my brain, there was so much that'd happened in the week that I really needed to process it. My fatigue, though, had a habit of clouding my judgment. I thought of Neelas' drink she'd first served me. That was good, like an instant pick me up. I could use one. The weight of today's events was pressing down on my eyes in the form of drowsiness.

And this...man next to me, whatever he was, a lunatic or a genuine being of spirit. I just couldn't deal with it right now or didn't want to. He was beautiful. Like one of my sketches. A figure from anyone's erotic dreams.

"Good. It's a nice evening and right now. At this moment, this is where I want to be, with you."

"Don't try to charm me, Mr....no name. After this chat, I'm going home to bed." His brows rose at that. "Alone!" I confirmed so as not to give the wrong idea. His head cocked to the side, grinning. It reminded me of my Marcus. The man gasped almost inaudibly and stepped back. I thought so. There was something about my thoughts of Marcus that disturbed him. Which put a few of the puzzle pieces in place; he was something of a spirit.

"I couldn't charm you even if I tried," he said, sounding disappointed at the broken prospect.

"Really? And why is that?"

"You won't like that answer," he countered.

"Tell me, I don't know you, and you don't know me. It's not like this conversation will amount to anything other than me walking away."

"Who is Marcus?" He said innocently, curiosity filling his voice and posture. He had returned to leaning in as he had at the bar. So close. That cologne again. So strong, sweet, and delicious.

"He's the reason I'm out!" I turned and walked off towards my home. Not looking back at the mysterious stranger who was an unnecessary confusion to my night, and my life in fact.

At a few steps, my meddling curiosity got the better of me, and I turned. The man was still there, just staring at me with a puzzled look on his face. I almost felt bad for being so rude. I was confident he had 'tracked 'me here. Whatever that meant, and that in and of itself, could not be a good thing. If he genuinely was a being from…somewhere else, then their idea of appropriate behaviour would deviate from ours. I stopped and stared back at him, unsure as to what to do. The puzzled look lifted, brightened to an easy smile again, and he walked briskly to catch up to me.

"I'm sorry," I said when he had reached me, "I was rude, and you haven't actually done anything wrong."

"There's no need for the apology. I should be sorry."

"So, did you read my mind or something?"

"I'll pick the stray thought up or 'something'; it's probably easier to explain over coffee?" Again hopeful, why did this guy even want to spend time with me? Against the better judgment of anyone on the planet, I nodded. If not, just to get some answers. And maybe make a new friend. Liar! My mind screamed. You know what's going on here. Even though…I said to myself, *This is new, and perhaps someone on the 'in' could tell me more about what I am dealing with.* Năinai wasn't here anymore, and weird stuff really wasn't Patience's wheelhouse. And my parents, bless them, didn't really have any answers. To them, my Năinai just did her thing, and they just facilitated the process.

"OK, coffee."

"Do you know a place near here? I am unfamiliar with this territory." Territory? Geez, this was going to be interesting. I guess some of my suicidal tendencies remained, doing silly things like this, or perhaps what Patience said had sunk in a little. I had been living a half-life, and it wasn't fair on me or to the memory of Marcus.

"I do know a place, but don't get the wrong idea." Unfortunately, I am pretty sure the one with the wrong and downright risk-filled ideas here was me.

"I wouldn't dream of it." Why did everything he said sound like a promise and a suggestive statement in one slice of dialogue?

***

Chapter 12: Interrogation

I pulled out my phone and opened the smart lock to my home. Ok, not the smartest thing letting a stranger in. There were animal attacks, muggers, and generally crazy people out there. This beautiful man could be any one of those. But no. Something in me told me no. That was wrong. He didn't want to harm me, but he was dangerous. I just had to be cautious. Nǎinai, I wish you were here.

I let him into my apartment and closed the door. He immediately noticed the red-fanned-out collection of books on my coffee table. I quickly ran and collected them and put them back into their place.

"Sorry, company really wasn't on the agenda for the evening, or any evening really."

"Your place is nice." He moved so quick I almost didn't see him move; a blink and he was somewhere else. Suddenly he was at my aquarium staring into the glass enclosure in absolute captivation. The little fish darted around. The neons zipped in an almost schooling pattern. The tiny blue, yellow and red shrimps crawled over the living plants at the bottom, cleaning up any detritus they could find that was edible. The beta swam back and forth, flashing his colours at our guest.

"These are amazing." Hadn't he seen an aquarium before?

"Thanks, you haven't seen an aquarium before?"

"I have; it's simply different when it belongs to someone. It indicates a lot about a person when they keep animals, especially when they choose to take good care of those animals." He straightened up and was suddenly in my kitchen looking at the calendar on the fridge. "Oh my," he peered closely at the envelopes but didn't dare touch any of them, "these, are yours?"

"Yes, they were given to me."

"By whom may I ask?"

"You can ask, and I might tell you, in exchange for some information."

"Ah, I see." My Năinai had been clear about one thing when she had had any dealings with spirits or supernatural beings like the Fae, it was best to keep things balanced, so they do not feel like they owe you or that you owe them.
"I am at your disposal, as I am a guest in your home." He reappeared on my couch faster than a flash. I was filing away these little details. Super speed? Hmm. Apparently can 'Charm,' what else?

I dialled into my phone a playlist of indie rock at a low volume. I was feeling even more tired. Hopefully, it would keep me up long enough for conversation with captain sexy mystery here.
"What is your intention with me? You were circling me in the bar, at the harbour side. Is there something that you are planning?"

"That is two questions, and I'll answer both," he patted the couch seat next to him, "my intention with you from the beginning is to get to know you. Honestly, and yes, I am always planning something. But nothing you need to think about. Like I said in the bar, I'm friendly."

"Friendly?" I plonked myself tiredly next to him, facing him, letting out an unintentional sigh as I did.

"Yes, I really don't want to hurt you; I actually don't have much to do with humans in general. These days I keep to myself."

"I know the feeling," I mumbled, "and another question…."

"Fire away."

"Cream or sugar?" That scored a laugh, which sent shivers through me, in all the ways I would feel guilty about later. I looked up at the postcard in the display cabinet to anchor me. And it did.
"Both, please. Thank you." I went to the kitchen to boil the jug. My fatigue was begging to be recognized. It had been a long day, but I

made my way to my kitchen and boiled the jug, the guy on my couch watching me the whole time.

"You realize I still don't know your name, and you are now in my home."

"I do realize; I also don't know your name."

"Mine is easier to find. I'm on several public records, which I doubt you are." He got up slowly from the couch and came into the kitchen, and leaned against the counter next to me while I prepared our hot drinks.

"Give me your name, and I'll give you mine," he said, looking straight into my eyes, with no cheeky grin, no joking smile, or sexy poses. I handed him a mug of hot coffee and held mine in both hands, both to steady my hands and to provide some kind of barrier between this handsome man and me. I stared back. Searching his eyes for something, any indication, waiting for my instincts to begin blaring the siren of, 'get the fuck away from this weirdo,' but none came.

"My name is Li Yīng; my friends call me Li, even though that is my family name, after the Li River in Guilin. My Nǎinai used to call me Xiǎoyīng." I blurted it out before I could catch up to the thought. Oh Shit!

"Her beautiful Flower or her little Hero. How remarkable." He translated. He didn't break eye contact, "And my name is Ayaka of the Zenko. Attendant to Inari."

"Your name means coloured flower, I think. My Japanese is a little rusty." He broke into that brilliant smile, and my heart skipped a beat, "Attendant to Inari," I said more to myself than to him as I looked down into my drink.

"Xiǎoyīng," he spoke it, and I felt it. A strange feeling of connectedness, like a tug on some essential part of me.

"Ayaka of the Zenko," as if in reverse, I felt a part of me tug an unseen but felt part of him.

"Well, Ayaka, I actually would love to continue this, but I'm actually wiped out. I'm barely keeping my feet. We should call it a night after our coffee."

"Ah, I see. Yes. But isn't coffee for staying awake?" He sipped his drink delicately.

"Yes, Ayaka," I said, testing out the name, liking the way it sounded and felt, "but I am actually drinking hot chocolate right now; you're the one who's drinking coffee."

"Trickster," he said, chuckling at the irony, "All right, let's sit for a bit. And then I'll take my leave."

We resumed our positions on the couch.

"The envelopes, who gave them to you?"

"My Năinai." His eyes widened, then deepened into a frown.

"Your Năinai, your grandmother? That is interesting. You know. I have a tale about a witch from many years ago who used to conjure such tools in her art. Would you care to hear it?"

"I would," I placed my drink on one of the white marble coasters on the glass coffee table; he did the same with great deliberation. And I thought to myself, he made a point to put it on a coaster.

"Well, long ago in the lands of China, there was a village that ran along a river," As he spoke, I could almost picture the area my Năinai grew up in, near the Li River in the ancient land of Guilin.

"In a village called Daxu was a young witch whose beauty was coveted by many, but her heart had already been given to a river spirit who lived on the banks of the river. He lived further upstream from the village. The village knew this but was happy for the crafts she learned from her fairy lover." In my mind, it all seemed so visceral. My artist's eye could always picture clearly: the river, the boats, local fishermen with cormorant birds. The mountains were like lumpy forest of covered pillars all around.

"One day, a group of spirits arrived from a foreign land. The village was frightened of them and asked the witch to use her skills to divine their intentions. But the spirits had hidden their intentions with powerful magic. And much of the witches 'energy was spent nourishing her unborn at the time child. So, by the time the witch had discovered their true plans, it was too late."

"What happened?" I saw her full belly, rubbing it and singing to her child within, a lullaby that my Năinai used to sing to me. Then I saw the spirits in my imagination, nasty things; they looked to my mind like pale spectres with white hair and fangs.

"She had gone to her lover's home upstream to ask him about the spirits. Even approaching his little cottage, she could sense the presence of the foreign spirits had been there. They had set fire to his small home. She found his lifeless body by the water, trying to reach towards the shallows. Her grief was immense. The scent of the foreigner's magic was all over her lover's corpse. She took his corpse and bathed it into the river, hoping to revive him with his native power, the river. It was impossible. They had drained his magic and left him for dead."

"So, what did she do?" I said, yawning but wanting to hear the story. I leaned my head on the back of the couch comfortably. I saw the witch, her pregnant belly, leaning over a beautiful man in the water, crying at her loss. I knew how she felt. So desolate. Angry.

"She chased them to the ends of the earth where their land lay. Then she laid a most terrible curse that burned inside their blood, ensuring death to them and all that aided them."

"That's quite a story, Ayaka." I found I liked saying his name.

"Well, my Xiǎoyīng, there's more. The spirits, it turns out, weren't without friends. Though their fate was sealed by the witch's curse, they had a curse of their own. A curse is known as a "twist of fate." It would turn a lucky star, for anyone born to her, into a damned star. A star that was so unlucky that misery would follow them wherever they went."

"I can't say I blame the witch. Those spirits sounded like assholes." He chuckled.

"I'm guessing they were there to kill her lover just for his magic."

"What happened next? This witch doesn't sound like the type to give up."

"You are correct; this witch did not give up. Though both curses remained in effect, the witch stared the fates directly in the face and laughed. She said, 'you might think you control the fate of my family, but I defy fate!'" He spoke the quote in perfect Mandarin.

"So, she did, and it's still talked about today with my people, that she did it with envelopes similar to those." My eyes were heavy now and wanted to close, but I tried so hard to keep them open. Why was my body letting all its defences down right this very moment?

"I don't think that was my Nǎinai. She was tough, but she wouldn't throw such horrid curses." I mumbled, then eyes closed. I couldn't open them. Perhaps I was exhausted from the events of the past couple of days. How could I let this happen? I was literally falling asleep in front of this stranger.
I felt my body being carried lightly and then gently placed into the waiting covers of my bed. I forced my eyes to open a little and saw through the dimmed lighting with Ayaka hovering just above me, looking down.

"Goodnight, my Xiǎoyīng." My eyes closed, and I snuggled down, smiling to myself for reasons I wasn't going to acknowledge just yet. Reasons that made my heart jump and my body quiver.

"Goodnight, my Ayaka of the Zenko." The sweet release of sleep washed over me—a peaceful feeling for the first time in a long time.

***

Chapter 13: Take Two of These and Call Me... (Sunday)

The morning sunlight streamed through the edges of the floor-length windows adjacent to the water view. I opened my eyes and rolled over, breathing in the heavy scent of Ayaka's cologne. It was musky and intoxicating.

The grogginess of sleep left me in a heartbeat as the memory of last night came back. I sat up and realized I was only wearing my boxer briefs. At the end of my bed was a bench/storage chest where my clothes from last night were neatly folded. How did I get into bed and undressed? I vaguely recalled solid and long arms wrapping around me like a heavy warm blanket and depositing me into bed. I did not remember undressing and neatly folding my clothes, which meant Ayaka had. Sweet, but weird. He'd seen me next to naked; I was sure that was violating... somewhere in my head... it should be, but it felt nice in truth. I had already been in therapy before and probably needed more. I looked around the open-plan room. There was no sign of him. A part of me felt not only disappointed but a little, almost empty.

I turned to my bedside to retrieve my medication from the top drawer where Marcus 'picture lay. I stopped. On the top of the bedside table was a large glass of water with one of my marble coasters under it. My cell was in its cradle charging, and next to the glass was two tiny pills. My medication at the daily dosage I required. Something about the whole scene made me sad, almost angry. Not at Ayaka's initiative or anything he had really done, but at myself. Although nothing other than storytelling had occurred between the apparent Japanese spirit and me, I felt guilty.

Opening my drawer, I pulled out Marcus's picture and let the tears come and trickle down my cheek, hitting my bare legs as I swung to sit on the bed's edge.

"Baby, I have no idea what I'm doing. I don't even know what to say is going on. I wish you were here. No matter what, you always had an answer for anything," I sniffled, trying not to "ugly" cry to myself at the start of my day. It could often set a tone of depression that hung around me like one of Patience's hangovers. A memory came, unbidden from my time with Marcus, a memory that I had put away…

My Năinai had passed away, and he had been there, holding me while I cried like a baby. Holding me tight. No matter how many times I broke down about the woman who taught me so much about finding happiness in this life. When I snapped and would throw unnecessary tantrums because I couldn't translate my thoughts or feelings to him the way I needed, he would just again grab and hold me and wait for the storm to pass. Then he would often suggest something absurd like going out for midnight apple pie at one of the twenty-four-hour bakeries that kept open downstairs from our apartment. It was that or a walk and a gelato cup. He always had some answer for my troubles. When MGV was in trouble, and our jobs were at risk; Patience was more stressed than I had ever seen her (at least until her sister was diagnosed); he had made us all come to our apartment and sit around with a pitcher of frozen margarita to brainstorm about an action plan. And one at a time, we had managed a solution for each problem. There had been something so comforting about his presence. So steady, even though he was one of the most spontaneous people I had ever known. When he was around, everything would work out somehow.
Except now… his picture didn't offer any solutions or silly distractions until the problems could be worked through. Though looking at his face, I remembered what Patience said: "He wouldn't want you living like this; he'd want you to be happy and in love again." Her relationship with Marcus was close, too, and she was qualified to make such a call.

"Marcus, baby, I really don't know what to do." Instead of in the drawer, I kissed the picture and placed it upright on the bedside to look at me. I hadn't done that since he'd passed away and the renovation had been completed. I took the glass of water and the two pills with the rest of my medication. Then I got up and put the glass in the kitchen. The cups and spoons we had used last night were washed and lay on a towel to dry. I had to smirk at that. He either didn't know how to use the dishwasher or just couldn't find it. But the gesture was sweet all the same. I turned to take my shower and complete my morning ablutions when I noticed it. The smell, his cologne… was also in the kitchen… where the bed was… the couch, lounge… everywhere. The scent tickled something empty within me that longed to be filled, but ignoring those feelings, I shook my head and promised to ask Ayaka about it. I hadn't seen him carrying a bag to hide a large bottle of cologne to spray around my house.

I went to complete my morning ritual, beginning with a scalding shower, brush my teeth, shave, and the rest of it. After dressing in jeans and a long sleeve T, my default outfit, I went to the bedside to grab my phone when I noticed something that I hadn't before while in bed. A tiny, folded piece of stock paper, the kind that my sketches were prepared on. It looked like a place card for a wedding reception. On its front in flowing calligraphy:

漓英 *(Li Yīng)*

With a stylized underscore of a flower in black ink. My name was written in Chinese characters. I opened the little card.

Thank you for last night; it was delightful getting to know you some more. I hope there will be more evenings with more stories. If that sounds like something, you could enjoy….

He'd left a cell phone number and signed it, *your Ayaka.*

My Ayaka….?

***

Chapter 14: Finding Happiness (Sunday)

There are some grave misconceptions that many straight people made about the gay world: relationships, sex, and all the dynamics of them. As a general statement, they try to classify it as they understand relationships. How many times had I heard, "So, which one of you is the man and who is the woman?" or "Isn't that too fast to move in together? You guys just met," "The age gap is kinda creepy; I mean, he's twice his age."

My answer is this: we are gay; we do it differently. You are straight, and you actually don't need to know any of it because we really don't want to know the details that you ask us for about your own love lives.

One of my favourites is how do you know which one is, you know…the "top"? Jesus Christ. As far as gays go, at least in most of the Western world, the gay way of dating and hookups was far more streamlined than the straights. We literally could dial up a hookup for a quick fix any time we want with the dating apps. No strings. Just sex.

It was so easy that some of the straight guys I'd met through Patience were dumbfounded. "It's *that* easy?! No waiting for second and third dates…buying dinners or long movies?" And I'd reply, "No, that'd just waste time they could spend boning." They'd look at me in rapped attention, not believing it.

Patience would laugh. She had learned off from the gays that if you wanted a good old roll around in the hay, meeting guys and getting to know them wasn't the way. All this is true, but what is also true is that gays have also streamlined falling in love. The often miscommunication that straight people experience in figuring out what goes on in the heads of people of the opposite sex? With the gays, it simply doesn't exist. Guys know, guys. Girls know girls. That's why it's easier and quicker. But quick doesn't mean romance is dead. Nor does it mean that it is any less beautiful or valuable to the people experiencing it. The only hiccup for us gays is really just defining a relationship from a hookup. Because sex is so readily available, it can lead to some misunderstandings.

I was fortunate when it came to relationships. I had some experience with guys in college, but everything seemed to click together so quickly upon meeting Marcus. Our love was simple and easy for both of us to see. We didn't need to worry about questioning if the thing we had was long-term or not; because immediately, Marcus had led the way. He'd taken my hand into years of loving bliss that I thought would never end. It was almost like a sick universal joke when we got the diagnosis that he had late-stage non-Hodgkin's lymphoma. My Nǎinai's words had echoed in my mind then, *"You're born under one of the unluckiest stars, my Xiǎoyīng ...."*

Ayaka's words from his story echoed with the memories. Though she'd reassured me that we controlled our own fates and could push past any barriers placed by fate, this barrier had been insurmountable. It had left me an empty husk that just wandered through day to day, going through the motions on autopilot. If not for the guiding light of Patience, her family, and my wonderful parents, that fugue state would have killed me.

So, why is this relevant now? Because the note I held in my hand could just be another cruel trick of fate, and I wasn't sure if I could handle another blow to my soul like that. Ayaka acted so charmingly and fascinating. Watching him talk and move so silkily around me tempted me to flow into whatever rhythm he played with his words and actions. He was the devil I didn't know. The beautiful and impossible dream that was trying to creep into my life. Then there was the other obvious problem. He wasn't even human, which didn't bother me as much as it really should, which probably made me the crazy one here.

"I love you, Marcus," I said with my eyes closed, hoping he could hear me, "I love you so much, I miss you every day, but baby, I'm so cold without you. My world is so cold without you. And either I follow you to the grave, or I try and live...."

Another memory I had suppressed on purpose pushed its way through my thoughts and made me take a deep shuddering breath:

He was weak, almost a skeleton, no hair, skin waxy sheen, and smooth. I was sitting there at his side, holding his hand, trying to avoid the offending tubes that tangled him while keeping his pain levels low and almost alive. It was just us now. My parents had gone to our apartment and Patience, her sister's house, to stay. I felt him move, so I lifted my head. Hopeful to see his eyes that had been closed for almost four days now. Yes, yes, there they were. My sapphire blue jewels looking at me. A tear that somehow manifested from the corner of his eye and rolled down his pale cheek onto the pillow, leaving a spot. He reached a bony arm from his other side and grabbed his breathing mask with his long fingers pulling it down.

"Baby, no, what are you…" he squeezed my hand.

"Shush love, and listen," he was speaking, oh god, though his voice was a rasp. I grabbed a cup of ice chips I had kept on his tray in case he woke up and placed some chips gently between his lips, still full but a little dry. He sucked on the chips until they melted into the water, which he swallowed, wetting his throat.

"Li, my baby, my Xiǎoyīng," he said, I could hear him, and he was looking at me; it felt like he was back with me again; I was smiling, the tears rolling down my face, "Listen."

"Ok, what can I get you? Anything? More ice, a juice?" I wasn't sure exactly what to do.

"Just listen, my love," so I did, just swimming in the blue eyes I had missed so much, "you know what is happening, don't you?"

"The doctor said that…."

"Baby, I'm going away, and we both know it," the tears were accompanied by whimpers. I began shaking my head and closing my eyes to banish his words, the doctor's words. "Open your eyes,

Xiǎoyīng. I want to see you." I did as he wished." Keep your eyes with mine; I need you to listen."

"Ok." I sniffed the most ungracious sniff but didn't break contact with him.

"I am going away soon. And I won't be able to keep you from the world's troubles. I need you to be ok, baby. I need you to take care of yourself." I nodded absently, trying to silently deny his words, "I need you to be ok, to be happy, to love again." I choked on my own breathing at that.
"I can't, Marcus, I won't, you're the only one," I was shaking with so much fear, anguish, and hatred towards the world in general for trying to take him from me.

"No, baby, I am only one! And I have been so blessed, so blessed," he was the one crying now, not just tears, his words were hurting him too, "so happy with you, you are the best thing that has ever happened, and there is not a moment that I won't take with me, know that, every moment. It was everything to me. You are everything to me."

"You're everything to me; please stop,"

"No, you need to listen and promise me," he took a rattling breath and swallowed, "Promise me you'll love again. You have to. You are too special, too beautiful to stay apart from the world. You must go on for me."

I could barely see him and tried to clear my vision, the tears obscuring everything.

"I will try, for you, I will do anything you want, Marcus, you are my world. I can't deny you anything. Just stay, please!"

***

Chapter 15: Supernatural Meets Donut!

My usual black leather jacket. At least I didn't look too bad. I remember Marcus 'advice about coordination, and he'd always said that when in doubt, James Dean everything but your hair. My hair. Shoulder-length black Asian hair. I'd had the sides and back shaved, and I pulled it up into a top knot that was probably never going to come back into style. But it was suitable for when the wind blew in Vancouver. The winds could really pick up, and having my hair fly around my face and in my eyes while crossing the road isn't something I'd want to try. Cell phone. Wallet, in which I slipped the little stock card from Ayaka. I decided it was going to be a "carbs" day all the way. Donuts.

Now, in Canada, there's a chain of famous donut 'cafes 'called *Tim Hortons*. They aren't the peak of donut glory, but neither were they scraping the bottom of the barrel when it came to quality. The bottom line with Tim Hortons was that they were consistent. You'd always get the same of whatever you ordered. I went across the road to get a box, sit by the water, and eat as many as possible. With that, the cake and ice cream from yesterday and the pizza from earlier, mingled with regular meals, I was probably going to end up a contender for the TV show "*My 600 lb. life*." Take that Ayaka, let's see if you want anything to do with me once I'm a giant heifer who needed to be transported by a crane and washed with a fire hose. I got my box of 6 Boston Creams and a large frozen raspberry lemonade. At least my brain freezes could be enjoyed without the mega embarrassment from the Freak club of the other night.

The sun was out, the air only slightly chilly. The sky was clear. I walked down to the harbour side and along the boardwalk seeing the families, parents wrangling their children from straying too far, or sunbathers (in this weather?) on one of the park hills. I always found that brave considering the Canadian geese, a regular sight in BC, would frequent the hill, any grass patch actually, and deposit goose turds everywhere. Cyclists and roller-bladers zoomed past alongside me in the cycle lane. I found a park bench and sat down facing the water. I unboxed one of the sinful delights and proceeded to devour it in less than three mouthfuls. Yup, 600 lb. life, here I come. I pulled out my cell and sent Patience a picture of my face covered in chocolate and custard. Then another of me shoving another into my mouth.

The phone vibrated a reply:

Patience Queen Bitch of MGV – 600lb life forever!!!!!!!

Then another message, a picture of her with Charity and Faith, covered in glitter.

My reply: *Ha! Glitter Bomb Hiroshima! You can't escape Squad Charity and Faith.*

A few more back and forth messages. One from Hope thanking me for coming to her party yesterday. I took a panoramic picture of the view around me: the harbour, the park, the trees. Then I sent it to Maman and Bàba. They loved seeing Canada's scenery. Sometimes I wished they could see the colours I could. Though it sort of complicated life, it made it beautiful too. I know they missed Canada, but Hong Kong was tempting for money, and Bàba would always find it difficult to retire. From a young age, he had been taught the value of having money by not having much.

Năinai had always seemed to just make ends meet and was constantly receiving gifts of food and clothes and such from the village in Guilin before she left. Bàba had grown up in mismatching clothes that were too big or too small and shoes on their last legs. It's not to say his childhood was rough. It wasn't. It had just been unconventional, but it had been the children he had grown up with that had shaped his opinion of money. They had always had what they wanted and often made fun of him. When he grew up, he vowed to himself his children would never have to think about those sorts of things and could focus on more important matters. It had become a bit of an obsession to earn money. But Maman and Bàba were happy more often than not. And at least they had the resources to come to Vancouver anytime they wished.

I went to take another panoramic picture, scanning my phone horizontally. Then something caught my attention; three benches away. A man was sitting casually looking out over the water. That is fine, of course; anyone could come here and do that. But this particular man looked out of place. He wore a suit that was tight enough to show a thick muscled build. Almost like it was a costume than an actual outfit. He had sunglasses on and had pale skin. He was obviously Asian, just very pale. Again, these qualities were not particularly remarkable. What really put him out of place was that he, like Ayaka, had hidden his aura. I couldn't see the colours around him. He likely wasn't human. He glanced my way briefly, nodding politely before turning back to the water.

I picked up the remnants of my donut sins and got up to leave. I didn't know the man. But he gave me chills. And he looked vaguely familiar. I couldn't pin it until I thought logically: *where would I have seen a non-human before?* The club - Crossroads. There had been that group of suits standing in the corner. They'd stood around the guy who had been sitting on the couches in the corner. This one had been conversing with the seated guy. I swear they were one and the same.

I walked briskly up the steps to the park with the families and more Sunday goers. I noticed another one across the park in conversation with one of the dads who kept his eyes on the playground, only half-listening to the suited guy's dialogue. He briefly slipped a look my way. I couldn't see any details other than Asian and pale. But I felt that chill again. My instincts were telling me something was not good about these guys.

Leaving the park, I saw another one walking in the opposite direction to enter the park and right past me. This time he did look straight at me. The chill came along with a slight dread. His direct stare at me felt like standing on the edge of a cliff, knowing the drop was below you even though your feet were on solid ground. I picked up my pace. These guys seemed to be all over the place. Why? I really had no reason to find out. The only thing I had to do was get to a familiar place. Hadn't people noticed these people? I mean, I know it's Canada, and people were polite. But when I saw one of the suits walked through a group of people, they parted to make room for him without even noticing.

The café! I headed straight for it.

I was trying to pay attention to everything in my entire surroundings. Had you ever tried doing that? It's actually exhausting trying to track all directions around you. I saw a few more of them. It really did seem like people were just ignoring them because they didn't seem to be hiding their presence at all. Just kind of milling around and flicking glances at me, watching, almost considering what their next move might be. Looking back, I saw the one who had walked past me standing there, just staring at me. This was all wildly fucked up mafia-type stalking behaviour. I was so focused on watching around me I almost missed the café.

I stopped and looked in. Fuck! It was closed. It was never closed on Sundays. The café was empty. I noticed a note taped under the closed sign: *To our beloved Patrons, The family is taking a much-needed break. Fear not, we will be back Tuesday, business as usual.*

The family is finally taking a road trip!!! It was cute. The family that owned the café worked so hard and always talked about taking a few days off to travel around BC and the mountains in Squamish and Whistler. Now they were doing it. I liked the family, mainly because their coffee was excellent, and they were sweet, so they deserved time off. But seriously! They picked today?! Random suits stalker day?

I should go home. I looked out from the café doorway and saw in every direction there was at least one of the creepy suits, men and women, all really pale and most wearing sunglasses. They were just standing there, staring. Not subtle. And freaky. I didn't want to bother Patience. She was helping out Hope and her family. I finally realized the price of isolation; you actually were isolated! And when some supernatural goons were encircling you, you were basically screwed. Any horror movie buff would be slapping me for making such rookie mistakes; I wanted to slap me! I didn't have my bear spray. Not that I was sure it would have any effect on these guys.

But at least I wouldn't feel so ridiculous. Argh. The last thing I wanted to be was a Bella Swann needing rescuing from every stupid threat because I couldn't think of a way out for myself. Think Yīng! Think!

What did I have? A cell. my wallet. Half a box of Boston Cream donuts. *Hmph*.

I steeled myself, reached into my Tim Hortons box, and pulled out a fresh Boston Cream. My heart was pounding. I didn't know how to deal with any of this supernatural bullshit, but there was no way I was going to be a Bella Swann. I rounded the corner out of the doorway with the most determined squint I could muster.

On the sidewalk in front of me and across the road were two suits. They both saw me; I looked behind me. Yup, the other one was coming towards me too. I stomped forward. The one directly in front of me lifted his sunglasses and showed his Japanese features, slightly handsome with his dark hair tied up behind him in a tail. He had the strangest grey eyes, almost silver. I filed away these details and carried on walking towards him, determined. A frown creased between his eyebrows, possibly confusion. His eyes were exotic, so were all their eyes, I bet. As I got to less than a foot away from him, it was into those eyes I pushed the Boston cream and broke into a run to my apartment building full tilt. Before I went into the entryway, I looked back; the suit I had creamed had his friends gathered around, the two non-creamed ones were laughing at their colleague who just looked stunned. Good!

Chin held high; I made my way into my building into the lobby. That's right. No Bella Swann here! Chin still in the air, I walked past the lobby couches and into a marble pillar that landed me on my butt on the lobby's marble floor. I looked around to see if anyone saw me other than the security and the concierge in the back office, whom I didn't mind seeing my clumsiness. I had bought them an espresso machine for Christmas which had bought me good favour for the next ten years.

Without warning, a pair of shiny and sleek men's boots squeaked up next to me. I looked up. And almost crab scuttled back but managed to restrain the urge. Ayaka looked down curiously at the tumbled heap that was me. He squatted down next to me.

"Please tell me you didn't see that?" I pleaded.

"I can pretend I didn't if you want," He reached under my arms and lifted me to my feet.

"I'm ok; I'm not an invalid," I said, trying to sound dignified and failing. Holding my head in the air was what got me a face full of the pillar in the first place.

"Of course, but you were rushing through those doors like the devil himself was on your tails." Tails?

"Well, he was. At least several devils. Or something. I dunno," I brushed my backside to straighten my jeans while he observed with his usual wry grin in place. Geez, he was tall. I hadn't really thought about it, but yeah, he was tall. His hair was tied back in a neat ponytail with some kind of clasp and pin made of what looked like jade. He wore casuals like I did. Except his shirt hugged every muscled curve of his chest and arms. Oh god, looking at him made it difficult to breathe.

"Devils?" His concern immediately replaced that cute grin.

"Um, I dunno, there were some suits out there; I think I saw them at Crossroads the other night," I swear I heard a growl escape his throat. He briefly bared his perfect teeth, giving me a glimpse of slightly elongated canines.

"It's ok; I can take care of myself."

"I'm sure you can," he said, looking pointedly at the pillar, then me.

"That pillar has had it in for me since I've lived here. One day, I'll win." A chuckle replaced the growl.

"I can't wait to see that showdown," he went quiet, and I looked at him, waiting for him to say something.

"Um, did you get my note?" He asked. Sounding innocent, but also trying desperately to hide the need for an answer. I bit my bottom lip.

"I did Ayaka." Oh, there it was. I thought it was a dream. When I said his name, I felt that imperceptible tug.

"Oh, I see," his usual enthusiasm and confidence seemed to fizzle a little, "I'm sorry. I was probably too forward. I shouldn't detain you, Xiǎoyīng." I felt the reciprocal pull of his words wrapping around my name.

"I do want to see you," it was like the sun had suddenly risen for the first time in his eyes, then at once, the typical cheekiness hid away that delight.

"Do you want to see me now?"

"Yes," I answered honestly. Failing to hide the burgeoning feeling that was escaping my control.

"Good. Do you have a tale about devils you want to impart?"

"Sure, but obviously, we should go upstairs to do that."

"You don't want to go somewhere? An early dinner?"

"Sure thing, but right now I want to go home and sit, there were weird men out there watching me, and it rattled my nerves, and right now, I could use someone just sitting with me, if that's all right; with you?"

"Of course, Xiǎoyīng."

***

Chapter 16: Home with the Zenko

For the second time, I invited the Zenko into my home. Only this time, it felt different. There was a heavy cloud of anticipation in the air, and my house smelled like him still. I plopped the box of remaining Boston Creams on my coffee table and sunk into my couch. How could I be so exhausted already? Stupid suits.

Ayaka settled in next to me. He leaned his elbow on the couch back, facing me.

"What happened?" he asked.

"Hmm, some suits from the club seemed to be following me. I went to the park to binge on donuts and eat my feelings away for the day…."

"Eat your feelings away?" The raw amusement in his question made me blush, I'm sure a beetroot colour.

"Anyway… I saw one a few seats away from me. I thought he was weird because I couldn't see the man's aura. And I remembered what you said, so I left."

"Smart Xiǎoyīng."

"Then they started kind of popping up everywhere, so I started to head towards a café I know. You know, be surrounded by people I know." He nodded at that.

"Then what happened," he was so close, but not close enough to touch, and part of me was relieved. His proximity screwed with my focus, and I needed my focus right now.

"Well, the intended destination was closed. Apparently, the owners chose today to take their mini holiday," I rolled my eyes at the bad luck. "Hence, I had to think of what to do because they'd kinda surrounded me," His face took on that feral snarl without the growl this time. I looked at his hand resting on the couch inches from my leg. Man! If this was a Grindr hookup, I would have grabbed that hand…possibly more of him by now. But no. Cautious is me!

"And…?"

"Um…I stomped towards home. I wasn't gonna be stopped from getting home."

"If you knew what they were, you'd probably be more hesitant to even approach them," he said matter-of-factly. As if the revelation of such should bring quakes and shudders to all humans around.

"Why? What were they?" He seemed to be considering an answer. And chose the direct approach. And he was right. Had I known, I would have probably changed my tactics and been a lot less brave/stupid.

"Vampires, I believe you call them here."

"Oh."

"Yeah."

"You mean…?"

"Blood-sucking supernatural killers."

"Oh," I smirked. The man looked at me questioningly.

"What?"

"Hmm, well, it's a good thing I didn't know what they were."

"Yes, as I said. But please call if you see the vampires again."

"I will. I almost forgot to add you to my contacts. I have your note here." I pulled it out and proceeded to create a contact for his number. He peered over at the screen, trying to see what I was doing.

I hugged it to my chest, "You can't see. I have my own naming system, and it's private." His eyebrow shot up at that.

"You don't want to use my name?"

"No, you gave that to me. It doesn't belong in my phone, I think." He looked smug at that admission.

"Thank you." He seemed to mean it. I'm sure I'd find out soon enough why. But I was beginning to gain a picture of the reasons.

"What I don't quite get is it's daylight out, and you said those were vampires…." I asked, trying to piece together a picture of Vampires existing in the real world.

"Sunlight isn't harmful to them in the strictest sense. It just seems to slow them down. Normally they are swift and strong."

"They did seem kind of, not at their best for Vampires. They were just following me."

"I think Xiǎoyīng, they were watching you," I wondered what implications that could have, vampires, stalking me in broad daylight, not afraid of-

"Ok, so it's broad daylight, and these things are out and about," he started to chuckle at my cavalier manner of which I spoke of the Vampires, "they didn't seem at all bothered by the prospect of witnesses."
"How perceptive," not that I needed validation from this hunk/spirit/creature on my couch, but it did send tingles through me to think I had impressed him somehow.
"Vampires have this…energy, I guess. They can influence their immediate environment and its occupants by making them ignore them. Among other things, it's quite the skill when you think of the possibilities." He paused, looking at me, and seemed to be ferreting out a detail in my face….

"You're not telling me something…." He said, his turn to be perceptive, reading my face clearly, too quickly. That was unnerving. But I had grown up with a Năinai who could read anything she wanted to, so I wasn't too shocked.

"Yes, but I want you to tell me what you were doing here when I got here. You realize It's slightly 'stalkery.'"

"I prefer 'trackery.'" He looked indignant at my jibe, "I wanted to see you. Now tell me what else happened." As if his answer was perfectly acceptable. I wanted to see many things; it didn't mean I could just turn up when I wanted…but then. I had to remember. This was someone who followed different rules, different social etiquettes than I was used to. Maybe I had to stop imposing my normality on him because it would be like me telling Baraz to stop drawing or Patience to stop being a bitch. Neither of those requests was fair or even possible.

"Ok, well, like I said, it's probably a good thing I didn't know they were blood-drinking killing machines because I attacked one with my donut." Confusion, disbelief, more confusion, then a loud, full laugh roared out of his pretty mouth, echoing around my apartment.

"You must be joking." He said, still laughing.

"Nope wasted a delicious Boston Cream too." He almost leaped across the couch, unable to contain some need with his grin so wide and his joy palpable. Then stopped himself short of touching. I flinched but not in fear, just surprise.

"Sorry, I just, it was something that made me feel, a lot." He shook his head, marvelling at me, "now I understand why you looked so damned smug until that marble pillar decided to burst your ego balloon." It was my turn to laugh now.

I couldn't remember the last time I'd laughed this much. This past week had been strange, but so much laughter had filled it; my heart felt a little lighter than it had in ages. The gloom that had settled on me was shifting slightly.

"Well, the stupid vampire gave me a look I didn't like with his stupid eyes." More laughs from the Zenko; he was going to fall off the couch, all grace and style gone!

"You know, those eyes are supposed to enchant and ensnare mere mortals," he put on a dramatic accent mimicking count Dracula. Then I too lost it, and of course, it was me, so I fell off the couch-

Ayaka's hand shot out and caught my arm, wrapping neatly around my sleeve to prevent my landing on the ground. Faster than lightning, he set me aright on the couch again.

"I'm sorry, Xiǎoyīng," he looked at his hand as he took it back.

"No, that's ok." I puffed, catching my breath.

"I heard Neelas," he murmured, "I don't want to do anything that might upset you." Oh shit. That's why he was always so close but never touching. Made sense now.

"I don't know much about it, but apparently, it's rare, and it doesn't do much but copy abilities of other magical people and such, so I am not sure it even applies to you, Ayaka." I looked at my hands, turning them over like they were someone else's.

"Being a Mimic is very rare for two reasons Xiǎoyīng." I was curious to hear more about this thing that I apparently was.

"Call me Aya, um, a few people do…but you can too if you like." I snorted. Again, that confused look, "now where was I…?"

"Oh, you're serious? Well, sure, Aya. I like it."

"My short name amuses you?"

"No, the fact that only a few people use it amuses me, it's actually kind of, um, I guess cool is the word? Or maybe Kickass?"

"Well then, I'm kick-ass." That smug look again.

"What were you saying about mimics?"

"Well, like I said, they're rare, and more importantly, not much is really known about them. I suspect Neelas was doing you a kindness by downplaying it, hoping you'd use the Eraser for your own good. There are certain transformative conditions which can change the nature of the ability too…." He said this last part so quietly that it was like he was saying it to himself more than me.

"Really?" I hadn't really thought about the Eraser much since that night. In fact, it now sat next to Marcus 'picture on my bedside drawer.

"Where I come from…."

"Japan," I said, interrupting. He looked from side to side, making himself look purposely sneaky.

"Sure, Japan. Well, where I am from, where all the beings you saw in the Crossroads come from, is dictated by energy."
"But isn't everything already dictated by energy?" I remembered my college physics classes the first year. Though mathematics turned me off the subject, the subject itself was interesting.

"Yes, you are correct, though, in some places, the energy is… harder? I think I can say. Less mutable or malleable?"

"Like here?"

"Correct again. Well, mimics are little bridges of those energies. It's how the copying happens. It's really quite fascinating."

"So that's the reason you wanted to hang out?"

"Not in the least," he was telling the truth, "I wanted to see you." Such a simple answer that had such heavy meaning attached to it. He kept saying it. Why? Seeing me for what? If I looked at this picture logically. He was a Spirit Being, so maybe immortal? Powerful? Full of magic, possibly? And could likely be and do anything he chose, so why me? It made me suspicious and a little puzzled. Like I said, I had to remember I was dealing with beings that were essentially alien to me—different rules.

"Is it bad for me? Being a mimic?"

"I can't say for sure. But I don't want to hurt you. I have been trying to not touch you. Plus, it is not polite to touch without invitation." A rule, possibly? Filed away.

"Oh," Did that mean he could never touch me? No way was that going to be my life. Another fantasy cliché I didn't want. *They're so in love but could never touch because of blah blah blah.* Lame! I felt almost defiant at that thought. Wait, what? In love? Back up!

"I'm not particularly good with touching anyways. I haven't been for a while," I admitted. Not really speaking to the guy, but to myself.

"I see," he reached over to the box of donuts on the coffee table and opened it, "I have to see what these deadly anti-vampire weapons look like."

"You're in Canada, and you haven't had Tim Hortons?"

"In my defence, I did just get here a few weeks ago and am still getting used to the place."

"Where were you before?"

"As you said, Japan. On business," His talk of business brought wild ideas about what a servant of a Japanese god would do. Some of the pictures were comical, others downright lewd. He picked up a Boston Cream, turning it in his hands like it was some delicate fossil first discovered and waiting for its secrets to come to light.
"I still can't imagine it. I have to see this again; you taking on a vampire with one of these and then strutting off like you're an unstoppable juggernaut." The laughter resumed. He replaced the

donut. I picked up the box and placed it in the fridge. Above the pizza box, which I have to remember, needed to go into the trash. I thought for a moment of something safe, pleasant, and public for us both to enjoy.

"Early dinner?" I asked. It was only four in the afternoon, but I wanted to be busy and not relaxing in my apartment with an… almost stranger.

"Yes, please. I know a great place."

***

Chapter 17: Red Robins

I looked around the décor, and it was my turn to be thoroughly amused by someone's choices. We sat in a booth with cracked red vinyl covering each of our seats. We sat facing each other. Aya's face beamed as the server came over with the menus. The server was a middle-aged woman with bleach blonde hair with extreme regrowth named Cora. She had her hair up in a messy bun. Her makeup was dated the same as the music playing on the overhead speakers (90's pop, complete with boybands and girl bands who were no longer bands). When she smiled, I could see a dire need for dental coverage. But I'll tell you, when she smiled at the two of us like it was Christmas morning for her, it was somehow sweet. She kept shooting, knowing looks at us, and then left us to decide our orders. I had to say, she was almost as endearing as my company, and I decided to tip her well already.

"This place is amazing, isn't it?" he asked hopefully. And I wasn't about to burst his bubble. It was too adorable to see his excitement. Plus, focusing on the auras always made places look like more than they were without the 'sight.' The colours wrapped around patrons and servers alike and were in full bloom. The crowd was typical fare for a place like this. Families and young couples, groups of college kids, carb-loading for whatever hellish assignments awaited them. The environment sported mainly red with rock 'n' roll memorabilia filling every available space on the walls. This, of course, clashed with what was playing on the overhead speakers. I doubted any of the patrons cared.

"Absolutely, Aya. You did well." I was not sarcastic because he had definitely added a new dimension to my week's whacky experiences.

"Did you see?" He pointed at the massive tower of onion rings featuring a prominent place at the top of the menu, "a *Jiin* of fried onion slices." *Jiin*? It was Japanese for a temple, I think. Perhaps he thought the onion tower was in homage to an onion god or something. It just made him seem almost innocent. What was I doing?!

"Wow, that's a lot of onion rings," I looked over the stack of fried goodies, "You must really love onion rings."

"I discovered this place in my first week here. I have come almost every other day. They have so many choices, and you can change anything you want as long as they have it in the kitchen." Every other day?

He, of course, had taken me to a local diner. It was known as Red Robins. If you can imagine Hard Rock Café and Denny's had a baby and gave it up for adoption to be raised by a fry cook, then you'd have Red Robins. But let's be fair, the food is delicious. I had made the odd run to Red Robins just for their burgers alone, or when Patience was still hungover well into the evening, and I needed to line her stomach with something quick, tasty, and easily digestible.

"So, what can I get you young gents this evening?" Cora sidled up.

"Cora, may I please have this *Jiin* of fried onions please, a Jammin' Bacon Burger, a Monster Burger, ooh… and the Red Robin Royal Burger, and then… let's see, the mountain high mud pie and the giant fudge filled cookie, um… and please may I also have the endless Lemonade?"

Both Cora and I stared gob smacked at the inhumanity of such a massive order. I knew exactly what I was going to do when that food arrived. I had to. It was my duty. I had my phone at the ready.

"Certainly, sir, and for you?" She indicated to me the shell-shocked companion.

"Um… an Impossible Burger and a strawberry lemonade, please."

"No worries, boys," she grabbed the menus and went to leave until Aya's hand was suddenly on her hand, the one with the menus. I swear I heard her squeak.

"Cora, it's a beautiful name." The waitress looked to me, unsure, then to Aya, absolutely enchanted.

"Why, thank you, um, my mother gave it to me."

"Your mother must have been a very knowing woman to give you such a powerful and strong name," his hand hadn't left hers, "do you know what it means?"

"I can't say I do, it's just been old Cora for forever and a day, nothing special here," her voice was cracking, nervous and excited, but then slightly sad.

"You were named after a Greek goddess. You see, it is derived from Kore, the bride of Hades. It represents the duality in women. At once, you are the beautiful maiden you are now, but if one could dig a little deeper, you would find a darker, more powerful woman. You are Something quite special if you ask me."

He released her hand then. She just stared, as did I. Her face was the colour of the general décor now, but she was smiling from ear to ear, "Beautiful name Cora," He repeated.

She positively skipped away like a little girl with the menus tucked against her chest like two treasures.

"What was that?" I had to ask. She may have flooded her proverbial basement with this stunning creature in front of me, touching her and then giving her probably the first compliment she had had in years.

"I haven't had the privilege of seeing the staff here in the evenings. They are quite different from those in the day. She is tired but exceedingly kind, and she needed to know what I told her." I shook my head, "What? Did I do something wrong?" He asked, confused.

"No, you have been doing everything right," I mumbled. And it was fast becoming a problem!
When the kitchen received Aya's order, they kept looking over to see how many people were in our booth and when they saw just us, they looked confused. Still, Cora assured them the order was correct and that they'd better get onto it.

I studied Aya's face. Still, his looks took my breath away. No wonder Cora was speechless; I bet the day staff had already written legends about the hunk who eats more than a football team and makes every old woman feel 16 again. He was studying my face too and appeared to be waiting for something.

"I've meant to ask about your aura," I said. Hoping it wasn't impolite to ask such questions: alien species and all.

"Yes?"

"Um…. can I see it? Am I allowed? Or is that breaking some etiquette? I'm sorry if it is. I'm new to supernatural beings taking me out to," I waved my hand around the general area, "ahh, extraordinary restaurants."

"I don't know if that is wise, my Xiǎoyīng," he looked apologetic and a little flustered, *My Xiǎoyīng?* "There are side effects."

"Oh, is it something that might hurt?"

"No, no, not at all. It's just, not everyone is like you, and not everyone will know what they are perceiving."

"Side effects?" Cora interrupted us briefly by setting our drinks down, "Thanks, Cora," I may as well have sworn at her or insulted her face for all she noticed me; she had only eyes for Aya. Could I blame her?

He sighed, then conceded as Cora shuffled off, "Ok, but this is the only time in a public setting, and you'll soon see why." Baffled, I gestured to him to get on with it while I sipped my lemonade. He looked around and then. Suddenly my sight couldn't see any other auras in the building…only one. The restaurant was briefly filled with a brilliant light. And then it was gone. Aya looking impassive and waiting again, but for what?

With the light subsiding and my usual 'sight' returning, I noticed we were no longer alone. A crowd of people had gathered around us. Almost everyone in the restaurant had moved to stand around our booth. Then as if some spell had broken, they looked to each other and us. Then they returned to what they had been occupied with earlier.

"Aya, what happened? I don't understand. They all looked so happy like they were high on something from the dispensary." They'd looked almost zombie-like if zombies could be happy. Or enthralled?

"Well, it is one of the side effects. Like I said, people perceive it a little differently to you."
"They looked like they'd seen heaven or divinity, I guess," he nodded.

"But not you." He sipped his drink.

"What do you mean?"

"My Xiǎoyīng, you saw it, they could not," he sipped again, eyes on his drink, "they could feel it, and you could not."

"What was I supposed to feel?"

"I'm not sure, but I guess the rapture they were feeling?"

"Oh," I felt like I had said or done something to offend him.

"It's ok, there's a reason for that. In fact, you expressed it last night." My mind went back to last night's events. The docks, our conversation, *"who's Marcus?"* he had asked…

"I couldn't charm you if I tried, and I wouldn't," he looked up from his drink, anguish, I think, marring his features.
"Your heart is somewhere else where neither I nor anyone could ever reach." Why the face? Anguish? Sadness? Why would he need to reach it? I wanted to get up and leave him again. To go to the safety of my quiet apartment and engross myself in a book or silly

TV drama, or maybe paint out my feelings until I was empty and there was nothing left to feel.

"I'm sorry, Aya." I felt the need to reach across the table and hold his hand. Wrap his slim long-fingered hands in mine. "Something happened to me that made me this way." A tear fell freely from one of his amber eyes onto the table, and for some reason, it was the most remarkable thing I had seen in my life.

"I know," he whispered, "a broken heart has the loudest cries one can hear." I realized suddenly that his tears, his anguish wasn't for him, but for me…? It was too much for me.

"Why me, Aya?" My feelings were wanting to break too, and I was also feeling those tears come again, but for many different reasons than before, "Why me? Why are you here? You are… what you are. None of it makes sense."

He reached across the table and, with his long index finger, swept it deftly under my eye and fixated on the single tear balancing atop it. And then focused on me and put his finger in his mouth. The act was so erotic and foreign, again such a strange and beautiful act given to me from this spirit manifested across from me in this diner. My hand this time moved of its own accord… and wrapped around his. I kept my eyes on his. I felt a jolt, like a small bolt of lightning, shoot through my hand up and down my spine and into my head, making me sway a little. He gasped at some unseen thing he felt too. He went to pull his hand back, and I held fast. He relaxed then placed his other hand atop mine. Then put them both to his mouth. "Xiǎoyīng." He breathed into our joined hands, "You should let go and guard yourself. Things with energy can be unpredictable, even though I am certain you are not in danger." He tried to pull away gently, but I held onto his hand as hard as I could without looking mental.

"Ayaka of the Zenko," it came so automatically, "I have been guarded as you said. Where no one could reach." I sighed. I had stopped feeling, living really, as Patience had put it: a half-life like a spirit wandering around without need or purpose. "So now I'm trying…. I'm reaching….or trying to…."

The air between us began to take on a different quality the longer I touched him. It was charged with feelings and energy we both felt. I wanted to do so many things right then and there, but we held still, just drinking in each other…

Cora chose that moment to bring over two trays piled high with Aya's order. His beloved onion ring tower she placed down, and whatever had transpired was put away temporarily. At the same time, she made room for plate after plate of food for Aya. Another server followed behind Cora with a tray and my humble order.

"Don't mind me, boys. Just enjoy yourselves. Food's up. Can I top up anyone's drinks?" I considered not tipping her for the interruption, but I did and still tipped her well. She was something special, as Aya had said. The years of hard life had just disguised it for a bit while Aya uncovered it for her to see again. That moment he had shown a stranger such kindness in a way that she would be reminded every time someone said her name. That was part of the reason I had reached across the table and taken this risk.

Our food-filled the entire table, and Aya's eyes were wide with delight, scanning the buffet of fried goodness to see which he would attack first. I took out my cell phone.

"Xiǎoyīng?" I was pointing the camera at him and leaning across the table towards him.

"Do as I do," I told him, he complied. I looked to make sure I could fit the food and both of us in. Cora saw me struggling to fill the picture frame with as much of the food and the two of as I could. She rushed over.

"Let me do that for you," she took the phone and aimed it at us, "Now smile and…cheese!" I saw her finger press the screen several times. She handed back my phone.

"Thank you, Cora," Aya said. Seeing her blush again was sweet.

"No problem, gents, just holla if you need anything else," she looked at the pile of food doubtfully, smiled, and shuffled to another table who was waving her over.

The photo did capture us both with the mountain of calories around us. It was about time I let Patience in on this little situation more. I showed Aya. He held the phone, looking at the picture like it was fragile and needed to be handled with care. His fingers were a blur as he pressed the screen briefly.

"Hey!" I admonished playfully, "What are you doing?"

"Sending this memory to my phone…" he pulled out his phone to ensure it had appeared on his messenger app, "when I typed in my number, another name came up…." I had the good sense to look embarrassed and shyly lifted my chin, to change my look to my usual dignified (but not really) look.

"I explained I have my own categorizing system in my contacts."

"Àiqíng gùshì..?"

"It's a Taylor Swift song I like, don't read into it." I couldn't meet his eyes. I was reasonably sure I blushed to match Cora's earlier display of colour. Furthermore, I was fairly sure he was reading everything into it.

"I see," He said, not buying it. Then handed the phone back, which I tucked safely into my jacket pocket until I remembered my reason for the selfie to begin with and whipped it out. A message to Patience: *600 lb. life is winning the day, baby!*

A reply came almost instantly: *Li! Who the Fuck is that!? He doesn't even look real. Surgery? Or just winning the genetic lottery? Jealous to the bone! This convo isn't over! Have fun, love you!*

My reply: *No surgery required for this one, long story. I'll explain later. Love you too.*

Aya was practically vibrating in his seat, looking at the food.

"Let's do this!" I said, like a general waging war on the million-calorie monster in front of us.

***

Chapter 18: First time

My parents, though my Maman was French, acted the way many Chinese families would at a buffet. It's a carefully thought-out strategic strike of getting as much into you until what you had eaten had far surpassed what you had paid. Seeing them leave empty plates, serving trays and platters in their wake, always reminded me of a twister rolling through a town only to leave debris and destruction.

Aya was something different. If my parents were a twister, then Aya was the perfect storm. He devoured his meal with gusto and abandonment while I daintily ate my Impossible Burger and sipped my lemonade. Cora came over, constantly refilling his drink. When we left the restaurant, Cora was fanning herself with a menu. The booth had been cleared of food, and only empty dishes remained. Aya had ceased his barrage on the plates briefly at times to offer me some. I ate the occasional onion ring, but watching the display was like seeing something from the nature channel, both beautiful and terrifying.

He walked on my left, and I felt his fingers entangling mine and squeezed. We walked towards my building past a myriad of convenience stores and restaurants. Like I had said, I was so lucky to be near so many of them. Aya explained that food was so scarce when he was a pup and struggled badly at times. So much so that their skulk had suffered losses. Zenko were all vulnerable when young. Their ability to defend themselves didn't kick in for a few years, so they looked like regular foxes for the first years of their lives. And when Aya had seen Red Robin, he couldn't resist indulging. His words made me wonder how old he was. What period was he born in? How long would he live? Would I be dust when he still looked like this model of inhuman perfection?

"Wait here, Li. I'll be right back." Without further explanation, he was gone, leaving me standing beside a small Japanese convenience store. I considered getting a cream freeze for Aya to see if he still had room for more food. Where it went was a mystery. His body was strong and lithe, like an athlete or Olympic swimmer. Ha! I wish. Stop imagining things, Li.

The fingers returned to mine and curled up to hold my hand again. It was like he could appear and disappear in the blink of an eye. We carried on walking. Up ahead was a bench for people to sit. Casually relaxing on it was a no aura suit. Trying to look busy.

"Excuse me again, Li," he was gone again. I turned to look again at the suit, and he was gone too. As before, the fingers curled into mine.

"Aya, what is going on?"

"We've been followed since we left your apartment, which I found considerably rude."

"Oh…so…"

"I removed them. I am pretty sure they were the vamps you encountered earlier."
"So sunlight really doesn't bother them that much? I was hoping they had forgotten and were waiting to become ashes. At least that's an easier explanation, Right?" Aya snickered.

"No, they're fine in sunlight, as I said."

Again, no one else thought their behaviour was weird when they were following me; no one seemed to notice them. Or if they did, they'd held a polite "not even listening" conversation with them.

"It's like they're not even there," I observed again.

"It's typical of vamps when they emit that sense of completely innocuous circumstance around them. It's part of their repertoire."

"Are you ok? I mean, they didn't bite you?" Another chortle at that naive question.

"No, no biting, they were just removed to somewhere else by me. It's rude. We are trying to have a lovely evening; at least I hope you are finding it lovely with me." I squeezed his hand in answer.

"What will happen now that I've touched your hand? Will I start acting unearthly charming to waitresses and stalking lonely artists? Sorry, 'tracking'…." I seemed to get him laughing often. That was a good sign.

"I am not sure. You may gain some temporary abilities from me. I don't think anything it's permanent with mimic magic; it's too unstable. It'll just fade if unused."

"Oh, that's a shame. I thought maybe I could have a superpower or something, like in the manga books I work on."

"You may, I don't know, but it'll be temporary and not likely strong. As I said, mimics are so rare there's not much known. Don't worry, you're still very human. Likely nothing will happen."

"What about your cologne?"

"Cologne?" His eyebrows raised at that.

"Yeah, it's strong. Whatever brand it is, they must have patented some good fragrance technology because my apartment has it lingering everywhere."

"My cologne? You like it?"

"I do, but it puts me in thoughts of you instantly like a trigger."

"I don't wear cologne, Li Xiǎoyīng." I stopped and turned to face him, surprising him. But he stopped to face me, even though my building was just across the set of lights we were at.
"You're telling me that's how you smell anyway? All the time?"

"Yes. It's something I can't really help without considerable effort."

"Not fair." I turned back to the crosswalk and pulled his hand along with me.

We came to the entrance of my building just as the rain started. The access to my building was undercover. I pulled out my key fob, unsure of what to do. We were facing each other again. Aya's eyes were trying to communicate something to me. My mind was picking up signals clearly, which made my heart begin to pound against my chest.

I need you to be ok, to be happy, to love again… Could I? Now, I have mentioned earlier that we gays do things differently, streamlined. But that doesn't warrant taking unnecessary risks, which is basically what this whole situation was—a risk. But I was beginning to feel again. Like when you sit too long on your foot and stand up, but your foot had lost some feeling and forgot how to support your weight. So you then move it around to reboot the circulation…it was like that…only fewer feet and more…feeling.

Then, I made a decision and asked, "Um, would you like to…."

With his supernatural speed, he had closed the gap between us, enclosed my face with his hands, so warm, his body pressed tightly against me. He was inches from my face. Was he going to… was I? This was going to happen. I had crossed some line back in the restaurant, some barrier with him that made this moment inevitable.

His lips pressed firmly against mine, then his tongue pushed into my mouth, massaging mine. When I say this kiss was like fire, I was almost literal. The jolt I had received from simply touching his hand in the restaurant was nothing compared to this. Heat poured from everywhere he touched, sending tingling sensations through my whole body, particularly my groin and all around my pelvic region. I was lost in the kiss, so wonderful, floating in a sea of pleasure, like nothing I had ever felt before. He pulled away abruptly.

"Breath, my Xiǎoyīng," he was right. I had forgotten to breathe, and my head was spinning; the sensations of warmth remained in all my erogenous areas. I gulped in the air and went in for more. He let me, again the heat of sensation swept through me. He pressed against me, his erection pressing against mine.

Absently I waved the fob across the scan pad, and the doors opened. We were in the elevator somehow, still kissing. Now that I remembered to breathe through the sensations, the kiss was longer. Already it felt like sex was happening to me, in me, and around me. Waving the fob at the elevator scan pad, I used my fingers to count up to the tenth floor and pressed it without breaking the contact. I never wanted that contact broken.

We were at my door. And then somehow inside my apartment. Then we were on the bed, Aya on top of me pressing hard against my jeans. When our shirts had come off, he kissed down from my neck to my chest, then nipples that he sucked gently. The fire of his kisses kept spreading through my whole body. He undid my jeans, and they were across the room. My erection pushed against my boxer briefs, he tore those off too and took me into his mouth, and I lost it.

My groans were loud and honest. This was the best feeling I had ever felt. Aya's hands all over me, His fingers squeezing my nipples. Then his hand ventured under my balls down my perineum to the entrance there. He momentarily let go with his mouth on my dick and suck his finger, wetting it, then resumed the madly hot mouth-work. His finger pressed against my hole gently and entered—another heavy wave of fire, no pain at all. There should have been pain of some kind, but none, only pleasure, so much so that my brain was finding it hard to categorize. Then two fingers, and I bucked against the welcome intrusion. His hand reached past my head to my bedside, to the second drawer, and pulled out the tube of personal lubricant that until now had only been used by me alone. Seeing something so plain and ordinary shook my head, clear of the pleasure storm that had enveloped me. I sat up.

"Aya," he looked up from my cock, sending a spasm of pleasure through it. He removed himself and sat up next to me.

"Yes, love?" Love? Oh god, my body was still spinning from the pleasure. I felt high. Like my drink had been spiked with Ecstasy.

"Aya, um, it is dangerous? To… you know?"

"Only as dangerous as it would be for a human with another human." He stated, confusion working into his brow. Neither of our erections was suffering my inquiry. But looking down his smooth tanned muscled Adonis of a body, then to the long thick throbbing enticement of his dick with a small tuft of pubic hair on the upper of its base. Manscaping? Everything else was smooth. I don't think I could have declined any proceedings.

"I mean, like, humans use condoms to protect against some illnesses that come with sex."

"Ahh, I see. Fear not. There is no disease that you or I could possibly transmit to each other; our bodies can't accommodate the same pathogens." He was stroking my shaft, and I wrapped my hands. Yes, both hands! Around his dick and tugged it. He sighed in pleasure. I was about to go down and pleasure him with my mouth, he stopped me.

"Love, I need you, I have wanted you upon seeing you," my heart was banging hard against my rib cage in time with the pulse in my dick. "There will be time for that, but I need you," he began kissing me again, reminding my nerves of the sensations he could bring about all over my body. He laid on top of me. I shook with nervous anticipation and heard the cap popped on the tube he had been holding and felt his burning fingers enter me again.

Although I knew what was coming, nothing - no stories, no explanations - could have measured up with what happened next. Aya gently lifted my legs over his shoulders, kissing me and holding me tightly against him; he pushed himself into me. It should've hurt, but it didn't. It was just the same fire of intense pleasure from his kisses, only more. His entry while going inside me took forever until he was all the way in, and his pelvis pressed hard against my body. He groaned in delight, as did I. With slow, easy strokes, the waves of ecstasy rolled through me from where his dick entered me up to my spine into the rest of my body. It was like my whole body was in orgasm already with him inside me. I was like a vessel that filled more and more with his thrusts, filled more with sensation. I closed my eyes tight. Feeling it all. He broke the kiss, but not the pace.

"Look to me, Xiǎoyīng, look to me." I did. Sinking into his gaze.

To describe what happened next required further explanation. As I said, the sex was like entering orgasm with every thrust. But when I locked gazes with Aya, something within both of us clicked together. He smiled down at me. I could only groan and sigh with pleasure as his eyes held me as firmly as his hands did my back and buttocks. Once I had tried a party drug that is popular with the gays called Rush. It would make the blood vessels in certain areas dilate, making inhibitions lower and sex more intense. That drug had felt only mildly pleasant compared to locking stares with Aya. He continued moving within me, leaning down to kiss me passionately often. Our cries of bliss were in sync and getting louder.

I climaxed and came without even touching myself all over my chest and stomach, getting some on Aya. He pulled out, and I felt so empty without him inside me. He leaned down and lapped up my cum, cleaning every drop then sliding back inside me. He continued while kissing me, making me taste myself on his lips. There were no words to encompass this moment entirely. I didn't want it to stop. I bucked as another orgasm wracked through me, and again he cleaned me off and kept going. I couldn't stop either, even after twice. Then his grunts of pleasure hit a crescendo, and I knew what was happening. I felt it. His body stiffened. His cock pumping cum into me, causing me to cross the threshold of orgasm again. This time he was so immersed in his own orgasm, he kept pumping until every drop had been deposited within me. Then he pulled out slowly and absently licked the cum again from my stomach and chest. It was such a natural gesture for him, tender but bestial. It was like he wanted everything of me in him too.

We both laid there panting, he atop me. Waves of pleasure still echoing through my nerves. They were slowly subsiding but with intense reluctance. He got up on his elbows and rolled off to lie next to me, kissing my face and touching me all over with his hands as if trying to keep contact. I did the same. My body missed him. We stayed like that for a time, then he leaned over and kissed me on the mouth passionately again with that fire, but with less urgency and more sweetness of intimacy. I could taste the saltiness of my cum in his mouth. This was weird but so intensely erotic and primal.

Then he got up, walking naked into my kitchen. I watched him as I lay there all tangled in the sheets, which had somehow occurred during the procession. Seeing him move put me in the mind of the sure and silent movements of an animal. But his naked body. The sleek sweat beaded all over his body, running down his muscled back then between his perfectly shaped bubble butt that bounced ever so slightly with his steps. I knew it, scanning every curve and inch I could see: a swimmer's body but more. Abs, pecs, deltoids, and all the others made him more than appealing; those muscles made him strong and irresistible… perhaps a fighter's body? So much more than a swimmer's body. His muscles were more well-defined all over.

He went to the kitchen cupboards knowing where the glasses were. He pulled two out, filled them with water, and brought them over. The full-frontal view was as breathtaking as the back, if not more. His long hair was plastered by sweat onto his shoulders, back, and chest. Seeing all the way down to his spent dick swinging back and forth. When I saw it, I wondered how on earth it could have fit inside, which earned me a twang of ache and wanting. That had been inside me!

He placed one glass on the coaster for me and another on his bedside. He looked at the photo of Marcus behind the glass of water. I knew he would have questions. And I would try to have answers. But right now, I wanted to bathe in the afterglow of what had just happened.

"Aya, that was epic!" I exclaimed breathily, not realizing I was still panting.

"Yes, it was, Xiǎoyīng. That is an apt description."

"Is it always like that? I mean for you?"

"No. It depends on the recipient." A brief flicker of sadness passed over his features and disappeared as quickly as it had come, "You are one of a kind." He breathed in heavily, sniffing up from my prone flaccid cock to my neck, "You smell like me. I can smell me inside you."

"It's amazing. I can't even think clearly, Aya. My heart is still pounding." I saw him coming closer to me, a feral smile showing a canine on one side.

"I smell me inside you, Xiǎoyīng," It was a statement of intent. He positioned himself atop me again and settled between my legs, "I need you more, please," he leaned down to kiss me. His erection stiffened against my hole again, bringing my cock to attention. This isn't normal, I thought. I hitched my knees higher and let him slide in much easier this time as his cum facilitated the entrance. Again. The fire came. The pleasure. The waves of ecstasy. And I lost myself in them again.

It happened another two times that night. I was aching from the effort, but I couldn't keep my hands off him, and he seemed the same for me. This wasn't normal, but right then, I didn't care.

***

Sleeping with the Zenko. Not the most intelligent decision I had made but was it the most exciting, erotic, and pleasurable experience I had ever had. Hells. Yeah, it was!

***

Chapter 19: The Loudest Morning After Pill

I opened my eyes to the amber glory of those of Aya, staring absently at the scar on my left wrist as he ran his finger tenderly up and down, a gesture that seemed so sincere and loving all of a sudden. He saw me awakened and shifted his attention to me. The entire room was aglow with light. I first thought it the sun. Looking around, it was Aya and me when I looked at my hands. I was sporting a glow. His scent and mine filled the air... I could smell my scent on him and he on me…. and I could recognize the scents. Now I knew what he meant by smelling him inside me. I could smell us now too. And it was having a similar effect that it did him. Every sense seemed enhanced. My 'sight' was in full bloom, with everything sporting an aura that was clearer than it had ever been. Perhaps this was what it meant to be a mimic.

Aya wrapped his long arm around my waist and pulled me in for a kiss. I tried to struggle, afraid of morning breath. But my mouth didn't taste the sour morning breath it would usually before brushing. I let him kiss me deeply, enjoying the now familiar sensations of heat rolling through my body to settle in my nether region, again awakening it to be ready for sex. His kisses became intense as he moved on top of me, again positioning himself between my legs, lifting them onto his shoulders. I felt him press once again against my entrance, and again he slid in easily as we began our ritual of sex as he allowed me to come twice before filling me again with his seed. It felt so good to be touched, but this intensity was much more like touching something vital in nature that had never been touched before.

Afterward, we lay again panting. Aya was looking at the photo of Marcus and stroking my scar again.

"Marcus," I said, confirming what I guessed he was thinking. He nodded, "I... I am sorry. I…" I went to remove the picture and replace it with the top drawer in the bedside table. By now, I was beginning to get used to the speed at which he could achieve some things as his hand snapped out and touched mine gently.

"No, keep it, Xiǎoyīng," I bit my bottom lip at his words, not knowing what to think, "those we love who are gone must be honoured and loved still. Not hidden." He took the frame from my hand and held the picture, one of my most sacred objects. He touched the picture as he did my scar, with such tenderness and care, tracing the outline of Marcus' face with his finger.

"You must love him still so much; I can feel it from you."

"I'm sorry, Aya, I didn't mean to mislead you or-"

"Li Xiǎoyīng, Love. No, no more apologies. There is room…." He pointed that same delicate finger he used to trace Marcus 'face at where my heart would be beating beneath my chest, "-in here for both, I hope. I will not intrude where I am not welcome, but I will respect your love for Marcus as I respect you." Of all the things that the Zenko could come up with, this was something I hadn't even conceived. So, I said the only thing I could:

"Thank you Ayaka of the Zenko." And I meant it. I really did. One night and I had lost my mind!
It was only then that I deigned to look around my apartment and noticed the post-coital carnage. Our clothes were strewn everywhere where Aya had thrown them in his urgency. My jeans laid across the TV, and my jacket somehow made it onto the kitchen floor. I got up, naked, feeling so comfortable with my nudity as he by now. He had settled something in me that had needed settling for a long time. I went into the kitchen and retrieved my cellphone from my jacket. I looked at the face, which somehow survived the throw across the room. There were two missed calls and 15 messages…. All from Patience. Oh shit!

I quickly ignored her messages and called her cell. Aya got up and came over to hold me bodily from behind, rocking gently from side to side.

"LI! LI!"

"Hey Pa-"

"OMG! I was going to call the police, I was worried, I tried calling and texting, and when you didn't answer, I thought perhaps you'd been eaten or something," I remembered the recent news reports.

"No, no, Patience. I'm good, I'm great actually."

"Oh…oooooh!" She laughed hysterically then, "don't tell me you and that swimsuit model…."

"Ah, yes…"

"Holy shit!" I heard a ding of an elevator on her end, "So tell me everything! He was something else!"

"You have no idea, or perhaps you do, owing to recent revelations." I laughed too.

"Well, I want to hear every gory detail!"

There was a knock at the door.

"So open up!" Came her drill sergeant command from the other side of the door, "Before I use my code and see things that are probably best kept!"

I panicked, trying to move away from Aya, but he wouldn't budge and held tighter. I hung up my phone. I looked up at his face seeing his usual mischievous grin. Whatever was going to transpire, he was sure to be entertained.

"One second, you screeching harpy!" I yelled to the door. I turned and kissed Aya long and hard, feeling that heat roll into my body. He obliged, and I felt him again stiffen against my leg.

"Aya, my best friend Patience is on the other side of that door. I am sorry, I need to…" and he was gone. I heard the shower turn on and looked around. I saw our clothing destruction had been tidied, and my underwear and jeans were spread helpfully on the end of the bed.

I donned them both and grabbed a shirt quickly, then rushed to the door. I opened it and clenched myself for the army of embarrassment that was my best friend.

"Where is he!?"

"The shower."

"I'm going in. I've gotta see this!" She went off towards the bathroom.

I knew beyond all doubt that she would burst in to see Aya stark naked in all his divine glory just to assess what had gotten into me last night, both in the literal and figurative sense. And I was glad she lacked Aya's preternatural speed as I reached her, picked her up and threw her onto my bed, and stood over her. We were both laughing like children at this stage. She sat up on her elbows, looking at me.

"Wow! You are positively glowing. This was something good. I need to ask him for tips!" She went to launch herself toward the bathroom in another attempt again. I picked her up and placed her on my bed, "This whole house smells like… Old Spice and CK one, or something else…. It's really nice. His cologne must be strong."

"It's not cologne," I admitted.

"Then what is it," she waved her hand dismissively, "Actually scratch that, just tell me, how you are doing." Ok, she was entering best friend mode now. Safe ground that should give Aya time to freshen up.

"I think I am terrific. I like him," I sat next to Patience and fiddled a little with a hangnail, nervous, "He makes me feel good. Like I'm not in a half-life anymore." She looked surprised and happy, but then a flash of sadness zipped across her gaze. I almost missed it.

"That's the best news I have heard since, well you know-"

"Since Marcus. It's ok. For some reason, I find it a little easier to say now."

"He must be good for you."

"I sure hope so," said Aya's deep but musical voice as he emerged from the bathroom fully dressed in last night's clothes drying his long hair with a towel, head to the side. At the same time, it cascaded down to one side. I heard Patience make a little squeak and looked at her. Her mouth might as well have been a cartoon mouth that had just dropped to the floor with its tongue rolling out, saying, "Hubba Hubba!"

"I'm Aya, and you must be the infamous bestie," he held out a hand. She took Aya's and shook it.
"That's me, Patience, the official guardian of this little troublemaker here and all that entails," she looked him in the eye, saying this trying to keep her voice steady. Patience wasn't easily rattled, but Ayaka's obvious supernatural beauty had taken her aback for a moment.

"Understood," he nodded, and something unspoken passed between them.

"Unfortunately, Aya, I have to steal Li away from you for most of the day," Aya cocked his head, "Because, for the first time in his entire life, Li has forgotten that he has a job." She laughed heartily when I gasped and jumped up from the bed.

"Oh my goodness, Patience, I'm so sorry, I'll-"

"It's fine, bub. Go get ready. You're late, but I am sure you are due a pass," Patience looked Aya up and down approvingly, "and this warrants a pass."

"Xiǎoyīng, I'm sorry, I should have realized you have responsibilities, how remiss of me," he looked genuinely admonished, which sent Patience into another bout of giggles.

"Aya, it's ok, it's my fault. I'll just jump in the shower while you two chat and compare Li's latest embarrassing moments with each other."

"Sounds good to me, Aya?"

"I don't mind if I do."

I went into the bathroom and was about to shut the door when Aya appeared as he did in a blink in front of me. He crushed me in another rushing kiss and hug, then was out the door to join Patience on the couch.

"Holy shit," I said to the steamed mirror that was quickly clearing thanks to the fan doing its work. I saw myself and my aura golden like the rays of a sunbeam breaking through a canopy. I undressed and looked at my naked self. The self that Aya had taken over and over again like he craved me more and more upon being with me. I didn't get it. But I recognized the luck of having such an ardent lover. I got in the shower and began washing. He had come in me so many times, but I felt no pain or discomfort, just like I was alive for the first time in forever.

I wasn't usually so reckless with casual sex. I had had various one-night stands over the past five years, nothing serious. Marcus' memory always outdid anything those guys had given me, and every time I had been careful to use protection. I put my hand on my head, feeling silly. I tried to admonish myself for the risks I had taken over and over last night….and this morning. But Aya, he wasn't human, and my sex-fueled brain had just accepted his explanation of different species, different pathogens without question. What an idiot I was. But would I do it again? Imagining those fiery kisses, hands, fingers, his body, and exhilaration at making love to me…. Well, I think you already knew that answer.

I also felt exhilarated at the thought and presence of him. It was all so new. So perfect and beautiful, like one of my manga covers. I didn't want to put a name to this feeling just yet until I had examined the situation first. I also had better hurry up and get into the living room before Patience said something that might chase this new beau away.

***

Patience had parked her car out front of the building, which technically was only for pick-ups and drop-offs. Still, the concierge had suffered the rage of Patience once too many and just let her do what she wanted when she visited. Patience waved goodbye to Aya, promising a beer and pizza night ahead. He agreed, and she waited for me in her car.

We kissed, more sedate, but no less erotic and heat-giving.

"Thank you," I said, "um…."

"Thank you too," He looked at me curiously, but also with that heat and fire from last night as he was scanning my face for something, "I have some work to do today, but perhaps we can see each other-"

"Tonight!" I interrupted, then blushed at my desperation.

"Tonight." He agreed. I exhaled in relief. Perhaps I could ride this pleasure train until it had reached its conclusion? Hopefully, I would be lying if I said I was cautious enough. I knew my thoughts and feelings were running at speed equal to Aya's when he had been zipping around my apartment inspecting the place that first time he was there.

I got into the car as Patience drove off. Aya and I watched each other for a bit. Then I noticed a suit standing across the road, looking at Patience and me in the car. Aya appeared next to him, and I swear the suit jumped and squealed. But it might have been my imagination. Then they were both gone. Perhaps that was Aya's work today. Relieving the city of vamps. I left the thought at that as Patience began grilling me about Aya. Until, of course, the questions became too crass for me to answer. We drove to work, to a day that held more promise than the days had before it.

***

Chapter 20: What's with a Little Patience (Monday)

We settled into our workday as per usual. Patience perched on my desk, clacking her pumps together as she did. I got out my sketches and then remembered that I hadn't even fixed the ones that had been fried in the scanner. Patience didn't seem to notice, which was a relief. In fact, she was staring off into the distance, considering something.

"Earth to Patience?" She snapped out of her daydream back to me, "Everything ok?"

"Hmmm, yeah…" she had snapped out of her dream state but sounded like she was still there, "it's just…Aya…."

"Yeah…?" Oh, I hoped she liked him. I could feel things I had hidden away for many years, and I didn't want to put them back into their proverbial hiding place.

"He's… not like you and me, is he?" My friend stared off again, possibly thinking of the ramifications of her words.

"What do you mean exactly? It's not like you to be this vague." I pushed to get some clarity from her so I could get on with my work. I had to catch up on these sketches to start a new piece that had been formulating in my mind.

"I mean, you know," she indicated us, then the room full of busy minions, "Us. He seems beautiful and sweet and very funny, but there is something alien about him like he's something else." It was then that she squarely looked at me. "I mean, when you look at him, it's like you only see half of what is really there."

"You are correct, but I would have thought you'd be more aware of such things than I," I raised one eyebrow, "Remember it was you who sent me to the Crossroads knowing it was different. As different as its Patrons." My eyebrow went up.

"True, but it's different when you have seen them in person," her answer seemed almost robotic as her mind's wheels turned, trying to put a puzzle together in her mind where the pieces didn't quite fit, "Speaking of, Neelas 'help, have you taken it?" She was looking away from me, "Because I sent you there to get your migraines and weird eye shit sorted."

"My eyesight isn't weird. It's just… ok, it's weird, but not entirely unmanageable. Patience? What's this about? I'll answer anything. You know that. And I'll always tell you the truth; just ask me. Aya is different, I know, but I think he likes me, and he's made me feel ok about the Marcus thing, better than I have felt since it happened."

"That's good, Li. Really good." Then why did she look so sad? Her eyes were looking at her heels, I think trying to avoid mine for some reason. "Please, consider Neelas 'help, potion, whatever she gave you. It might be for your own good." With that, she slipped off my desk and sighed.

"Whatever the deal is with Aya, please be careful. You know you're more than family. And I don't want to lose you. The world that Aya is from might not be what we expect. He seems great, really. Just be careful," she repeated.

She click-clacked past Cherry, her assistant, who looked at me and shrugged. Perhaps Patience was in a mood? She seemed like she got along with Aya. Although it was comforting, she was looking out for me. If there was one person I'd want on my side in a fight, it was my gun-toting ride or die, Patience, the badass bitch. She had seen how precarious my grip on things was firsthand. I rubbed the scar on my left wrist as I sometimes did. It was a constant reminder that I always had to check myself and not fall again into that place of helpless self-destruction.

I buried myself in work for the rest of the day. Patience came out of her office once and asked if I wanted lunch. I had to decline. I was close to finishing the sketches I had promised. She hadn't even mentioned them, which meant something was really bothering her. She had done so much for me, especially when Marcus passed. She even headed up the reno to clear the apartment of Marcus 'stuff and put it in storage. Whatever was on her mind, I would keep an eye out to see if I could do something.

As I finished my sketches, I took out my personal sketch block. I began the preliminaries for a painting I had wanted to do for a few days now. Something that I needed to get out of my mind.
When the day wound down, Patience came over leaning on my desk.

"Hmm?" I intoned my question to her.

"It's knock-off time, and I've got your sketches. They look amazing as usual. I sent them off to the author to green light, and she seems pleased. So, pack your shit. We are out!"
I guess I was leaving to head home then. I shook my head at the almost bipolar nature of my bestie.

The car ride was strangely quiet. Patience just engaged in polite chit-chat and smiled, trying to hide whatever was bothering her. Finally, when we rounded into the entryway to my building, she turned to me. A purposeful look on her petite face:

"Dinner, you, me. A girl's night per se on Wednesday." She said simply.

"Yes, of course, Patience. I'd love to. I've missed our girls' nights. Although…" I said playfully, "Whatcha cookin'?"

"Penne Pesto Pasta, your fav, and I have a bottle of champagne to celebrate."

"Celebrate?"

"Yes, two occasions," perhaps this is why she was so distracted, "One, Hope is undergoing a very promising new treatment soon that could fix everything." My smile must have beamed contagiously to her because she couldn't help but reflect it. "And two, your new boyfriend, who is a real stunner," she groaned, "So much so that I am almost jealous and am gonna get hold of Heath and take it out on him!" By taking it out, we both knew what she meant: make him her man-bitch for the evening while he screamed for more.

"He's not my boyfriend. We're just…."

"Are you sure about that?" She nodded to the entrance to my building. And there stood Aya in all his magnificent unearthly splendour. The whole picture could have been a photo in GQ magazine with his muscles showing through his dress shirt and pants. The only thing that was out of place was the Red Robin takeout bags and soda cup holder. He saw me and gestured happily to the food. It was too cute.

"Is that Red Robins again?" Patience peered through my window side to look.

"Yes, I think it's probably a permanent fixture in his day."

"Wow."

"Yup."

"I guess there's gotta be something. Otherwise, your boyfriend would have been too perfect, and I'd have to steal him." That earned a joint chuckle.

"All right, I'll see you tomorrow. I'll come to pick you up again if you like." Her offer was a usual one but seemed more important somehow. My instincts were being sharp on this one.
"Sure thing, see you then. Love you, Hag!"

"Love you too Fag," and before people get all huffy at what she just called me, we routinely insulted each other. It was part of our relationship. If I allowed her to call me fag, that opened the opportunity for me to be absolutely vulgar with any retorts. I would never choose to be PC with my bestie on any given day.

I waved her goodbye and then turned to my "boyfriend"? Still not sure about that label.

"Aya!" I couldn't contain my joy at seeing him, "You made dinner!"

"That I did," he gestured to the fast food in the bags he was holding, large bags…with probably a lot of food, "I hope you don't mind."

"Not at all. A man who cooks is way sexy." We both laughed at the joke. My heart started pounding so close to him again. My thoughts all day were of the celestial level sex I had enjoyed with him literally all night long and some this morning.

In the elevator, he leaned in to kiss me as he did, fully with tongue.

"Mm," he mumbled through our kiss, "You taste so good, My Xiǎoyīng."
I wasn't sure we'd make it home until the elevator dinged my floors. Aya must have moved us at lightning speed through the door again, food on the counter and then on the bed. And we were again at each other like animals.

This time his urgency was primal, and again the clothes flew off us. I loved it. His touch was heaven itself. He kissed my neck then gently rolled me onto my stomach then pushed my knees up underneath me until my ass was in the air facing him. I was nervous but bursting with magically enhanced arousal. I felt his lips kissing around my ass cheeks, nipping slightly, which gained him groans of pleasure from me. And suddenly…. with one quick movement…. A certain taboo was broken. His mouth went in between my cheeks, and his tongue lapped at my hole, sending more shudders of pure bliss vibrating through my body. His tongue darted in and out, fucking me with it. It was so much I began stroking my cock, hoping I didn't cum too soon. It felt so good. Just as I was nearing a climax, he pulled away. I heard him spit, likely on his hand, then spit again. I felt it on my now tender hole. He leaned onto me to kiss my neck and nibble my ear, then gently thrust his cock into me, and as before, my body welcomed his. I suddenly felt complete as he moved in and out of me, rising up and holding my hips as he continued fucking me. God, I loved it. I loved everything about it.

"Do you want me to cum inside you, my Li? Tell me you want it. Tell me you want my seed; it's all for you!"

"Yes, oh god, please, I need it!" I grunted furiously, rubbing my cock, which was about to burst with cum all over the bedsheets.

"Ok, my love, I will give it to you always," He thrust in hard, and I felt his cock pumping cum into my hole as before. The fire and feeling running through me like a drug, and as it did so, I came all over the sheets.

We both collapsed onto each other. And for some reason, we began laughing at our ridiculousness. We couldn't stop. We were addicted to each other. We were each other's drug.
He fondly stroked my side, running fingers all the way up my shoulder and down to my thighs. He seemed to drink in my very essence every time we made love, but I his as well.

"The food," I said absently, still drowning in the sea of gratification.

"Oh yes, I will prepare it." He moved like lightning, and I barely heard the scraping of a plate as the 'gourmet 'meal Aya had brought was laid onto my dining table, which was never used. He had moved the orchid to the kitchen bench safely away from the acts of feasting that would begin soon.

I got up, as naked as he, and we enjoyed eating Red Robins for a second time together.

Aya spent the night again, and we repeated the night before. We only stopped to move the activities into the shower, then back to the bed. I should be exhausted from last night and tonight, but all I could feel was the throbbing life force inside me.

"Aya?"

"Yes, love," Love? I liked to hear it, but still, it was something that needed tending to later. He kept saying things like that. We were lying on our sides, spent and facing each other. We were just talking nonsense and laughing. It was divine, but I needed to know some things.

"Um, I know you're different, and there's a likelihood that our…." I struggled to find the words that were accurate to what we were doing, "lovemaking has passed on some things… traits onto me."

"Oh, yes," his eyes were closing and opening slowly like an animal that was happily resting in the sun, "well, that may happen. I am sure it will be ok. Such things are temporary usually."

"Hmm, what kinds of things could pass on to me?"

"Good question, love," he was thoughtful for a moment, "well, heightened senses likely, small things. Mimics aren't powerful. They just seem to take on energy signatures for a bit, you understand?"

"Sure. Um, is there anything else?"

"Now, it is improbable, but you might be able to adopt some of my skills."

"Skills? Like…?"

He shuffled a little closer to me. It was like watching one of those CGI scenes, but more subtle, not slow, just as if something fundamental in reality was changing and being accepted by the new reality happening in front of me. Aya's long black hair began to shorten in length, moving up to a length closer to shoulder length. The colour lightened slightly to a black-brown hue. His Amber eyes deepened into black, and his skin paled somewhat. When the change was over, it was more than just looking in the mirror. I reached out to touch his face, which was actually my face and hair. Then I ran my hand over a body that was identical to mine.

"Remarkable. Aya! This is amazing." We both sat up as I examined him. He had changed into a copy of me right down to the last detail, including the shape of my cock and the roundness of my little ass.

"You're beautiful, aren't you, my love?" He reached his hand to touch my face and pulled me closer, "Truly beautiful."

"I don't know about that. You're out of this world, Aya." Still touching my face, a thought occurred to me, "Is this just an illusion? Like you're sending the idea to my mind? Or is it a whole, physiological thing you've done?"

"Everything that is you, I am; in this shape, down to the last cell." I was dumbfounded. The world I was entering into was so magical. I thought of my Nǎinai and what she must have been through in her life and how much contact she might have had with the Fae. She was 112 when she passed away. It was more than likely she had known all about the vampires, the Aya's, and maybe even about the Neelas ' in the world.

He pulled me closer still. Then started to kiss me as he did, full of fire and hunger. We laid down, side by side at opposite ends, and I began to take him into my mouth. It was strange. I knew the shape and curve of the dick because it was mine. He reciprocated immediately. His mouth was like his kisses on my cock. The fire and feeling suffusing every part of me. When we both came, I tasted him and immediately swallowed, wanting every part of him in me. To be part of me. He did the same.

"I love the way you taste, my love," he whispered, kissing my cock as it began to go flaccid, spent as he was. He was still wearing my form, and when we sat up again, he adjusted his appearance back to the gorgeous being I knew.

"Aya, you are amazing. But why me?" A part of me wanted to cry. It was a question I had posed again and again, not just to him but to myself. It seemed as if he was breaking through the barriers that I had built up for the past five years and doing it with such ease and abandon.

"It's you, Li Xiǎoyīng. It's always been you." Confusing words that sunk in slowly as he wrapped my naked body in his arms as we laid side by side: his hot body behind me, his pelvis tucked tightly close to my ass, his face buried in my neck, kissing me and whispering to me, "You're so beautiful, how could I look past you. You're mine now. Please be mine." I wanted to. This magical creature. This beautiful man. Oh god, I wanted to. But what did he mean?

The thought of Aya made me feel alive again. Before dropping off to sleep with Aya's arm wrapped around me, holding me close, I looked through the dim evening light, illuminated only by the open floor-length window's city lights and the bio lamp from the aquarium. I looked at Marcus 'photo, the shadows of the night dancing across his features. Slipping into unconsciousness, I thought I saw his smile widen a little and a feeling of pride imparted from somewhere. A place I couldn't reach just yet. Not yet. Marcus? Am I ok?

***

Chapter 21: Work Late (Tuesday)

Patience crashed our slumber party again, though I was ready for her this time, showered with my messenger bag slung across my shoulder. She came through the smart locked door using her code with three coffees. One black for her and two mochas, explaining that she didn't know what Aya wanted, so he'd have to enjoy what I liked. This suited the Zenko fine as he sat on the couch with her sipping from the takeout cup.

"Stay here in bed if you want to Aya, I've texted you a code for the door." Even though every time he's wanted to drag me into the bed from the downstairs entrance, we've just somehow magically made it there. The door offered little obstruction to Aya.

"Thank you, my Xiǎoyīng. You and Patience enjoy your day."

"Will do, Aya," Patience said, saluting him while heading out the door.

We kissed, long and hard until the torturous moment that I had to drag myself away from those lips. My jeans were uncomfortable and showed my obvious tumescence through the fabric. I hoped the neighbours weren't riding the elevator at this time.

Patience just smirked when I got into the elevator with her. I sipped my coffee shyly, avoiding her look.

The day was a productive one and zoomed by quickly. It likely did so because I was still on my Aya high. I hardly registered talking to my workmates. I'm sure Cherry had told me some story about her girlfriend inviting her to go away to Whistler for the weekend, or Todd mentioned some current events. But between my 'sight' filling the world with a psychedelic mess, my heightened sense given to me by Aya, the flashbacks of him transforming into me…. and then what we did after occupied my full attention. I didn't even notice the drawings I was creating at my desk.

It wasn't until Patience interrupted my thoughts that I stopped to see what I was doing.

"Wow, nice work Li," she hissed through her teeth, a sign of approval, "I swear your talent makes me so jealous sometimes." I looked at what she was referring to. It was a stylized picture of a fox encircled by a figure I hadn't finished outlining yet.

"Cheers, what's up?"

"Well, while you've been in lala land today, the office ended its day." What the fuck? I looked around the office and saw everyone packing their bags or switching off their monitors and heading out the door.

"Geez, I didn't realize."

"It's ok, lurrve will do that to you." I had a mock look of exasperation.
"*Luuurve*! Who said anything about Lurrrve! I'm surprised you even know the word Patience," she scoffed at my comment, "BTW, how's Heath? How's his *Lurrrve* for you."

"Argh, shut up, he won't stop texting to meet again."

"Well, if your *Lurrve* wasn't so good, he wouldn't come back for seconds, thirds, and I've lost count, young lady." This initiated a laugh we both enjoyed.

"Come on," she said, grabbing my bag and slinging it over her shoulder, the same as her handbag, some red monstrosity that cost more than her Tesla probably.

When we arrived again at my building…

"Well, look who's waiting for you…." I had hoped and half expected to see him there, waiting for me, "does he have a home other than your bed?"

"You know, I honestly couldn't tell you," I answered truthfully.

"Well, with a face and body like that, I'm sure he could find a 'home,'" she used her fingers to indicate the inverted commas, "in any bed." She giggled, probably not knowing she was needling my insecurities.

"Yo nasty bitch."

"Don't you know it! Hey, don't forget dinner tomorrow night. Just us. No Heath or Aya. We've gotta have a proper catch-up."

"I wouldn't miss it," I was out of the car with my face still in the doorway, "At least the food will be better than the company."

"Hah!" she threw an empty coffee cup at my head that bounced off and fell on her car floor, "See you tomorrow, I do have Heath over tonight, so I won't be able to pick you up tomorrow."

"No worries, say hi to your *Lurrrrve* muffin." She yanked the door closed and sped off.

I turned to the waiting Zenko.

"No dinner?" I asked jokingly.

"Well, I was hoping we could try something new tonight."

"No Red Robin? Goodness." I wondered what culinary delight Aya had in store for me tonight. He grabbed me and held me close, kissing me with his usual fire.

"I missed you," he said through kisses. Missed me? He was so forthright. He wasn't scared to share his feelings. Perhaps another cultural difference between our species? Which reminded me I would have to do more research on him and his kind.

"I missed you too," and I meant it, even though the words sounded strange to my ears.

And as before, the heat overcame us, and we were in my apartment on the bed again. This is something I wanted to get used to. To have every day, I thought as Aya was on top of me, moving in and out of my body. I want you, Aya. I want you every day. Please stay. Don't ever leave. I want to be yours. Please stay!

"I'm here, my love," he whispered in my ear while we made love for…. I had lost count of how many times and how many ways. Had he heard my heart's words?

After some time in bed, I was hungry and so obviously was my bedmate.

"I want to try a new way of getting food." He said excitedly. What did he mean? My mind flashed to a fox hunting rabbits or breaking into a henhouse.

"Yes…" I said, suspicious but knowing again that this was probably going to make me laugh.

"I want to order in! You know, make them serve the food to your door!"

"I'm familiar with the concept. What did you have in mind?"

He grabbed his phone, which had been lying on what I was beginning to think of as his side. He showed me on the screen a coupon he had received in text. Where had he been, living under a rock in Japan before coming to Canada? At times he seemed so worldly and then at others, so innocent like everything was new to him. The coupon showed two for one pizza deals with Dominos. I was trying not to chuckle.

"And look, you can make them put anything on it. There's a whole list of ingredients here," Aya was enthralled by the prospect, flicking through the possibilities, "Marvelous! Simply marvellous! I have eight of these vouchers that I have been saving."
"Saving for…?"

"For us! So, we can have a feast right here! They bring it to your door! Isn't it amazing?" My smile was so broad and genuine, not at the miracle that was pizza delivery, but at this Japanese anime character, who'd come to life and was fast becoming my own personal miracle.

"That is truly one of the sweetest things I have heard in a long time."

"Well, my Xiǎoyīng, only the best for you." I think he meant that….and I think to him, Dominos was the "best," which made his words doubly sweet.

I proceeded to help him order the pizza online on his phone. When it came to entering the codes, I entered it, and then he said. "Love, you have to enter the rest."

"The rest?"

"The promotion is 'two for one' - you have to enter all eight; otherwise, we won't have enough."

Oh…. oooooh! I had forgotten his ravenous appetite entirely for sex was almost rivalled by his desire for fast food. I did as he bid, and we ordered sixteen pizzas—all different toppings. A minute after we placed the order, his phone rang. It was the pizza place, just confirming 16 pizzas to this address.

When the pizza delivery person arrived, it was a lovely Indian girl, whom we tipped generously for hauling the pizzas to our door. I had to take a selfie with Aya and me with the sixteen pizza boxes piled up on my dining table, a slice in each of our hands about to devour…and snap. I then sent it to Patience: *Let's see who becomes the size of a bus first! 600lbs 4eva!*

Her reply was also a pic…of Heath's dick. As Heath was African Canadian, Aya was fascinated by it, and seeing such a prominent and dark member intrigued him. I completely understood the fascination. The texting had to end there, lest it devolves too far into a Pornhub rival.

***

Chapter 22: Champagne with a side of WTF (Wednesday: End of Day)

The day began without the interruption of Patience. The end result was Aya and I taking a shower together. I found out how strong he actually was physically as he lifted me with my legs wrapped around him, my back cushioned by his other arm. The hot water just added to the enjoyment of our sex. Why we couldn't keep our hands off each other, I didn't know. But I really didn't care right now. He wanted me for whatever reasons, and I wanted him.

I got to work late. Patience was waiting for me on my desk in her usual spot.

"You're late, Li." She said, more playful than reprimanding.

"Sorry Patience, I -" I tried to think of a good reason, "I…. my fox ate my homework?" She snorted a response, obviously finding it funny.

"I am sorry."

She put a hand on my shoulder. I felt her squeeze it through the fabric in reassurance.

"It's ok, Li, you have needed this, and I truly am happy for you. But remember we have dinner plans tonight."

"Haven't forgotten, I can bring dessert," She was walking past her assistant Cherry who looked enquiringly at me. I shrugged, not knowing what to tell her. My world was a vast magical sexy mess, and I was ok with that for now.

"Nope, I have everything sorted, just bring yourself," She shut the door to her office at that. I saw her auric glow through the frosted glass. My heightened sense heard her take a seat as the lumbar support office chair creaked with her little weight. Then I heard her open one of her desk drawers. I saw the glow I had almost forgotten about. The light from the package when my 'sight' had broken free from my self-imposed restraints, without the pain of a migraine. It looked like she was holding it in front of her looking at it. She did this for a full, maybe five minutes before the glow disappeared and I heard the drawer shut. My phone buzzed.

Patience: *I meant to ask, have you taken Neelas' Eraser yet? It's a good idea to make sure your new life with Aya starts off without those pain-in-the-ass migraines (winky face emoji, eggplant + spray + peach emojis).*

Texting from her office? This wasn't unheard of if she were on a call that she couldn't be bothered listening into. But my enhanced hearing couldn't hear anything of the sort.

Me: *I haven't yet. Apparently, there's more to what the Eraser does to me than I knew. Perhaps I can explain tonight at dinner since it's a you and me gossip fest.*

Patience: *Absolutely. Now draw something worthwhile (LOL face).*

During my lunch break, I called Aya.

"Hello?" he answered, "is that you love?"

"Yes, it's me. How's your day going?"

"It's going well. I hope you don't mind. I went home and got some extra clothes and such and dropped them at your apartment…?" Oh my god. So, when I said gays move quick, this is a perfectly normal pace for us. We own the rights to whirlwind romances no matter what the movies say. Perhaps it has something to do with the fact that before being gay was widely accepted, we had to enjoy whatever we could before being burned at a stake or tortured for loving our own gender. Who knows?

"Perfect." My heart was pounding, and my body began to miss his touch again, "I have a girl's night with Patience tonight, just her and me. Dinner Gossip, that kind of thing." There was a space of silence.

"OK, love, I will miss you, but please have fun and give Patience my regards."

"Sure thing," there was another space of silence that I wanted to fill with three little words I was feeling all too soon but couldn't and wouldn't quite articulate yet. Yeah, too early and insane, so instead, I said, "I will miss you too, Ayaka of Zenko." That gentle tug of identity as I spoke his name.

"Xiǎoyīng," the reciprocal tug, "You enchant me as always." His breath through the phone sent a shiver through me and down to my loins. It caused me to harden in anticipation, "Perhaps we can meet up later? Maybe go out for a stroll along the water?"

"I'd love to. I'll see you then."

"Bye, love, have fun." His voice was almost sad as we finished the call. Although I liked that he was sad without me already, the idiocy of presupposing the nature of his feelings did not escape me.

Who was I to say if he's even sad? He's a being from somewhere else. And even so, why would it be I who made him feel so? Look at him Yīng, he's a veritable God compared to any other male you'd seen, met, or shagged. One could only wish.

***

Patience had dropped me off home to get ready for her dinner. She had seemed so lost in thought and also a little sad. What was with people? Was I the only one feeling good today? A nasty, awful idea emerged from my subconscious: Maybe it's just the balancing of the universe. You get to feel good, but at the cost of others feeling bad.

"Shut up, brain!" I said out loud. It echoed around the shower. Talking to myself. In the shower. Like a nutter. Meh. I stroked the scar on my left wrist. Technically I had already gone over the edge before, so at least I'd be in familiar territory. I thought sadly of the fragility I sometimes felt within myself. The same fragility that had led me to take a razor to my wrist. I breathed in deeply. Remember you are ok, Yīng. You are ok. You need not feel that feeling again.

I dressed and prepared to leave. Same outfit, different colours. White leather jacket, black t-shirt, grey jeans, with a pair of black boots, the Christian Dior ones that Marcus had insisted I had needed way back. No pang of guilt or overwhelming sadness came to me thinking of Marcus. This was new. I went and kissed his picture by the bed, remembering Aya's view on Marcus 'memory. While in the closet, I found a small area that Aya had made for himself for an extra pair of boots and some shirts and pants on hangers. My entire home smelled of both of us. The spicy, sweet smell, like incense and perfume, mingled together.

***

I walked up to Patience's townhouse. It was easy to pick out of identical habitats around hers. Her Tesla was usually parked on the road where the gate was, even though she had a below-ground parking space. Her home was pretty modern, with three stories and a rooftop balcony. There were identical buildings on both sides of the small street. These homes were worth a tidy penny, and Patience had told me it was family money that mainly had allowed her to purchase the house. Vancouver prices, especially for a three-bedroom townhouse this close to the waterfront, were almost as high as those in Hong Kong. Into the millions of dollars.

I entered the tiny courtyard. It was tidy with potted Japanese maples and a small table and chairs that were never used. Patience liked to be outside on her rooftop courtyard instead.

I let myself in, hollering, "Honey, I'm Home!"

"Up here, tiger!" She was in the upper courtyard. It was quite a lovely rooftop garden. The ground/rooftop was paved with large grey slate stones. A small dining table was placed near the street edge. There were planter boxes dotted around with little sculpted mini-hedges. A sizeable outdoor heater sat next to the table, offering enough heat that pushed the Vancouver evening chill away into the night.

The table was set for two: one setting at the head, back facing the street, and the other next to the head. A champagne bucket sat between the two placings. A large bottle of Cristal opened. Wow, that was an expensive beverage. She must really have a celebration in mind. Patience had received that bottle from a grateful author a year ago and had been waiting for, I guessed, this occasion.

The table itself had tea light candles floating in small globe-type glass bowls, all in a row down the table, arranged with an exuberant centrepiece. Patience was puttering around on the dining end of the table, grating parmesan cheese into a bowl.

"Wow, you went all out!" I said, looking around at the display.

Then, not looking up from her task, she replied, "We have two important things to celebrate and a lot of catching up that's gonna require booze and pasta." She nodded to the bottle of champagne. She had already poured a glass for both of us. She must've done it before I even got up the stairs. Understandable. In this world, there were probably 4 things that Patience loved the most:

Her sister Hope and her family, Dereck and the Girls
Me
Her job
Champagne

I was guessing the order of the last three went up and down depending on her mood, though I had always known her sister Hope was number one with her family. I couldn't blame her. That family had drawn me in as one of their own so easily. I loved them all. I knew I could never have a family of my own. It was a dream that Marcus and I had wistfully thought about, but after Marcus died, so did that dream, and I just adopted Hope's family as its replacement. Those two little angels that were Patience's nieces had enchanted me from the moment I met them. When they called me Uncle Li, it called to some paternal/maternal part of me that made me want to love and protect them from all the ravages of the world.

"Sit down. Dinner's almost ready."

My auric sight saw the whole affair in a technicolour mirage. I'd never seen tea-light candles like these. The glow left trails of their own energy in a mist on the table. The flowers held their own green auras, tightly hugging their physical counterparts. Patience was grating the cheese, looking fuchsia, almost red, intertwined with strings of black smoke.

I had always wondered what that meant, but I had never got a chance to ask Năinai before she passed. But Năinai had seemed to like Patience for the most part, if not guardedly, so it couldn't be anything terrible. The champagne in the glasses appeared to sparkle like the glittery mass to my "sight." Looking like the glitter bomb I had experienced with Charity and Faith at Hope's party. Both glasses had a purple haze around them. Interesting. I had never seen champagne with my sight. No wonder people liked It. It had strong auric energy of its own. It'd be interesting to ask Aya or Neelas if champagne had any inherit magical properties.

Patience sat down at the head of the table, of course. She was dressed in a tight black Gucci dress with her hair made up in a bun with elaborate tendrils framing her face, making her look almost like a child but beautiful all the same. She would have wanted me to say she looked dang sexy, but tonight I thought she looked like a girl, full of innocence.

I heard a slam, as did Patience, that made her jump slightly from the street. But street noises up here were normal. We had once witnessed the Ragnarök vengeance of a drag queen, making it abundantly clear to her recent ex that his triflin 'ass wasn't wanted or needed. Said ass had received the business end of her heels. It had been funny and impressive to witness from this very rooftop. Ah, Vancouver a hub of diversity and now magical wonders, apparently.
Patience focused her gaze on me, her smile unreadable.

"Tell me about Hope's new treatment," I inquired, "You've been holding out! If it can help fix everything, how on earth could you keep it a secret! I'm impressed."

"I will, but first, I want to toast to you, my lovely friend, Li," her eyes filled with tears as she lifted her glass, and I followed, "you have overcome so much. I never thought you'd make it out." Patience took a deep, shuddering breath. "You are so sensitive and loving that the world doesn't deserve you. But seeing you so happy. Your light is back, Li." She stared at me, her eyes pleading somehow, "I am toasting to you and Aya. May you both become the Happily Ever After we have all been wanting for you." Her words touched me, that tears rolled down my cheeks. We brought the flutes together in a clink.

"Stop!" The strength of the sound made me freeze.

Patience's eyes went wide, looking panicked, almost afraid, looking over my shoulder to the courtyard entrance. I turned to see Hope standing, panting at the doorway. Her scarf had come around her bald head. She was so frail. She was looking past me to Patience. The look in her eyes: Have you ever seen a mother of any animal defending her young from a larger and scarier predator in a nature documentary? That persistent lack of fear and readiness to sacrifice was evident in the eyes. Those were Hope's eyes now. Like she was ready to protect something precious to her.

She stomped across the courtyard so hard and fast that it was hard to believe that there was that webwork of cancer that was ravaging her body according to my 'sight.' She got to Patience and gave her a loud slap, using her whole body. Her strength, though limited, was completely behind it.

Patience's glass flew out of her hand onto the paving stones shattering. I saw blood on Patience's lip as she leaned away from the attack. Hope then stomped towards me, and I flinched, afraid I would receive the same treatment. Instead, she snatched the glass out of my hand. She tossed it over the edge of the rooftop courtyard to the waiting Tesla below, where it landed with a muted crash.

Hope, looking almost crazed and went back to her stunned sister, whose face was streaming with tears now, was fully crying now.

"Get over here!" Hope demanded as she grabbed Patience in a crushing hug. A green flash caught my attention briefly behind them, "This is not the way!" She yelled.

Then she pulled Patience to the side, as a roaring sound from the street below filled the night, the loudness and impact of it smashing windows on both sides of the road below. While causing those further away to rattle. A fire ball bloomed into the evening night from below the courtyard on the street, almost cutting off the sound to everything else.

Hope kept pulling her sister away from the edge. I rushed over to see, except then I heard what sounded like a giant mosquito buzz past me in slow motion that somehow pushed me back so hard I fell on my back.

I was as stunned as Patience had been after her sister's surprise assault. Time seemed to rush back, and my shoulder stung more than a mosquito bite. I touched it with my hand. It was wet. I looked at it. My white leather jacket was covered in a crimson red. I could smell the coppery smell of my own blood, and in the distance, Patience's blood. My heightened senses picked up the scent of blood and made my gorge rise in my throat.

My head was spinning. I was dazed. And I tried to shake it off. My hearing was also not working right. I just heard a roaring in my ears. I tried to sit up.

Patience and Hope were both there; my hearing seemed to be returning slowly. I could make out their voices, though they were muffled. Patience was reaching for me, and Hope slapped her hand away and gave her a look so severe it froze her in place. Hope came over to check on me instead.

"Li? Li? Honey? Are you ok? Can you hear me?" She said, pushing down on my shoulder that suddenly felt like she was pushing a thousand bee stings into it.

"Ouch! Shit! What the Fuck!" I tried to sit up, but she gently pushed me down.

"You've been shot, honey." I looked over to my left shoulder where she was pressing. Her hands were wrapped in cloth napkins. I reached over to move her hands, "No, don't. Li, sit still."

"Patience, don't just sit there. Call 911, we need an ambulance and probably the police," I saw Patience's face again show panic, "someone blew up your car Patience and shot Li. We need police and an ambulance. Also, tell them there will be a body on the roof directly across the street."

It was the first time I had seen Patience so…un-together. She got her cell, where it had fallen from the dining table in the ensuing chaos. She brushed it off and began the process of arranging very human, very ordinary things.

***

Chapter 23: Healing in the Hospital

I was taken to the emergency room. They tried to give me something for the pain, then something to get me to rest as I kept moving about. But the longer I waited, the better my shoulder felt.

Another very human and familiar face that made the orgasmic week seem a fevered dream. My mother's friend, Dr. Pia, came in looking like a mother who wanted to slap her child for swearing. Except I was the child, and the swearing was, "not calling her to tell her I was doing fine."

"And this is the result, Li Yīng!" She said, literally telling me off like a child, "A gunshot!? Your parents are going to be livid!" Her musical, Hindi accent incited memories of dinners with her family and mine and holidays. Oh shit. I had been a dick to hers and to my family for a long time- while I had been allowing my own wallowing in a well of self-pity and grief. Had my mind been so broken to forget all these beautiful people in my life?

"I'm sorry, Aunty. I…." She wasn't my aunty by blood, obviously, but as our families had gotten close, she'd demand that I call her "aunty." And she had definitely been an aunty to me since I had been in Vancouver. But, man, I was such a dick!

"That's Doctor Pia to you! Young man." She smiled then and lifted the bandages on my shoulder, frowning. She pressed the call button and waited for the nurse.

"Nurse Ginny, what do I see here?" She showed the nurse the wound.

"I think a scar from some kind of punctured wound, likely from a bullet."

"Correct - a scar. Why was I told that my nephew (our families had been 'close' in that sense too where her children called my parents uncle and aunty as well) had a serious gunshot wound - fresh?"

The nurse gave a look similar to what Patience had when facing her sister earlier.

"My shoulder does feel better, Aunty," the nurse came back with a folder that held my file and some pictures they had taken upon my admission. Aunty Pia looked at the photos, then at me. Then she rechecked my shoulder.

"Nurse Ginny, I'm taking this case over; you can go do your rounds, please."

"Isn't that a conflict of interest if you're related?" Aunty Pia turned to the nurse, and the nurse seemed to shrink into her scrubs like a turtle.

"Do we look related, you silly girl!" Oh my, there was definitely a resemblance to the Iron Fist of MGV publishing, Patience. Perhaps they were related, no matter how improbable that could be.
"No, doctor." After a brief discussion, the nurse left. Aunty Pia sat next to my bed. With a heavy sigh. She flicked through the folder several times, then took out the photos and handed them to me.

"What's this?" I asked, shuffling through the bloodied images.

"These are your shoulder upon entering this ward Li," all gunshot wounds have to be reported and documented like this."

"Oh" was all I could say as the picture formed of a delicious Japanese god-like figure in my bed and what that might mean here.

"Your shoulder shows healing from a wound maybe a few months from now? Six months? But definitely not an hour ago. It doesn't make sense to me as a doctor." I nodded, "But I had seen some strange things when your Nǎinai helped my family out with her…. Ways of doing things. So, I was introduced to new possibilities." She stood up then, "I have my rounds, but I'll fix it so you can be discharged with minimal fuss and no questions. I'm not sure what is happening here, but you need to talk to your mum and dad. And for god's sake, don't go getting shot again."

She was about to leave, then turned back around and placed a small plastic specimen jar on the tray table. It held a large chunk of squashed metal, "And take that with you. And bloody well call us for dinner, we all miss you, Li Xiǎoyīng." There is something about mothers, teachers, and doctors when they use your full name. You know you've screwed up and feel obliged to make amends.

"Yes, aunty. Thank you."

"Say hi to your mum for me. She is still talked about here as a legend in nursing."

"Will do," I promised. Aunty (Dr.) Pia had also left pictures of the mess on my shoulder.

***

I was still in shock. A car bomb; A shooting; a Crazed cancer-riddled mom slapping people and throwing champagne. I found both sisters waiting for me in the waiting area. Patience's face was all red and blotchy, while Hope's face, though unmistakably tired, looked stern. It was a face I had seen her use on her girls when they had been misbehaving beyond acceptable limits.

Patience went to move towards me, she looked so relieved, but a hand on her chest from Hope stopped her. It was Hope that approached.

"Are you all right, Li? What did the doctor say? And why aren't you in bed?"

"Apparently, it isn't as bad as it had looked at the scene…?" I lied but shrugged, unable to really answer.
"That's wonderful. Come on, we'll take you home," Hope put a hand on my back to guide me out, "do you have anyone who can stay with you tonight, Li?"

"I…" Patience tried to chime in.

"No!" Hope yelled, silencing Patience, "No," she said again, quieter. We climbed into Hope's SUV and buckled up. I was in the back, and the sisters were in the front.

"I do, I think. I'll call him when I get home."

That reminded me. I was wearing what looked like a donation shirt. Clean and serviceable, but not mine, of course. My jeans had some blood still on them. Seeing it was weird, like seeing ketchup stains that needed cleaning, but nothing significant. Obviously, my mind was still catching up with the events of the evening.

Then I remembered, "My phone?"

Patience handed me the phone without a word. It was dirty, but otherwise, it had survived the rooftop craziness.

We rode home in relative silence, which was weird too, as I tried to wipe the spots of blood off my jeans with a licked finger. Hope and Patience were always chatting and laughing together. But somehow, the dynamic had changed, and Hope had taken charge of something that I wasn't privy to for whatever reason.

"You wait here," Hope commanded her sister harshly. Hope proceeded to help me up to my apartment. My shoulder was feeling better but was so stiff that I still had trouble using it. She opened up my apartment using her code, carried my messenger bag and a plastic bag with my jacket and ruined t-shirt sealed in it. She placed both on the counter and turned to me.

"Li, I am so sorry," she turned to me, her smooth, waxy face, still pretty but obviously tired beyond all reason. Her eyes were streaming tears down her cheeks like two little rivers. It was unbearable seeing her cry.

"I don't understand," I said, shaking my head, moving to comfort her, but she waved me off.

"You will, but in the meantime, give Patience some space. She's got a lot to think about."

"Why did you hit her?"

"Because I'm her sister and love her more than anyone will, and she needed it," Hope sighed.

She must be nearing her limits herself. Her medications took it out of her, but hopefully, the new treatment Patience told me about would work soon, "The police are looking into everything, just so you know to expect a call or something. They may want a statement."

"Wait. Did I hear you say there'd be a body across the street?"

"You did."

"But, like…what?!"

"Don't worry about it, Li. What matters is you are safe. And that is all that matters."

"Oh," I still didn't get it. But I was actually exhausted and just wanted a shower and bed.

"I'll leave you then. But Li, be careful. You are family, and we love you. The girls love you. Dereck thinks of you as a brother. Be careful."

"I'll try, but in my defence, I hadn't known there'd be a car bombing and a shooting this evening on the menu; otherwise, I would've skipped Patience's cooking." She chuckled. The strength from earlier was leaving her as the awful disease gripping her body, and its harsh treatments once again claimed her back. She turned to leave.

"Thank you, Hope!" I called after her, but she had already closed the door. She'd never miss a chance at politeness. Leaving without a proper goodbye was very unlike her.

I stripped off, leaving everything on the floor of the living room, and went to shower.

While I washed, I touched and considered the scar that had formed on my shoulder. It was only a dull ache now. So, what? Did I have Wolverine's healing factor now? Could I survive diving into a woodchipper? Ew, why would I even think of that? But as both Neelas and Aya had explained. This stuff was temporary and much weaker than the source. This led me to think, what else did the source, Aya, have up his sleeve?

I dressed back into the borrowed shirt and some boxer briefs and called Aya.

"Love! Oh, I'm so glad you called!"

"Hey, um… something happened today…."

"What happened, my love?" His concern was evident, and it felt nice to have him worry for me even though it had been… What, a few days? Geez. Moving fast much?

"Please don't panic…."

"Wow, now I'm obviously gonna panic," yeah, he might. Hmm.

"I was shot." The phone disconnected. I frowned, looking down at it. "Okay… he took it rather badly," or well, depending on the next two minutes…

I was only guessing. Still, a knock at my door answered which. I opened the door and was swept up into powerful, gentle arms that laid me onto the couch. Aya proceeded to sniff me, probing me with his eyes and nose. Then prod me all over my person, which made me giggle hysterically as I was very ticklish at times.

"Don't move love, I want to check you over." He continued prodding then came to my shoulder.

I heard a rumble in his chest, then the growl of an animal, his mouth opened, exposing his slightly elongated canines. He tore through the cheap fabric of the borrowed shirt. He was inspecting the puckered scar on my left shoulder even before the pieces of torn fabric had settled on the floor—another rumbling growl. He kissed the scar, still growling.

"Aya?"

"Someone shot you?" He said through clenched teeth, looking up at me. I saw his amber eyes change into more orange, then red. He continued to issue that rumbling growl, like a guard dog meeting an intruder. I was feeling a heat coming from him. Not like the heat, we felt together when we had sex, but a literal heat. Like I was standing next to open fire.

"Yes. They did."

"Tell me everything." I did. I tried to explain the whole evening right until the scar caused such a fuss in the hospital. Through the entire tale, he continued to growl, and when he heard about the explosion, his eyes flared again, and another wave of heat flowed off him.

"I don't know why any of it happened. I'm so confused and tired."

"I have some suspicions, Love. But perhaps you should stay home tomorrow and not go to work."

"I think being shot and exploded warrants a sick day, sure."

"Good," He kissed me, and we ended up tangled together on the bed, which almost ended the way it usually did, but he pulled away, "I have got some work to do. I want to stay with you, love, but it's necessary work."

"It's ok, Aya, I'll be fine. Thanks for stopping by anyway," I looked away, kind of disappointed, horny, and missing him already.

"But if anything happens, this time, call me."

"I would have, but my cell was taken away when I got to the hospital."

"No love, Call Me. My name."

"Oh, why? Is it like a bat signal?"
"Ah, this I know. A popular cultural reference. Yes, a bat signal. I will come."

"So, Patience knows your name. Can she call you?"

"No, for two reasons: One, I gave you my name and not her; and two, the way we said our own name when we gave them proffered them the power they now possess."

"I see, so could you bat signal me?"

"I'm not sure. Perhaps we will try some day. But for now, love, I have to depart." We kissed again. I let him out, which was more of a formality considering he probably could just disappear or something.

***

Chapter 24: Sick Day with Mr. Djinn (Thursday)

I worked from home the next day, calling the office to let them know. The gossip had already gotten around, so Cherry had already arranged the leave for Patience and me. At the same time, Todd went around spouting theories about Patience being in a secret mob for tiny people. Asshole, but it was kind of funny.

Just doing sketches that seemed utterly irrelevant to my thoughts and reality right now. I was deeply worried for Patience. I had no clue what had transpired yesterday, but Patience was my bestie and probably needed me. I desperately wanted to call her. But I heeded to Hope's words. Something about what she had said last night echoed with some secret truth. I needed to give Patience some space.

While I fumbled through trying to work on the new painting I was formulating, someone knocked on my door, a shy but one that I knew.

"Come in, Baraz!" I called.

Baraz used his code to come in.

"Hello, Li."

"Baraz, where's your mum, and why aren't you in school?" He looked at me sheepishly. He was wearing pj's, and it dawned on me. Someone else was having a sick day.

"She is at home working in the office. I am sick today, so I thought I would come to see you." He held up his little enclosure, which held the nefarious biting monster, his Pacman frog. I waved him in to sit next to me on the couch.

"What exactly is your illness today, so I know what flavour soda to give you?"

"I had a migraine last night. It's like a headache, but worse, and mother didn't want me going to school anyway."

"Ahh… yes. Those terrible things. You know I get them too?"

"Really?"

"Sure do, but I manage them well now." Although "manage" wasn't really the word for what my current treatment plan entailed.

I got up to the fridge and opened it to peruse the selection of terrible sugary drinks in stock. I noticed my fridge was suspiciously clean, with no old pizza boxes or half-eaten takeout. The sodas were topped up, and there were vegetables in the crisper and apples and oranges in the bottom drawer. Had Aya moved in sneakily? I should mind or feel weird about it, but my big brain and little brain were in agreement that neither could find a reason to feel anything other than elated. Therapy is becoming more likely as the days with my Fae lover carry on.

"For migraines, we have cherry, cola, lemonade lime, grape, raspberry, and orange."

Ok, so soda was not suitable for migraines at all. In fact, it could make them a lot worse. But any sufferer of migraines would tell you that there was this moment of need for some kind of sugar high after an attack. I had always craved candy or soda after a big attack. Though I always balanced it out with plenty of water as well.

"That's a lot of medicine for migraines, Li. Perhaps just orange." I brought it over with a metal straw in it, save the turtles and all. I also put a large glass of water next to it for him. I sipped my cola with my own metal straw, "Thank you, Li."

"Welcome, now what's up?"

"Hmm, nothing. I just came to hang out and see the fish," he looked over at the fish, then blushed a little… "and to find out if you have replaced me with a new friend?" I snorted, and he looked at me, shocked that I'd laugh at such a severe subject.

"Baraz! You are irreplaceable! I'd never give you up. We are Bros for Life, right?" He perked up, and we did the fist bump explosion. "You need to know, you feel like my only little brother, and I won't let you go quite that easily. Besides, who else are you gonna complain about this little asshole to…. Oops, my language, Ahzi!"

"But you do have a new friend. I have seen him."

"Yes, I do. He is a friend like Marcus was."

"He is your husband?"

From the mouths of babes! Parents really shouldn't coddle and hide explanations of the gay world from their children. Kids had such a simple understanding of the universe that we somehow gave up as we got older.

"Oh my, I don't know about that." It was my turn to blush this time.

"I remember Marcus was fun to hang out with too. Maybe he can be my friend like Marcus was?" He looked a little sad. It was then that the selfishness I had imposed on others has come to the fore again. Baraz had missed Marcus too. The little man was so wise and sweet for his age.

"I am sure he would love that. He's quite something else."

"Hmm, my mum saw him in the hall once and said he looks like a Djinn." He was referencing the middle eastern mythology of the earth-bound spirits that were between heaven and earth.

"Your mum may be right, but I think he's a good Djinn."

"Yeah, he looks ok," he proceeded to take Azhi out of his little enclosure and put him on the coffee table. I moved my art supplies off to the floor. The yellow and pink blob sat there eyeing up prospective targets for biting.

"How do we know he's a good Djinn?" I asked Baraz, curious what the boy would say.

"Well, in the stories, some Djinn would play tricks and cause deaths, but I think your Djinn isn't like that."

"And why do you think that?"

"Because he would have done it already." He said it like it was the most obvious thing. Because it probably was.

We chatted about frogs and Djinn and then my fish some more until my phone buzzed.

I looked to see Aya's text: *Is it ok if I keep you company today?*

Me: *As long as you don't mind that I have a guest. The neighbours' son, Baraz.*

Aya: *Be there soon! (smiley face/ emoji/ winky face).*

"You're in luck, my friend," I said to Baraz, "You get to meet my Djinn after all!"

"Yus!" he said, pumping his fist in enthusiasm, "should I tell mum?"

"Hmm, sure, I guess? But perhaps after."

"Ok. The Djinn won't eat me, will he?"

"No, sorry, he only eats Red Robins and pizzas as far as I can tell."

"Oh, a modern Djinn. That is good."

There was a polite knock on the door. I was so excited to see Aya. My body ached for him, as did…. my something else? My soul? I had Baraz answer the door for fun.

"Ah," Aya leaned down to be level with Baraz, "You must be Baraz that I've heard about." Aya held out his hand, and Baraz shook it.

"Yes, sir, I am," he was trying to look staunch and unshakeable. Perhaps he really thought Aya was a Djinn. I guess he wasn't too far off it.

"A pleasure then, young sir, may I enter and see my friend Li Yīng?" "Friend? Isn't he your husband?" Oh god. My face turned so red, but my heart fluttered for a moment in excitement.

"Almost Baraz, there are formalities to observe first, of course."

"I see. You may enter." This was so cute. I felt that Baraz was trying to play the part of a big brother to me.

"Thank you," Aya bowed, acting as serious as Baraz. He came in and went to the fridge, retrieved a cherry soda with no straw, opened it and downed the whole thing, then placed the can in the recycling bin under the sink. Baraz had not taken his eyes off him.

"Sir?" Aya looked at Baraz curiously as he led his inquiries on the Zenko, "Are you a Djinn?"

A laugh issued forth from Aya as if Baraz had said the silliest and funniest thing ever.

"A Djinn?"

"Yes, sir."

"Well, no, I am from Japan originally, so I can't be a Djinn."

"Untrue, sir, you could be a Djinn born in Japan." The logic was simple and adorable.

"He's got you there, Aya."

"Interesting. And what would you do if I were a Djinn?"

"It depends. Are you a good Djinn?"

"Define 'good,' young Baraz."

"Do you want to hurt Li?"

"Never." He said this seriously.

"Do you love Li?" I choked on my soda and panicked.

"Always."

"Then you are a good Djinn," I said it before: from the mouths of babes. Baraz's simple way of defining the world….my world. This is why the boy was one of my favourite people.

"Just like that?" I asked, "Suddenly, he's good. What if he's lying?"
"Everyone knows there are things even a Djinn cannot lie about. Their love for someone is one of them. My mother told me that's how many Djinn were tricked into getting trapped, like that old story of Aladdin's lamp."

"You are wise indeed, Master Baraz." Aya offered another bow and sat on the rug next to him, "Now I feel I have been rude in not introducing myself to this little fellow here." He indicated to the tiny pink and yellow blob that was Azhi. Baraz picked him up.

"This is Azhi." Aya eyed the little frog, who eyed him back. Then raised a finger to the frog's mouth, "N…."

I cut Baraz off with a quick shake of my head, just to see the next few seconds unfold.

Azhi did not disappoint and leaped at Aya's finger clamping onto it. This called for more bellowing laughter from the Zenko, who fell on his back on the rug waving the frog who stubbornly clung to his finger slightly, laughing some more. This sent off a chain of laughter from both Baraz and me. The frog finally didn't like being hung above a mocking Zenko and let go, plopping onto Aya's chest. He picked the frog up with both hands as if holding a fragile Faberge egg. He daintily gave it back to Baraz.

"He's a brave creature. A defender of his home. His name suits him well." Aya explained.

"Yeah," agreed Baraz, "I've gotta head back now. I'm sure you guys need to do husband stuff, whatever that is." He shrugged at that statement.

"Yes, we do Baraz, it was a pleasure meeting you." They shook hands again. I led Baraz to the door, and again he surprised me by wrapping me in one of his hugs.

"I really like him, Li," he whispered.

"Yeah, me too," I admitted. And then Baraz left.

"That boy loves you, Xiǎoyīng. He sees you like family."

"I am fortunate to have those people in my life."

"Now for that husband stuff…." Aya looked at me hungrily as he crept over to me, then towered over me. I felt myself stiffen quickly…. yes, husband stuff.

***

Chapter 25: Whodunnit (Friday)

Aya actually rode an Uber with me after I insisted on heading to work. My mind needed something to focus on. Spending all day in bed with Aya would be great, but it wouldn't pay the bills. When we got to the building that housed the MGV publishing offices, Aya escorted me to the elevator and gave me a long boner-inducing kiss, making me regret getting out of bed. My auric sight could barely see past the light suffusing my body that was undoubtedly from my Zenko. It made me feel so special thinking that he was with me when I went about my day.

"Hurry home, my love," he said as the elevator doors closed. It was only then I noticed I wasn't alone in the elevator. Cherry was there.

"Holy shit! That's your boyfriend?" Her mouth hung open.

"Aren't you gay?"

"Yeah, that's what I thought," she laughed and patted me on the back, "Well done, Li, he's …Wow!"

"You have no idea," I mumbled.

"Phew, I'm pretty sure even Fee would want to give that a go." Felicia was her gf. Cherry, being what the gays call a lipstick lesbian, was all heels, skirts, lipstick, makeup, and pretty. Her name was really Cherry. It suited her deep red hair and pale complexion. I suddenly felt a little insecure looking at her. She was a gorgeous specimen of a woman, and Aya might be bi for all I knew. Shut up, insecure brain!

"What?" she said, looking me up and down, and as if she read my mind, "Oh honey, that man saw no one else coming in here. He only had eyes for you." I was relieved but pretended not to hear. I just smiled shyly at her. Really?

***

Todd stood over me in all his sweaty glory. He was swabbing his face with his customary tissue.

"Li, what are you doing here? We know what happened. You're not expected to come to work for a bit, I'm sure," he had stopped to update me on the office gossip and current events.

More bear attacks, this time closer to my area of town. And given what I now knew, I was going to ask Aya about it. He was sure to tell if it had anything to do with his side of the tracks.

"I'm ok, Todd, really, but I'm still waiting for the police to contact me. I haven't heard anything."

"I swear, I'm right about Patience. She's the head of a midget mafia."
Smirking at his comment, I wondered if there was some truth to it. Not the midget part, but why had Patience's car been targeted, and how had Hope been there at that exact time? In fact, running the event through my head without the distraction of Aya, a few details came to light.

Had Hope not pulled Patience to the side, the shot would have gone right through Patience's chest. I was sure of it when I measured in my mind where Patience had been standing, where I had been, and where the bullet had hit me. What the fuck! God, I wanted to call Patience, but Hope had warned me off, and I was going to respect her words. There was something about her behaviour that evening.

Around mid-morning, two people I had never seen before came in - a man and a woman. Their look suggested cop/detective. Something about the way they dressed and the way they scanned around the office. I was at the water cooler when I saw them come in. They asked one of the visual techs for directions, I guess, who then pointed directly at me.

Well, I said to myself, this might shed some light on the whole situation. The two strangers came over to me with what they must have thought were friendly smiles. But I had painted enough faces to know expressions. They looked grim.

"Mr. Yīng? Li Yīng?" The woman asked. Again the common mistake was people using Chinese last names as the first, hence my friends calling me Li.

"It's Mr. Li. And yes, can I help you?"

"We hope so. We are with Vancouver Police Special Investigations. This is Dt. Sean Winder and I'm Dt. Sergeant Nat Bates. We've called your boss, who's given us permission to use your conference room." They both flashed their police badges.

"Ah… ok?"

The guy broke in, "We have questions concerning the events of Wednesday evening at Ms. Bakker's residence."

"You're not in any trouble Mr. Li. We just have some details that need clarification."

"Sure thing."

I led the pair to the conference room. We sat at one end while the female Dt, Nat (did she say her name was?), produced a folder.

"We are just trying to piece together the events. Can you describe what happened last Wednesday evening?"

I did. The two detectives made notes while I spoke. They also looked somewhat disappointed. I had obviously not given them what they were looking for. Perhaps I should tell them to ask the Vampires that had been stalking me? Or my Fox Spirit Boyfriend/Lover? If only they knew.

"And it shows on record that you were shot." Simon pitched in, his head down, writing then snapping up to give me a piercing look. At least it was supposed to be piercing, but I didn't feel any kind of intimidation or fear. In fact, I kind of felt indifferent. Perhaps because my mind was elsewhere, worrying about Patience and Hope. Curious about a body on the opposite rooftop. And maybe the motives of Vampires following me.

"It wasn't serious," I pulled my shirt up to show the bandaged shoulder, "I think the doctor said it just scraped me, but it hurt like a motherfucker." They both chuckled.

"Yup, even a nick can sting," said Dt Nat, "So you've given your account of events. They seem consistent with other witnesses. We wouldn't normally tell you, but this case only has two loose ends, and they, as far as we can tell, might be cases of mistaken identity. Both Ms. Bakker and her Sister have been very cooperative. Considering the events, we just wanna make sure nothing like this happens again." I had seen on TV shows like The Blacklist. When interviewing people, the investigators often would allow little details to be revealed to test the reactions of possible suspects.

"Mistaken identity? Patience and I were shot at, and someone blew up her car. That's friggin 'weird."

"I agree," said Dt Nat while her colleague continued writing notes, "So what do you make of this?"

She opened the folder and tossed some photographs to me. This made me jump out of my seat in fright.

"What the fuck?" They both looked at each other, judging my response probably, and came to some agreement unspoken.

"You don't recognize this person?"

"No, no, I don't, ahh?"

"Yes, Mr. Li?"

"Why is there a champagne flute stem sticking out his forehead?" My voice was shaking a little, and the adrenalin of the fright made my hands shake a little.

"We were hoping to find answers from you, Ms. Bakker, or her sister," said Dt Nat.

"Lab techs have a crazy theory that they say explains what happened completely," Dt. Simon finally stopped writing and looked at me as I retook my seat. I pushed the pictures of the dead stranger away from me, "the man in the picture is a contract killer and hasn't ever been found active here in Canada."

"Oh," Seemed to be my new catchphrase of late when dealing with people, but what else could I say?

"According to the techs who looked over the scene, a broken glass that had been sitting on the roof of a parked car just shot up when an explosive charge detonated. The techs are sure that it had malfunctioned when it exploded. We are not sure who the intended victims may have been." Dt Nat took over as Dt Simon just shook his head as if he heard an old joke again.

"Apparently, the stem from a broken champagne flute flew up and hit the shooter square in the forehead, killing him instantly. But he managed to get off a shot that missed whoever it was intended for."

"We are just collecting information, but we'd like to speak to you again soon." Dt Simon handed me a card, as did Dt Nat. I took them. They got up to leave.

"Wait, that's it?" I asked, confused.

"Should there be more?" Dt Nat countered.

"No, I mean, none of this makes any sense. We are normal people (lie). Why would anyone want to hurt Patience, let alone hire some random killer? It doesn't make any sense. I'm sorry, but I'm worried about my friend. What if someone tries again?"

"Your friend is staying at her sister's, and we have a patrol car there round the clock. We'll make sure they're safe." I breathed out in relief. I had been worried about Patience but had been too afraid to call and upset Hope.

The detectives thanked me and made their leave. My colleagues came rushing over, talking all at once, wanting answers. Asking all sorts of questions, which I didn't have the answers for.

"You shouldn't even be here, you fool!" I heard a familiar voice screaming from Patience's office.

"I had to come to get it, otherwise,"

"What, Patience!? He might find out!"

What the fuck? Who? What?

"No, I just, I dunno." I heard Patience whimper. Who was this woman who was my best friend? Patience had never whimpered all the time I'd known her.

"You wanted it all to disappear. After what you tried to do!" Hopes voice was enraged. I don't know where the woman got her energy.

"I just wanted to…." Hope cut off her explanation.

"Did you even ask me? I should have a say in this!"

"I know."

If it weren't for my enhanced sense, I wouldn't have even heard the conversation let alone Patience's whispered comeback. All the office could listen to is muffled yelling from the Top Bitch's office. But I could hear the whole conversation. I couldn't even believe Patience had risked coming here, although she had been a gun-toting tough mofo since I'd known her. She had had a gun license since she was allowed to apply, and I was pretty sure Patience owned more guns than she was licensed for.

"Li is family, Patience," Hope said, calming down obviously.

"I know."

"No, you don't, obviously, but you are gonna tell him."

"I can't!" I could hear her muffled crying, but Hope would have none of it.

"You will! Or I will! It's better coming from you after everything! Now get your shit together!"

With that, the frosted glass swung open and out stalked Hope. Again, she was running on anger and frustration. I went to go after her but changed my mind and turned to Patience's office door that was now closed.

I approached it. Despite what Hope had said to me, this was my best friend. I hated knowing she was in some kind of pain. I didn't care what their conversation was about. I knocked and tried to open it.

"Patience? It's Li." No answer. "Come on, Patience, let me in. Whatever is going on, we'll work it out." No answer. "Ok, well, I'll text you later. I've finished another set of panels, so I'll go home if that's ok." Still silence. I could hear her quiet sobbing, trying to keep it to herself.

What would I do without Aya's "blessing." It made me feel really sad knowing Patience would have a smutty comment about Aya's "blessing" inside me, and we couldn't laugh about it right now.

"I'll text you and try to call you later. Love you!" I turned from the frosted glass. Half the office had stopped their work and were watching me curiously, and something in me got mad.

"What are you all looking at! Get back to work! This isn't a playground!"
They all snapped into motion, pretending they all hadn't been rubbernecking. Cherry and Todd were remarkably busy looking at something right in front of them. Fuck it. I loved my job. But I loved my bestie Patience more and would keep trying. I packed my stuff. Then went to her door.

"Patience, please let me in. Please bub. Whatever it is, we have always fixed it together." No answer.

Patience was a strong woman. I had to have faith that whatever was going on, she could handle it. But I was going to call and text incessantly like a fucking stalker until she answered.

I left the office. I noticed some missed vid calls from Maman and Bàba. 8 missed calls—only them. I dialled Aya's number, which went to voicemail instantly. Weird. I tried again. Same again. Huh. Strange. I called an Uber and headed home alone.

***

Chapter 26: The Reckoning (Friday)

My smart lock clicked open as I stepped into my apartment. I breathed in deeply our scent—my Aya and me. I tried calling Patience, the phone rang but eventually went to voicemail. I then decided to order on Doordash from Tim Hortons. A Craveable chicken sandwich, a frozen raspberry lemonade, and a box of six Boston Cream donuts. I knew I would have to pull out the big guns to get a response from the stubborn woman.

While I waited for the food to arrive, I tried calling Aya again. Voicemail. Hmph. I checked and double-checked the messages. Nothing. From either Patience or the Man that was called my husband last night.

I called my parents. They picked up immediately.

"*Wei*," I was greeted with a barrage of expletives in French that I could barely translate as my mother offloaded the entire French curses dictionary on me. I switched to French.

"Maman!" I yelled to get her attention. She stopped." What is going on?"

"*Espèce d'idiot! Tu t'es fait tirer dessus et tu ne nous as même pas appelé! Qui sommes-nous pour toi? Est-ce que tu en as quelque chose à faire?* (You silly boy! You got shot and didn't even call us! What are we to you? Do you even care?)" Somehow it sounded more dramatic and sorrowful in her native French.
"Pia told me everything. Why didn't you call us immediately?" Um…sorry. It's because my boyfriend gave me magical powers that could allow me to survive leaping from a skyscraper, but only temporarily…. "What were you thinking? You didn't think that's what!" The tirade continued until she had spent herself and was crying at the screen, *"Mon garçon, mon beau garçon (*My boy, my beautiful boy*)!*"

"*Marguerite, bouges-toi!*" Bàba snapped in French at her. She moved. He switched to mandarin. It was easier for him than

Cantonese, "您媽真擔心 (Your Maman is just worried). Pia said some pretty disturbing things, and we were waiting for you just so you wouldn't feel pressured. But a shooting. That's serious, boy. You call no matter what."

"I know, Bàba," Maman had made me teary-eyed too. I sniffed, "I'm really sorry," I called in French to my maman in the background. "*Je suis très desolé* (I'm so sorry), Maman, really I am. *Je t'aime beaucoup*." She just reached vaguely towards the camera as if trying to reach through and stroke my face.

"I'm sorry. A lot has happened, and I am not even sure what to tell you," It was true. Where the hell do I start? The doorbell buzzed, and I went to get the door. My Tim Hortons delivery had arrived. I set it on the counter and went back to the dining table, where my phone was propped up to continue suffering the wrath of my parents that I rightly deserved.

"Show me," my Bàba demanded, "the hole, show it." He was angry but trying to hide it. I couldn't blame them. As I had noticed with Baraz, I had been so selfish. I took off my shirt and removed the bandage. There was barely an outline, "Where is it?"
"I told you it was nothing, just a scrape that healed already," I replaced the completely unnecessary bandage.

"Someone tried to shoot Patience, apparently. The police are as confused as the rest of us."

"That's crazy. Patience is a good girl! Why would anyone want to hurt her!" Oh yeah, Bàba was angry. His face was red. I had suspected he and my Maman viewed Patience as their wee girl, possibly as my wife if I ever stopped being gay. Hey, my parents were progressive, but they dealt with things in their own way, even perhaps by making crazy unspoken and unrealistic wishes of their own.

"I hope they catch the asshole!" my Bàba yelled.

"What happened to Patience? Is she ok?" I was about to say she was ok then Bàba beat me to it.

"Someone tried to kill her, Marguerite!"

"No!" She looked as furious as my Bàba. Ok, maybe my parents did view Patience as their little girl, but whatever, *"J'espère qu'ils auront le bâtard!* (I hope they get the bastard)" she said. I swear the way my Maman spat these last words, I could visualize her strapping on a Kevlar vest, slinging some semi-automatic weapons and a rocket launcher over her shoulder. Then going full Rambo on their ass.

"They've got him, guys." That stopped their angry babble for a moment.

"That was quick!" Bàba said.

"Well, someone got him."

"Huh?" My parents said almost in unison.

"A freak accident of death by champagne glass on a rooftop across the street."

"What?" Yeah, my parents were confused. Welcome to my week, guys! We talked more about this. Then the crime rate not being so high and the animal attacks that had been happening. I assured my parents I was okay. Then they asked the most innocuous question that they'd asked so many times on these vid chats.

"Are you doing ok, my son?" When my face broke into a wide grin, my Maman gasped and covered her mouth in shock. My Bàba just smiled and looked away from the camera, then back again, trying to hide the tears welling in his eyes.

"I am Maman and Bàba. I'm doing really good." My Bàba couldn't control a tear that fell down, and he didn't stop it, just continued the conversation as though his eyes weren't streaming, and so were mine, "Yeah, I'm happy."

The relief and love pouring from the screen filled me with so much joy. They had seen their son, their broken boy try and take his own life. Then when that was unsuccessful, he stumbled through the last five years in a haze of grief and regret.

"I am so sorry for the…." I was trying to articulate my words and having trouble, "- since Marcus…." yeah, I was fast becoming a blubbering mess.

"It's ok, my son," My Bàba assured.

"Je t'aime tellement mon fils, (Love you so much, son)" my mum kept saying, her passionate French side taking over that she couldn't say much else.

"I'm really sorry." I yelped out. They just shook their heads and said they loved me.

"Now go be happy and call your Maman more. She's crazy, you know." My Maman playfully slapped the back of my Bàba's head while he pulled her down from behind the couch onto his lap laughing. They were so happy. I could tell my Bàba was delighted to see me smile and his wife to be relieved. It had been a miserable five years I had put them through.

When someone made a choice to take their own life, it's a personal choice. Yeah, it's selfish but also deeply personal. It could be for the silliest of reasons, but also for the largest of reasons. A mind could be coaxed to conclude that there was none other than the final exit in many ways. Mine had been grief, missing my Marcus and just wanting to see him again. This had taken a heavy toll on those I loved, but you'd never see or feel that at the time of ending it all. You just wanted the pain to stop.

We signed off not long after. Patience had been right. I had been living half a life, and it had been screwing with my loved ones. No more. I would do as my Bàba had insisted and be happy as best I could.

I tried Aya's phone again. Voicemail. I sent him a bunch of texts, then realized they had started to sound incredibly desperate. So, I stopped, trusting he'd get back to me.

I set out the food on my bench and laid out the donuts. Then I used a popular app I had downloaded that superimposed your face onto any scene, action, or static image. It would then meld it so well it looked almost real. I found the scene I wanted and took the picture, which was perfect. I then photographed my personal feast. Then I cropped and added the fake me behind the food. The result was my face on the body of Fat Bastard from Austin Powers in all his greasy obese glory seated atop my counter with the Tim Hortons haul. The final touch was a text box: *600 lb life 4ever?*

Hopefully, she would see it and get back to me. I hadn't gone this long without talking to my bestie.

While I waited for texts from my Bf or Bestie, I decided to go and use my tub for the first time in ages.
Stripping down, I looked in the full-length bathroom mirror at my body. The body that Aya had constantly been enjoying. I saw the glowing aura all around me—Aya's aura. I felt so sexy thinking of him. I started to get an erection, but I wanted to save it for him tonight. I still didn't understand what he saw in me. My body was toned but kind of skinny. Tanned or pale depending on the season. My face, I guessed, was pretty enough, my hair shoulder length. Not as gorgeous as he thought. I turned to the side. Well, at least my ass was worth killing for. I knew that that part was something guys loved. I even loved it. Perhaps my ass had magical powers to ensnare supernatural beings of all kinds.

That made me think briefly of the Vamps that were now mysteriously absent from everywhere I went. I suspected that was a result of Aya's efforts. Perhaps that's the work he did while I was at MGV during the day. Did that mean if we became a permanent thing, I would have to support us both? I could. I knew that much. I earned very well. But it made me laugh: "No, my husband isn't a deadbeat gold digger. He hunts demons while I go out and earn a living."

I turned some more, curious of my own body more than ever before. Then I saw it. Crawling up my spine like an ugly black tree. It was the webwork of black veins curling up my back and stopping at my left shoulder blade.

If you've ever seen the scars of lightning victims, it looked like a black ink-coloured version of that. At first, I didn't believe what I was seeing. I moved closer to the mirror. And looked on in horror. It looked like the cancerous veins that I had seen on Hope, and more vividly remembered, all over my beloved Marcus.

"No," I whispered, trying to banish what I was seeing. Moving closer to the mirror, I saw tiny lights moving from the base of whatever this was and spread into the upper branches of the mass. The root of the black veins went right down between my cheeks and into the area that had brought me pleasure all week. What the Fuck!

The veins were pulsing with light. Whatever it was looked alive, and it made me feel ill. I went to the toilet and expelled everything I'd eaten.

"No," I said again in denial. I rushed back to the mirror, "No, please, not me."

I was feeling faint from throwing up, but also from the shock of the discovery.

Five minutes later, I was out the door dressed and ready, the Uber arrived, and I headed to my destination. This was not something that could happen to me too!

***

Doctor Pia, or Aunty Pia as I called her, shut the door to the exam room.

"So soon, Li, you flatter me. But perhaps we should have a family dinner instead, huh?" I half-heartedly laughed.

"What's the problem?" She was in doc mode now, and I couldn't think of anyone else who might help.

"I think I might have caught something, Aunty," I started to cry.

"Shh, shush now, Li Yīng," She hugged me, then pulled me away to look at me square on, "Whatever is wrong, we can figure it out. Now, what makes you think that? Don't be shy. This is between you and me now. I won't tell your parents. This is personal, not like the gunshot."

I went to the exam table and undid my jeans, my tears uncontrolled now, and pulled down my jeans and underwear.

"Darling? What am I supposed to be looking at?"

"Um…you can't see it?"

"What I can see is your adorable little butt!" She slapped a cheek with her latex-covered hand. I pulled my top further up so she could see my back.

"Is it there?"

"No, honey, whatever you're trying to show me, I can't see it."

I felt confused and pulled up my underwear and jeans. By this time, I had no shame about showing myself to Aunty because I was scared. Really scared.

"Have you been sexually active, darling?" I nodded, "Condoms?" I shook my head. She just marked onto the clipboard what she needed.

"It's ok, darling, we will figure this out. But no more unprotected sex for a bit, huh?" I nodded.

"I'm gonna order a full panel of tests for you. We will look for everything, ok?" I nodded again dumbly, "Don't worry, Li, most times these scares are nothing, but they help us remember to be careful, ok?" I nodded again.

What was I - a bobblehead? Yeah, a dumb bobblehead who had unprotected sex with an alien spirit being from Japan…? Even in my head, it sounded stupid.

For a few more minutes, I was there as a Lifelab's tech came in and took a pint of blood in vials for the tests. I had to pee into a cup and leave that with them too. By the time I was done, Aunty Pia had kissed me on the forehead, hugged me and said, everything would be fine and that she would call me with the results as soon as they were done.

I numbly got into another Uber and went home.

***

It took me three tries before I got my own code right and got into my apartment. Then I remembered that my cell could unlock it too. Geez. Yup, I was an empty bobblehead doll right now. I went into the kitchen to get some water, suddenly thirsty. I walked past the calendar. No envelope for me to open. Not until tomorrow.

"Năinai! Seriously!?" If there was a time for guidance, it would be now.

I tried calling Aya, voicemail. I sent him one last text that we needed to talk about, and it was serious. I tried calling Patience, and hers went straight to voicemail. At least I knew she would be safe at night at her sister's home, with a patrol car outside.

I went and had a shower hoping this was some silly humiliating hallucination. The mirror showed me otherwise. The prominent black veins were still spread across my back. Pulsing, mockingly. That could not be anything good for me.

After my shower, I got into bed and stared at the picture of Marcus. Had Aya given me something other than some of his "skills?" He had said that our diseases weren't compatible as we were different species. That had made so much sense at the time, but now I felt foolish. Really stupid. I touched my back. I couldn't feel anything veiny. Maybe it'd be gone tomorrow. My head and heart agreed that it was a stupid notion, and I needed to do something stat.

"Please, Marcus, let it be gone tomorrow." I prayed to my love, despite my brain's misgivings. Aya wouldn't hurt me. I was sure. In fact, he had said he loved me so readily to Baraz. It had sounded so sincere. Baraz approved. So had Patience.

But what if…. the whole thing was a convoluted lie, or some of it at least? No. that couldn't be it.
But what if he did hurt your body, gave you something, and made you sick? No…. but I still had a veiny mass curving up my spine. I rolled over, ashamed to look at Marcus on the nightstand. Ashamed of myself for being fucking happy. Who was I to be happy?! I could feel the dark cloud rolling in across my soul. So familiar and unwelcome now, but still rolling in.
Perhaps I was crazy, and this was all a bad dream?

With that, I went to the bathroom drawer, where I kept some other prescriptions that I hadn't needed in a while, specifically after my self-inflicted brush with death. I looked at the bottle, Diazepam. Yup. That'd do it. I choked down two with a mouthful of tap water and went back to bed. It wasn't long before I saw the blackness of sleep take me away from black veiny, invisible infections, shooters, bombers, and basically all of my worries.

***

Chapter 28: From a Cocktail to a Doctor's Note (Saturday)

When I awoke the following day, my head was so groggy. I almost forgot the past couple of days and had reached across the bed for Aya, but the empty space gave me a cold and sobering start.

I opened my bedside drawer and got out those two tiny pills that kept me from succumbing to the more profound depression I was prone to. There was no glass left on the bedside for me. Anyone else who had met Aya would have probably felt intruded upon when he had thoughtfully left the glass on his first night here. He had gone through my stuff and found my meds, and made sure I took them when he was here.

But I found it sweet. I found it charming because it is what I had needed. I had also rationalized that perhaps, as I had thought earlier, the different rules of social engagement between species might have something to do with it. It was probably insulting to not go through people's things and ensure their crazy meds were taken the next day? It had been so long for me that my neurosis was literally dictating itself the moment I woke up now. I had gotten attention from guys but had politely disengaged any romantic possibilities with them. Aya was the only one I had let in, at least in a romantic way. And there was a possibility that he might have made me sick.

I texted both Aya and Patience, requesting they call, text, or meet. Then I tried calling each. No answer again.

Checking my back in the mirror in the bathroom, it was still there. The black veins were so stark against my skin, they appeared to taunt me. I almost let the tears come. But I took a deep breath, followed by my morning shower. While under the blessed scalding water going about the simplicity of washing my body, I was considering if Aya had given me some kind of supernatural STI, could I deal with it? My feelings for him were still there, growing, like the weird spiderweb of black veins in my back.

Maybe they were connected. Aunty Pia hadn't seen any veins. Knowing her, she would insist on my lab work before anything else.

Aunty Pia had known Maman and Nǎinai, and both had had an enormous influence on her life. Hence the "Aunty" part. I needed to stop feeling sorry for myself. That hadn't gotten me anywhere in the past 5 years. I needed a plan of action. And the first action was info gathering. That was what a smart hero would do, right? But where to start?

***

Where it all started.

It was Saturday morning, and the air had a slight chill to it. I went to the Crossroads, stepping lightly down the stairs. It had been more difficult to find earlier, but now with my auric sight on pretty much all the time, I could see exactly where it was. It glowed brightly, a beacon beneath the brownstone building in which it was housed.

When I got to the landing, I looked around. I swore this was the place, but there was no door on any three surrounding walls. This couldn't be right. I ground my teeth in frustration and pounded my fist on the brick wall, where I was sure had been a glossy black door when I had entered the bar. The world was having a joke at my expense.

"Ha!" I said a little too loudly. Stepping back, I saw a black door on the brick, only painted on the wall. Hmm.

I turned around. The wall behind me sported a mural of a house, mid-century maybe? White with one of those wrap-around verandas. The paint on the brick wall was faded, as was that on the black door painting, almost disguising their presence. Perhaps this was a magical thing. Argh! Not giving up yet! I promised myself.

"Hello?" I yelled.

"Coming, just a sec," a deep, gravelly voice answered from somewhere near…. I spun around. Where did –

The house mural wall seemed to bulge out slightly as the outline of a large, muscular man came into view. He stepped out of the painting and was still putting a tight black t-shirt on as if he had just gotten out of bed.

"Whoa!" was all I could really say to that. Magic was cool! And then not, as I absently touched the lower of my spine. His aura was deep green and tightly packed against himself, then abruptly it vanished, hidden.

"Ah, yes, I remember you, young one." The large handsome man leaned slightly in, "Only the Fae can summon me… or someone who has had considerable contact with one." He sniffed, "I'm guessing the latter?"

"Um, hi, can you help me please?" my voice was rushing out. I suddenly realized that this was a place where myths met reality and scared me slightly. Enough to make my voice tremble. There was that and the panic of the black stain on my back.

The bouncer squinted his gaze at me, then his beautiful ebon face softened: "Hey, hey, it's ok. I think you are probably looking for Neelas, right?" I nodded, "Come on, sweet thing, you look like you need a drink anyway." His large palm slapped against the wall, which bulged out and shaped itself into the black door I had seen on my first visit to the Crossroads.

"How…? How do you do that?" I was looking wide-eyed up at him and his handsome face with utter amazement.

"Ah, yes. It's not something humans get to witness often. In fact, most of them can't. Their minds flip it around until it becomes something that fits their usual perceptions."

"So, they make an illusion of something in their heads to ignore something that might be a little weird."
"Well put," he said, placing a hand on my shoulder and leading me through the door. This time he came in with me. The club was deserted, and it dawned on me that I was in this place, and no one

knew I was here. What an idiot. Horror movie 101, don't go anywhere alone! You'd end up dead! Rookie mistake. I didn't even have a weapon. Lame again, Yīng!

The giant tree vibrated with an energy that was so much clearer without the patrons filling the place with their own stray energies. When I looked at it, it felt as if the tree was regarding me as well. And I had a feeling of warmth and connectedness coming from it. It was like the feeling I would get from my Nǎinai whenever we would spend time together. Stern, but kind.

"Yggdrasill likes you," Bouncer said, leading me past the giant tree, "she's not the original Yggdrasill obviously, just a piece of the larger whole as you could say. But she's been giving you the equivalent of 'a loving look'." I shrugged, unsure what that meant, but knowing I did feel it all the same.

I had heard of Yggdrasill in stories and books about Norse gods. And, of course, in the recent Marvel franchise. The tree between Life and Death. It was a magnificent sight still, and my breath caught while staring up into her branches overhead.

"Come, little one," he said, gently pushing me towards the bar, "Neelas is getting the bar ready for tonight." I heard the clinking of bottles as someone behind the massive wall-length bar was shifting glass around.

"Neelas?" The bouncer half-shouted.

"Here! Just a sec!" The sound of something smashing, "Shit!"

Neelas 'head popped up over the bar, "What's up?" then she saw me, "oh hi! Our resident mimic! How're things?" She was dressed in a tank top and jeans, with a pair of what looked to be steel-toed boots.

"Um…"

"I think he needs our help Neelas." Her smile was quickly replaced by concern.

"What's going on?" she asked. She held a towel in her hand that she wiped her hands on before placing it on the counter.

"Have a seat, son," the deep-voiced bouncer led me to a stool, and I hopped onto it while he sat next to me. I then realized these were probably the very seats Aya and I got acquainted with. A small pang. Why hadn't I heard from him?! Or Patience? Best friend and pseudo-boyfriend going AWOL when needed. Dang!

"Um, I think I might be sick," my voice came out in a croak.

"Oh dear," Neelas tied up her loose blonde hair into a ponytail and came around to the front of the bar next to the bouncer, who just sat there squinting slightly at something he could see but wasn't commenting on.

"I, um, something happened, and I remember you used to be a doctor and…." Neelas looked quite concerned but also curious.

"I don't practice medicine anymore, my friend, at least not in the conventional sense. I'm sorry."

"No, you see, perhaps if I show you?"

"Sure."

I got off the stool and pulled up my long sleeve t-shirt to expose my back.

"I'm sorry, buddy. I don't see anything unusual."

"But I thought," I said helplessly, "you'd be able to see."

"Oh…I see." She gestured to the bouncer to look from her side. He took a sharp intake of breath.

"Something?"

"Yes," He answered simply, taking on a grim tone.

"I can't see what you are both seeing because, as I told you, I am 100%, rawhide human. I have no abilities whatsoever. Only training in the fields that apply to both worlds," she explained. She reached over the bar and grabbed what looked like a metal lip gloss container. She opened it, and I could smell the mix of herbs and spices and oils in its contents. She then smeared some under each eye, then a line on her forehead.

"Give it a second. It'll work." She said as if that explained the smelly lip gloss she was smearing on her face, "Ah, I see. Wow. That's something else." My heart dropped. It was something terrible. Had Aya really made me sick? Did he lie about no STDs between us, just so he could fuck me without protection? I felt like such a fool! No Yīng, relax! You don't have all the facts.

"What is it?" I asked, panicking.

"I am not entirely sure, but it looks like your energy body and the physical body is reacting to something. I'm not an expert on these things. I've only seen something like this once before, but the case and circumstances were nothing like yours, so I don't think it applies."

"Will your Eraser get rid of it?" Desperation filled me.

"I don't think so. I'm sorry. In fact, it may do more harm than good. Save the Eraser for when whatever this is, is out of your system."
"So, it can go away?"

"I didn't say that. But I know someone who might be able to help." She reached over the counter and grabbed a fishbowl of business cards, fished her hand around until she found what she was looking for then handed it to me.

"He's a doctor, but not the kind I was. In layman's terms, a Witch Doctor. But he's outstanding. Everyone uses him in this area, and some people come from worldwide and beyond just to see him. He should be able to help." My spirits lifted. He would know. He would help. Maybe it was nothing. Maybe Aya and I could just be together and enjoy each other. Aya wouldn't lie to me. But you just met him Yīng ….

Neelas saw my smile and wrapped an arm around my shoulder.

"Look, Hun, you're gonna be fine. This world we are part of is strange, beautiful, and dangerous, but it's also full of wonder, miracles, and some great people," she nodded to the bouncer, who grinned then winked at me. I did feel slightly better, "There is one catch, though," there had to be, didn't there, "He's incredibly expensive, but you'll get results, and that's what you want."

"What kind of expensive; ballpark," I said skeptically. I didn't want to get scammed, obviously. Though I felt like I could trust these two, I had just met the Fae bouncer and the ex-Dr. Neelas. I had also trusted Aya, and now I was back here pleading for help, so, yeah, skeptic.

"He may ask for money, but it's unlikely, he's like," she nodded towards the bouncer, "You know, they have a different currency than ours."

"Currency…"

"Yeah. He may ask for a favour, which sounds small, but it could be anything he wants you to do. He's not evil. In fact, he's quite the opposite. But he must get equal to what he gives, otherwise, and I quote: "*The imbalance of exchange will demand to shift back to balance, and it will demand loudly*!" She said the quote dramatically as if this Witch Doctor had said it to her several times, perhaps in some tutorial-like setting.

"I see." I was getting the picture. It wasn't a total loss, just another step. I had to keep going.

"Now, a drink!" Neelas called with glee, "Your usual?"

"I have a usual?"

"You do now!" She laughed, leaping behind the bar. The bouncer roared in laughter. Before I knew it, the colourful confection of alcohol was sitting in front of me, waiting to be consumed. Why not? I was feeling like crap, and this carnival of madness in a glass balloon might be just what the doctor ordered…. Get it? Ha!

***

Chapter 29: Death by Dim Sum (Saturday)

The hunky bouncer was helping me up the stairs of The Crossroads. I called up an Uber to collect my drunk self and take me home. Before it arrived, Neelas came out and asked to exchange contacts. She said she wanted to know the outcome of the Witch Doctor appointment or if there was anything else she could do. Neelas and 'Mr. Bouncer' made me feel a little bit safe, or that could be the alcohol, but it was nice. It was like the feeling the giant tree had given me upon seeing it for the first time without the crowded auras of the patrons that frequented the club—a type of friendly affection. The Uber arrived, and Mr. Bouncer helped me pile in. And I was sure he had grabbed my ass as I climbed, but it was again, probably the alcohol.

***

When I got home, the buzz of alcohol was still in full effect. It was fun, but I had to sober up and decide what to do about this Witch Doctor. He was "expensive." Possibly in trading your soul kind of way, although Neelas did say he was one of the good ones.

I stumbled into my open shower, barely remembering to remove my jacket and pants at the last minute before the water poured on me. Phew, I was really drunk, but at least I was coherent enough to remember my phone and the business card Neelas had given me. They were my veritable lifelines now. I didn't care that I was wearing my shirt and boxer briefs. I just sat there under the powerful jet of hot water, waiting for the room to stop spinning.

OK, so the shower did give me a little time to clear my head. The doctor would likely ask for payment upfront—a Witch Doctor. My Nǎinai wouldn't ask for payment when she did her work, but she wasn't Fae, as far as we knew. But she would take gifts, and when I thought about it, people would give her extravagant gifts of jewels and precious statues or stones sometimes. Gran didn't care about material things. She just made sure those things could be liquidated and turned into college funds and other essential items like rent or food.

A Witch Doctor. I wonder if Nǎinai knew one or even this one. It was then I realized the day. I rushed over to the calendar. Yes! It was today! I took the red envelope carefully from today's date and went and sat on the couch. There was only a date, no exact time. So, I was to open it anytime today. And I did just that.

Xiǎoyīng Bǎobèi (precious),

You were always such a light in my life, and I have done all I can to protect you from the clutches of that bitch fate. You have gone through a hell of a time recently, I'm sure. My sweet boy. We all have challenging moments. We must rise from those and become something more. You are to be something more. Trust Nǎinai. There will be a tough decision to make to help someone who needs it. Do your best, boy, and that is all I can ask.

By now, you will have received a contact to get some help. I wish I could help personally, but I can't, and this is the best I could do from here.

Ps. The Witch Doctor has been paid in full. He is open on Sundays. Go see him.

***

My Nǎinai was a very singular woman. She was someone like no one else and the most fantastic person I had known. She had a gift for knowing too accurately when things of import would happen and could sometimes leverage those situations into becoming an outcome she liked more. This premise ruled my Năinai's life.

Năinai grew up in Guilin in Daxu, a tiny village I had only seen once that looked like it was out of a Chinese period drama. It had all the original buildings preserved and used by the residents. Cobblestone streets and old bridges. It was magnificent and only a hint of what it was like when Năinai was a girl. She didn't talk too much about her youth, but it raised more questions than answered when she did. I spent so much time with Năinai that she became my best friend growing up. I had a few friends while in school, but I always liked hanging with my Năinai more. It always seemed that she understood me better than everyone else.

Every year she would gather some homemade red packets and give them out. No one would know when they would receive one, but they were so grateful and often in tears when they did. It was always a vital piece of information that would help them in some way. Leverage the outcomes of things. Sometimes these events were manipulated to avoid death itself.

Năinai's red packets themselves were always beautiful. Exquisitely crafted treasures. Dyed red with gold hand-painted designs. Each one was unique. The designs themselves were personal to the receiver of the packet. When my Năinai first started teaching me to paint, I saw things that drew me to them, like flowers, insects, fishes, and birds. Sometimes it would be an exciting mushroom or plant. I never felt like I'd be as good as her, but it didn't matter. She always let me help her make the packets, guiding my hands to create the right picture. During these times, she would tell stories, and I would sometimes paint what I heard about in these tales.

There was a little story that my father told me about Năinai. She had learned her craft from the spirits around Guilin and used it to help those around her.

Now, as mentioned, Năinai's predictions were spot on. Sometimes down to the minute. I remember so clearly that she had demanded that we all go to her favourite dim sum restaurant. We were all to attend, including Marcus. My parents had to cancel various meetings, but they entertained the notion. I was ok dropping anything for Nǎinai. If it wasn't for her, I wouldn't have my gift for drawing and painting, nor would I have a career.

Seated around the dining table eating and laughing, Nǎinai asked, "Xiǎoyīng Bǎobèi, where is your husband?" She actually had called Marcus my "husband" from the moment she met him. It was typical Nǎinai, just skirting centuries of tradition to accommodate her own worldview.

"He'll be here, Nǎinai," I replied, "He's just finishing up work."

"Well, he needs to hurry, I'm on a tight schedule, and I need him here."

"Really," I giggled, "for what exactly, Nǎinai?" I gave her a sideways look. My Nǎinai's sense of humour was often inappropriate. Still, one wasn't allowed to tell anyone over 100 years old what to do, even if what they had said would make a pirate blush. They had earned the right to do whatever the hell they wanted after surviving a century.

"He's gonna be my packhorse." Everyone laughed, not knowing exactly what she meant but hearing her say it in such a lascivious manner was worth every syllable.

Marcus did come in puffing and apologizing profusely in the Mandarin he could manage to Nǎinai.

"Sit next to me, my boy." She demanded, patting the empty space next to her.

Then, as he was about to sit down, she looked plainly at the group and proceeded to grab a handful with her tiny hands of Marcus 'ass cheek before he sat down.

He yelped slightly but was used to the harassment by now, "Just checking if he's firm enough for the task." Another round of laughter. Did I mention Năinai was one of the most inappropriate people you'd ever meet too? Well, then it warrants me saying it again.

The dinner proceeded as these things did. Suppose you had never been to a Chinese restaurant filled with Chinese people eating noisily and talking about everything all at once. In that case, it could be quite a sensory overload. We were always happy when eating, and it really brought everyone together. They passed and shared food from their culture that was both tasty and filling.

Năinai somehow had an appetite always, even though she was now 112 years old. Still sharp as a tack and so independent that she rode the sky train and buses wherever she wanted to go. We never worried for Năinai, any brute dumb enough to give her any trouble was likely to wind up in a ditch somewhere. Or, if they were lucky, apologizing profusely for crossing the little biddy.

"I have something for everyone," Năinai yelled in Mandarin in the general direction of a particular waiter who kept looking over expectantly. I had seen him here before. He was an exceptionally cute Chinese boy with a porcelain complexion, likely in university and working here part-time. Năinai took a liking to this boy the moment she saw him and took no pains to say the most embarrassing things to him. Why did he put up with it?

He came over, and Năinai pulled a hundred-dollar bill out of her purse and shoved it down the waiter's front apron pocket. Then she proceeded to take out a red envelope and slide it in after the big tip she'd given. Then she offered a few instructions to her nervous minion. He went off while we all looked at each other confused.

He came back with a food trolley, not containing food, but a stack of red journals and a silk box. There was another box there too. My Năinai's jewelry box and a large manilla envelope with my dad's name on it.
"Now, Marguerite, you know you are my *nǚ'ér* (女兒/daughter) by marriage and purpose," she gestured to the waiter. He lifted the

jewelry box off the dining trolley. And placed it in front of my Maman. She had a hand to her mouth.

"Nǎinai, no! This is…"

"This is yours. I won't need it." My Maman tried to protest some more, but Nǎinai ignored her and handed my dad the big manilla envelope with his name on it, "Here, érzi (兒子/son), this is all my stuff on paper. It's in order. I had a lawyer friend go over it. I have some land in Guilin that you or Xiǎoyīng Bǎobèi might want to check at some stage." Again, Bàba tried to say something, but Nǎinai was on a roll and ignored the other person.

"My boys," she turned to us and smiled, "I am so proud of you both." I loved my Nǎinai, "马科斯 (Marcus)," she looked a little sad all of a sudden, frowning a little, seeing something only visible to her, "I'll need you to help your husband with this next part."

"Of course, Nǎinai," Marcus said dutifully.

"Xiǎoyīng bǎobèi," yeah, everyone in my family knew Nǎinai favoured me, but it didn't bother anyone. She was fierce in the protection of her beautiful little flower. So, my parents were glad to just be there to enjoy raising me with her, "My yíchǎn (遺產/legacy)." She gestured to the books and silk box on the trolley.

"I always told your parents you had more important things to do than pop out babies and marry a girl," she looked at me with pride on her face. Like the day she had first begun teaching me to paint those red packets.

"Well, kids aren't off the table yet," Marcus piped in, looking to me. Of course, I'd love to raise a wee Marcus, girl, boy, in between, whatever fate decided, or we could adopt. I grinned at him. Maman and Bàba looked like they were bursting with excitement over this proclamation. They'd written off grandkids upon Nǎinai revealing my sexuality to them. Nǎinai gave Marcus a long look. She put her hand on his and held it without saying a word.

"Marcus, my boy, if you would be so good as to help my Xiǎoyīng Bǎobèi take these with you to your home?"

"Sure thing, Nǎinai," he complied readily. He'd been trained early in the mysteries of my Nǎinai.

"But Nǎinai, what's this about?" My Maman asked.

"Yes, well, I will be too busy, you see," she gestured again to the waiter, his name was Hung, who looked uncertain, "Just humour an old woman, young man," she said quietly, smiling up at him. He pulled her chair out for her. Nǎinai had pre-arranged a lot for this evening. This was some occasion she had been planning.
The waiter sat on her chair then gently lifted her into his lap. He looked a little nervous. The restaurant had a lull of quietude over it. The conversation had stopped as if nature has asked for quiet as a monumental moment was about to happen.

Nǎinai sat happily on the waiter's lap. She took his arms and wrapped them around her. Geez, she was a naughty old witch sometimes.

"Nǎinai," I scoffed. I loved Nǎinai, but this was going a bit far. The boy, Hung, cut me off by putting up his hand.

"It's ok," he said. He hugged my Nǎinai tightly all of a sudden, "Thank you for everything!" The waiter looked both sad and grateful all at once. My Nǎinai's red envelopes had the most profound effects on people. This was a classic example of how grateful people were to her.

"Not many people get to go doing the thing they loved," she looked at everyone at the table, "and you all know I loved my men more than anything, at least until my Xiǎoyīng bǎobèi came." It was true. There were still stories about Nǎinai's voracious appetite for men in her time and how she'd caused many a wife to worry. But I also suspected she was giving us one of her double meanings. Because I didn't miss the red envelope that Hung had, nor the blatant look of gratitude on his handsome face. She loved helping people.

"To go…?" I felt my stomach drop.

"Boy!" She said sternly, "You know it has to happen. Remember what you have to do," she waved at the gifts on the food trolley, "Hung, you have such nice arms. Thank you for giving an old woman a cheap thrill before heading away." My parents looked slightly annoyed, my Bàba particularly.

"Ma Ma, please don't joke around -"

"Death is not a joke, my son." She closed her eyes while Hung started humming what seemed like a nonsensical tune at first, but then I realized it was an old Chinese lullaby she used to sing to me. Hung was rocking side to side with my Nǎinai, smiling contently. Whatever her red envelope was for him, it must have been a doozy!

And that's how my Nǎinai went on her own terms. Held by a cute boy who was kind enough to humour her, surrounded by her loved ones. She went grinning like a pumpkin. By the time the paramedics had arrived, she was already gone.

I had gone hysterical at that point, and Marcus had held me so tight while I flailed around so I wouldn't hurt myself. My Maman cried into Bàba's shoulder. At the same time, Bàba stood resolute, holding back the tears until he could acknowledge his legend of our Nǎinai was gone.

***

Part Two
Chapter 30: The Witch Doctor (Sunday)

The doctor touched my back lightly while I stood spread eagle for him. He opened up and examined the whole area as best he could. There was a series of hm's and ha's.

"All right, Li," He knew my name, "pants up. And yes, I know your name. Obviously not your 'name' per se." I shuffled back into my briefs and jeans and did up my buckle.

"Have a seat," I did. I was so scared. What had the Witch Doctor found? "I need to ask you some questions, and you need to answer them honestly, ok? This could be a serious matter for you." I knew it. I knew it. Aya had given me something. So used to it now, I let the tears roll down my cheeks.

"Ok." I agreed.

"Now: Have you been having unprotected sex with any of the Fae? These can be creatures like me that are," he looked a little embarrassed at saying it, "to you unearthly and beautiful?"

"Yes," I said simply.

"I see. Now I see you have a strong 'sight.' How is it now?"

"Um…it seems a lot more under control, but I can see more details than before."

"And your other senses, anything new?"

"I can hear and smell things better."

He grabbed a tissue from a box he had handy and dabbed my cheeks. Then handed it to me. I sniffed and tried to daintily blow my nose and failed.

"I see. Now Li, you don't need to worry," I looked up from my tissue at this lighthouse in my storm of momentary misery.

"Really?"

"Yes. What has happened to you is exceedingly rare, but it's not permanent."

"What is it? I'm scared, doctor… Dr. John," I sniffed again noisily, "My friend patience, her sister has something like this all over her, and she's dying of cancer and my late…" More tears. He waved my comments off.

"I mean it—nothing to worry about. Let me explain. For humans generally, there is no pathogenic risk with unprotected sex with the Fae. That's why so many of them do it, it is basically risk-free, and of course, humans love it." He smiled to himself. I had the suspicion he had his own personal experiences to go by.
"That's what he said." I sniffed, remembering his words. So convincing, but according to the doc, Aya was in the clear.

"And he was right, under most circumstances. But you are not just a normal human, are you Li?" He asked.

"Neelas, the bar lady says I'm a mimic. I'm not sure what that is."

"It's a gross oversimplification of a complicated genetic anomaly. Mimics are rare for a reason. They tend to not survive past the manifestation of their abilities." I remembered my Nǎinai always making sure she waved incense over me before and after entering the house. She said it was cleaning out things that cling.

"A mimic is more of a conduit condition. You can copy different energies, yes, but there is a time when the copying becomes more assimilated to your energy body."

"When is that?"

"When you agree for it to," I considered this.

"So, he wouldn't have known it would happen?"

"Hmm, unlikely. Not much is known about mimics, but even if he did know, he probably thought it would subside, as I've told you. It's like a sunburn. It will go away."

"Wow! Thank you!" I held his gloved hands in mine, "Thank you!"

"My pleasure. I need to ask Li," he went over and sat down at his desk. "I'm just taking some notes. This question is important," he scratched into a notebook, "exactly how many times did your Fae partner and you have unprotected sex. It will determine how much time it will take for it to subside."

"Oh," memories of heat, scents, grunts, and groans of pleasure shot through my mind, "um…a lot?"

"OK, an approximate number? Also, when did the relationship start?"

"Sunday week it started," I started counting the number of times. The doctor watched my counting on my hand. His eyes went wide as I kept counting, "maybe 23, 24 times? There was a lot."

"Li, what kind of Fae is this? That's a lot. Fae generally doesn't enjoy the company of humans more than a few times. It's due to their long lifespans. They are a little ADHD with sex and relationships and move onto partners frequently." Hearing this detail jabbed at my insecurities some. Perhaps I was just some fad that Aya was entertaining until he got bored.

"Um, he's a fox, a Zenko he said." The doctor paused with his pen and frowned a little, then nodded. And scratched some more notes. "Ok, Li, my friend. That ends the appointment. Your condition should wear off as long as you abstain from contact with any more Fae for two months." Two months?! WTF? It might not be as impossible as I initially surmised. Aya hadn't even returned my calls. Maybe he was an ADHD Fae like the doctor said. All fast and furious then gone.

"Thank you, doctor. Thank you. I appreciate it." He had allayed my fears a great deal. And for that, I was extremely grateful.

"Like I said, my pleasure. Don't worry about your bill - it's all settled. In fact, if you need anything in the future, just make another appointment."

"Sure thing, doc." I was feeling a little lighter as I stood up to leave.

"Two months Li," he waved his pen at me, "Do it, and you'll be fine, no permanent damage done. Just close the door on your way out. Stay safe, Li!"

I did as he asked. I was in a bit of a cloud of thought when I re-entered the waiting room with its strange incense and spice smells. The clientele had changed since I'd been in with Dr. John. The space was empty except for two men seated on one of the couches near the far wall. One was dressed smartly in a lovely, tailored suit. He filled it out well. Slim, but not skinny. Underneath that suit whispered some kind of predatory strength. He looked directly at me as I exited the office, and recognition dawned. I saw his jaw clench. His companion was dressed in a white hoodie and white jeans and white shoes, tapping his foot furiously on the floor, which put me in the mind of an addict tweaking. He looked exactly like the other.

Identical twins. They were the pair from Crossroads the first night I entered. He had been staring then. His twin saw me and was about to get up, but his darker counterpart put a hand on his brother's white jeans, holding him down and pushing his chest against the back of the chair at the same time. The white-clothed twin grunted in annoyance. My initial thoughts were that their faces were Romanian: pale skin, prominent nose, wide jaw, and high cheekbones. Though they did possess these silvery grey eyes that somehow flickered to blue with the light. But they were both staring at me as I left. Shivers ran up and down my spine. And I wished my boyfriend (maybe my ex-boyfriend) or my best friend were with me more than anything.

***

Chapter 31: The Sunday Confessional (Sunday)

The ride home in the Uber was uneventful. Thankfully, the driver accepted my silence as permission to listen to his classical music on his stereo. I felt miserable. How could things have changed from heavenly to hellish so quickly? Well, at least my veiny mass growing up my spine would go away, provided no more Fae sex with Aya, or anyone for that matter. I didn't want anyone anyway (big fat liar!).

Dialling the number for my local Chinese takeout, I ordered just a few dishes. Noodles and vegetables, pork wonton soup, and some fried rice for later. Another shower, and I would be ready to settle into my misery alone tonight.

There was a knock at my door, sounding tentative. It couldn't be Baraz. His family had gone out for the evening for dinner, having sent me an invite, but I had to decline as I was at the *Doctor's* office. That elicited a barrage of concerned texts from both Baraz and his mother. Baraz's father sent a text later apologizing for his nosy family. It was exactly what I needed.

Then who was at my door?

I went and looked through the peephole and almost ripped the door off its hinges when I saw who it was.

"Patience! Where the fuck have you been?!" She still had that smacked puppy look but came in quietly. I almost hugged her, but she waved me off with a half-smile.

"We need to talk, Bub." She said, sitting on the couch, not looking at me.

"Ok, but I've been so worried about you, what's been-" she held up a hand

"Actually, I need to talk." She was seriously struggling with something. I had never seen her like this ever.

"Li, I am so sorry. I am so sorry," she broke, like a damn, and started balling into her hands. I rubbed her back, and hopefully, it felt comforting through her giant pink fluffy wool sweater.

What the fuck was she wearing? These were clothes we'd wear at a slumber party we'd occasionally have at her apartment. Where we'd binge on horror movies and laugh at all the dumb mistakes the characters would make, resulting in their demise. At least her purse matched.

I grabbed the tissues, and she grabbed a handful, doing a re-enactment of my recent ugly crying. I brought over a waist bin and sat it next to her. It was going to be needed, I could tell.

"Li," she sobbed, "my dear Li," never had I ever heard her voice so defeated, "I did something awful."

"Oh, Patience, of course, you have, but nothing that warrants this drama, you know we can fix anything –"

"No, this is unforgivable."

"I'll help you hide the body, Patience, I promise! Just tell me!" my voice was rising in anger, I could tell, and I was getting silly and hysterical. I breathed deep.

"Something terrible to you!" She looked at me, her puffy face and red eyes wet with tears.

"No, you haven't. I'm ok, Patience. Whatever it is, we'll fix it. I don't care what you've done. I love you, and that won't change –"

"Don't say that!" She snapped almost viciously, but the anger wasn't directed at me. Still, at something else, "I almost, I was going to…" her sobs took over.

"What patience?!"

"Killed you!"

Silence as she looked at me, eyes wide. Seeing my confusion. I smirked. She had me on. Of course, she was. She didn't seem to be joining my smirk.

"The gunman?" I asked in a whisper.

"No, not that. I'm pretty sure that was for me." Maybe Todd's theory about midget mafia was correct. Shut up, brain, let her finish!

"Why, though, why would someone try to kill you?"

"Probably because I tried to kill you." She repeated it. It sounded weird. Not like the jokes we usually played on each other. They were words that weren't making sense even though the language and structure were acceptable. They seemed to be….not part of my reality, of my Patience.

"No…" I said, offering a strained smile and shaking my head, waiting for the punchline she'd deliver to make everything better.

"Yes… but Hope…" I remembered Hope bursting in like an avenging bald angel. Then the full-bodied slap she had delivered to Patience so strong it had cut her lip, "Hope stopped everything."

"How? What the fuck? You're not making sense, Patience." The girl was making less and less sense.

"Shut up and listen. You're special, Li. Unlike anyone on earth, I think. You do this thing that is so rare that it's kind of coveted for various reasons."

"You mean my weirdness."
"Yes, but the deeper weirdness, they call it 'Mimicry.'" Ha. There it was again—stupid latent talent. Good for nothing power.

"Oh," this I had heard so many times lately. I was special. Yeah, unique like the 'short bus' kind more like it. At least that's how I felt at the moment.

"You're able to take on other energy like no other being and not just copy them." Patience blew her nose and disposed of another tissue. "I wasn't sure at first, but then I tested it, and it was true." Tested it? Patience was not some kind of witch. She was just a bitch! Who was not making any sense right now!

A flashback of the scanner losing its life along with the unexplained power surge in the office…

"That was you with the scanner? You're like a Fae or something?"

"No, nothing like that, but my family has something that has followed us through the generations."

She stared at the wall opposite her, not really looking at anything but recalling details.

"I saw my grandparents, my parents, aunties, and uncles all waste away into death. Not dignified old age death, but the embarrassing messy death of disease."

"I know, I'm sorry, Patience," I tried to sidle closer to her and put my arm over her shoulders.

"Don't touch me, Li," she whispered, not angrily, just an instruction. "Haven't you thought about why we have never touched? Best friends? I pretend like I do not do 'touch-feely,' so I won't touch you, Li."

"Oh ok," a weird statement that had layers to it, "That's ok, Patience, I'm ok about that. You're my ride or die." She scoffed at hearing that.

"Or die? Li, we've been friends for years, right?"

"Yeah, you're family to me, not just my friend." She flinched back at these words.

"My family was cursed. Many years ago. We did something horrible, at least my great-grandparents did. Apparently, it was to get them a leg up, financially, I dunno." She shook her head in disbelief. "It just seems like only a silly story until you see it happening to everyone around you."

"A curse!"

"Yes, Li, a curse. A real live magical curse. It runs through our genes like some kind of sick death stalker."

"I don't know much about curses, Patience, but Năinai told me they didn't last that long. Only mighty beings can make curses like that."

"Yeah. Beings. Vengeful beings. But I found a cure for it, Li. Hope is dying, and she will be gone soon. I've seen it happen often enough. And I knew that while being your friend, I might see or hear something to help. I even tried to ask your Năinai about it, but I know she pretended not to understand my broken Mandarin."

"That's great, so Hope's gonna be ok?"

"No-Li, Hope is going to die, as am I, as is Dereck, even though he's not blood, it seems to touch the family like that. Even the girls, Faith and Charity. The whole family will die off."

"It's cancer, Patience," I said quietly, "it's a curse, yes, but it's cancer, something that happens to even the nicest people." She knew I was talking about our Marcus.

"It parades around as cancer or some other wasting illness, but the results are always the same," she wiped her eyes. The tears had stopped. "Death."

"But you said you found a cure for this apparent curse. Why haven't you used it?"

"I was going to Li, I really was," she was quiet again, her voice a hissing whisper, "I was ready to. I had it right there. I was seeing

Hope dying, and my nieces, those precious girls," She was reliving something in her head.

"I got a potion from Neelas. A potion of transference, she's gonna fucking hate me too!" My whole body suddenly went cold as my subconscious started assembling a puzzle that had been occurring all around me.

"You were going to put the curse on someone else….. me?" She nodded, "That's not possible. The energy I can only copy but not take it on. I saw a doctor today that told me all about it."

"A doctor?"

"Yeah, he was cute too," I said, almost forgetting the nature of our conversation.

"They are, aren't they, Li? Like angels, their faces can make you do anything." Yeah, beautiful, like your wildest fantasy…

"The doc said that the only way energy can set up shop in my energy body or whatever is for me to have some kind of agreement with it." I was trying to remember his exact words, "It's something to do with permission or intimacy." A pang of heartache as I thought of the black veins and no contact with the creature that was fast being considered as an ex.

"I know Li." She said. She reached into her purse and threw a pill bottle and a small empty potion bottle like the one Neelas had given me.
"What's this?"

"The reason you're gonna hate me, Li. The reason you should hate me. I even fucking hate me." I picked up the pill bottle. It had no label, so I opened it, and two pills fell into my palm, one blue, the other looked like a smooth aspirin. I recognized one of them. That ice filling my stomach spread as I was guessing what the other pill was.

"Viagra and Rohypnol?" I asked. She nodded slowly. Still staring at the wall. The details of that evening came back. I was numb.

"Hope knew, she knew, Li," she shook her head, "your Năinai told her everything." She laughed the empty laugh of someone who had nothing left to take or give.

"She saved both our lives that night, Li," I remembered the bullet. It would have hit Patience in her heart if I had my guess. The shot for a sniper wasn't a tough one. Across the street, a clear shot. Hope had pulled her to the side to avoid the bullet, which had hit me instead. I still had it in my draw in the bathroom. Hope had first grabbed my glass and tossed it behind Patience onto her car below.

"You saw the photos didn't you, Li? From the detectives?" I had. Putting together the events, the forensics had a pretty accurate account of what had happened then.

"I did."

"You know that only your Năinai could have that kind of predictive and manipulative capacity." She was right, right down to the stem of the champagne flute. Holy shit!

"You….were going to drug me, rape me, then give me cancer?" I said dumbly.

"I'm sorry Li, it's fucked up, I know, but I couldn't lose Hope or the girls –"

"Stop!" I shouted, "Just stop talking." I couldn't fathom it—another information overload. My best friend admitted to planning to rape and murder me! Her best friend! I was shaking like a leaf. My adrenaline filling me. I had to get away from this woman, get away from everything I thought was mine!

Everywhere I looked, I saw betrayal even in my damn kitchen where Aya and I had made love on the counter and then devoured piles of pizzas. Where was Aya now! Now that I needed the goddamned creature! It's probably like the doc said. Bored now. Moved on.

And now, the woman whom I had trusted. I had let into my life more than anyone other than Marcus, who had plotted to rape and murder me. It was like a bizarre telenovela, but I was the butt of every one of the victim roles! Within me, a seal was breaking—that darkness. I ran my finger over the scar on my left wrist. I remembered Patience as I was fading in and out of consciousness, making an effort to rescue me, save my life…. So, she could what? Do all this? I snarled!
Without a word, I got up and left my apartment, not even taking my phone, wallet, or keys. I didn't fucking care!

"Li, wait!" yelled Patience. Patience. The woman who was there when Marcus went. Who held me, had she? She had, but when I thought about it, there was always cloth between us. A sleeve, a glove, a jacket. She was right. We had never touched…until that day at Below Ground.

Of course, I didn't wait. The lift opened as soon as I approached it. I got in and stared at Patience with the most venomous look I could muster as the door closed, and I pushed "L" for the lobby. Fuck off, Patience, you traitorous filthy harpy. I stalked out of the elevator. My hate building within me, along with that dark cloud of feeling that was usually held in check by medication and the careful support of my friends and family. Was. Oh yeah. This was a comfortable feeling. Alone, hating the world. I've been here before.

As I walked as purposefully as I could to the large glass entryway door, I heard the sound of a bang behind me. I turned and saw Patience at the entryway to the stairwell panting. Bent over, her purse in hand. She looked absurd with her oversized fluffy pink sweater, activewear tights, and running shoes.

"Li! Wait!"

Wait for what Bitch? More lies. More reasons to hate you and the world? No thanks. I kept walking and exited my building. I didn't know where I was going. Maybe to Crossroads, at least she couldn't follow me there. But then what if I ran into Aya, and he was with his new freshly "tracked" target. Fuck him too. Ok, I was irrational. There could be a reasonable explanation for the Zenko to have gone off the grid for three days. Wait, it was only three days? Seemed like forever.

"Wait!" I heard the desperate panting of Patience behind me. Change your tune bitch! I hoped she had a heart attack running. Unlikely…. and a part of me whispered. Also, untrue. A portion of me wanted to believe we were still best friends. Taking the piss out of everything and everyone. Going to work at a job where we were both at the top of our game. So much so that we could slack off half the time…No! Rape. Murder! Fuck That!

Hope and the Girls…she'd said. Yeah. Hope and the girls. The one thing in this whole nightmare that deserved better. How did she even know that sex would result in a transfer of, oh god, it made me sick. Everyone was using me, my body! Fuck, who cares!

The night closed around me with its night-time noises. I could hear Patience still behind me. I glanced briefly behind me. Yup, the fluffy pink box was still following me, trying to catch up.

"Li…" she huffed, out of breath, "There's more," what more could there be?

"The people who tried to kill me…." I didn't want to hear anymore.

I spun around and watched her approach me, just so I could say, "Fuck off Patience. It's over! You killed it! At least you managed to murder something this week. Cross that off your bucket list."

She stomped toward me, her purse floppy around like an annoying pink appendage.

"They were trying to kill me because they knew what I was going to do to you!"

"I'm sorry 'they' didn't succeed." More venom. I could barely see through the tears. *Argh*. I hated myself sometimes. Trying to act all tough and mad, and tears came as usual at the worst time.

"I know, but this isn't about what I did. Those people. They're dangerous."

"How could they be more dangerous to me than you!" I screamed. I wanted that to sink in.

I was so busy yelling at the filthy witch I hadn't noticed the two Cadillac Escalades that had pulled up right next to us. Their shiny expensive bodies lining up one behind the other neatly next to the sidewalk. Ok, in any movie, we all knew when we saw this, we'd run. Yeah? Well, Patience and I looked at each other, and we did just that as the car doors slammed behind us. The streets around us were residential, but the back lot of shops lead onto Davie Street ahead with a narrow alley onto the main road…. and a crowd.

"There," I said. Ok, so I hated Patience, but I wanted to finish our fight good and hard, so it'd never revive itself ever. And to do that, we'd have to avoid whatever new menace had decided to enter my life.

We got to the lot, and one after another, suited men and women appeared all around us. Patience kept running past me until I grabbed her sleeve.

"What?" I waved towards the suits encircling us, "What are you doing, Li?"

"Patience, these are vampires. You can't see them yet because they make humans ignore them with their 'vampiness', I think. Aya said."

"Oh," She was still peering into the dark, trying to see something that wasn't there until an invisible switch flipped in her mind, and she gasped. "Holy shit!"

She opened her purse and pulled out her pride and joy, a Sig Sauer 9 mm XL with a little sight on it for accuracy. "Lucky I brought my anti-vamp kit then." Ok, yeah, I wanted to hate the woman, but that was cool.

They stood there waiting. Then one came forward; This vampire looked vaguely familiar.

"I must insist you come with us, sir." He said, authority filling his voice. He was used to being listened to by these people and respected. Yeah, I recognized him. And I was feeling foolish and angry tonight. Why the hell would I want to do anything anyone told me. Tonight, I really felt like destroying the world, not coming quietly with a vampire.

"Well… Sir," I said sarcastically, "I seem to remember mashing a Boston Cream in your face last time, which should give you an idea of what I'm gonna say next: Go Fuck yourself! I'm busy eliminating one parasite, and I don't have time for a pile of new ones in my life."

Patience smirked, and much to this vamp's chagrin, so did some of his colleagues. He gave them a look akin to the one I had given Patience earlier.

"Sir, time is of the essence. You must come with us. We aren't here to hurt you."

"So, surrounding me in a parking lot in the middle of the night with your," I counted, "six fucktards is what…?"

"You have been very hard to get in touch with," He said as if that would convince me to come with him, "and as I said, time is of the –"

"- Time is of the - I've got a newsflash for you. Time is always of the essence for us mere mortals! So, as I said, fuck right off, all the way off!"

I wondered if I'd get my throat ripped out. Let's be honest. All the words were just false bravado. I was scared, but I was also pissed off, so the two feelings were fighting for dominance. The Escalades pulled into the lot. The drivers stayed in the cars with the engines still running.
The vamp with the mouth and words stepped suddenly next to me so fast I hadn't even blinked. He grabbed my arm in a vice grip: "I'm insisting!"

A metallic click and a tiny pink woman came into view, holding a gun high aimed at the vamp's face. Her stance was steady, not shaking at all. She'd loved her guns for longer than I can remember.

"I don't know what or who you are," her eyes were locked onto him, her hands steady, "but I do know that if I fill your head with enough holes, you'll cease being a problem, now let him go!"

Ok. So, this guy's voice had spoken of authority. Still, he'd never heard Patience wrangle the entire Art and Visuals department on a strapped deadline with military precision. The vamp flinched but didn't let go. My estimation of Patience's ability to intimidate went up a few notches. She made an evil blood-sucking dick head cringe.

The vamp tried to pull me away with such strength I could barely resist. Then his head snapped back, once, twice, and a third time, as the shots echoed around us. His grip slackened. I grabbed her sleeve again and made the run. Then they closed in on us.

***

Chapter 32: With a Little Patience (Sunday)

They moved so fast, too fast to track with your eyes. In less than a second, there were six of these things around us, then on us in varying capacities. One seized Patience's wrist, the one with the gun, and pulled. There was a sharp crack, and Patience's scream pierced through the night. She had dropped her weapon. A guy vamp had picked up her tiny body with one hand and tossed her against a cement block wall. I wasn't sure if the trash bags underneath her actually cushioned a fall.

My heart sunk. Was Patience ok? Like they had planned it all, three vampires had the passenger sides of both vehicles open, facing me, ready to receive guests. They seemed to be ignoring Patience now and advancing on me with some trepidation. Maybe they didn't know what or how much power I had been given. The one that Patience had downed twitched on the ground next to me, and two vamps appeared next to him, took him, and loaded him into one of the cars. That car drove away; I guessed they assumed that three vamps could handle Xiǎoyīng.

The three remaining vamps faced me.

"Come on, guys, we've wasted enough time. It's time to go," said one of the vamps, a fresh-faced looking Japanese woman (by fresh-faced, I mean, pale like death and smooth like marble). She would have been pretty if not for the fact that she was a killer leech in a human shape.

That really pissed me off. They had tossed my filthy murderous rapey ex-best friend around like she was nothing but a bag of shit. For some reason, I couldn't let that just stand.

"Come on, Mr. Li, we aren't here to hurt you." One of them said.

"Tell that to Patience!" They, in unison, looked at her.

"Collateral damage, we're sorry, but we are strapped for time," another chimed in.

While they were looking at Patience, I leaped to her prone form. They realized I had nowhere to go, so they just appeared standing there. And then I realized….

"You're not allowed to hurt me, are you? Or touch me?" That got them.

"We have ways, but we'd rather not use such force." Gosh, these dicks were really something. So arrogant.

I leaned down to Patience.

"Patience? Are you ok?" I heard a whispered mumble, "What? I can't hear you." She mumbled again. I leaned in further.

"Take my hand, Li!" she said slightly louder. The other vamps heard.

"Get her away NOW!" One yelled. I didn't see who.

Patience grabbed my hand, and I let her. A jolt. A big one. Like touching an electric fence. It flowed up my arm. I held tight to her hand, remembering the scanner at the office. Two vamps closed in on Patience this time. One was the one that had forced her to drop her gun and had probably crushed her wrist. Another was the female vamp—the only other identifier. The third stood there watching the two. Amused.

They both put their hands on her, I didn't know what would happen, but I was only guessing the nature of what had taken hold of Patience's lineage. I grabbed the sleeve of the vamp closest just as she was about to yank Patience away from me.

I heard the tearing of fabric and then, "What the fuck!" I glanced to her enough to see her clothes tearing themselves and somehow tangling her in their folds until she looked like a bundle of bloody laundry with limbs. Well! That was some meaty curse her family had!

Another jolt from the hand I held, and I yanked on the pony of the other vamp without even bothering to look at what had happened. I only heard a wet pop and felt something wet hit my face. I stood up defiantly. Shaking. Scared. Ready to wet myself. But I wasn't gonna just sit there and take what these guys dished out. I couldn't be that person… I couldn't be… a Bella Swann!

"I'm not Bella Swann!"

Hearing the most unlikely of war cries gave the remaining vamp a slight pause, and I jumped at that one. The one standing at the passenger door was next to his compatriot in a blink. God, these assholes moved quickly. The vamp I had leaped at put his hand out to stop me, which I grabbed happily—a jolt.

And suddenly I was fast too. I was behind the vamps. I pulled one away with little effort and watched him sail into the Escalade with a metallic thud. Then whatever jolt from the vamp that I had copied went away just as quickly. I looked around. Another Escalade pulled up, and the doors opened. So unfair!

"Get her out of here now!"

The vamps waiting at the open doors of the Escalades moved too fast as I tried to intercept. But there was no speed left or vampy strength. One grabbed Patience and hefted her over his shoulder while the other, a hefty-looking vamp, veered towards me with a large body bag.

They tossed Patience into the car, which sped off. The vamp that approached me did so carefully as not to touch me. Before I knew it, two vamps were on either side of me, pinning my arms to my sides. They had pulled the body bag vertically around me like a cocoon.

Oh shit. No. Not like this! Patience!
"Patience!" I screamed, "No, you fuckers! Give her back!" the tarp body bag was being zipped up. The vamp doing the zipping looked

up at me apologetically while the two vamps on either side held me firmly in place.

"It's gonna be ok. We aren't gonna hurt you, Mr. Li." The vamp doing the zipping said as the zipper reached my neck, "Now close your eyes for a while; we will be there before…."

His words were cut off by a mouth-to-mouth kiss. I saw his eyes bulge in realization. Vamps had super speed, super strength, but not all of them were super smart, so it took him a few seconds to realize that a skinny gay Eurasian had planted a full kiss onto his lips. It took him even longer to understand what that meant.

Those seconds were all I needed. And I head-butted the motherfucker! And tore through the tarp body bag, quickly pushing the vamps on my sides away from me. They fell, obviously only expecting human-grade strength for the bagging of one Mr. Li Yīng.

I turned to run, then was spun around by a bloody nosed upset vamp who punched me in the chest. I heard a crunching sound. Felt the air leave my lungs, felt my chest explode inwards, and funnily enough, felt myself flying through the night into the same cement block wall that had caught Patience. I heard another crunch. Light flashed before my eyes, and I had trouble focusing. The pain was too much. My vision kept trying to shut off, as did my breathing.

"You idiot! He wasn't to be damaged!"

"He caught me by surprise. I just reacted!" I heard a dull thud and the grunt of pain that sounded familiar, probably from the guy I'd planted a kiss on. I looked at them, my vision swimming. My head pounding, but my legs weren't listening when I told them to move.

"I'm not Bella Swan!! You hear me!" I screamed, groggily, "I'm a fucking Hermione Granger! And where is my Ayaka! That fucker should have texted me back by now!"

"What did he say?"

"I dunno... he hit his head pretty hard. We'd better get him back. We are so screwed. He's not supposed to be damaged."

"Of that, you are absolutely correct!" A voice yelled. It was filled with menace and power. It boomed through the night and filled the air and my mind with thoughts of heat and death. Again, I tried to focus. I saw a golden glow in the distance. Saw a silhouette that seemed like someone I knew. But I was finding it difficult to stay awake. Was it an angel? A god? God...I didn't like god, so it couldn't be him.

"Shit!" I heard a vamp say. Then the whole parking lot was lit up by a brilliant orange glow, and I felt heat on my face and saw there was someone I knew. Who was it? I couldn't tell or remember. My head! I saw the three vamps who had tried to detain me turn black suddenly and then flew away like dust. I started laughing.
"Haha! Told you fuckers," I coughed. Argh. My mouth tasted gross, all tangy like blood, "I'm no Bella Swann!" My breathing wasn't working properly. I couldn't feel anything below my waist, but my chest felt backward.

"No, you are not my love. You are my Xiǎoyīng. Only mine. And I've got you." Someone was picking me up. Cradling me like a baby. I couldn't think of who. But he felt warm. And smelled like heaven and spices. I supposed going to sleep wouldn't be so bad, "Don't sleep, my love, hold on and stay awake."

Aww, I didn't want to. I felt so tired. And my head hurt and felt wet. There was someone I was worried about too. I couldn't think properly.

"Almost there, my love, stay with me," the voice sounded so kind and loving, but I didn't want to stay awake. Couldn't he tell I was tired? Why else would he be carrying me? And then I drifted.... into a nice quiet place.

***

Chapter 33: The Fox Den (Monday)

I felt a warm buzz filling my head. Like bees were buzzing around my brain. The feeling moved down to my neck, pain! Excruciating, I was sure I screamed but couldn't hear anything. Further down…. then I heard voices.

"How much longer!"

A desperate, angry voice snapped. I liked this voice, but I don't remember it being angry ever. His voice reminded me of…. something sweet, like smooth… chocolate?

"It'll take as long as it takes," a sigh, another voice I knew. Who was it? Someone young, good-looking, in a beach-surfer kinda way. Oh, he seems hot…. but not as lovely as… "I don't know how much intimacy you two had, but there's enough here to work with, trust me." Intimacy? The buzzing continued, and in some ways, it felt nice. In other places, it ached.

"I do, you know that," a sigh. I heard a seat being shifted closer to me, "It's just, I can't," then the desperate voice sounded more so. "I can't lose him, doc. He's…. You know?"

"Yes, I know. Have you told him yet?" Presumably, the doc speaking now.

"No, I can't, not yet. What if….?" What do you have to tell me?

"You should, life is short for mortals, and things can happen. They are so fragile." Down to my chest, the buzzing feeling spread, more pain, worse than before. My chest felt like it was filling up with pain. The buzzing warmth moving down further.

"Is it working?"

"Yes, now just wait!" Surfer beach bum said.

"You came as soon as I called and didn't even quote. John? You always quote beforehand."

"Yes, I did, and no, I didn't." The Doc said.

"But you must. There must be balance."

"This little one has had someone shift the balance enough that I have to do this."

"I see."

"Go outside. You're distracting me. I'm a doctor, not a marriage counsellor, even if you are my friend."

The chair next to me moved and suddenly. I felt the absence of something fundamental to me, "Now Li, I know you can hear me in there," this man knew my name, "I have done all I can, but now, you have to do the rest. Wake up for yourself."

I heard the snap of latex gloves, then I felt one laid across my forehead and felt the press of lips against my head through the latex, "You can do this, and that kiss is from your Nǎinai."

My Nǎinai? Where was she? Oh yes, Nǎinai. She'd know what to do…. But she was gone… So much was gone. Was there anything to come back to? Maybe. And I guess a "maybe" could be enough for now.

***

I opened my eyes. This wasn't home. I sniffed. It smelled good, like a spicy cologne…. I tried to move, and a large hand gently pushed me down.

"Not yet. You're still weak, Li. Stay still." I looked over to the voice. It was a handsome man, sun-bleached hair and a tan that spoke of surfing as often as one could during summer. He was attractive, but I felt disappointed. I had wanted to see someone else. But whom?

"What happened?" I vaguely remember having a terrible dream of monsters. Patience being stolen away by them. Oh yes, Patience. Patience, My friend Patience….

As I clung to that thought, pieces started to come together. Slowly at first, then all at once. The vampires. Me running my stupid mouth. Getting thrown. Crunch! Patience. Betrayal. Oh god, that hurt. Almost as much as losing Marcus. Was it true? Yes. She had admitted to everything.

A face appeared over me. I must have been lying on a bed. A comfortable bed. The face was heaven incarnate. A smile that would melt the wings off angels and make them give up their chastity just for a kiss of those perfect lips.

"Aya?"

"Yes, love." He replied. His eyes searching all over me, "Doc?" I felt a teardrop fall from one of his amber eyes onto my cheek.

"His memory is coming back slowly. It's typical of the kinds of injuries he sustained. Mortals don't survive what he went through." Mortals? Survive?

"Aya, where were you?" I started to cry. Like a baby, but I let the tears come, "I called and messaged? Where were you?"

"Love, I'm here now. I'm so sorry."

"But where were you?" I pleaded.

"We can discuss that when you are better, love. Just lie still."

"No, he can sit up now. That area is ok now." The Zenko lifted me gingerly and laid pillows behind me.

"Zenko, go get him some water." The doc's command sounded almost like he was telling Aya off. Aya went off to somewhere I couldn't see, presumably to get water. At the mention of water, I realized that I was horrendously thirsty.

"Li, I need to ask you some questions. And as before, you must be honest if I am to help you."

"Ok… sure," I said, trying to take in my environment. I was in some kind of alcove where the bed was set up… it looked like a basement that had been remodelled into a small apartment. It was actually well done. Functional and open. Painted white like my apartment. The beams overhead had been painted to blend with the walls as much as possible. On the beams were the occasional bonsai tree—really detailed remarkable specimens If I was any judge.

"Li, did you and Aya share names?"

"Y-yes, we did. It was something we did early on. I'm not sure of the meaning to you guys, but it apparently means a lot."

"That it does," he nodded, "Anyone can say your name, and it won't do or mean anything unless it's given. In our world, ceremonies, even small ones like that, have meaning that can cause changes that you might not understand."

"What do you mean?" I was tired. My eyes wanted to close, but I wanted this information, I needed it, "We shared names, and then when we said them. There's a weird feeling, like a tug on myself…except inside." He nodded again.

"Li, listen to me very carefully. Don't give your name like that to anyone else. It's dangerous."

"Ok, sure," he didn't look convinced by my response, "No, I'm serious, I won't. This whole thing has been a nightmare, and I'm not even sure I want any part of it anymore." Doc nodded again.

"One more thing. As your doctor, I have to give you advice that is for your overall wellbeing." I was listening. "Once the Zenko energy leaves your body in a few months, take an Eraser potion. It'll wipe out your abilities. There's a reason why mimics are rare. It's because they often get used for rituals that end up with them either dead or so empty, they go mad." I nodded, taking it in, "Because if you have any more energy like that put into you, it could cause permanent damage." I nodded again.

"Doc? Thank you," his smile was warm.

"You're most welcome."

"Oh wait, I have a question."

"Yes, Li?"

"Why do vampires just kind of stand around when they are trying to capture something or someone?"

"Ah, good question, Li. Vampires are hunters. They are gifted with speed, strength, and durability. With the blood they consume, they can heal almost any wound. It's quite remarkable," he considered my question some more. "Vampires also can glamour the area around them. It's to make humans forget they're there, or part of the natural surroundings, or even part of a conversation they're having, among other things. It's one of their 'go-to 'skills. They use it constantly, almost unconsciously, and when they meet an individual such as yourself, it confuses them slightly. So, their once certain and powerful actions become clumsy. If not for that, I fear you'd be dead today, even if they'd wanted to keep you alive. They live on the edge of instinct and sanity, which can lead to massacres on occasion," he looked like he wanted to say something else and was unsure.

Still, in the end, he said something odd, "Li? What do you know of Foxes? As an animal?"

"Um… admittedly not much."

"Aya is closer to his nature than you may realize. Just remember that in the days to come. It could be the difference between the taking of one of two paths for you."

"I see. Thank you, doc." He smiled down at me again.

He got up, "Right back to the office for me. Li, consider what I said." Again, I nodded as Aya came in with a large glass of water.

"Thank you, Dr. John. I really appreciate it. Coming on short notice and everything."

"You know I didn't do it for you. I did it because it was the right thing to do and because he needed me." He went to go, then looked at Aya directly as if communicating something important, "I will leave you two to talk. Stay well, Li, and Aya stay outta trouble."

I couldn't see where he exited from my view in the bed, but I heard a door close. At that point, Aya had blinked to my side and was holding my hand. With one of his, then pushing the glass of water to my lips, I drank with his aid. Then he placed it on the bedside cabinet.

"Li! My Xiǎoyīng, I'm sorry I wasn't there," he looked genuinely mortified.

"Where were you, Aya? You have no idea how much I needed you there, things happened, and I know we haven't known each other that long…but I thought…maybe…."

"I know, I know. I can't… tell you just yet. But everything is going to be ok."

I took the opportunity to look at myself. I was naked except for my boxer briefs lying on a bed. Ok, this was happening way too often with strange hot men. My whole body, legs, feet, stomach, and arms had giant bruises all over them. I ached all over when I saw them and let out a cry in pain.

"Don't move just yet, the Doc does good work, but it takes a little time."

"What happened? Where's Patience? I need to call Patience. They got her, Aya! They got Patience!" I tried to get up to do what I wasn't sure about. But Patience was in trouble… should I even care? Well, apparently, a part of me still did.

"Here," he handed me one of those cheap prepaid burner-type phones, "Call her now if it'll stop you from wiggling."

"You don't know…they took her," I must have looked panicked because he unwrapped the phone package and set it up to work straight away and passed it to me. I tried to hold the phone, even my fingers were bruised, and I couldn't move the flip mechanism of the phone (old school cellphones, I missed them).

"Give me the number, love." I did, and he dialled it and then handed me the phone. I heard the call tone, and then someone answered.

"He- Hello?"

"Patience!?" It was Patience's voice. I felt relief. It flooded through me, then was quickly followed by disappointment, not in her safety but in her betrayal.

"Yes, it's me, Li. Where are you? Are you ok?"

"Scrap that, are you ok? Tell me now." I countered.

"Yes. It was the weirdest thing. Once they had me, they asked me where I was staying. Then said it wasn't me they were interested in and that they weren't trying to hurt you. I told them to get fucked, and then they just said that I wasn't of consequence. I don…"

"Yeah. They wanted me for something. I don't know what. But you're, ok?"

"Yes, Li," she sounded relieved too, so happy to hear my voice, I guess, but I didn't want to give her the wrong impression, "I'm with Hope and the Kids. Dereck is working. But I'm ok."

"Good," I snapped the phone shut. And threw it to the end of the bed.

"Is she ok? I need to know what happened, Xiǎoyīng."
"She's fine. But a lot has happened, Aya. It's a mess." More tears. His gentle arms wrapped around my bruised body, so careful not to move me too much or touch a particularly injured area. But he held me.

"What's been happening, Love?" I sniffed as I usually did in my ugly crying sessions, and Aya passed me a box of tissues.

"I need a mirror Aya. A long one."

"Oh," he said," I think I know what this is about." He went away for a moment and came back with a full-length mirror facing me on the bed. I turned as much as I could without too much discomfort and saw still the veiny stretch up my spine. It wasn't black, though, but almost looked like a suntan mark, but darker. But it was still there.

"It's going away," I said, relief flooding through me, "Aya, you made something happen to me, and I was so scared, and you vanished, not cool!" I touched the area. He replaced the mirror to its home. Then came back.

"Yes, it'll go away a lot sooner, thanks to the doc. He used the residual energy from me to heal your body. You were in terrible shape, Li. I was scared too," He looked down at his hands as he settled into the chair next to the bed, "I couldn't do anything to fix you. Your body was so broken! And like a straw doll, all…flimsy." He looked miserable at the prospect of not being able to do something to help.

"How bad was it?"

"Um… I don't know if you really wanna know Li. It was terrible. I don't even like thinking about it." First, a little memory of the crunching of bones, and then I was flying through the air, then more crunching and pain everywhere.

"Ok, but, um…you aren't like, bored of me?" Yeah, my priorities were screwed. But apparently, I had had significant head trauma, so that's my excuse.

"What?! What's that got to do with anything? Of course not!" he looked up at me, smiling and putting his hand on my forehead. His hand was warm and comforting, "That's what you were worried about?"

"Well, my priorities are different from everyone else. Mortal peril is on like… sixth on the list," I made the admission as Aya chuckled, shaking his head in bewilderment.

"The doc says it will clear up on my back in two months. But I should… you know… not… be with you anymore for a while because it might cause permanent damage. Did you know?"

"No, Xiǎoyīng. I told the truth; I had no idea my energy was dangerous for you like that. I'm so sorry." He buried his face in his hands, his long hair hanging down, hiding him away from me, "I never want to hurt you, Xiǎoyīng. Never!"
"Ok, Aya." I put my hand against his head, trying to stroke his silken hair. But didn't really succeed as everything about my body still didn't work properly.

"Oh my Xiǎoyīng, I'm sorry. I didn't know. I thought it was just like with other humans, and my energy would just dissipate after a while." He looked at me. His beautiful amber eyes running tears freely down his cheeks.

"In that case. Everything is ok."

"What about Patience?" Aya asked. He'd really taken to Patience's brazen nature and found her fun, unfortunately.

"I'll explain later, Aya." I closed my eyes, feeling so tired. My mind began to drift blissfully into a pain-free place… sleep, blessed sleep.

Yes, that would be a good idea. Aya replaced one hand on my head and the other over my heart. As it was meant to be.

***

When I opened my eyes again, my Zenko guardian was waiting, hovering over me. Grinning with delight.

"Li Xiǎoyīng!" He pulled me to him and hugged me hard. I was expecting the pain of all the bruising I had seen earlier, "Only two hours! That doctor is enormously talented!"

"Huh?" I said dumbly. He let me go and went to retrieve the mirror again. No bruising. Wow. I had slept for two hours, and this was what I woke up to. Awesome.

"My beautiful Xiǎoyīng is back!" He leaped into bed with me, kissing me so hard all over….. he began to abandon his clothes and pull down my briefs…. And then stopped. And recovered himself.

"Oh, Xiǎoyīng. My beautiful and heroic boy. I'm sorry." He climbed off, taking that taste-filled fire from my mouth and my body. Both our erections standing to attention, nasty reminders of our frustration.

"It's ok, Aya. It's ok." We both almost forgot. We were so used to jumping each other. It had become a natural part of 'Us' as a unit. Doc's words came to me, "*Aya is close to his nature,*" I breathed in deep. Calming my hormones and blood rush. He appeared to do the same.

"We'll figure it out." He said reassuringly.

"Yeah," We could just use condoms, which was fine. But the fire came even when we touched. Although….

"Aya…?"

"Yes, my love."

"When my back is all cleared up, I'll take the Eraser potion. Then we can be together, like properly as a couple?"

"You'd do that for me?" He said, saying it like I was giving up something important. I wasn't, not compared to what I wanted with him. What I was hoping to have with him…

"In a heartbeat, Aya." He went to launch at me, stopped himself again, and growled like an animal, frustrated. I laughed, "Yeah, I know, right. Two months! Argh."

"I will wait for you, my love." His earnest expression, I wanted to believe, had to, despite what I had heard about the ADHD nature of Fae like him. His body seemed to be vibrating with intensity.

"I need you to do something for me, my love," his face went serious. "You need to stay in my home for a little while until I straighten out this vampire problem."

"Sure, but why are they after me? Doc said that mimics are rare because everyone uses them up like tissues and disposes of them."

"An apt description, yes, basically. But it's more complicated than that. Just make sure you don't go outside. The Vampires know where I am but cannot enter this place uninvited. It's my Demesne. Protected by Inari."

"May I use your bathroom?"

"Of course, my home is yours too." He led me to the bathroom, simple and functional. Shower stall, bathtub, sink, and toilet all in a tiny area. All modular, clean and white. The tiles were black and white all over the back of the shower/bath and floor.

"There are some clothes on the towel shelf for you." Then he left me to clean my broken self.

***

These clothes were new and fit well. Aya had bought them just for me. Ha! They were exactly what I'd wear right now. Jeans and a long-sleeved black t-shirt. That was extremely sweet of him. There was a black hair tie lying next to the bathroom sink and a comb. The comb was actually one of those old-school-looking jade combs. I did my hair in my usual lazy top knot. I was tempted to put the comb in. I didn't mind feeling a little femme occasionally. Then abandoned the notion of remembering it might be something important to my Fox Spirit.

Also, next to the sink was a cup with a toothbrush in it. And next to it a new one still in its packet waiting to be opened. My heart was beating with each tiny revelation of thought that had gone into this moment. I used the toothbrush and came out of the bathroom. Now I could have a good look at Aya's home. It resembled a mini version of mine with an open-plan kitchen in one corner largely. An alcove that housed the large bed and bedside tables. Another area was designated for a sectional that faced the stairs leading upstairs to the main house. A black glass fireplace had been installed below a flatscreen in the wall below the stairwell.

The whole look was contemporary but warm. He had browns and blacks for throws and cushions and bedding. The Kitchen cupboards were dark wood, while the flooring was a uniform wood. Light. But not the pale grey oak of mine. The lighting made the whole place feel like it was above ground. Its layout was strategically placed to provide sunlight to the areas that needed it the most.

Aya was tending to one of the bonsai whose branches actually hung down past the beam. He was snipping it here and there and putting the waste in a basket in his other hand. What he wasn't using was a ladder. He just stood there on the air, like it was another landing built into the empty space.
He saw me and came down slowly to firm and happy earth, where things could make more sense. Levitation, add to the list of Zenko things.

"Hey, my beautiful and heroic flower," He hugged me, then went and put the basket in the kitchen sink to tend to later, with his snips. He washed his hands and dried them on a towel, "Did you find everything?"

He came over to me. I nodded.

He picked me up and breathed in deeply: "Mm, you still smell right. You smell like you and me." He kept breathing in my scent. It felt so right for some reason.

What he didn't know is that I was doing the same, enjoying the scent of him, "I missed you," I said into his ear.

"And I you," he whispered. The beginnings of erections separated us again, "So tell me what happened with Patience. Is she ok? You were manic when the doctor was trying to treat you, despite your injuries. You were trying to wiggle away and were yelling for Patience."

We went and sat down on the couch. And I told Aya. At some points, he growled like an animal, angry. Then when I was done, he sat there impassively waiting.

"I don't know what to do," I said helplessly. Repeating the situation had really upset me. It made me feel stupid, angry, and like I was missing a piece of myself. More ugly crying. Damn!

"Patience did what she did out of desperation. If she had achieved it, the consequences would have been horrific. I doubt she'd have been able to live with herself." Aya was right. And then he said something that surprised me.

"Patience had to choose between the love and future of her best friend and the love and futures of her family members. You have told me there are pups involved."

"Yes, Patience has two nieces. Hope's children."

"If what you say is true, then those girls would suffer the same fate as their mother and likely Patience's fate as well." Yes. It was true. And I loved those little girls. Hope was terrific….and Patience.

"I think you and Patience do need that girls' time you mentioned. Just to talk about this. There's more to this story, I suspect." Again, he was right. I just sat there soaking it in.

"I think I'll do that. But first things first, I need to wait out a two-month quarantine with the temptations of Lust waltzing around in front of me." He laughed.

"I don't waltz. I skulk." He winked at me, and I felt like we were settling into that rhythm we were beginning to achieve initially.

"Food!" He announced. What was even the time? And I was starving. My body had only slight aches now. While showering, I'd checked out my vein scar and saw it had indeed lightened and was going down. Thank goodness. Two months, then Eraser. Then Aya and I could give it a go. A real go. I hoped he'd want to.

"Well, I am in your territory now, so what do you suggest?"

"Our territory," he corrected me automatically. "I thought since we are in Chinatown, why not…Chinese?" Oh my, my bf was a serious food addict. Wait, we were in Chinatown?

"Yum, sounds perfect." He went to a kitchen drawer. I followed, seeing him open it and pull out a binder labelled "Takeout." I laughed. He looked at me, wondering what was so amusing, "How very organized." He had put all the takeout menus he had discovered and put them in an order he seemed to understand. Then turned to a Chinese menu with reverence.

"Here it is. The restaurant is close, but it doesn't deliver. So, I will zip out and get it for us. You stay here, obviously." He kissed my forehead, "Can't have you wandering the streets and getting stolen away."

We perused the menus, and I ordered what I usually did: noodles, vegetables, and wonton soup. And Aya, no doubt, was gonna bring back at least one of each item on the menu. These restaurants must love him! He had probably been singlehandedly steering the Canadian economy in a more positive direction just with his monstrous appetite.

"I'll be back soon, love. Help yourself to anything." Another kiss and my magical lover was gone.

Again, I felt his absence. I sat on the couch. I was considering watching TV or snooping… Yeah, It's only fair to snoop. So, I did. Which turned up nothing nefarious. Although I found he had put a whole new Me-sized wardrobe in half the closet and in half of the drawers. They were new clothes, not mine… had he moved me in? Ha! I laughed. Maybe we could be a real thing. He was a being from another realm whose motives would likely remain a mystery.

He did have a cupboard with a shrine in it, of a large orange Japanese temple gate. The shrine was to Inari, the Japanese god. I knew Inari was important to him, but he had not spoken much of him. Still, he had set Inari in place of private solitude where he no doubt meditated with his god. I went to the bedside drawers and was about to open one when I heard an unfamiliar ringtone. I looked around and found the prepaid burner was the source. Maybe Aya had forgotten my order or something. I answered.

"Hello?"

"Hello, Mr. Li." I froze. Unsure of what my reaction should be. My body was so tired from healing. My mind was also exhausted from the constant adaption of new supernatural facts being shoved at it. So, I simply echoed the greeting.

"Hello."

"My name is Kentaro. I am the reason you've been plagued by vampires of late," the voice had a mixed accent. It was still a pleasant voice. The kind that could talk you onto, or off a ledge, "And for that, I'm profoundly sorry."

"How'd you even get this number? I opened this phone like an hour ago?" I wasn't inquisitive. I just wasn't sure what to say yet. I was still gathering my thoughts and trying to come up with ways to draw information so we could deal with this nonsense once and for all.

"You do realize, Mr. Li, you are dealing with Fae from other worlds and places. With that comes other resources your human technology hasn't caught up with yet."

"I see. Well, nice chat. But I've got to...."

"Mr. Li, please a moment of your time." He said silkily on the other end.

"I don't think so. You broke Patience's hand!"

"That was an unfortunate accident." Something clicked in my head at that moment talking to this non-breather on the other line.

"Did you send a contract killer to kill my best friend?"

"Yes," He said, not even trying to hide it.

"Then we are done...."

"She was going to kill you, Mr. Li. We had to act." Ok, that sounded almost reasonable, but I still hated this guy and his idiotic cronies.

"What do you want? You've been stalking me and chasing me, and one of you apparently put me at death's door!" I shouted down the tiny phone's mic.

"That individual is no longer an issue. But Mr. Li, if you'll permit me a moment of your time to explain."

"Fine, but the next words out of your pointy mouth had better be good otherwise, we are done here."

"Mr. Li, you have been lied to, by everyone including the Fox!"

"Oh."

***

Chapter 34: When the Light Becomes Shadow

"I don't understand, and I don't know why I should even believe you," I said, more skeptical than ever. Vampires in most stories could not be trusted!

"It doesn't matter if you believe me or not. The results are the same. Let me explain," my curiosity peaked, but cautiously. After all, these bloodsuckers had menaced me and my ex-bestie.

"Haven't you wondered why the Zenko was at Crossroads in the first place?" My stomach dropped. No. Please don't say anything that might change it. Aya…. "Every Kitsune is special in its own way, which can make them very useful as a resource."

"Get to the point. I'm losing interest, Mr. Ken."

"Aya has a talent for tracking. A supernatural talent. The kind that is so accurate that he is well known throughout our…ah…. 'community,' I guess you could call us." Tracking… this word itched at my memory.

"He's a fox. Of course, he can track." The voice of Kentaro sighed in impatience.

"He was tracking you, Mr. Li."

"Yes, he said that…."

"Whatever he told you is a lie, Mr. Li,"

"How do you know what he…" he cut me off again.

"Because I hired him to track you." Ice slid up and down my spine. No. No. No. No!

The vampire continued in his even, cold tone, like a computer spouting off facts.

"Didn't it strike you as strange? You were at the Crossroads. You saw the calibre of clientele. They are mainly Fae, otherworldly beings. They are more beautiful than anything you had ever seen, correct?"

I didn't bother answering. Mr. Ken knew he was going in for the kill. Unfortunately, vampires seemed to be able to find the metaphorical jugular as well as the physical.

"We are beings of beauty, darkness, and light, angels and demons of temptation and dreams," he continued mercilessly, "and one of the most beautiful in the club fixes his attention on you? A human? Do you know what the Fae think of humans in general? They are a dirty, smelly, inept race of self-destructive miscreants. Zenkos are no different. They are Fae too. Why would he be interested in you unless I had instructed him to be?"

There it was. The dagger, sliding neatly into my heart and into the new dream I had been carefully trying to cultivate away from my conscious mind so as not to ruin it. I felt it keenly.

And the vampire knew it. My insecurities welled up, almost happy to be confirmed as correct. Why would anyone want you, Li Yīng? You're a broken toy that someone would only want to play with for a time before throwing you away.

"No way, why would he? I mean you…."

"Because we needed to find you, Mr. Li. You are quite a rare commodity." The doc's words came floating back with Aya's…*I tracked you here*….and *Mimics are rare because they get used….*

"Why would he have spent time with me if he had already tracked me then?"

"Because it was required. It's probably easier to show you. There's a car out front waiting for you."

"I don't think so. Whatever you say, I can't just trust your words. Aya wouldn't do that to me."

"You're right. You shouldn't trust just my words, ask the Zenko yourself, judge his reaction for yourself."

"If you're right, Mr. Ken, then that means…."

"That you were lied to." He hung up the phone at that, leaving me with a miasma of nasty questions that began to dredge up the pall of darkness that Marcus 'death had shrouded me in for five years.

Absently, I realized I had missed my meds. But that didn't matter, really. I had to ask Aya. He would tell me what Kentaro said was a lie. I sat on the bed. I was shaking again. The panic closing in as it used to before my meds had been prescribed to me. I started breathing in and out. Focusing on that. The door opened and closed.

"Love. I'm back," Aya's grinning, pretty face poked around the corner and saw me on the bed.

"Xiǎoyīng, my love, what is wrong? You're pale and shaking?" He blinked next to me. Settled a comforting arm around me. Pulled me to him. I froze at his touch. He felt my body stiffen instantly and pushed me gently to face him. "Xiǎoyīng, my love?"

"Ayaka of the Zenko," I said in barely a whisper, but he heard, "I'm going to ask you something once, and I need you to be honest with me." He froze this time.

"Ok, my love." He said stiffly.

"Were you paid to find me? And be with me?"

He remained stiff, staring at me. His amber eyes were sad. His face beauty incarnate. Again, I saw a tear trail down his face, it was beautiful and distracting, but that spell was losing its hold the more I looked at him and remembered the horrid vampire's words.

"Who told you that?" he said in as much of a whisper as I had.

"You haven't answered me, Ayaka!" My voice rose now, "Is it true?"

"Yes, my love, but…." I pushed him away from me. And stood up.

"Seriously?! The whole…" I couldn't voice it, my wishes, my torment. Marcus came into my mind, and I immediately felt like I had somehow betrayed him, cheated on his memory. I was feeling ill. So wrong. Everything was wrong! Darkness clouded into my mind. Shoving away the light of hope that had begun to kindle there.

He came to me, and I could dimly hear his sweet voice, but it was drowned by the roaring in my ears. Finally, I spun to look at him in the eyes. He was crying, reaching towards me, and tried to pull me towards him by the wrist. The gesture was light, but I slapped him away.

"Don't touch me!" My voice was a growl.

I opened my mouth, and I screamed at him. Like a madman, loud, it came out like a roar of pain, hate, sadness, and loss. I turned towards the door. He blinked to the door and put his arm out.

"You can't leave love, please!" he pleaded, "It's dangerous!" Patience's exact words… *You can't go because it's dangerous…* Well, it seemed every time I heard those words, the damaging blows had already been dealt.

"More dangerous than being here? Being touched by you?!"

He stepped back as if I had slapped him, and I took the opportunity to pull open the door and climb the steps to the open air and street above.

Across the street was an Escalade, the same as I had seen the vamps use before. I didn't care. I stormed across the street, not caring if a car hit me. A suit opened the passenger door, and as I slid in, Aya came leaping out across the road. Yelling after me "to get back." And "please, we'll fix it." And "please, I am sorry." And "please…" Whatever!

***

Chapter 35: Where Villains May Lie (Friday)

Patience… Ayaka….

My soul closed up as I accepted the depression and anguish engulfing me. I cried. I had cried so much lately. I was getting sick of it. I was sick of myself. Looking around the car, the vampires had the good sense to stay quiet. I barely registered where we were going, but the drive seemed to be a long one. I don't know why I had gotten into the car. Perhaps I no longer cared what happened to me. Did I?

We pulled into an area I had only been once called Point Grey. Exclusive and expensive. We drove a little more, but I was hardly paying attention. Why was I even in this car? I should've just gone home. And then what? Be alone? Be stalked some more for being this thing? Perhaps visiting this vampire crew would conclude this dream I had been living in the past week.

A large automatic gate loomed before us. One of those iron ones with ivy growing on it, but it was well maintained. So were the grounds as we pulled into some vast estate. It was getting late, so the only details I could make out of the house were a new build. And it was a modern, glass and concrete monument. Reminiscent of some of the recent award-winning Japanese designed architecture. Integrating wood, steel, concrete, and glass into a layered affair of rectangle blocks stacked three-story high but stretching off into the distance. The house had huge full-length windows. I saw the inside occupants milling around and going about their business.

We stopped at an entrance to the compound—double wooden doors with a concrete slab for a bridge across a very shallow artificial stone-filled water moat. My door opened, and I got out. Barely focusing on the vamps around me. For all I knew, I was going to be the main course for an orgiastic dinner party. Meh. I was way past caring. Patience and Aya… both the people I loved… Yeah, loved! There it was, and unfortunately, my heart had opened up at the wrong fucking time and to the wrong fucking people.

"Mr. Ken will see you in his sitting room if you please." I followed the vamps into the house.
The interior was minimalist but opulent with no expense spared, adorned with grand paintings and sculptural masterpieces. The entryway held immediately in view a Robin Wight's Dandelion Fairy sculpture or an excellent copy, at least.

I was taken to a large recessed sitting room, white and sterile. Less lived in. But the furniture was modern and comfortable, though I wasn't a fan of white leather couches. I found leather always stuck at the worst times to your butt. The sofas were sectionals forming the three sides of a square, with the couch-less side looking out to face a backyard area that I couldn't see much into.

Dominating the wall to my left was a giant flat screen. On the opposite wall, another sculpture anchored on a raised part of the floor. It looked like a copy of Paige Bradley's Expansion. But thinking of where I was, these 'copies 'of modern art were probably the real deal. It was a nude woman in a lotus-like pose, with the fissures of light that shone through her.

Sitting on the TV side of the couch was whom I assumed to be Mr. Kentaro. I sat directly opposite him, allowing the coffee table between us, a large glossy black slab of veined marble.
One vamp then whispered into Kentaro's ear, and he nodded. He was the vampire I had seen in the doctor's office waiting. His Romanian mixed heritage is more pronounced in this stark environment. He also looked younger in this light.

"You came of your own volition."

"Yes," I wasn't in the mood for chit-chat, "what do you want?"

"Ah, yes, the direct approach. We need your help, Mr. Li. Specifically, I need your help." He sat there just looking at me. Gauging my reactions, I supposed.
 "My *Ani*(兄)… sorry, my brother is sick, and only you can help him."

"I see. Another curse?"

"Yes, but this one is mostly self-inflicted, but the fault lies with another."

God, did everyone have this cryptic nonsense in the spirit world? No wonder Năinai was so blunt. She had probably hated dealing with things like this. I wish she were here now. This situation made me miss her so much.

"Your friend Patience, I guess not so much a friend now, tried to take the opportunity before we could and almost succeeded."

"Yeah, and…?" Get to the point. I was beginning to hate the magical world.

"You no doubt have heard about the animal attacks in Vancouver lately?"

"Yes, of course. Everyone says it's a bear or something."

"Not a bear, but my brother." Oh, dear. "The missing detail the authorities haven't wanted to be released was that most of the bodies were exsanguinated." *Eww.*

"Isn't that what you guys do. You're vampires?" I said, laughing. No one else laughed but me.

"No, at least not anymore. There's no need. We live in an age where donors are plenty and supply is abundant. So we have no real need to hunt. And when we do, it's for sport."

"So mauling isn't common for vamps now?"

"Not really. In fact, it can lead to the offending vampire being put down," he looked a little saddened. "My brother is the only family I have." He said, gaining some sympathy from me.

"Come with me, Mr. Li. I need to show you something." The escort of vamps fell in behind as we got up, "That won't be necessary. We will be fine gentlemen and gentlewomen," he said to the cronies (PC, cute). They dispersed. It was he and I. He appeared to seem a little different without the cronies around. Almost like he was acting a little less….old? I guess? Odd. I had a feeling that under this cold exterior was a moody, petulant child.

"My *futago no onii-san* (双子のお兄さん/twin brother) and I were born in Southeastern Europe some years ago. We were purchased by some human traders who moved us to Japan, where a Japanese family adopted us after paying a large sum. They couldn't have children of their own, and we were so young. Our birth parents were probably dead, and we would have followed. We were lucky, I guess. Most kids in our situation wouldn't have been."

I kept silent, letting him tell whatever he needed to tell. We were walking down some stairs now into the basement area of the place. If he indeed were a villain, he could continue this monologue that hopefully would result in his downfall at the end of this story. If only.

"When my brother and I were twenty-two, we were having dinner with our family in the outdoor courtyard of our home. It was a clear, warm evening. I can still smell the evening air and hear the chirps of the night insects and frogs."

We got into an elevator which immediately began to move without any pushing of buttons. Mr. Ken turned to me, "When the frogs and insects suddenly stopped, I knew something was wrong. And so did Daisuke, my brother. They came so fast! I couldn't fathom what was happening until it was done. Our Japanese parents, our staff, everyone was dead, some killed by archers but most with their throats ripped out. So now when I said that Vampires don't do such things anymore, it's mostly true, except for certain circumstances."

The elevator stopped. He allowed the elevator door to open, and we entered a large room. Like a basement viewing room. Looking kind of like an underground parking building. The type in police stations but much more extensive, with a one-way mirror. The viewing room took up one whole side of the structure. Inside was what looked like an apartment, nicely appointed with every amenity. A bathroom was on one side through a door. And a couch whose occupant was watching TV. It looked like one of the many streaming services, Netflix probably.

"Our parents in Japan," he carried on, "had gotten into some business dealings with an organized crime syndicate, kind of like the "Yakuza" you hear about." I had guessed the ending already but let him tell his own tale. "My parents had messed up somewhere along the line, and debts of one kind or another needed paying. So I guess eventually it got out of hand." He sighed as if tired of the story himself.

"The syndicate took us. They took us because my brother and I were considered treasures to our parents. It was later that they and we found out my Daisuke was a mimic. So they thought to use him as a resource." Ok, revelation. Interesting. He indicated the duplicate of him sitting watching the TV behind the glass. "In the end, they had to turn us both because we were too much to handle, and Daisuke was getting sick too often with their use of him." He looked at his brother.
"I love my brother Mr. Li. There is nothing I wouldn't do for him. After he turned, he was miserable. He hated being a vampire."

"Who wouldn't? It's not exactly what the media make it out to be."
"Exactly," he smirked, "But we really hadn't had much of a choice in the situation," he put his hand to the glass, and his twin looked up.

He switched off the TV and came to the glass. He put the mirror of his print in the same spot on the other side of the glass. The gesture was simple but felt intimate. Twins had a bond beyond most relationships. At least that's what my Nǎinai used to tell me. She had once even told me stories about twins and their special connections. It was something only twins could understand.

"When Daisuke fell in love," he sighed, "I wanted to be happy for him. At least I tried to be…. He seemed so joyful, like before our Japanese parents died…." He breathed in and looked at me with sorrow in his eyes. "When Aya and Daisuke got together, it seemed so magical. I hadn't seen Daisuke so happy…." Mr. Ken had tears, strange pink tears welling in his eyes, "I just wanted my *Onii-san* to feel joy, be happy." Oh god! It hurt again, the Aya betrayal.

"They enjoyed each other's company, but Daisuke was more into Aya than Aya was into him. So Aya tried to end it with him. I think Aya thought he was doing the right thing…."

"What happened?" I asked, mesmerized by the twins, so much so that I wanted to trace my fingers down and around their hands and fingers. Their story was so sad. And they were actually quite beautiful. There was something about Ken's eyes when he looked at his brother. His twin. I got the feeling Ken was the younger of the two. And if this was so, he missed his big brother. These were the kind of vampires that I think teen fiction writers would want to meet. Beautiful and tortured.

"Daisuke didn't take it well. He didn't understand that a Fae often is promiscuous by nature and would move on just like that," he took a breath. "I tried to protect him from this, but I couldn't."
"Oh, I see." Yup. I knew it was all too good to be true.

"My brother tried to plead for Aya to take him back…." He was struggling to say something, to find the words, "Then Daisuke did something that hurt himself. Inside and out. He wanted so much to be with Aya. It seemed almost an obsession. He bit Aya and tried to use his mimic nature to turn himself from a Vampire to Kitsune."

"Is that even possible?"

"I don't know. It didn't work anyhow. The energies were incompatible, and it drove my brother's mind over the edge. His energies are so out of balance he is never going to be in his right mind."

Kentaro pulled his hand from the glass. The vampire looked so sad, so in anguish. Daisuke went to sit on the couch again like a robot. He was fully crying now. Not the ugly kind of crying like me. Just silent pain-filled tears that fell as crimson drops from his silver-blue eyes.

"My brother often escapes hunting like a wild animal. He uses a mixed combination of Kitsune/Vampire and Mimics abilities to do so. And as you have seen in the news. People have died, and they will continue dying, and my brother will continue suffering."
Not good. People had died. Aya had a bf before me? Of course, he did. He probably had a whole harem of beautiful men and probably women too at his beck and call. Fucking Fae. Fucking Aya!

"So how am I supposed to help? I don't know anything about this stuff."

"Your knowledge base isn't what I need. So many symbolic acts, even small ones, can have great ramifications in our world." Indicating the'"supernatural world,' I guessed. It was as the doc had said.

"There is a ritual that could restore my brother's mind and energy to a vampire and likely even get rid of his mimic ability and the residual kitsune powers in him at the same time."

"I'm guessing this ritual involves me."

"Correct." He looked at me evenly, "But as I said, symbolic acts are important. This ritual will not work without your cooperation. The agreement is essential."

"Ah-huh." One eyebrow goes up, "This isn't some kind of simple new age wave the sage, and that banishes the bad energy kind of ritual, is it?"

"No."

"It's the more blood sacrifice type deal, isn't it?"

"Blood is everything to vampires, so yes."

"I see. And would I survive this process? I mean, vampires aren't known for their reputation of leaving mortals alive, you know."

"Yes, I know, and that is the question, Mr. Li."

There was a commotion at the entrance to the underground crypt/bunker/interrogation bedroom. Both Kentaro and I turned to see Aya burst through the elevator doors. Like literally burst through the doors. The metal had melted to slag on either side of the doorway. Flames were licking the edges of the blown-out opening as he charged into the room. He was followed by a veritable army of suited vamps who all piled around him. Restraining him.

"Yīng, please!" he pleaded, the same look I gave Patience I sent his way, but he didn't falter, "Xiǎoyīng, don't listen to them! They're lying!" Who wasn't lying to silly Xiǎoyīng these days? You lied. Patience lied. Who cares?! And stop using the name my Nǎinai gave me!

"Are we Ayaka?" Kentaro interrupted, "Did you not usher my brother into this state?" he waved at the figure in the enclosure watching TV. The figure stood up and sniffed the air and, in a blink, was at the window nearest Aya. He was sniffing like he smelled something delicious and irresistible. "You also promised on your honour to help remedy this malady you helped inflict on my brother!"

Aya looked at Daisuke on the other side of the glass, then cast his eyes down in shame.

"Xiǎoyīng, please, don't listen to them. You could die."

"Aya, you lost the privilege of addressing me when I found out you were paid to…." I was livid. I couldn't finish the sentence.

"It's not like that. Please! Let's go, and we can go home together. Please!"

OMG. Home together. My gaze softened. I looked up at Aya, home? With me? Yes? Are we a home together? Could we be? Please say something to put this feeling of desolation away, Aya… please. Please tell me we could go home to our magical castle in our fairy tale and live happily ever after… My soul wanted to crawl out of the black pit of hatred and betrayal and find that string of hope… but couldn't find it.

"Mr. Li, do you know why you are the only candidate to qualify for helping my brother regain his sanity?"

"Don't do this, Kentaro!" Aya growled. He struggled, and I saw smoke rising from the hands of the vamps that held him, "Don't!" They were struggling to hold him. Chains were produced suddenly and wrapped around the Zenko.

"We need more than a mimic, Mr. Li. We need a mimic who has been suffused with a particular Kitsune energy. The only energy that is compatible with Daisuke's. Can you guess which?"

The nail in the coffin. Kentaro had said it and knew what it meant. Had he done his research on me? Yeah, that was a huge possibility. The little broken and fragile mimic. The one who would fall so quickly into the Zenko's honey trap. But it had worked. The words had hit home. Right where they needed to. I was back in that place. The door to my soul slammed shut. There was no escaping it. I ran my fingers along the scar on my left wrist. That place that could make all the feelings go away.

***

Chapter 36: The Sacrifice

It's hard for people to understand what goes through a person's mind when choosing to end it all. It's even harder for me to describe when I have actually done it before. When Patience had found me in a pool of my own blood, I was too weak to say it, but I had wanted to say, *"It's ok, it's my choice, Patience. You had nothing to do with it, ok? I want to see Marcus. I miss him too much."*

Life just seemed to pile upon you, and you couldn't see past your own pain no matter how hard you tried. Marcus had been my life. My Future. My Light. And when he left, darkness fell across my world. It had swallowed me whole and shut everyone out. But slowly and surely, Patience, my parents, even Baraz's family, and of course, Hope and her family had pulled me out, bit by bit. I was still broken, but I was able to stumble forward with life.

But then, tonight: Patience, who had saved me from me, had planned on raping me and giving me cancer to protect her family. Still, I couldn't really reconcile my feelings on that, but I knew those feelings spoke of raw hurt.

Ayaka… he had also slowly but surely, bit by bit, helped me to feel safe and secure. Bit by bit, to hope for a future with someone. And bit by bit, made sure that I'd fall in…. That I'd betray Marcus' memory. It felt sick to think about. I felt dirty. Tainted. I was disgusted with myself—my dirty body. My heart felt blackened and dead inside.

Ayaka had lied. He had been paid. God knew what the delivery of a mimic chump went for these days; to fuck me enough until I had enough kitsune power to perform a ritual to fix a situation he had helped bring about. Probably through being an insensitive jerk during the breakup. I bet he had used it. That line that just drove people into a murderous frenzy: *It's not you; it's me!*

Bitterness and spite could lead people to do awful things. It could lead them to do stupid things. Self-destructive things. Permanent things. Led them sometimes softly and gently by the hand or roughly to a single conclusion.

***

"Xiǎoyīng …." Aya's voice again faded as that roar of emotion filled my ears. I could hear my heartbeat in my ears, like a drum beating fast.

"My precious Xiǎoyīng…." Another distant echo. Then hearing myself say.

"What does the ritual involve?" It sounded muted like I heard it all underwater.

"No!!!!!" Aya again? Maybe. It had become a guttural sound like an animal in pain.

"It is quite simple, Mr. Li. You transfer your energy into my brother, enough of it for his to…. re-adapt again. It's kind of like a reset button in his energy body. But that access could only be given to a mimic that is filled Aya's energy signature." He said that last bit of driving another stake into the heart of what was my dreams of Aya.
"Will it hurt?" I said, almost a whimper.

"It shouldn't. Vampires mesmerize their prey before consuming, so they can't feel a thing."

"Oh, ok. Is that like that ignoring thing you guys do out in public?"

"Yes, it is." He seemed impressed by my knowledge of the subject.

"Then it's going to hurt."

"It will only work if you comply. Otherwise, that act is useless," Kentaro put his hand on my shoulder and turned me away from the Zenko. Aya was now struggling against the chains that had been wrapped around him. He had begun barking and screaming. His long hair flying around his head like a dark corona. His aura seemed muted. I could see it struggling against the chains, but it couldn't break past them.

"Don't worry, Aya, I'll clean up your fucking mess," I said under my breath.

Kentaro led me to a secure door and typed in a code on the keypad. I looked back. I didn't recognize Aya anymore. He had changed into a rust-coloured foxlike beast standing on all fours, struggling against the chains, whimpering and howling. He had a bunch of tails, like a peacock fan spreading behind him. I just took one look in those amber eyes and slipped into the enclosure of a vampire madman.

Kentaro was beside me. He was looking at me. He didn't quite have the emotionless, cold look he had sported outside the enclosure now. Instead, he looked hopeful, almost like a little boy behind those cold eyes.

"Two things, Mr. Li: one, you may survive this because of the Kitsune energy your body has absorbed. It can heal you at an alarming rate." Was there any left after one of your goons threw me into a wall?

"And the other thing is that you will be ok. Mimics are stronger creatures than we give you credit for. Remember that."

***

The door into the enclosure was at the opposite end of the room where Daisuke was sniffing at Aya's scent, which he obviously smelled. But a stronger scent of it was coming from me because I was in his enclosure. He couldn't see outside because the glass was a one-way mirror that ran the length of his 'bedroom.'

"Aya!" he screamed, almost rapturously. Suddenly he had me in his arms. Like a vice, I couldn't move, "You came back to me, my love. I've missed you!" I looked into the wild silver-blue eyes of Kentaro's twin. He was looking more through me than at me. He saw some kind of illusion in his head.

"Um, hi Daisuke," I said, now nervous and wanting to leave and renege on this decision immediately, "you can put me down so we can do the ritual now?"

"Ritual?" He said, his breathing wild, "I'm here to make love to you. Like we always do." Always do? Likely Aya had played the same with Daisuke as with me. Poor Daisuke.

My shirt was gone from my body somehow. Only the sound of torn fabric traced its passing. He held me tight, so I couldn't move and was kissing all over my chest. His kisses had a coldness to them but felt so good. He was licking my chest, and an angry part of me wanted to fuck this vampire right in front of Aya, just to show him how much he'd hurt me. Ok, so he was good-looking, and I could have gotten a slight boner, but I should also focus on getting the hell out there. What had I done!

"I missed you," he said, ceasing those teasing kisses on my nipples and chest then looking into my eyes.

His mouth moved so fast my brain barely registered the movement. It was on my throat. I felt his fangs pierce my flesh and then warm wetness running down my front and back. I was struggling like a wild thing now, but it was like working against a granite wall.

Then a sound I'd heard once while pulling weeds out of Patience's garden when the roots were stubborn, and then the plant would come loose. The sound met my ears, and Daisuke came away from my neck with a wide grin on his face and a chunk of something in his mouth. Pain filled every nerve in my body! I couldn't move my neck to look. My throat, I guess, was filling with liquid. I wanted to cough but couldn't. I could only feel the pain of something essential gone from my body that shouldn't have been removed.

As he moved in again, the images started flowing. They weren't mine; they were his. He and Aya together entwined, enjoying each other, Aya then telling Daisuke no, and I could feel Daisuke's heartbreak at that sound. I felt his mind, not unlike mine. It was fractured in grief and loss. Loss of his parents in Japan, loss of his ability to control his actions… loss of Aya, who had seemed so promising as a mate. Loss of his other half…. his twin. His twin, he felt keenly aware of him but missed him so much.

For Daisuke, it was hard finding someone to love. He just felt so awkward around his own kind. He didn't like being a vampire. The thought of blood had made him feel ill every time he drank. He and Kentaro had not been given a choice when they were made into Vampire. It was forced on them. Daisuke, a mimic, had to say goodbye to his humanity and the light and fun that human interaction could bring. When he had met the Fox Spirit, it was only because Aya had dealings with "their business." Aya had taken a liking to him, nothing serious, just the usual male-to-male attraction that could be solved by some fun. If Aya had known what would come to pass, he might not have taken that route. Daisuke had fallen so quickly for the beautiful fox spirit. But it wasn't just that.

Daisuke had been so focused on getting away from his nature, his mind felt too focused on any solution. Aya did not want to lead the young vampire on. As a mimic, Daisuke figured he could change what he was by taking enough essence of Aya into himself and become a Zenko too. As he'd later find out, the problem was that the two energies within him could not settle. Instead, they would end up twisting his mind and binding his mimic abilities into madness. Daisuke had become more feral than ever and started going out on wanton-killing sprees just to satisfy his thirst. He had become purely instinctual and obsessed with Aya, only wanting to consume more of him.

As the images flowed, so did the energy of the vampire who had locked onto my neck. It was a cold, empty feeling like putting your hand into a bucket of freezing water and pulling it out only to have lost feeling on the tips of your fingers. It permeated through me. It was dark energy, and I did not like it. It didn't help my body or soul. It just poured in, causing a stalling in any helpful process within me as Daisuke emptied me of the last of Aya's offerings. The foreign energy sneaked into my soul and found a place, then curled up, like a snake, waiting. The foreign energy felt like an aberrant mix of Aya's, Daisuke's, and another energy… similar to mine.

As I felt the last of Aya's original offerings to me leave my body- it was then that I knew I was going to die. Whatever transference of energy coming from Daisuke was too much of a mix of vampire, kitsune, and mimic. I was dying.

I could also feel not just a stream, the last systematic pumping of my blood leaving my body. Daisuke didn't want to waste it and was lapping as much as he could. My eyes were too heavy to stay open. In the distance, I heard breaking glass and more yelling. *Eww.* Metallic taste and smell all over me. Daisuke's tongue felt weird, mixed with the pain on my neck that wouldn't respond.

Dimly I saw Daisuke fall onto his butt on the ground and was looking at his hands in wonder, then looked up at me, horror on his face.

"No, no, no!" he was saying. No, what? The damage was done. And so was I, Daisuke. Look at the mess we made!

Kentaro was there dragging away his twin. Both arms wrapped protectively around him. He also looked panicked, but his eyes were only on his twin. I thought I was on the floor. I couldn't feel anything. My hearing had gone. Probably didn't need it anyway. But wait… no, I could hear the odd noise. Steps, more yelling.

Ayaka was leaning over me, sobbing, I thought and had picked me up. I was against his chest. This would mess up what he was wearing.

"Xiǎoyīng, my love! Don't leave me! Please! Come back to me!" He was crying. Well, he shouldn't have done what he had done! I would never have left him. We could have had our castle….

"You're mine Xiǎoyīng! You gave yourself to me! Come back to me!" He was rocking me. I think I was moving somewhere, but I no longer could see. Everything seemed so unimportant now. It was just comforting… dark… like falling asleep. Oh, this feeling again. Perhaps this time, I could stay asleep. That'd be nice.

***

Daisuke: Beautiful and sweet. A vampire, but not.

He hated the life of parasitism. But when I met him. His soft nature and kind ways drew me in. He looked like a pale angel with his strange European face and blue-silver eyes. Like the humans I had enjoyed, I wanted to enjoy Daisuke. He obliged. In fact, he seemed to throw himself into spending more and more time with me. I liked his enthusiasm, and we had so much fun, just hanging around the human cities, going to human attractions like markets and wildlife reserves.

Then I moved into the city away from my home. The temples in Kyoto were so isolated, and the human interaction was limited. When I moved, he was thrilled, as his clan lived in the town. I wish I had seen it sooner, the signs that poor Daisuke was falling in love with me. Okāsan had said that one side always knew before, and I considered that perhaps it was Daisuke. But my heart knew better. So, I broke off our romantic ties. He was devastated. He begged me to stay, and I almost wanted to. But I knew in time he would be able to find someone of a better match. Daisuke's twin brother Kentaro hated me for hurting his brother like that. I couldn't blame him. I hated myself for making Daisuke feel unworthy.

Then sweet and beautiful Daisuke did something I did not expect.... he tried to take my blood. To him, it was a way to possibly become Kitsune. I am not sure if that would even work, but he hated being a vampire so much and blamed that for our relationship ending. However, he did take my blood in a vicious attack I hadn't expected.

We were at my temple on the outskirts of Kyoto. It was beautiful, serene, and had the kindest monks tending it. They ate only vegetables, that was how much they loved nature. Daisuke had met me there. I had gone back, hoping to put distance between us for his benefit. We were sitting on the steps of the entry to one of the temple ponds. It was one of my favourite places to sit, and here with him made me wish we could be a mated pair. He had said he was sorry for not understanding sooner that we couldn't be together as we were. I was happy to hear him say that. At least someone would make this sweet boy happy. And then he kissed me, with the passion we had used in our lovemaking. I thought it was a goodbye kiss…. And then he struck.

The bite had been swift and brutal, tearing into my neck. I remembered I had screamed, and the monks and my family had heard. They were there in a second. Daisuke not only took my blood but a large amount of my energy. That moment of my acceptance of him kissing me had left me open to his vampiric attack on my power. When he had stood up in bloody triumph, it was horrific. My body was slowly trying to seal the damage made by Daisuke, but the wound was so deep, I was having difficulty closing it up. I remember feeling the energy in Daisuke change. Then seeing him turn to face me, with a manic and bloodied grin marring that pretty face. Something had changed. It had twisted the Daisuke I knew. Made him into something terrible, something powerful, and something utterly insane. My family leaped into action to rescue me and defend the monks and our temple.

Daisuke was quick. So fast for his kind. So powerful due to the stolen energy and his own Fae powers. My sister was the first to miss her opportunity to subdue him, and she paid with her life. He drank of her briefly, then spat it out as if it tasted foul to him, and then while she struggled to claw at his face and summoning the foxfire, he gave her neck a sharp twist. Snap. The next was a monk, then another. The carnage was everywhere. I was trying to move. But my wound was so severe that I was still losing so much blood.

Kentaro appeared from somewhere and subdued his brother easily, who screamed like an animal. But upon seeing Kentaro, something in Daisuke seemed to calm instantly. He still held that look of a person who has lost their mind, but the other vampire seemed to have some supernatural way of calming him instantly. Kentaro had looked afraid, not of his brother but of what he had become. The look Kentaro gave his twin broke my heart. Kentaro looked like his life was at an end upon seeing the mad creature that was his brother. There was blood and wounded everywhere. Vampires cared little for others, and I knew Kentaro would leave in an instant. I hissed his name. His hearing was such that he'd be able to hear from even further than where he stood, holding his brother in place. He had paused. Then turned to face me.

"You," was all he said. And was about to go.

"Kentaro, please, save them! I know you have the resources to do it! Please!" The wounded monks that were left didn't have time, and my family carried my sister's body away.

"No!" he said simply and again turned to leave.

"A favour! Ken! A favour! From a Zenko!" He turned back, and his grim look was replaced by a smile, almost as feral as his brother's had been. We Zenko were naturally known to be more powerful than vampires in general. If it weren't for the stolen energy that suffused Daisuke's body, he wouldn't have stood a chance. But he had it and had used it. Killed and destroyed my home and my human and Zenko family. A favour was nothing if Kentaro would help them all.
"I'll save them." He had said.

- Ayaka

***

"Xiǎoyīng, my beautiful flower," almost a familiar voice. I was standing on a small hand-built dock. In the end, facing the water was a woman in traditional Guilin garb. Silver headdress, elaborate and intricate, sitting atop her head. Her dress was yellow silk with the accompanying attire of her people. She turned, and I knew who she was. Though she was young, about my age, perhaps younger, at least she looked that way.

"Nǎinai!" I ran to her and held the small woman, who looked like she was barely twenty, "Why do you look so young? And I love this dress!"

"Well, my boy, this is how I was when I was a girl," she swished the garment left and right so I could hear it jingle and see it sparkle in the sun, "I was pretty, wasn't I?" I nodded in complete agreement. I could see why my Năinai had been a little heartbreaker in her time.

"Where are we, Năinai?" I asked. At least this woman would never betray me. I had missed her.

"A place I haven't visited in a long time. A place where I was the happiest and the saddest." I looked out and saw Guilin stretching out along the Li River.

We went into a tiny stone house, simple with stone flooring all made by hand. We sat at a simple wooden table, each on our own little stool.

"Năinai, I have missed you so much." She grabbed my hand. It felt real and warm.

"I have missed you too, my boy," she looked around, "But I keep myself busy." I laughed, imagining what trouble she was putting the other side through just to amuse herself.

"So much has happened since you left," I started to cry. Năinai let me cry, scooting her stool closer to mine so she could wipe my tears with a square piece of gold silk. The gold material had a red embroidered dragon and phoenix intricately woven into it. She always let me cry. Never told me it was weak to cry.

"I'm so sorry about Marcus, dear boy."

"Is he here, Năinai? Can I see him?"

"I'm afraid not yet. Marcus is further away. This isn't the other side, my boy," she indicated with her hand, "this is an in-between place, "but I can tell you, Marcus is ok. He's in no pain. He watches over you when I cannot."

"Oh, ok." I couldn't hide my disappointment. It was warring with the elation I felt at seeing my Nǎinai. I looked at the square of silk in her hand. It was beautiful—a lovely piece of craftsmanship.

"I see you got yourself mixed up with the Fae. God, they're a pain in the ass, aren't they?" We both laughed at that, then she saw me looking at the square, "This was a gift. It's beautiful, isn't it?" I nodded, then answered her question.

"You're telling me, Nǎinai. Those Fae are all twisted plans and plots and silly agendas that get everyone hurt but themselves."

"Really…?" she looked at me slyly, "But themselves? Is that what you think? There are more stories here than yours, Xiǎoyīng."
"Nǎinai, why is this your place to be in right now? Another story?" She laughed, recognizing my sneaky passive-aggressive slight.

"Now you're beginning to ask good questions, Xiǎoyīng. You were always so clever," she folded the square, and it vanished into the folds of her outfit.

"I didn't tell you. I didn't tell many people that I was once in love with a Fae, much like you are now." She seemed to be looking off into the memory. "He was the most beautiful creature I had ever laid my eyes on. It wasn't just his appearance, but also his soul Xiǎoyīng. He was so kind and gentle. He seemed to love everything about life." She seemed to snap back to me.

"Oh Nǎinai, I don't think I'm in love, I mean…." She smacked the back of my head lightly.

"Now, Yīng. No lying. Nǎinai always knows." She looked ahead, staring out the open door of the tiny river home, "It's a long story and one you'll soon discover, I'm sure. But the point is, love is part of life and living, my Xiǎoyīng. The best part."

"Are you saying I should forgive him?"

"Him? Perhaps. You know, even the best person will do the worst things for love, even if it means sacrificing themselves too." I was thinking of both Patience and Aya. And I was also totally confused as to which she was speaking about, if any.

"Am I dead, Năinai?" Remembering the Daisuke moment of his mouth holding what I was sure a piece of me in his mouth.

"Do you want to be?" Then, she asked, "Remember when Marcus came to the other side, and you tried to join him?"

I looked down, feeling ashamed, and nodded. Năinai held my wrist with such care and stroked along the scar there.

"I was there, watching your pain. I wanted to help, to stop you, but I couldn't. You had chosen, but you didn't pass on. Then, finally, Patience came." Yes, I remembered how that story ended.

"I always liked that girl, you know." She sighed. "What a terrible decision to have to make…." I had the feeling she was giving me cryptic and annoying advice that I would no doubt have to follow through with later.

"Yeah, me too," I said sadly.

"You can come with me and leave this journey or go back. But things are never going to be easy on either path." Năinai seemed to be waiting, just making conversation as she sometimes did. Waiting for something she knew was coming but couldn't push.

"I don't know, Năinai, aren't there some things I should do?" I remembered the box of red packets left unopened waiting.

"Exactly," She looked like she was beaming with pride.

"Well, what can I do?"

"Again… Exactly!" Năinai was jiggling up and down, making tinkling noises with her outfit, "what CAN you do. My boy! I taught you skills you didn't even think you'd need. But I also gave you all the tools you'd need. So be smart, and don't be a victim. You are no Bella Swann!"

OMG! My Năinai had been watching that too. Or perhaps she'd seen the movies. Who knew?

"No! I'm not. You're right, Năinai."

"Always am, my boy… well, mostly. Your Năinai has made a mistake or two in the past. But I want you to ask yourself when the time comes. 'What can I do?'"

"I love you, Năinai," I hugged her tightly. It was weird hugging her as a young girl. But hey, Năinai can be anyone she wants here.

"I love you too, more than anything," she pushed me away to look at me, "and remember this when you forget what to do about things, just tell yourself: It's not about me. That idea will lead you through the most terrible of hells that life might think to throw at you."

"Yes, Năinai, I love you!" We hugged again. I didn't want to let her go. But the whole feeling was slipping into a watery mirage that ended in blackness again. I heard a beeping. A steady beeping. Hmm. What was I going to open my eyes to this time? A goblin hoard trying to disembowel me, perhaps?

***

Chapter 37: The Rebirth

Few moments in a Kitsune's life are more pivotal, more profound than finding one's mate. As a species, Kitsune are known to be sexually prolific. This is true and does not end upon finding your mate. It's just that prolific drive is localized in a monogamous sense.

For Kitsune, we do not limit our sexual impulses to the need to breed only. The act of sex is one of pleasure and can be enjoyed beyond the constraints of gender roles. Human men try to gauge their prowess and virility based on the females they encounter. I have heard them call these females the fairer sex. Indeed, when told that one enjoys the 'fairer sex,' the whole concept is subjective. For when I saw Li Yīng for the first time at Crossroads, he was, and would always be, to me, The Fairest of them All!

- Ayaka

***

I could feel something warm and pure filling one side of me. It felt like sunlight and liquid pouring into me. In my mind's eye, I could see it filling the recesses of my mind, my body, and my soul....

Where it found… waiting for it… something dark and unnecessary. The light didn't waste time as the snakelike presence reared up to defend its newfound place in me. The sunlight poured over it, not burning it away as one would expect but covering it, exposing it. Whatever it had been was scared and primal and had only wanted a place to call its own. The two energies met and spun together, finding a balance that wouldn't typically exist but now did. Those two energies then sought out a third more native energy within me. A small light that was all me. Again, it covered it and made it part of them.

***

I risked one eye and saw the fluorescent lights of a harsh office-type environment shine down on me and bloody hurting. I looked to my side and saw one of those heart monitors from the medical dramas to my right. There was a bed next to me. A line connecting me to that person. A bloodline. I looked closer; the person was me. He looked just like me. I shook some stupid clip thingy off my finger, which caused the heart monitor to emit a horrific tone.

The person next to me opened their eyes. I marvelled at the likeness. The clone looked at me, unsure. Then looked at the line from me to him. I looked at it too.

"Ouch, shit!" Delayed pain reaction? My neck felt like it was missing a whole side, and trying to hold my head up was too much for it. Finally, I collapsed into the bed.

"Xiǎoyīng?" Whispered a little shy voice. Not sure what kind of an answer it would get. It sounded like me too. "It's me, Xiǎoyīng. It's me. I'm here."

He had gotten out of the bed and was standing over me as a nurse in scrubs came rushing in.
"Move." He commanded. He reattached the clippie thing. Then buzzed for a doctor.

One apparently arrived, wearing a lab coat. He was either that or a mad scientist. He looked me over and shone a light in my eyes. Kentaro joined him.

"How is he?" asked Kentaro.

"He'll live despite the odds; this kid beats the odds somehow..." The doctor shook his head.

"What hospital?" I tried to ask. My voice wasn't working right. Why was I constantly waking up sore and sick lately? It was stupid? But Nǎinai had said to me. Don't be a victim. So, no more.

"You're still in my home Mr. Li."

"I want to go home," I said petulantly.

"You can travel a short distance, Mr. Li," said the doctor, "but you'll need assistance."

"I can provide everything," assured Kentaro. God, I was tired. But I wouldn't have these monsters dictating my fate anymore.

"*Mnmfslke*," I mumbled.

"Huh?" Kentaro said, "Get him home and take all the necessary precautions to ensure his recovery."

"Thank you, Mr. Li." Fuck you, Ken. I said in my head. I was hoping vampires could read minds. Unfortunately, if they could, I could not tell. He had seemed to have lost that haughty demeanour he'd been sporting on our initial introductions.

The nurse returned and removed the bloodline linked to my clone, who pulled it out of his own arm and stood up. As he did, his appearance readjusted into that of Aya. My lip quivered.

"Aya…" I hissed, "you!"

"If it wasn't for the Zenko, you'd definitely be gone, Mr. Li," Kentaro stated. "He saved your life." I gritted my teeth and snarled. Unable to do much else. Kentaro looked uncertainly at me, "Such as it is now." He frowned at me.

"I'm sorry, Xiǎoyīng!" He pleaded some more, "Please forgive me…." I ignored him. Just growled like a maniac as I was wheeled out.

***

Saturday: Re-Awakening

So apparently, Kentaro had the hookup when it came to everything. He had his own private army and apparently a mini-hospital inside his compound, fully staffed.

I was driven home in a large black van converted into an incognito mobile medical facility. I was so doped out on something they injected me with, it felt like I had floated all the way back home. I have no idea how they got into my apartment. I remembered mumbling that they were invited, but then I was in my bed—all snug and warm. Everything was as it should be, except for the fact that days were missing, and I had one of those wheely IV bags stuck to me delivering something I needed. Though I was not sure what. At one stage, I vaguely remember seeing the doctor from Ken's stupid house in my home, briefly replacing the IV with the assistance of a stupid nurse. But, of course, everyone around Ken was stupid.

I remembered seeing Baraz enter my apartment through the warm haze, come over and ask if I was ok. I had felt his warm little hand on mine for some time. I wasn't sure how long. Then he went and fed the fish—such a good boy. I remembered hearing knocking on my door and Aya yelling for me to let him in, not that he could not just come in himself. I ignored everyone and just floated on a warm drug-filled cloud.

At some point, I rolled over and saw Marcus smiling at me from his picture. Such a lovely, sweet smile. I saw my phone sitting in its cradle by the bed, charging. How did it get there?

Sunday: I am sure a day went by, or maybe two. It felt nice just floating in warm nothingness. Someone again must have changed my little IV baggie. I couldn't remember, though. But, like I said, the drugs were good. I could quite happily get used to them!

Monday: There was a vague noise at the door, and it opened. Two figures entered.

"Neelas, hi! Can I offer you a drink?" I slurred through my muddled speech. She was there with Mr. Bouncer. He really was quite stacked. I would not mind taking a ride on that!

"What's wrong with him?" Even his deep gravelly voice promised it would be rough and fun: "Why is he getting a boner?"

"Huh? Oh geez. He's high as a kite," she pulled out two bottles, like the ones she used for her potions, and stuck a separate hypodermic needle into each one.

"Hey, cutie!" I slurred, "You can join me right here," my arm flopped around and then across my body.

"I'd love to oblige you, little one, but I can't," The Bouncer leaned closed and sniffed.

"He smells different, Neelas."

"I know, I mean, I can't smell him, but he should, given the circumstances." She plugged the needles one after another into the IV line, injecting one vial of blue and another of red fluid into it. "With the number of mixed energies in him, he should be dead or in the same boat Dai was in!"

"Oh, those look pretty…." I said, "What did you do, you naughty bar girl!" I giggled and let my head lull to one side.

"Kentaro, you fucking prick!" She said, looking into my eyes, "I swear. I like this kid! If he goes, I'm gonna take out the vampy mafia ponce myself!"

"I'll help, sweetie. This kid has been through the wringer," I heard him leave my side. Shame, I looked. Yup, I had a boner. Meh.

" Would you look at that…" The deep voice of the Ebony Fae rumbled from my kitchen.

"What?" said Neelas.

"This calendar…" Ah, yes, that delicious black god must have found my Năinai calendar I kept every year since she passed.

"Oh…."

"Yeah…. He has so many of them." Why was he impressed? It wasn't a nice colour! All gold and red. It didn't match anything in my house. I missed Năinai.

"How much do you know about the red packets?" Neelas said.

"Not much, I haven't gotten one myself, but I know Dr. John got one once, said it was worth everything to him."

"Wow. Where do you suppose the kid got them?"

"Hell if I know, but I feel like we did something important by coming here, Neelas."

"Yeah. Aya was insistent we check on him, and good thing we did." She leaned over me. She was pretty for a naughty, naughty bar girl. Sticking needles into my little baggie thing. She shone in each of my eyes. I complained and waved vaguely at her to leave my eyes alone.

"Aya… eh… never seen him like that," the bouncer said, moving back to my side. Their conversation had been a boner killer. But that is ok. Sleep seemed preferable anyway.

"Me neither, Hexter." Hexter? Cute name. Was that Mr. Bouncer's name? Like a magical non-psychopathic serial killer name.

They had left. I was not sure. But I just lay there still swimming in my warm haze of euphoria until I did fall asleep.

***

Chapter 38: Patience, Patience (Monday)

I woke up. Yay! I was not dead. I think. I did not feel amazing, but I didn't feel shit either. So, win.

The first thing I did was send my parents a text letting them know I was sorry for not calling earlier. I would as soon as the time zone permitted later today, usually in the evening. The second thing I did was to check my neck. I had bandages all around it, and someone had put a neck brace on me. My body felt strange. Everything felt strange. I looked under the bandages and saw an ugly red welt with scar tissue all over it. It looked almost like I was burned flesh all over one side of my neck.

I decided a shower was the next best thing to do. I cautiously showered, careful to avoid touching or getting anything on the ugly marks around my neck. I redressed the bandages around my neck when I had dried off. I got dressed. I had not checked anything else. I did not want to know. Not yet.

I was also starving. I got my phone and saw my inbox of messages had maxed out, and I had almost 200 missed calls. Whatever! I shuddered to think of the havoc Aya's blood was doing to my body. I had not had the guts to check. But I would eventually. Doc had said to stay off of the Zenko, but Aya had taken that choice upon himself. I remembered him telling me: *Down to the last cell…* and I guess it was true. I had to remind myself to stop in and thank both Mr. Bouncer and Neelas when I could. I don't know what she did, but she seemed more capable of handling the supernatural than the supernatural did itself. LOL.

I checked my Nǎinai calendar, and there was an envelope for today. Well, Shit, Nǎinai! It didn't have a time on it, just my name and today's date. So I opened it, and what it said really annoyed me. But the instructions were clear and the final message: *Remember Xiǎoyīng, It's not just about you!*

I went over to her silk treasure box and opened it. An envelope had come loose from the stacks and was sticking up from its corner. That's the one! I thought.

I went down to my favourite little Korean Café with the great coffee and adorable service. It was a nice day. The sun was out, and the sky was clear. I ordered my usual café mocha and omelet. I scarfed it down in no time. I was still hungry, so I ordered pancakes. Delicious! Chocolate chips and tons of maple syrup. Gone. I hadn't eaten in days. Although I was still hungry, I didn't want to make myself sick. I sat there, content to sip my coffee and just enjoy not thinking for a bit. Ha! I was probably supposed to work, but I wasn't going to. I had been torn apart by a vampire, for Christ's sake. My job could wait. And then there were the other reasons to take a break.

A shadow fell over my little corner table. Admittedly not a large shadow, but a shadow, nonetheless.

"May I join you for a moment?" I looked up. Patience stood there, her arm in a cast, looking down. I let her wait…. "Ok, I guess not," she turned to go.

"Sit!" She stopped in her tracks. Then turned slowly. Cautiously stepped to the seat across from me and took a seat. I let her wait again for as long as I felt petty enough to.

"The police came and said the case had been closed." Ok, change of subject but whatever, "And they had been reassigned. The patrol car is gone now." It was Patience trying to pass on idle chit-chat, though this news was welcome. I couldn't be bothered with telling the authorities that a secret cabal of slightly inept vampires was to blame for the shooting and the malfunctioned bomb that blew up Patience's Tesla.

"I know why you did it, Patience. I get it." I had given it some thought. And yeah, she had to choose. It wasn't fair, but she had had to choose. To her, there was no other choice. She wasn't an expert on curses. She only knew of one cure to save her sister's whole family; wherever she got that knowledge from was anyone's guess. The cost of a cure? It was at the low, low cost of one best friend.

"Ok," She said quietly, "I'm really so-"

"No!" I hissed. Something in me stirred. Something new. A part of me reacted to my hatred of this situation. She looked into my eyes, and something about them scared her. She backed up a little in her seat. "No more apologies. It's just words. It means nothing against actions."

"You're right, Li." She admitted. But stayed there, ready for whatever I was going to dish out.

"I really loved you, Patience: every foible, flaw, and contradiction I loved. I loved your family, Dereck, Hope, the Girls. I loved them all."

"I know."

"No, you don't know. Because you can go back to them. Your sister will love you no matter what fucked up plan you concocted. But that little piece of a family I thought I had built into my life is gone. You took it away."

"No, but –"

"What, you think I can just come to family barbecues still? Birthdays? Christmas'?" I snarled at her. "You took that away from me! You took my best friend from me!"

She sat there silently. I let the full ramifications of her actions sink in. Her eyes were wide as that new feeling reared up inside me again. I wondered absently what it meant. Meh. It could wait. "How long did you know?" I asked, keeping my voice quiet, even.

"A few years. But I wasn't sure it was all real, you know?"

"Years. So, for however many years, you were stringing stupid Li along until you had everything you needed." She kept quiet. I took that as admission, "The perfect murder actually because magic isn't traceable by the police." I laughed. She flinched at my laugh.

"I want you to know something, Patience, what you took was unforgivable. What you tried to do in and of itself was evil and sick. I might've seen past it, I don't know, but what you took…."

I let that hang as I got up. I then slammed a red envelope on the table in front of Patience's stunned figure. She stared at it dumbly, but I didn't have to offer her any explanation. I didn't owe her anything. So, I just left her sitting there.

***

Chapter 39: The Debt (Sunday)

If I was indeed going to move from fucking victim to... well... the other one, non-victim, then I needed to stop being so passive about the situations that had been presented to me.

I got out my Nǎinai's treasure box and her journals. I laid the journals out one by one. I started at the earliest one, and for the first time, I began to read the sporadic account of my Nǎinai's life. As I had said, they weren't entries of "Dear Diary" nonsense. It was Nǎinai. She did everything for a reason. So, anything that was written here, she knew I'd read it someday.

***

A knock at the door sounded. Then the doorbell. Both sounded polite, almost apologetic. It had shaken me out of the land of Guilin and magic that my Nǎinai had transported me to in her journals.

I reluctantly looked through the peephole. Well, there's a weird and unwelcome surprise. But I was curious enough to open my door.

"Yes...?" I answered.

"Good Evening Mr. Li. Do you mind if we come in for a moment?"

Kentaro was standing there with his brother. They were wearing their opposite colours as I'd seen them initially. I guess it must be a twin thing. I don't know. Then I thought of something. I would try one of the things my Nǎinai had mentioned in her journals.

"As long as you abide by the laws of hospitality while you enter this dwelling." Oh yeah, Nǎinai's journals had been handy.

"Agreed," they both said as they crossed the threshold into my home.

"You have a nice home," said Daisuki shyly. He looked at me, and I swear he looked embarrassed.

"Thanks. Look, guys, what can I do for you? I literally gave my life to you, so I don't know what else I can offer you. Tea, coffee perhaps?" This earned a smirk from Kentaro, whereas Daisuki just sat on the couch looking out the window. Something unseen and dark now linked us. I could feel it. Similar to the name thing with Aya, just more imperceptible. There was something about Daisuke that, well, that I had the feeling I liked too. Though he was acting pensive, he looked and felt totally different from the madman that had torn me to pieces days ago. He risked a look at me and gave me a shy smile. Not apologetic, but more.... personal.

"We just came by to thank you formally," Daisuke said. There was more to his words, but he stopped there. Ah, I see. I had done something monumental for them, and now they were indebted to me. "Well, you're welcome. So, you can go now. I don't really wanna relive the trauma of having my throat ripped out," I said, getting worked up. Daisuki hung his head.

"I'm sorry, Mr. Li," Daisuke said. He seemed so different now. His brother was powerful and sure of himself when he was twisting thoughts and words into a feasible conclusion that he had designed. At least, that is how he appeared to be. But Daisuke, on the other hand, was sort of sweet. I sat next to him.

"Look, Daisuki," he looked up at me, hopeful, "Your apology is accepted, but you needn't be sorry." He looked confused, "You see, Daisuki, this entire circus was orchestrated by your brother and his sick little foxy cohort. You were not in your right mind, so you didn't have a choice."

Kentaro inhaled sharply. His mouth became a line on his handsome face. I went on. Unwrapping the bandages around my neck. Then running a finger along the lines of scar tissue wrapped around the whole right side of my neck. Lines of ripped flesh that had knitted itself together enough to give me life again.

"And, your brother also gave me his name, which covers some of the debt incurred." Another sharp intake. Oh yes. I remembered. These details Nǎinai had told me were important. *Even the most minor conversation can give you a kingdom if you listen hard enough.* It was a quote from one of her journals.

Kentaro stood facing me straight, looking at me in the eyes. This was something no Bella Swann could do. Stare a vampire down. But I stood, and I did. Yeah. I thought so. He wasn't as sure as he pretended to be.

"I want you to remember something, Kentaro (feeling that tug on his essence gave me a little bit of a thrill). You manipulated me," he opened his mouth to say something. I put my hand up to his face before he could. There was a mist falling lightly from my hand and disappearing just below it. Yeah. That feeling I had in the Korean café was there. Almost wanting to be let out. Like a scream that needed its voice.

"I know I have a fragile mind. Something that has troubled me all my life. It's made me sensitive to many things, but you took my mind, and you twisted it to your agenda, and you used my heart to do it. Aya? You put him in my path so you could make me a blood and energy body match for your brother." I narrowed my eyes. And I think he saw whatever had rattled Patience earlier.

"And I would do it again!" He said, losing his composure. Ah, so my assumption was right. A petulant child was hiding under that icy exterior.

I could feel it more within me now. Then, as I stepped closer to the vampire, I heard the distinctive sound of ice crunching under my bare feet.

"Of that, I have no doubt. Kentaro (the tug again), but you made a miscalculation," he looked to Daisuke, who didn't move or say anything. I suspected that Daisuke understood, mainly because he now had pieces of me swimming through his body, healing whatever damages had long plagued him.

"That little fragile mind that you played with so easily, it still stood up to your goons the other night, even without weapons or backup. I stood up to your vampires with all their strength and power," I practically spat that last word, "just imagine what I could do with this fragile broken, and unhinged mind of mine," I was approaching him now, tapping my head. He was backing up toward the entrance of my home. I opened my mouth and showed him....

"If I did have power!"

He blanched at that as the temperature in the room plummeted, and steam motes flowed from my mouth and nose as if it were a crisp frosted winter morning in my apartment. His eyes locked onto the lengthened canines glittering in my opened mouth. No longer a victim! Frost was forming all around us, looking like translucent snowflakes that had attached themselves to any surface available. I had no idea how, but it felt like me, somehow.

"Daisuki, I will call on your brother for a favour in the future. Remind him of today."

Daisuki nodded, knowing what had just happened. I said this without looking to Daisuke, but still staring at his twin, my new canines bared slightly. The temperature dropped further in the apartment, and I could hear the crackling of tiny layers of ice forming from the moisture in the air on things within my immediate vicinity, including Kentaro's terrified face and angelic face.

"You may leave now." Blink, the vamps were gone.

***

Back to my reading. My Năinai's collected knowledge was actually really cool. And the more I read and saw in her books, the closer I felt to who she was and to who I was. She had told me what was needed of me. The past couple of weeks might have sucked, but perhaps it was all necessary. Because there were things I needed to do, and it wasn't all about me.

By the evening, I had cleared through most of her journals. My reading speed had increased. Cool! I bet I could clear a bunch of textbooks in a day if I wanted to! They were definitely going to require more intense study, though. Significantly since things had changed. I had changed…
I decided to ring Maman and Bàba. I checked; they'd sent a reply text letting me know they were looking forward to speaking with me.

I called them on vid chat.

"*Wei!*" They were there—my beautiful parents.

I told them I had been unwell for a few days, but I felt much better, which was technically accurate. I wore a turtleneck to hide the scars as best I could from them. Really, they just wanted to know I was ok. And strangely enough, I was. I wasn't good, just ok. Moment by moment, I was making it through the day so far. The next ten minutes, then the next. I told them I was finally reading our Năinai's journals, which they hadn't even been privy to read. They were curious. I just told them they looked like details about Năinai's work and some of her life before dad was born. Seeing them was comforting. It grounded my attention a lot.

"How's Patience?" asked Maman. I stumbled a little with my thoughts, "Everything ok? Is Hope ok?" I was holding back tears.

"I saw Patience this morning down at the café. There is some family stuff she's dealing with for a while. Hope seems ok for now. I'll check on them soon." Hope. I wondered….

"Good man," said Bàba, "Something is going on? Something different?"

"Yes, Bàba." I wasn't about to lie outright about things like this. Saying I wasn't skipping meals was different from lying about life and death situations, "I am ok, but there's been a lot going on here."

"Is it to do with that shooting?" Bàba asked, "Ask about the bears!" chimed in Maman.

"Yes, about the shooting. And the bears had been taken care of."
Again, technically accurate.

"If you need anything or want to come home to Hong Kong, you know you can. It's an easy fix."

"I know, Bàba, thanks. I might actually be taking time off and coming soon anyway. We can do dim sum and buffets until Maman bursts." They both laughed at that. My parents and their food….

Unbidden a stray thought of someone else who loved food….

"I just have to sort a few things out here, but I am planning a trip soon, ok?"

Maman was bursting already but not from food but excitement. Bàba was a little more composed. Still grinning at the news.

We signed off. Yeah, Hong Kong might be a nice respite from monsters, lovers, and traitors.
I went to my closet and pulled out my paints and stock paper. My mind was swirling with images that needed paper. It wasn't until I had the paints out that I noticed….

The colours… the auric sight… where did it go? I looked around the room and focused a little, remembering what those blurred images and outlines looked like. Then, that wave of colour covered my vision, exposing the unseen energy world to my sight once again. I gently pulled it in. There was no straining; it just quietly went back in, and my vision cleared to normal human 20-20 vision.

"Huh, isn't that hell of a thing." I knelt over the paper on my coffee table, scratching away with a pencil. My hands were moving at an insane speed. Another Hell of a thing! Like my reading speed. Cool!

I remembered the curves and colours of the images in my mind that begged to be given form. I was working so fast I lost track of time and saw the city lights blinking through the floor-length windows. I had completed the piece in record time. A piece that would usually take a week to do if I worked non-stop. Somehow it just flowed onto the page. I looked at the image. Oh yeah, it was beautiful. It spoke of so many feelings, so many experiences that had happened and promised more to come.

I had let the feelings guide my pencils and paints just as my Năinai had taught me, and the result needed time to dry. I'd used similar paints to the ones I gave Baraz and some acrylics. I left it there to dry. I got the calendar off the fridge and folded it carefully as to not disturb the envelopes. I placed it on the counter. I retrieved the silk box with the rest of the red packets and put that on the counter. Then Năinai's journals.

There was a lot to do. But first, I needed to check something I had been avoiding since waking up strapped to an IV bag in my own home.

I went to the bathroom and stripped down naked. The full-length mirror stood there taunting me. I saw on my neck the puckered scar all-around one side where Daisuki had taken a bite out of. I wondered if that would ever go. Perhaps there was enough of Aya's energy or whatever in me to take care of it? I turned my back, afraid of what I'd find.

There was still a mark on my back, creeping up and around my spine as it had before. It wasn't black. It had changed to something else. I moved closer to the mirror. It had carried on over both of my shoulders now, but it didn't have that ugly malignant look as it had before. From my ass to where it ended at my shoulder, it looked like a cherry blossom tree, with roots curving around the shape of my buttocks and a twisting trunk that spread into branches across my shoulder blades. I saw tiny buds at the apex of each branch and the indications of blooms coming soon.
Wait, what?!

***

Chapter 40: The Last Envelope

Afsaneh, her husband Elham, and Baraz were seated around their large dining table.

"Afsaneh, you have outdone yourself!" I said, meaning every word. She had cooked *koobideh*, ground meat, and spiced kebab with *tahdig* as a side, a type of Persian fried rice. So delicious. I loved their food and always finished my plate. This time Afsaneh readily filled my plate again, and down it went.

It had taken some time, but we had moved the aquarium into their living room which Elham kept going over to and staring at the serene little animals going about their lives in the aquatic world we had put together for them. I don't think he had ever had pets, and he was secretly glad his son was obsessed with animals. Baraz was over the moon to have more pets in the house. He loved the fish and knew how to take care of them.

"How long will you be gone, Li?" Asked Elham. He was such a hardworking man that I hardly ever saw him. But when I did, we always had a good laugh, "I hope it's not too long; Baraz needs someone to play with Azhi, that damn frog!" He shook his head, not knowing what to think of the strange pink and yellow monster.

"Yeah, Azhi," I reiterated, smirking.

"Where is Mr. Djinn, Li? He hasn't come in a while?"

"Shush Baraz, don't be so nosy. Sorry Li, he's been asking to see your friend again since he met him."

"You know Djinn, they come and go like the wind." Ok, that elicited a laugh from both mum and dad, but Baraz was left wondering what was so funny.

"Baraz?"

"Yes, Li," he was sitting next to me at the table like we were best buds. It was sweet.

"What did you think of Mr. Djinn?"

"I liked him, Li, and I know you liked him too."

"Yeah, I did, but I don't think he felt the same," I said sadly, but still keeping my tone light.

"You're right. Mr. Djinn didn't," Ok, didn't expect that, "He felt more; he said he loved you, Li." I blushed.

"Baraz, stop," his mum chided, "Sorry Li, he can be such a gossip sometimes," she smacked his hand lightly with her fork and gave him a pointed look. "I don't know what's gotten into him."

"But mum, Djinn can't lie about who they love; that's the rule."

"He's got you there, darling," said Elham. Which earned him a look also, "The Djinn are tricky, but when it comes to love, they have to be true. It's written. They can't help it." Well, if only Aya had been a damn Djinn instead of a sneaky-ass Fox Demon.

"Regardless, what's done is done," I said. I raised our tea glasses, "A toast to friends," I gestured around the table, "and family…" we raised our tea, and all said, "*bé salamati!*" and drank. It was a term spoken for good health to all at the table.

It was such a lovely meal with such a sweet family. As I shut my apartment door, I looked around my apartment. The fridge was cleaned out and had my latest masterpiece taped to it. Gosh, I was silly. Such a stupid man doing such a thing. But as my Nǎinai had said, the soul of the picture would create itself through my brush strokes.

I had my travel wallet with all my cards, passports, and Hong Kong ID, my various currencies in cash. I had also put my medications in there. If there was a time to be on these pills, it was now. I slipped it into my messenger bag, which would get attached to my carry-on roller luggage. I usually travelled with clothes, but I only added my toiletries and such into my carry-on. The rest of the room was reserved for something more precious. I zipped Năinai's journals into one side with my picture of Marcus and the postcard from France. They fit perfectly. I picked up Năinai's silk box, feeling quite purposeful, and spun on my heel to put it into my luggage next. Only, my heel slipped somehow, and I fell onto my ass on the kitchen floor.

"Ouch!" I cried. Năinai's box had spilled its contents. In the past, I would have panicked because Năinai would have packed them just so. But upon reading her journals, sometimes these things happened to add the right mix to items. So, I gathered the red packets all up and put them into their rows in the silk box. Though it didn't make it any less irritating.

Then I crawled to my luggage to avoid another spill. In they went, and I zipped the whole case closed, then clipped it shut with the TSA lock. Finally, I put it upright on its four wheels. I slung my messenger bag over the handle, which had a convenient attachment.

I stood up and looked around—my apartment. Too much had happened. I would probably come back and sell it. Who knows? But right now, I was just going to lock up and have Baraz check on it now and then.

Looking around, I saw those twinkling city lights. So beautiful. I switched off the lights and locked up behind me.

***

As I had before, I went through the threshold of my lover's door and into what I had considered our territory now. I could smell him there, but I couldn't feel him. I looked around in panic, seeing the place had changed. His aquarium was gone. There was no bio lamp illuminating the night. His display cabinet was almost empty, only a few trinkets remained, but the journals and silk box were gone.

"No, please. Don't go!" I said to the night in general, hoping against all odds that he would hear my plea. I had tried calling his true name. I felt the pull and then nothing each time, "Come to me, my love!" I pleaded for what was probably the millionth time.

I looked at the fridge expecting it to be blank, knowing he'd take the red and gold calendar with him. It wasn't blank. Taped to it at four corners was a painting. It was painted with watercolours with some acrylic I could see. He really was talented. It showed a cherry blossom curving around the left edge of the painting. The backdrop was dreamlike, and brush strokes here and shading there make it look like the two figures were lying on silk sheets but in an ethereal world.
The two figures were Yīng and me. He was curled up tucked against my chest, and I was using my body to encircle Yīng's. Written vertically on the side in flowing Chinese calligraphy: If Love is truly lost, it can never be found.

I had cried so much since that night. When I had seen Yīng's throat being ripped away by that creature. I remembered tearing through the ranks of vampires and their silver chains that were able to hold me until then. It hurt, but it didn't matter. I was in my bestial form and leaped at the glass, all heat and fury. The glass shouldn't have broken, but I'm guessing the heat from my foxfire had something to do with it. I had sped as fast as my nature could take me, the other vampire, Kentaro, just ahead. I remembered him pulling his brother away from my Xiǎoyīng's prone form.

My Xiǎoyīng lying there blinking up at me. His beautiful face, so sweet, so gentle. His throat half missing. His blood had slowed its pumping to a trickle now, and I could feel his heart slowing to a stop. And when it did, so did mine.

Vampire speed is mainly unmatched by other beings. I could sometimes work as fast as they, but certainly not for any length of time. The vamps took Yīng's body to Ken's personal hospital wing. And quickly staunched the wounds. They tried to restart his heart. But, unfortunately, there was nothing left in him to restart.

Blood. They'd needed blood. He would hate me more than he already did, but that didn't matter. He needed to live. I needed him to live. The world was much less a place without someone as filled with light, humour, and what I hoped was love for me. The love didn't matter as long as he lived, though. I could live with him hating me, maybe, if he lived!

Upon seeing my shift, the vampire medical crew got the plan immediately, understanding Zenko physiology as well as a human's, I'd wager. A line was set up between us, so I could give my Xiǎoyīng the life he needed but knowing what my energy had already done to him... this might be the tipping point in his body. After that, who knows what or who would wake up?

I took the precious piece of art from Yīng's fridge and hugged it. The tears running down my cheeks. How could a Zenko cry so much? My Okāsan had always said I was sensitive. And that it was a gift from Inari. It helped me see the world as it should be seen. But hugging the painting, I didn't feel like I saw anything it should be. He was mine. My love. Why!? I had messed up royally. But I would never let it happen again. I had to tell him. I didn't know how it was going to play out, that I would find him...

I put the painting on the floor next to me, then realized what I was doing with such a precious object. It shouldn't be on the floor. I turned to pick it up with the reverence it deserved. Lifting it gently off the cold floor. As I did, I noticed the glint of something. I quickly placed the artwork gently onto the counter and leaned down to look.

Under the fridge was a red packet. I frowned. Indeed, my Yīng wouldn't have left one intentionally. They were precious objects. And even more special to him because they came from his Nǎinai. I pulled it out, then thought, well, it would give me an excuse to track him, to return it to him. He'd be grateful even if he didn't want to see me ever again. At least for a moment, I could see his face before disappearing from his life forever.

I looked at the envelope. It was hand-dyed and painted. On the front was a painting in gold, similar to the one Yīng had painted and left on the fridge. This work was so delicate and intricate. Instead of Yīng's form being encircled by mine, it looked the other way around, and my form was that of a fox. That woman was a marvel. Along the side was some calligraphy. Not in Chinese characters, but in Japanese kanji. A true marvel. It had my name and Yīng's name, and today's date, alongside that: "Don't be so lazy, you can find anything!"

These packets were known to be extremely specific, and for them to be used, the instructions had to be followed. In a blink, I was gone. My senses guided my body to the location. It wasn't far.

– Ayaka

**

I stood at the water's edge on the boardwalk, looking at the yachts floating peacefully in the night. Everything around me felt so vivid and alive. Living in a world of auric confusion, these new sensations weren't too overwhelming, just added to the newness I would have to get used to. Those same senses picked up on something close and then behind me from one moment to the next. I didn't turn. I couldn't trust myself to do the right thing. I could hear a heartbeat….and my own matching it.

"Xiǎoyīng…" He simply said.

My heart stopped suddenly. Aya came to rest his elbows on the railing as I had, looking out over the water. I stretched down to my luggage and turned to leave. He didn't use his speed, just gently reached out and took my hand. My heart was beating again, as it always did with him. I was a mix of anger, attraction, hate…. and love. Oh yeah. I had to face it. I did love him. I also had to face this demon… at least once before going. So, I did.

I saw his face; it was pained but still beautiful. His skin so smooth and hair so long and silken, and amber eyes that glowed slightly in the night. A face that would bring kingdoms to their knees, a face that time itself would be still for. He would probably always take my breath away. That I couldn't control ever. And that was not a good thing.

"I… I can't… Aya…" He grabbed my face in both his hands and leaned in, our foreheads touching. I didn't struggle.

"I know Xiǎoyīng, I know. I have committed unspeakable acts against you both knowingly and unknowingly," I placed my hands over his. Warm. Mine were cold from the night air, I guessed. He smelled so good. No!

"Yes, Ayaka, and I can't forgive you," My cheeks were warm, god. Did I have to be crying all the time? My thumbs stroked his cheeks and picked up the tears streaming down his eyes.

"Why My love, why?" It was a pitying sound, a sob, and a whimper combined, "Please forgive me."

"If I do, then what? What does that make me?" I said, trying to rationalize what we were both saying, "It means that I let go of what you did, how you treated me. It means I accept what you did. Accept being hurt needlessly."

"If you give me one more chance, Xiǎoyīng, I will honour it with my life for eternity," he breathed; I wanted to reach up to his lips and take them with mine. I didn't move, though, and neither did he. "I will give you everything I am. Just forgive me. Please." I knew he was pleading. It didn't give me any pleasure at all. On the contrary, it just further broke my heart.

"Ayaka… Ayaka, my beautiful god, how could you?"

"I didn't know what was happening. Please forgive me. I had no choice, your heart had stopped, and I would have given more than what I did to hear it beat again."

"Wait, you think I'm upset because you saved my life that night?"

"Aren't you? I took the choice from you…."

"Ayaka, my sweet little fox, you silly thing," I wanted him. I wanted to forgive him. But if I did, would I just be another lame stereotype of the "damsel" needing a knight? Did it matter?

"That never crossed my mind Aya…." I pulled his face from mine, and he resisted for a moment, but I needed to look him in the eyes. "You deceived me, lied to me. Did you even… I mean…"

"I have loved you from the moment I saw you, Xiǎoyīng." His voice and tone went from desperate to severe in a heartbeat, "That was why I didn't know what to do. I was just biding time to figure out something. You weren't meant to go with the vampires… with Kentaro ever. You were supposed to stay in our home safe! Until…." He hissed as he uttered Kentaro's name. Our home? "You were just gonna keep me at your house until something else worked out," I smiled, almost seeing the animal logic behind his behaviour, "What were you gonna do, take out the entire vampire cabal?" He just looked earnestly at me.

"You were?" he shrugged helplessly.

"How could I not? It's you. From the moment I saw you…."

"I want to forgive you, Aya, but…." I took a breath wanting to believe him, "how can you say you loved me from the start? That's not possible."

"Xiǎoyīng, Foxes, once they fall in love, it's forever. We can't help it. We can and will only mate with the One. That's how I knew it would never last with other partners and tried to be honest."

"I want to believe it, Aya…."

"Then do it. You won't regret it ever. I will give you everything you want. Anything, please be mine again." I honestly didn't know Aya was this serious. His tears, his voice, everything screamed of a man who had no other choice but to be here right now with me.

I ignored any thoughts or words of reply. Instead, I just did what I had to.

I pulled him to me and kissed him, "I love you, Ayaka of the Zenko." His sobs barely broke through the kiss as his long, strong arms wrapped around me and pulled me tight.

"I love you, Xiǎoyīng. I'm yours. I'm yours forever. Take me, please."

"And I am yours Ayaka of the Zenko. I can't let you go!" The pull and push of our spoken names felt different like they were becoming something more. We kept kissing, the heat and love pouring from us.

"I love you," he whispered again, kissing around my ear and neck, "I love you, I'm yours, Yīng, I'm yours. I loved you the moment I saw you. I loved you instantly!"

I just let him kiss me while I let the sensations I had missed so much fill me again. His scent, heat, shape, and attraction clear as he pressed his erection against me.

He pulled away, and it took me a moment to gather my wits. He seemed to be in the same head spin I was.

"I… I have something… for us," Aya said, reaching into his jacket. I wanted more of the kissing and, hopefully, the stuff that followed, but when he pulled out a red packet, all thoughts of that vanished.

"What? Where'd you -?" I took the proffered envelope that bulged slightly and read the front. It was for both of us, "Oh, Nǎinai…."

"Yeah…"

"There's a time here. It says after 6:30 am tomorrow, or today if you look at the time." I had pulled out my phone and saw it was after 3 am. So I took the lead and pulled the Zenko against me, "Upstairs now…" I whispered through my kissing. I had to, we had to.

And there it was, we went into my closed-up apartment at the speed of a... well... Zenko Fox Spirit. And you can guess where that leads...yup...the bed.

***

"Xiǎoyīng, my love," he was tracing the pattern on my back, "this is a cherry blossom."

"Yes, it is Aya," he was, of course referring to the magically created tattoo decorating my back.

"It's stunning, have you seen it? Close?"

"I like it enough, I mean, I think it's permanent now, but it could be worse," I was tracing my hands on his naked chest. "Guess I could get a tattoo artist to do something with it."

"Ah, I see, hmmm, I think you need to see…." He lifted me up, and I laughed, telling him to put me down. My naked and beautiful god took me to my bathroom and set me down to stand naked before my full-length mirror. There was something about our energy that was the same. I couldn't pinpoint it just yet. He stood behind me, in all his naked glory. He turned me slightly to my side with my back facing a clearer view in the mirror. There it was, the twisted design curving my spine, except where the branches extended. Instead of the buds from earlier, they had white and pink blossoms that were raining down as if in a real moment with a slight breeze. I touched it. My hand didn't disturb the scene.

"What the fuck!?" I grinned, actually enjoying the scene. The mark had wholly become the scene of blossoms in the spring.

"My love," he kissed me again, "I really hope our recent reunion is not marred by this event."

"Not at all, Aya; this is pretty cool. Is this what it means to live in your world?"

"Actually…my love," his voice sounded a little graver… "It's what it means to be Fae." It took me a moment to grasp his words and their possible meaning, "Come, let's to bed; we have a little more time."

And that little more time was spent doing one thing a few more times.

***

6:29 am: What the Dawn and Clear Skies May Bring

The morning sky was clear and blue, with no clouds to be seen. There was no breeze, and somehow the boardwalk was people-free—no early joggers or dog walkers for once.

"I'm ready," he said, handing me the packet to open. It was a little bulkier, and they sometimes were depending on what Năinai placed in them. I opened the top end and tipped the contents into my hand.

A folded silk piece of material slid out. Ha! Of course, you did, Năinai! I unfolded it gently and found a tiny pair of gold scissors and some red string.

"Look at that thread work. It's so intricate," Aya pointed to the design of the dragon and phoenix on the silk material. I looked up at him. Then, I held it up to him.

"You understand Ayaka of the Zenko?" He nodded.

"I do," he said those perfect words as he took the tiny scissors and pulled a stray lock of my hair into his hands gently and snipped a length of my hair, "My Xiǎoyīng," He held the hair between his thumb and forefinger. I took the scissors from him, and I, too, cut some of his long silken hair and cut a similar length.

"My Ayaka of the Zenko," I held it up to him. I took both locks of hair and the string my Năinai had left us and wound it tightly around both locks of hair, binding them into one. Then I tied an elaborate knot that resembled a butterfly. He took the knotted hair and wrapped it into the silk, and kissed it. And I took it from his hand and kissed it. Then we held it together and came together kissing, feeling that tug we felt with our names, except now they were together. Like two parts had come together and wouldn't be moved without the other.

Drops of water pattered down onto the water and onto us as we kissed, "I love you, Xiǎoyīng," and "I love you," I said through the kissing. It was pouring now, soaking us. We came apart then. I looked up, there were no clouds, but the rain kept coming down all around.

"Inari had blessed this union," Ayaka said, smiling like it was his wedding day because, well, for both of us, it was. I put the silk package of our little ceremony into my messenger bag carefully. My Nǎinai was one cunning woman.

Life and Death. These could change one's perspective on everything. It can bring about a change in you, similar to what I had seen with the boy transitioning in the Below Ground café. Your priorities became different, and what was essential and needed in your own personal world became crystal clear.

"Aya, my love," I hoped he would understand. It felt good to call him my love too.

"Yes, my love." Ok, his smile was so wide and contented like a predatory cat on the Serengeti. One that had just taken down a gazelle and finished eating their fill. Now said cat was basking in the sun, their eyes half-open and closed in pure primal joy. Suffice to say, he'd probably be ok with whatever came out of my mouth next. "I still have to go." His face fell, "But you are coming with me, aren't you?" Then, the grin resumed on his beautiful face.

"Absolutely…. ah, where are we going, my love?" His arms had wrapped around me possessively, and I didn't mind because I wasn't just his; he was Mine!

"China Aya, we are going to China."

"Oh…" he looked perplexed and a little worried. "Why China, my love? We can go anywhere in the world, and even to some places in the Universe only open to us…" Tempting but as I had recently been reminded:

"Because Aya, I have a task to accomplish," I turned to the water, seeing China in my mind's eye, "As an incredibly wise and stubborn lady told me: It's not always all about me."

"Ah, I see, a quest. Well, this will be fun," Aya pulled out his cell and began texting. I gave him an inquiring look, "I am just texting my tenant Caeyr; he'll need to watch my place and take care of my bonsai while we are journeying." I nodded, but a tenant? Hmph. First, I had heard, and my jealous side reared up and decided I would most definitely be screening this 'tenant' myself. I sucked in a deep breath, remembering our excitement of what lay ahead. Well, I guessed someone had to live in the upstairs of Aya's basement level place.

"Yes, I hope it's fun too, Aya." Still staring off, I couldn't help but feel the sense of trepidation and excitement. Yes, a quest.

***

Made in the USA
Middletown, DE
30 June 2021